About the Authors

...cia Thayer was born in Muncie, Indiana, the
...nd of eight children. She attended Ball State
...ersity before heading to California. A longtime
...ber of RWA, Patricia has authored fifty books.
...s been nominated for the Prestige RITA® award
... winner of the RT Reviewer's Choice award. She
...s travelling with her husband, Steve, calling it
...rch. When she wants some time with her guy, they
...e to their mountain cabin and sit on the deck and
...e world race by.

...as far back as she can remember **Michelle Conder**
...ed of being a writer. She penned the first chapter
... mance novel just out of high school, but it took
...tudy, many (varied) jobs, one ultra-understanding
...d and three gorgeous children before she finally
...n to turn that dream into a reality.

...le lives in Australia, and when she isn't busy
... she loves to read, ride horses, travel and practise
...isit Michelle: www.michelleconder.com

...*ODAY* bestselling author **Karen Rose Smith** has
... over ninety novels. Her passion is caring for
... rescued cats, and her hobbies are gardening,
... and photography. An only child, Karen delved
...oks at an early age. Even though she escaped
...ory worlds, she had many cousins around her on
...nds. Families are a strong theme in her novels.
... about Karen at karenrosesmith...

Animal Magnetism

Animal Magnetism: Reclaiming Her Love

PATRICIA THAYER

MICHELLE CONDER

KAREN ROSE SMITH

MILLS & BOON

Special thanks and acknowledgement to Karen Rose Smith for her contribution to the *Montana Mavericks: Rust Creek Cowboys* continuity.

ISBN: 978-0-263-28179-8

MIX
Paper from
responsible sources
FSC™ C007454

This book is produced from independently certified FSC™ paper to ensure responsible forest management.

For more information visit: www.harpercollins.co.uk/green

Printed and bound in Spain
by CPI, Barcelona

THE REBEL
HEIR'S BRIDE

PATRICIA THAYER

To the newest addition to the family, Finley Steven.
Hero material for sure. And to his mother, Daralynn.
You never stop amazing me.
Thank you for another fine grandson.

To Dr. Michael Pahl.
Thanks for all your help with this book

CHAPTER ONE

HE'D always been told he was too cocky for his own good.

On a sunny November morning, Brady Randell hobbled out to the porch with the aid of a crutch. His left leg was bandaged from his last surgery and covered in a removable cast strapped from his foot up over his knee to his thigh. It served to protect the damaged bone so it could heal properly. If it ever did. Three months since the accident, and he wasn't feeling so damn cocky anymore.

With a groan Brady dropped into the Adirondack chair. This was about as far as he traveled these days. He was tired of doing nothing but sleeping, eating and sitting around. Oh, yeah, he forgot about going to therapy twice a week. Or maybe he should call it torture.

After all his hard work, he hoped for a payoff, some good news when he saw the doctor next week. With a little luck he could get the cast off and finally be able to walk on his own again.

"Wouldn't that be a miracle," he murmured in frustration.

He sighed, recalling the vivid details of the accident

that had caused him to drop right out of the sky. He'd barely had time to eject from the cockpit before the crash of his F-16.

Brady tensed. He could still feel the bone-bruising tremors; hear the death screams of the powerful aircraft disintegrating as it plowed into the desert floor. He'd gone over and over in his head what he could have done differently. What had gone so terribly wrong that day?

Was this possibly the end of Captain "Rebel" Randell's air force career?

Now instead of being in the cockpit of the Fighting Falcon, he was parked on a porch of the foreman's house outside San Angelo, Texas. His daddy's home, the Rocking R Ranch. After Sam Randell's death, it now belonged to him and his half brother, Luke, who, after thirty years, he'd finally met. Since the accident, Brady had needed a place to heal. He thought a remote, inherited ranch would be perfect for a loner like him.

Brady stared out toward the barn and corral area where his new sister-in-law, Tess Randell, was working one of her horses in the large arena. She rode like nobody's business. Watching her skill and grace was the treat of his day. That and being left alone.

Brady closed his eyes and leaned back. Not that he was going to get any peace and quiet staying here. He had family coming out of the woodwork. Up at the main ranch house Luke lived with his bride and readymade family—a young daughter, Livy, Tess's father, Ray, who had Alzheimer's and kept referring to Brady as Sam's boy. And Aunt Bernice, who spoke her mind and could cook up a storm.

They weren't so bad, but the six Randell cousins who lived in the neighboring ranches with all their wives and kids were a bit much. And there were lots of kids. Evidently, there wasn't much else to do on the ranch during those long nights.

With a groan he shifted in his chair, recalling the last time he'd spent the night with a willing woman. It had been too long.

"Excuse me, are you all right?"

At the sound of a female voice, Brady's eyes shot open. He blinked and focused on a pair of big, emerald-green eyes staring back at him from the edge of the porch. They belonged to a petite woman dressed in snug jeans, a white blouse and a denim jacket. Her hair was the rich color of cinnamon, cut just at her jawline, and wayward strands brushed against her full lips. A black cowboy hat sat firmly on her head.

He swallowed the sudden dryness in his throat. "I'm fine," he told her.

"I heard you groan and—" she glanced down at his injured leg "—wondered if you were in pain."

Damn right he was. "I'm fine," he repeated.

She gave him a half smile and his heart began to race. "Then I apologize for disturbing you."

This woman could disturb a man in a coma. She looked like every man's dream. That was if you were into fiery redheads. Oh, yeah. He sat up straighter. "Are you lost or something?"

She looked around. "I'm here to see Tess Randell."

Brady glanced at the oversize case she was toting. Great, a solicitor out in the middle of nowhere. "If you're here to sell her something, she's busy."

The woman shook her head and raised an eyebrow. "Actually, I was invited. She called me."

"Right."

Her shoulders tensed. "If you'll just direct me to Tess Randell, I won't bother you any longer."

From the corner of his eye, Brady saw his sister-in-law hurrying toward them. "Looks like we'll both get our wish," he told the pretty intruder.

Tess rushed toward them. "Good, you found us," she said a little breathless. The statuesque blonde wore her long hair tired back in a ponytail. "Did you have much trouble with my directions?"

The redhead glanced at Brady. "Nothing I couldn't handle."

Smiling, Tess's gaze shifted to him. "Have you two met?"

Before Brady could speak, the woman said, "We haven't had a chance."

"Brady, this is Dr. Lindsey Stafford. She's the new veterinarian taking over Dr. Hillman's practice while he's recovering from his hip surgery. Be nice, or you'll have to answer to the Randell cousins, especially Travis. He went all the way to Dallas to find her." Tess turned to the redhead. "Lindsey, this is my brother-in-law, Brady Randell. He's a captain in the air force."

Lindsey fought her nervousness. Not because the

man was drop-dead gorgeous, but every time she met another Randell she was afraid someone would figure out who she was.

"It was nice to meet you, Brady." She held out her hand.

He shook it. "Same here, Doc. You'll excuse me if I don't get up."

She nodded, not missing the sarcasm in his voice. "Hope you have a speedy recovery."

Those midnight eyes locked with hers. "Not nearly as much as I do."

"Well," Tess began, "I better take you down to the barn." She turned to Brady. "You need anything?"

"No, I can manage."

Tess nodded. "If you see Luke, tell him where I went. Come with me, Lindsey."

Lindsey quickly followed Tess along the path. She didn't want to have any more conversation with the man.

"Sorry about my brother-in-law," Tess began. "He's recovering from an accident and is a little antsy with his confinement. Of course, that doesn't excuse his rude behavior."

"You don't have to apologize for him. I'll just keep my distance next visit."

Tess Randell was beautiful to begin with, but when she smiled she was gorgeous. Tall, with long legs, her every movement was graceful. Everything Lindsey always wanted to be. But at twenty-nine she was resigned to the fact she'd stopped growing at five-foot-three, and her freckles across her nose would not suddenly vanish.

They arrived at the pristine white barn and walked

inside. Lindsey looked around the well-kept area where new-looking stalls lined both walls. She followed Tess down the center aisle to a section that was designated as the grooming area. A stable boy was washing one of the horses.

They continued past three beautiful quarter horses that peered over their gates to see the visitors. "These are horses I board and train, and their owner has given me permission to call you if I feel the need."

"Good." Lindsey stopped to pet one of the equines. "I'd hate to think about something happening to one of these beautiful animals."

"That's the reason I'm so happy you came here to practice."

"I was lucky to get the chance." She walked alongside of Tess. "I don't have much experience yet, and this will definitely help build my résumé." And she never dreamed she would get the opportunity to meet the Randells. It was a chance she couldn't pass up.

"The vet you interned for in Ft. Worth gave you a glowing recommendation. That's good enough for us." They stopped at the stall of a young bay stallion. "This here is Smooth Whiskey Doc. He's my number-one concern. I hope to have him compete in the NCHA Futurity."

Lindsey was mesmerized by the beautiful golden bay horse. When she went to him, he showed no shyness and came to the gate to greet her. She set her case down and he immediately nudged her hand. When she rubbed his muzzle, he blew out a breath.

"I think I'm in love," Lindsey said with a big grin.

But her thoughts suddenly turned to the brooding Brady Randell.

"Be careful," Tess warned. "He's fickle."

"I don't doubt that for a second," she said, remarking about both stallions.

Whiskey bobbed his head as if to agree and they both laughed. All the time, Lindsey was looking the animal over. He was about sixteen hands high, his eyes were clear, and his coat shiny. Well cared for.

"What seems to be your problem, big boy?"

Tess swung open the gate and walked in beside the horse. Her hand smoothed over his withers across his back and down his rump. "It's probably minor, but I didn't want to take a chance with this guy." She talked soothingly as she leaned down to reveal the gash just below the hock on his hind leg.

"I was working him in a cutting exercise and he got clipped by a steer."

Lindsey ran her hand along the horse's rump as she crooned to him. She didn't want to get kicked because the animal was nervous. Tess did her part, too, to keep Whiskey still.

Lindsey examined the open wound closely, then asked, "When did it happen?"

"About a week ago. I've been treating it with the normal antiseptic cream and clean bandages."

"You were right to call me. In a few more days, this could have really gotten infected. I believe a strong dose of antibiotics will clear it up, but I want you to stop training for a few days."

Lindsey went to her bag. "I've looked over Dr. Hillman's file on Whiskey. He was examined just a month ago, but I'll give him a quick check just so I can get familiar with him."

Tess looked relieved. "That's fine with me."

After the exam, Lindsey gave Whiskey a glowing report. They came out of the stall in time to see a man walking down the aisle. He was tall with a muscular build, coal-black hair and a cleft chin. Obviously another Randell.

"Luke," Tess called, love shining in her eyes. "You're finished with the meeting already."

"Not exactly." He leaned down and kissed his wife, then looked at Lindsey. "Hello, you must be Dr. Stafford. I'm Luke Randell."

She nodded. So, another cousin to Jack's boys. "Lindsey, please. Nice to meet you." Oh, my, another charming Randell man. Suddenly Captain Brady Randell came into her head. Correction. Not all were charming. Some were just too damn good-looking.

Brady stood leaning against the porch post as he watched for the redheaded vet to come out of the barn. Hell, why not? How often did a pretty woman—who wasn't a Randell—come around? It was the most excitement he'd had in days. Besides, he had nothing better to do.

That wasn't exactly true.

He glanced toward the large house on the hill. There were several cars parked in the driveway, probably for another business meeting with Randell Corp. He'd been invited to attend, but he'd declined. He wasn't into numbers and budgets. That was his brother's show.

All Brady had to do was sit back and let everyone else handle things. Hadn't that been what he'd done since he arrived here? Just sit around and heal. Isn't that what he wanted? Silence and solitude so he could think?

He raked his fingers through his grown-out regulation military cut, then across the two-day beard along his jaw. He'd let himself go to hell. Suddenly he cared, because a woman showed up here.

The sound of laughter brought him back to reality. He looked toward the barn to see Luke and Tess, escorting the pretty vet down the path toward the house.

Great. Why hadn't he gone inside sooner. The last thing he wanted was for them to find him here. But before he could make his escape, his brother spotted him.

"Hey, Brady." He waved and they started to the porch.

He froze. "Hey, Luke."

They arrived all smiles and Brady suddenly felt left out. "Have you met Lindsey Stafford?"

He nodded, trying to balance his weight using the post. "We've met already."

The redhead looked up at Luke and smiled. "Brady mistook me for a salesperson."

"Really." Luke stood there looking smug.

Brady refused to let his brother outmaneuver him. He could sweet-talk as well as the next guy. "Well, Doc, no one said our new vet would look like you. I guess you could say I was blindsided."

Lindsey could see through Brady's sudden charming

attitude. Well, she wasn't going to let him have the upper hand. "Believe me, it won't happen again," she told him, unable to understand why he seemed to dislike her so. "I should get back, Mr. Randell," she said, then turned away to go with Tess and Luke.

Before she could make her departure, she heard a curse and a thud. She swung around to find Brady Randell lying on the porch floor.

"Brady!" Luke called. He was the first to reach him. Lindsey followed behind him.

She knelt down beside Brady, who was lying flat on his back. He tried to raise his head, his face strained in pain. "No, stay where you are," she ordered.

He grimaced again. "Who made you the boss?"

"Are you going to fight me for the title?" She was eyeing the leg in a cast. "Did you twist your leg?"

"No, I fell on my arm, trying to catch myself," he said, still fighting her to sit up.

Once again, she pushed him back down. "Lie still," she ordered, then reached for his arm.

"What the hell are you doing?" He tried to pull away.

"I just can't resist you, Mr. Randell. So lie there and enjoy the attention."

Brady's angry gaze went to his brother, but Luke just held up his hand in surrender. "I suggest you listen to her."

"Then make it quick. And if you're going to get familiar, you can drop the mister." With a groan, he did as he was told.

Lindsey checked his arms and good leg, happy to find nothing broken. But she soon discovered a lump on the back of his head. She had him open those piercing brown eyes. Although they weren't dilated, he could still have a concussion.

She turned to Luke. "Seems nothing is broken. Could you help me get him on his feet and inside?"

"I don't need help, Doc," Brady continued to argue.

"Come on, Brady," his brother urged. "You need to listen, or I'm going to take you to the emergency room."

Brady grumbled and finally sat up. Lindsey couldn't help but notice his hard, flat stomach that his dark T-shirt didn't hide when his bomber jacket fell open. His chest and arms weren't bad, either. With Luke and Lindsey gripping his arms, they managed to get him to his feet.

Lindsey immediately felt his strength, his power and his masculinity, too. The sudden feelings he evoked surprised her. He was definitely not her type of man. Too dangerous.

Tess handed Brady his crutch, and Luke helped his brother inside the cottage. Tess and Lindsey followed behind them and into a small living room that was cluttered with newspapers and magazines but clean otherwise.

"You want to go to your room or stay out here?" Luke asked.

Brady pulled away from his brother, made his way to the sofa and sat down. "I'm fine right here. So you all can leave."

Tess and Luke looked at Lindsey for confirmation.

"He's got a small lump on his head," she told them. "But his pupils aren't dilated."

"No concussion," Brady said. "So go."

Luke looked at his wife. "If you stay for thirty minutes, I can finish up the meeting and be back here."

"But Livy's bus is due," she said, and glanced at her watch.

"All of you go," Brady demanded. "I'll be fine alone."

"I can stay until you get back," Lindsey offered.

"Oh, thank you, Lindsey," Tess said. "I promise I'll be back soon as I pick up Livy."

"I'll get back as soon as the meeting is over. And I'm still thinking you should get checked out," Luke said, then followed his wife out the door.

Suddenly Lindsey was alone with this overbearing man.

"Well, now you're stuck," Brady said as he lifted his cast-covered leg onto the coffee table.

"I'm not stuck," she denied. "But it would be nice if you tried to be civil."

"Why should I? I just want to be left alone."

"And I'm sure you will be when your family learns you're okay. When do you see your doctor again?"

Brady started to say it was none of her business, but found he liked her being here, though not exactly under these circumstances. "In a few days."

"Let him know what happened today. In fact you should call him and tell him."

"Lady, that's not going to happen."

She gave him a stubborn look. "I'm not the enemy here, Brady. So you aren't going to run me off. Not until I want to leave. That will be when Tess comes back."

Brady studied her for a few minutes. Lindsey Stafford was different than most women who hung around the base. Those females were overeager to please the hot-shot pilots. This woman had a take-me-as-I-am-or-not-at-all attitude.

"Maybe I've been a little hard on you."

Those big eyes widened in surprise. "You think?"

"Okay, I plead guilty. Now please sit down. You're giving me neck strain from looking up at you."

She sank down in an overstuffed chair across from him. "That's a switch."

Brady felt his mouth twitch. "Get picked on for your size, huh?"

She glared. "Not since seventh grade."

"That's a lie," he said as his gaze combed over her petite body. "What do you weigh? A hundred pounds?"

"One hundred and ten. I work out to build muscle. The added strength helps in my profession."

He'd like to see those muscles. Dear Lord, he was pathetic. "Why aren't you working with dogs and cats? It would seem easier."

She shook her head. "I love horses. My mother and stepfather are horse breeders. I grew up around them."

"Where are you from?"

She hesitated for a second. "North of Fort Worth. Denton. What about you? Have you always been in the military?"

He nodded. "All of my life, and we moved around a lot. Dad was career air force, so I went into the academy after high school. I always wanted to fly."

She motioned toward his leg. "Is that how you were injured?"

He hated to think about that day. "Yeah, I had to eject from my aircraft and my landing wasn't the best."

"Well, it looks like you're on the mend."

He stiffened. "It's taking too long. I want to get back in the air."

Lindsey had heard some of the history of the Randell family, but Brady was a surprise to her. There was actually a Randell who wasn't a rancher. "So you're going back?"

"Why shouldn't I? I'm one of the best."

"And so humble, too." She forced a smile. "I'm sure the doctors are doing everything possible. Are you?"

His eyes narrowed. "What does that mean? Of course I'm doing everything, and that includes a lot of rigorous physical therapy."

"That's good." *Just keep your mouth shut, Lindsey*, she told herself as she looked around. *Where is Tess?*

"You don't like me much," he said.

"I barely know you, Captain Randell." And she wasn't sure she wanted to.

"You should know that I'm very good at what I do. And I plan to continue flying for the air force for a long time." He set his injured leg on the floor. "Sitting around a ranch house isn't for me."

"You don't seem to have a choice right now. So maybe you should use this time to count your blessings that you survived your accident instead of taking your anger out on every unsuspecting person who happens to cross your path."

"How the hell do you know what I've gone through?"

Lindsey was going through her own personal pain, too. Her stepfather didn't have such a rosy future.

"You're right, I don't, but I know you're healthy, with a family who loves you, and all you're doing is complaining."

His stony look told her that she'd gone too far. "I should go," she said. "I'm sure someone will be here shortly."

She stood, but before she could get to the door it opened and a little girl came running in.

"Uncle Brady, Uncle Brady. Mommy said you fell down." The little blonde went running to the stoic man on the sofa. "Are you hurt?" she cried.

"No darlin', I'm fine. I just tripped over my big feet and bumped my head."

The girl's worried look didn't leave until her uncle showed her the damage. "See, it's just a little bump."

The child leaned down and kissed it. "There, that will make it better."

Then it happened. Brady Randell sat back and a big smile appeared across the handsome face. Lindsey's heart leaped and she tried hard to remember the man with the bad attitude.

The little girl turned to her and smiled. "Mommy said you're Whiskey's new vet. I'm Livy Meyers Randell. My new daddy married my mommy and 'dopted me."

Lindsey smiled. "Well, it's nice to meet you, Livy Meyers Randell. I'm Lindsey Stafford."

"Hi, Miss Lindsey." A smile beamed on her cute face. "Thank you for taking care of Whiskey, and Uncle Brady."

"You're very welcome."

The child put her arm around her uncle's neck. "Did you know I'm gonna marry Uncle Brady when I grow up?"

You can have him, Lindsey thought. "Isn't that nice."

Lindsey hadn't planned to be gone all day, but she also hadn't planned to babysit an injured fighter pilot, either. That was until she'd been pushed aside by a five-year-old girl. It didn't matter her age, that female had already staked her claim on the man. What had amazed Lindsey was how Brady Randell's whole demeanor had changed when the child walked into the room.

She smiled. So he wasn't the tough guy he pretended to be.

Tired, Lindsey walked into the cabin the Randells had given her to use during her three-month stay. The one-bedroom structure was located in the Mustang Valley Nature Retreat. This cabin had been designed as a romantic getaway.

A big, river-rock fireplace, plush rug and overstuffed love seat were the centerpieces of the main room. The bedroom consisted of a large four-poster bed with satin sheets and an abundance of candles. It connected to a bathroom with a whirlpool tub that easily held two.

Definitely for a couple.

It was off season, so she had the place to herself except for the herd of wild mustangs that roamed freely in this area.

The only drawback was she had to park her SUV at

the top of the rise and walk or ride down in a golf cart.
There were no vehicles allowed in this area.

Hank Barrett, the patriarch of the Randell family,
was adamant about keeping his wild ponies protected.
Lindsey felt the same way. So many people thought of
them as nuisances, but the Randells had made sure this
area was going to be left untouched.

No development in this valley. Ever.

Luke Randell was the project manager for a gated
horse community being built on the land that edged the
valley. But the project had many strict rules.

It was dusk, and Lindsey looked out the picture
window at the scene below. Picking up the binoculars
off the sill, she focused in on the grassy meadow. She
sighed at seeing the half-dozen mustang ponies grazing
peacefully.

Her chest constricted at the incredible sight. How
could Jack Randell ever have left this place? More importantly, after all these years, how could she get him
to come here? Back to his home…his boys.

CHAPTER TWO

THE following week Brady got some good news. At his doctor's visit the day before, he learned his fracture was healing well. Well enough that the bulkier cast had been replaced with a walking cast, so he could finally put weight on his leg. That meant he could get rid of the crutches and use a cane. And start more-intense therapy.

Finally it was time to get back in shape so he could get back into the cockpit.

Brady had also succumbed to Luke's badgering and gone along as he toured the construction site. He cursed as the golf cart bounced over the uneven ground. He grabbed the frame as he nearly flew out of his seat. "Hey, do you think you could have missed a few potholes back there?"

Luke grinned as he continued to maneuver the vehicle along the ridge. "Just wanted to make sure you haven't fallen asleep."

"Not the way you drive." Brady zipped up his flight jacket to help ward off the morning chill. "Besides, I don't need any more injuries added to my list."

His brother gave him a sideways glance. "I might have to call on the pretty veterinarian to come by. Seems she's the only one who can handle you."

Brady tensed. Not one of his proudest moments. "I didn't need to be handled by anyone. I was fine then and I'm fine now." He hadn't seen the hot redhead since that day. Probably a good thing. If he let her, Lindsey Stafford could be a powerful distraction.

Luke stopped the cart, then he sat back with a sigh. "Now, is this a view or what?" He motioned with his hand. "What do you think?"

Brady looked through the grove of ancient oak trees that shaded part of the valley below. A creek flowed around the sturdy trunks and through high, golden meadow grass.

In the peaceful silence, Brady felt a calm come over him. "Not a bad view." His gaze went to the other side of the rise where a small cabin nestled on the hillside. Farther on was another log structure, and another nearly hidden from view. "Who lives up there?"

"That's the Mustang Valley Nature Retreat. It's part of our holdings, too. There are about a dozen cabins that are rented out through the summer months. Some of the construction staff is living there now. And also your Dr. Stafford."

Brady refused to take the bait. "Why? Can't she afford to rent her own place?"

"Since she's here temporarily, Hank offered her one of the cabins for her stay."

"How temporary?"

"Just until Doc Hillman is able to handle his practice again." Luke stole a glance at his brother. "Tess would love for Lindsey to stay on permanently. Maybe it's because she's a woman, but she likes how Lindsey seems to take extra time with Whiskey."

"I take it the stallion's leg is healed, since I saw Tess working him yesterday. Is he okay to compete?"

Luke nodded. "We're headed to Fort Worth this next weekend. Tess is entering Whiskey in the nonpro NCHA Futurity. But don't worry, Bernice will be here if you need anything."

Brady hated everyone hovering over him. "I've managed to take care of myself most of my life, and I can handle it now."

Luke glanced down at Brady's new cast. "Seems you can get around better, too. How is the leg? Giving you any trouble since you've been walking on it?"

Sometimes it hurt like hell. "No. Between Dr. Pahl and the therapist conferring, I haven't been allowed to do much. But I get to start real therapy next week." His therapist, Brenna, was Dylan's wife, another cousin. She hadn't been easy on him so far, but he liked that about her. She'd warned him about starting out slow. He wasn't good at slow. He needed to get back into shape again, and fast. Granted, the wide-open beauty of Mustang Valley was peaceful, but he needed the vast sky through the cockpit of his F-16 to feed his soul.

"Is everyone around here related to us?" Brady asked.

Luke leaned back. "Just about. It takes getting used to, having all this family."

If he and Brady had anything in common, it was that they were both only children. "Being in the military, we moved around a lot. I didn't have a chance to make friends, so most of the time it was just the three of us."

"You had plenty of family—Uncle Jack's family—our dad just chose not to come back here."

Brady knew that he and Luke would never agree about Sam Randell. He'd abandoned his oldest son, but in truth, he wasn't around much to be a father to his second boy, either.

"So Dad chose a military career over ranching. I bet that didn't make a lot of people happy," Brady said.

"And he chose your mother over mine."

And me over you, Brady thought as his anger started to build. In truth, Sam had chosen his career over everyone. "Look, Luke, I thought you and I were okay with this. Whatever happened between our parents didn't have anything to do with us."

Luke stared out into the valley. "I'm okay with you, and our partnership. It's still hard sometimes." He let go of a long breath. "But like Tess said, I'm back home now." He turned to Brady. "And I finally got to meet my brother."

Brady wasn't about to get all mushy over the reunion. "And about a million cousins. Man, is there something about this valley that causes all these kids?"

Luke arched an eyebrow. "You got something against kids?"

"I don't mind one or two, but a squadron is a bit much."

Luke laughed. "I thought the same thing when I first came here. But they're all great kids, and our cousins are good parents. I believe it's because of their foster parent, Hank Barrett, who was a big influence on them. A lot more so than Jack Randell."

Brady smiled. "Oh, yeah, our uncle, the famous cattle rustler."

They both remained silent, reflecting on the past, when they spotted two riders. Brady recognized Tess on Lady and beside her another woman. A redhead with a familiar black hat.

"Looks like we have company." Luke leaned forward. "My Tess and your favorite doctor."

Brady groaned, but he found his pulse racing as he watched the two approach. Luke got out of the cart and went to his wife as she jumped down from her horse. Tess smiled at her husband, but when Brady turned his attention to Lindsey, she didn't show him any kind of special feminine greeting.

Good. He wasn't going to be here long enough to get tangled up with a woman. She wasn't his type, anyway. But as the redhead started toward him in her form-fitting jeans, cream-colored sweater and black nylon vest, his body suddenly called him a liar.

"Good morning, Mr. Randell."

Okay, he liked her a little, especially her attitude. "Since you've had your hands all over my body, don't you think you could call me Brady?"

She stopped next to the golf cart. "And since you're not that familiar with mine, you may call me Dr. Stafford."

He arched an eyebrow, letting his gaze speak for him. "The day isn't over yet."

She finally smiled. "How about Lindsey?"

"Oh, I don't know, I'm kind of leaning toward sexy doc."

She frowned. "Only if you want me to hurt you."

He glanced toward his brother and sister-in-law to see they were out of earshot. "When it comes to a beautiful woman, the last thing I'm thinking about is pain." He climbed out of the cart and stood in front of her. "I'm more a pleasure kind of guy."

Lindsey didn't like Brady Randell so close, but she refused to back away. "How about we stop the innuendos and try to have a normal conversation?"

He nodded. "Nice weather for a ride."

"Yes it is," she told him. "Tess invited me to go along to help thin the mustang herd and check for injuries. We're going to meet up with Hank Barrett and some of your cousins."

"So you're going to play doc?"

"I don't *play* doctor."

He raised a hand. "I only meant I wish I could go along and see you in action. But all I'm traveling in these days is this cart."

Lindsey knew the confinement had to be hard for Brady. She glanced down at the new, smaller cast. "It looks like you're making progress and will be back in the cockpit soon."

"That's what I'm shooting for."

She could see the cocky determination on his face. No doubt he looked even more handsome in his flight jumpsuit. She glanced down at his worn jeans, then upward to his straw Stetson. He wasn't a bad imitation of a cowboy, either.

"Maybe if your doctor approves, you could go out for a short ride. Nothing strenuous, of course. But I bet Tess has a gentle mount."

"I'd take anything at this point."

"Can you drive a car, yet?"

He nodded. "Since it's my left foot, yes, but only if it's an automatic. My '67 Chevy Camaro back at the base is a stick shift."

She never doubted that for a second, or the fact that the vehicle was a hotrod. Brady Randell was definitely not her type. She was all about settling down, safety and animals. He was a death-defying jet jockey with no intention of letting grass grow under his boots. She looked up into his piercing eyes and her heart went crazy. Okay, speaking from a sensual aspect, this man was any woman's type.

She really needed to stay clear of him.

"I should get going. I have appointments this afternoon." She turned to find Tess lost in her husband's arms. They were exchanging kisses and whispered lover's secrets. The couple seemed unaware anyone else was around.

Brady came up behind her. "Those two are like that all the time. I hate to say it, but it makes me a little jealous."

Lindsey felt Brady's breath against her ear. The warmth of his large body shielded her from the cool morning. She closed her eyes momentarily. Yes, she longed to be part of a couple. To find the right man. Someday.

Right now she had other things to think about. Top on her list was the true reason she'd come to San Angelo, and her time was limited to find the answers she needed. Getting involved with a man would only complicate matters. She finally moved away from temptation.

"Tess," she called. "We need to get going if we're to meet up with Hank and the others." She glanced at Brady. "I'm glad you're doing well."

He leaned against his cane. "Like I said, I wish I was going with you, Doc."

"Maybe when your leg is healed," she promised as she backed away. Was she crazy?

"I'll look forward to it," he called. "I'll work to make sure it's soon."

Lindsey was still chiding herself when they reached the edge of the valley. There was high grass mixed in with thick native mesquite bushes. Ancient oak trees arched over the riding path like a canopy filtering the sunlight. The November day was brisk, causing her skin to tingle. She felt exhilarated.

Her thoughts returned to Brady. She hadn't expected to see him again so soon. He'd looked considerably better than the last time. He'd shaved and was dressed in jeans and a gray U.S. Air Force sweatshirt under his bomber jacket. In a cowboy hat, he looked cocky and sure of himself.

"How are you holding up?" Tess asked as she rode up beside her.

"I'm fine. In fact if I could schedule it, I'd ride every day."

Tess smiled. "I come out to check the ponies every week during the winter. I could saddle up Dusty and bring him by the cabin for you."

"If I'm not busy, I'd love it." She patted the seasoned buckskin gelding, remembering her childhood days at the ranch. She loved the freedom of riding. It had been her escape from a lot of problems, especially during her parents' abusive marriage. "You sure you don't mind me borrowing Dusty?"

"Anytime. Since Dad can't ride anymore, I appreciate anyone who exercises him."

Lindsey's heart softened. Tess's father was in the beginning stages of Alzheimer's. "Good. I'll let you know my schedule."

"And maybe you can help get Brady up and riding, too."

Lindsey glanced over to see Tess's smile. "Shouldn't he walk before he gets on a horse?"

Tess shrugged. "Maybe he can do both. We're willing to try anything to get him out of the house. Luke managed today, but not without a lot of prodding."

She couldn't imagine the captain doing anything he didn't want to do. "It's a start."

"Since the two had never met until a few months ago, both Luke and Brady are still getting to know each other. If their father, Sam Randell, hadn't left them both the ranch, I wonder if they would have ever met."

"Then it's good they have this opportunity."

"I feel the same way," Tess said. "Although they do

have very different views of their father. Luke was deserted by Sam when his parents divorced. Brady had him around most of his life."

Lindsey rested her hands on the saddle horn, letting Dusty take the lead. "Sometimes there isn't a choice."

"There's always a choice," Tess murmured, then pointed up ahead. "There's Hank, Cade and Chance."

Lindsey knew Hank Barrett was the one who'd taken in the three Randell brothers, Chance, Cade and Travis, to raise after their father, Jack, had been sent to prison.

As they got closer to the men on horseback, Lindsey could see the strong family resemblance between the brothers. It seemed all Randell men were tall, with that rangy, muscular build. The square jaw and cleft in the chin was like a brand, telling the world who they belonged to.

She'd met Chance and Travis earlier, but Cade looked even more like the man Lindsey had called Dad for the past fifteen years.

The difference was these men shared his blood. She didn't.

Jack Randell was only her stepfather.

Just as soon as Jack and her mother returned home from their vacation and discovered she'd gone against his wishes, he wouldn't be happy.

It wasn't as though she'd planned to come to San Angelo. It had been curiosity that had her go to the job interview. She told herself she only wanted to meet Travis, one of Jack's sons. Then she found herself accepting the position. After all, it was only temporary.

* * *

Hank Barrett sat back in the saddle and watched Tess approach with the new veterinarian. Ever since Travis returned from Dallas singing Dr. Lindsey Stafford's praises, Hank had been anxious to meet her.

He smiled as the redhead rode closer. She was easy on the eyes, and if there was one thing he appreciated, it was a pretty female, no matter what the age.

Hank greeted Tess. "Hello, Mrs. Randell."

"Good morning, Mr. Barrett," she answered. "Hi, Cade, Chance."

Chance touched the brim of his hat in greeting. "Tess." He glanced at the redhead. "Dr. Stafford, nice seeing you again. This is our other brother, Cade. And this is Hank Barrett, the one who started the mustang project."

Hank nodded at the petite woman who sat comfortably in the saddle. There was something about her name that was familiar. "Dr. Stafford, I'm glad you could join us.

"Please, everyone, call me Lindsey." Her horse shifted sideways. "And thank you for inviting me along today."

"Well, Lindsey," Hank began, "I hope you still feel that way if the ponies don't cooperate. They've been known to be stubborn."

The doctor rewarded him with a smile. "I hear old Dusty here is pretty good at cutting out his target."

Cade reined his roan back. "I guess we'll know soon enough if he likes to chase wild ponies as much as cows." He grinned and Lindsey tensed, once again seeing the resemblance to his father.

"I'd say we better get going," Chance said, pointing to the herd off in the distance.

Lindsey looked at Hank for direction as they started down the trail.

"We'll let Chance and Cade take the lead," he said. "Wyatt, Dylan and Jarred are at the other end of the canyon to drive the herd toward us."

"I'll just follow you," she said.

Hank nodded. "Okay, let's go and get us some ponies."

They rode off, and Lindsey felt she was taking a step back in time. To see the wild ponies in their natural setting. This had been another big draw for her to come here. She just didn't realize how much she would already love it.

Two hours later Brady sat with Luke in his truck, waiting at the temporary corral at Hank's ranch, the Circle B Ranch. He was still wondering why he'd come. Of course, it beat the alternative, sitting back at the cottage. That had been what he told Luke, anyway. Not that he wanted another chance to see Lindsey Stafford again.

"They're coming," Luke called as he climbed down off the railing.

His own excitement growing, Brady got out of the truck and looked to where his brother pointed. He saw the riders on horseback, chasing after the ponies. An assorted mixture of paints, bays and buckskins. Over a dozen as far as he could see. But he couldn't find Lindsey.

"There's Tess," Luke called.

It was easy to catch his sister-in-law's long blond

hair. Then he spotted Lindsey's black hat. She was riding drag, a bandana tied around the lower part of her face to help filter the dust.

"Come on, bro, help me with the gates." Brady was glad he could finally manage to do something useful. He followed his brother, took one side and swung open the metal gate. It had been a while since he'd been around horses, but he knew they could be unpredictable at best. The first two ponies arrived and went into the pen, but the third and fourth decided to turn off.

Hanging on to the gate, Brady yanked off his hat, waved it around and yelled to turn the horse back. Then Chance and Cade showed up to take over. Finally the last of the ponies were in the large pen and the gate shut.

His cousins climbed off their horses and everyone went to the corral to check out their finds. Brady's gaze was on Lindsey. She dismounted and walked toward the metal railing with the old guy, Hank.

Barrett looked the part of mentor, father and grandfather. He didn't have to demand respect, but he got it. He wasn't a Randell, but he'd earned the title of family patriarch.

He nodded at Brady. "Good to see you up and around."

"It's a start."

"Well, if you get the doctor's okay, you can go out with us the next time."

Brady nodded. Chances were, if he was strong enough to chase wild mustangs, he'd be hightailing it for the cockpit of his F-16. "Thank you, sir," Brady said. "I'd like that."

Hank turned back to Lindsey. "I think we got ourselves a good-looking bunch this time."

Lindsey avoided Brady's gaze and went up to the gate. "I'm worried about the paint. See how he favors the right front leg?"

Brady looked, too, but he had to watch closely to see the slight limp.

"It could be a pebble. I'm going to have to examine him, but I have appointments this afternoon."

Hank agreed as he checked his watch. "Tomorrow, then. We'll separate them so they all can be examined and inoculated. How's that with you, Doc?"

"I could come by tomorrow afternoon for a few hours."

"Good, it will give us time to see which ponies are worth the time to saddle break."

"Why are you saddle breaking them?" Brady asked.

"So we can sell them at auction. Since we have to thin the herd, we want to find good homes for them."

Brady had his eye on a gray stallion that didn't like being confined in the pen. He kept moving back and forth along the fence.

Hank waved the group on. "Everyone is welcome to come up to the house for lunch. Lindsey, I hope you can join us."

"I'd like that." She pulled out her phone. "I just need to check my messages." She hung back from the group.

Hank looked at Brady. "How about you, Captain? I wouldn't mind hearing a few F-16 stories."

"I might have one or two that are worth repeating." Using his cane, Brady managed to fall into step beside Hank. Although his steps were awkward, he was happy to be able to get around. What he couldn't understand was why he was feeling drawn to this family. Not to mention one vet.

They made their way into the compound where a large ranch house stood. It was painted glossy white with dark green trim. The barn and other buildings were also white and well kept.

"Nice place, Hank," Brady said.

"Thanks. My boys run things now. In the summer months we open it as a dude ranch of sorts, but it's a working ranch." He grinned. "You'd be surprised what people will pay just to do chores like a ranch hand."

Cade joined the group. "Yeah, Chance, Travis and I had to do the work for nothing growing up."

"It built character," Hank told him.

Cade laughed. "Well, I sure got a lot of that, then."

Brady listened to the teasing between the brothers and Hank. Suddenly he thought back to how much his own father had been away during his life. All the baseball games he'd missed, the birthdays and holidays. As a typical kid he did a lot to get Sam's attention. Most of it didn't work, until he got into ROTC in high school, then into the academy.

"You boys turned out okay," Hank said. "You've settled down with pretty wives and have families."

Brady glanced over his shoulder and caught sight of Lindsey hurrying to catch up, so he hung back.

"Do you have to run off?"

"No, I can stay for lunch. But I have a two-o'clock appointment."

"Good, that will give me time," he said.

She frowned. "Time for what?"

"Time to convince you I'm not a total jerk."

"Really." She looked skeptical. "You think I should go easy on you?"

"No, but I'm hoping my Randell charm will win out."

She smiled. "So the average guy doesn't have a chance over a Randell?"

"That's right."

They took slow, easy steps toward the back porch.

"Well, I disagree on that theory," she said. "Jarred Trager, and Dylan and Wyatt Gentry do all right in the charm department."

Brady fought rising jealousy, recalling how his cousins had been flirting with her earlier. They had their own wives. "That just goes to show you a Randell wins out."

She stopped and looked confused. "But they're not Randells?"

He nodded. "Yes, they are. Seems Uncle Jack had three more sons."

CHAPTER THREE

AS HARD AS LINDSEY TRIED, she couldn't hide her shock. "Really" was all she could come up with.

Brady gave a sharp nod. "Evidently Uncle Jack was quite the lady's man when he was out on the rodeo circuit."

"Have Jarred, Wyatt and Dylan always lived here?"

Brady shook his head. "About half a dozen years ago, Jarred Trager showed up. He had found an old letter from Jack to his mother that talked about their affair. He came here and met Dana Shayne and her son, Evan. They married a short time later." He shrugged. "That's the condensed version that Luke gave me."

Lindsey took easy breaths as they continued on toward the Barrett house. She walked slowly so Brady could keep up, and so she could try to absorb what he told her. Had Jack known about his other sons?

"You say Wyatt and Dylan are your cousins, too?" She should have seen the resemblance in the men.

He nodded. "After their mother finally told the twins who their father was, Wyatt came to San Angelo looking for Jack, too. Wyatt ended up buying Uncle Jack's half of the Rocking R and found Maura Wells and her two kids, Jeff and Holly, living in the rundown house. A few months later his twin, Dylan, arrived after he'd been injured bull riding. He ended up marrying his physical therapist, Brenna. Who, by the way, is putting me through torture these days."

They reached the porch and he turned to her. "You seem pretty curious about the Randell family."

She shrugged. "The Randells are a big part of this valley. As an only child it's interesting to hear about a large family."

"Yeah, aren't we just one, big happy family."

"I'd take them," Lindsey told him, trying to act light-hearted. It was difficult. From the beginning, Jack had warned her and her mother about his shady past. She also realized that her stepfather needed to know about his other sons. If only to make amends with them.

Suddenly the back door opened and Hank peered out. "There you are. I was wondering if you two had gotten lost."

Brady used the railing to climb the steps. "No, I'm a little slow these days."

Hank smiled. "I thought you were just hanging back to get some time with a pretty lady."

"Well, that, too."

Lindsey felt her heart accelerate, but she put on a smile. "Well, now that we're here, how about some lunch?"

Hank ushered them into a huge old fashioned kitchen. Sunny yellow walls were lined with maple cupboards. The white-tiled counter gleamed, and a tall, older woman was busy setting the table.

She turned and smiled. "Hello, you must be the new vet, Dr. Stafford. I'm Hank's wife, Ella."

"And I'm Lindsey."

Her friendly brown eyes searched Lindsey's face. "It's nice to meet you. Hank said you were pretty, and he's right."

Cade walked by her. "Hank says all the women are pretty."

"That's because all the women around here *are* pretty." Hank hugged his wife to his side, kissing her cheek.

Ella acted as if she were pushing him away. "Be careful, Lindsey. Hank will be wanting to know if you're a good cook, too."

Hank tried to look indignant. "I hardly know this woman. But if she can cook up any special dishes, I wouldn't mind sampling them, say at our next family get-together. Thanksgiving is coming up."

Cade grinned as he took his seat at the table. "Watch what you say, Hank, or Ella will have you sleeping in the bunkhouse."

The group hooted with laughter, and Lindsey quickly realized she'd been had. "Well, sorry to disappoint you, Hank, but I spent all my free time studying the last few years. So my culinary skills are sorely lacking."

Hank sighed. "That's going to make it harder for you to get a man."

Lindsey was too stunned to speak, but Tess did it for her. "Hank Barrett, stop your teasing. We want Lindsey to stay, not run her off." She turned to Lindsey. "Please sit down, unless you want to clobber Hank first."

Lindsey walked around the table. "I think I'll wait until I have some big instruments in my hand."

The table broke into another round of laughter as she took a seat next to Tess and Luke. Brady managed to snag the seat next to hers.

He leaned toward her and murmured, "You sure know how to hold your own, Doc. I should call you when I'm being chewed out by my commanding officer."

"I can't imagine that ever happening, not with your sweet disposition."

Those dark bedroom eyes bore into hers. "I'm workin' on changing that." He grinned. "Give me a little time, and my charm will melt you."

Lindsey knew Brady was more dangerous than any of the Randells. Because he was the one who could get to her. And when he discovered who she was, he wouldn't be happy. None of the Randells would be, not when they learned that Jack had hung around to play the doting father to her.

Brady hated being cooped up. That was the reason three mornings later he headed down to the barn. He needed the exercise. He'd been lifting weights to keep in shape, but hanging around the cottage was driving him up a wall.

He told himself it wasn't the possibility of meeting up with Lindsey and Tess coming back from their ride. It was just to take a walk. He ran into the groomer washing Lady and ended up helping with some of the light chores. He found that working his muscles felt good. Just being able to complete a simple task helped his mood. By the time an hour was up, the temperature had warmed. He'd shed his jacket and was mucking out a stall when Tess and Lindsey came into the barn.

Both women were laughing, their cheeks flushed from the cool weather as they led their horses. Lindsey spotted him, and her smile dropped.

Tess spoke first. "Brady, what are you doing out here?"

"Earning my keep," he told his sister-in-law. "It's about time I did something around here."

Tess glanced down at the cast on his foot. "Just so long as you don't do any damage."

"I've been careful, *Mom*," he teased.

Tess fought a smile and lost. "Well, you can go out and play." She turned to Lindsey. "I hate to run off, but I need to meet Livy's bus. Juan can handle the horses until I get back."

"Not a problem, I can stay and take care of my horse," Lindsey said as she took the reins from her. "It's the least I can do for you letting me ride. So go on, go get your daughter."

"Thanks." Tess smiled as she backed away.

"I can help, too," Brady said.

"There's no need," Lindsey said. "I would hate to take you away from your job."

Brady didn't back away. "Then after I help you, you can help me. There are two more stalls to clean. Unless it's too dirty a job for you."

She made an unladylike snort. "I've probably

mucked out more stalls than you've seen. I grew up on a horse ranch."

He took Whiskey's reins from her. He loved to see her get riled. It made her eyes turn a deep emerald green. "You probably have. We didn't live very long on our ranch."

They walked slowly to the stallion's stall. Right next to it was Dusty's. "Where was your ranch?" she asked.

"We had a small place in Utah not far from the base. Dad bought it with his reenlistment bonus. With the help of a foreman, he ran a small yearling operation for about four years. I was ten when he was sent overseas and had to sell the place." He wasn't sure why he was telling her this. He tossed the stirrup over the seat and unfastened the cinch, then pulled the saddle off the horse and took it to the stand outside the stall. After Lindsey pulled off Dusty's, he took it. He liked moving around, being active. He found his balance was a lot better.

"Thanks." She went to work on the rest of the tack. "It's a shame you never got to live here."

"Dad never told me about the Rocking R until last year when he got sick."

"Had he been ill for long?"

Brady shrugged, remembering the hulk of a man who had slowly faded away after he retired from the air force. Even his wife, Georgia, hadn't been enough to keep him happy and at home. She'd died alone.

"Dad ignored the doctor's advice," he told her. "After he retired, I don't think he cared much if he lived or died." He gaze met hers. "They say I'm a lot like him. All I've known is the military."

Lindsey paused at her task, hearing the sadness in his voice, seeing it in his eyes. She suspected coming here and meeting the Randells had been overwhelming for him.

She suddenly thought of Jack. What was going to happen to him, when he was too stubborn to help himself? Well, she couldn't let that happen, not without doing everything possible, at the very least to get him to see his sons.

"Are you okay?"

Hearing Brady's voice, Lindsey pushed away the wayward thoughts. "I'm fine. Just thinking about how lucky you are to find your brother," she said. "And to be able to come here, and be with family."

He snorted. "Hell, I knew nothing about all these cousins. Dad never talked about them. Most of the time, it was just Mom and me." He shrugged. "We moved around a lot. But, hey, I got to see the world before I was in high school."

"Too bad you never got to come here."

He straightened. "My dad had to go where the air force sent him. That's the way it was then, and the way it is now. You go where you're assigned."

Lindsey nodded. "I bet your dad was proud of you."

He blinked, as if the question caught him off guard. "Hell, I guess so. Why so many questions?"

She had no doubt this man didn't share much about himself. "I'm just curious."

"Okay, here's the lowdown. I'm a fighter pilot in the U.S. Air Force. I'm qualified to fly F-15 and F-16 and at this time stationed out of Hill AFB in Utah." He moved closer. "Do you want my rank and serial number?" He reached inside his shirt and pulled out his dog tags. The chain dangled in his hand as if to taunt her.

"No, I think I have enough info."

She returned to her task of removing the gelding's bridle, a little embarrassed. She didn't have any business questioning this man or thinking about developing any feelings for him.

"Family is important, Brady. Get to know your brother and cousins before the chance slips away."

"I don't seem to have a choice, for now, anyway." He looked down at his injured leg. "There's no guarantee that I can go back to flying."

"Even if you can't fly again, there are other careers in the air force."

"Not for me." A muscle tightened in his jaw. "It's who I am. It's the only thing I've ever wanted to do."

"Flying can't define you as a person, Brady. It's what you love, yes, but not who you are. You can do something else, or go wherever. Maybe even live here."

"I hardly see myself as a rancher. I need a little more excitement." He relaxed as his dark-eyed gaze settled on her face. "Of course, if you'll be around…"

She was caught off guard. "My job here is temporary."

A slow, lazy grin appeared. No doubt a sample of the Randell killer charm. "Yeah, but you could make it permanent. Everyone wants you to stay on." His gaze moved over her. "And I could make a point to come back here for an occasional visit."

Lindsey refused to react to Brady's arrogant comment. She had other worries. For one, would she be welcome after they learned her real reason for being here? "You'd be wasting your time, Captain."

His dark eyes narrowed. "Why? Is there a man back in Fort Worth?"

She looked at him. "Yes, there is someone back home."

Brady hated being caught off guard, and he was truly blindsided by Lindsey Stafford. The only good thing was that Tess walked into the barn before she could tell him about her man.

He grabbed his cane and headed out the door. He didn't like the game Lindsey Stafford was playing. With women in the past, he set the rules. No attachments and no commitments. Have some fun, then walk away. So far there hadn't been any fun, but he sure as hell was doing the walking.

He should have known she'd be trouble the second he first saw her. He climbed the porch steps, went into the cottage and didn't stop until he got to the kitchen and pulled a can of iced tea from the refrigerator. After a long drink, he worked on calming down. He was going to erase her from his head. But he doubted anything would do the job.

What surprised him was why this even bothered him. She was leaving in a few months. So what? He was going back to his base in Utah. And besides there were other women…a lot of women.

A knock sounded on the door, but he ignored it. When the knocking continued he figured it was probably Luke or Tess. They wouldn't give up. He finally went and pulled open the door.

Damned if Lindsey wasn't standing there on his porch.

"Did you forget to tell me something else?"

She didn't act sorry. "Yes. Before you took off, I was about to mention that the man in my life—"

"Believe me," he interrupted, "I'm not interested."

She didn't move. "The man is my stepfather."

His heart began to race. "Your stepfather?"

"Yes. He's been ill recently, and I don't want to make any long commitments away from home."

Brady watched the sadness play on her face, and the sudden tightness in his gut caught him off guard. He reached for her and pulled her inside the house. Closing the door, he pushed her back against the wall.

"Do you know you had me crazy, thinking all sorts of things?"

She blinked as her breathing grew rapid. "You didn't let me tell you anything else," she whispered.

Her slim body was pressed against his, reminding him how long he'd been without a woman. "All I want to know is if you have someone special in your life, a husband, a significant other, a friend with benefits." He raised an eyebrow, praying she'd give him the right answer.

"No, none of the above."

Brady's resolve disappeared as he cupped her face and lowered his head to hers. "Maybe we should work on that," he breathed just as his mouth closed over hers.

She tasted sweet and sexy at the same time. He

hungered for her like no woman before. He couldn't get enough of her as his tongue dove into her mouth. Lindsey murmured something deep in her throat and her arms slipped around his neck.

Brady slid his hands inside her coat, under her sweatshirt to her bare back, and pulled her as close to him as possible. The imprint of her breasts against his chest nearly drove him over the edge.

He still needed more. His fingers traced across her warm, soft skin to her breasts. The material was thin enough to feel her pebbled nipples through the lace. This time he groaned.

With a gasp, he broke off the kiss and sucked air into his starved lungs. He tried to slow the drumming of his heart as his gaze searched hers to find the same need and raw desire.

"You shouldn't have done that," she breathed.

He shook his head. "Probably not, Doc. But my common sense doesn't seem to be working right now," he assured her as his head lowered to hers again.

Lindsey had called herself every kind of fool by the time she made her way back to the cabin. She'd managed to escape Brady Randell's arms, but just barely.

Once inside she leaned back against the door and shut her eyes only to relive the man's mind-blowing kisses. The feel of his hands on her skin as his mouth expertly caressed hers turning her into a whimpering teenager. What in the world had possessed her to go after him? To soothe his ego? To poke at the lion in his den?

She could still see those dark eyes, and that sexy grin spread across his face, looking as if he'd just conquered Mt. Everest. Lindsey groaned. She didn't need this kind of distraction to add to the already complicated situation.

She hadn't come here to get involved with a man, especially a cocky jet pilot with an ego that needed to be stroked. Well, she wasn't stroking anything of Brady Randell's. He wasn't her type. She never could handle a casual affair, no matter how good-looking and tempting the man was.

It would be wise to keep her distance. She needed to focus her attention on Brady's cousins. Jack's sons.

Lindsey's thoughts turned to her stepfather and the phone conversation she'd overheard during her last visit home in September.

Ever since Jack's first leukemia diagnosis four years ago, she and her mother had kept a close watch on his health. She'd recalled her stepfather's year of intense chemotherapy. How they'd almost lost him. He pulled through, and had been in remission for nearly three years. Until this last checkup.

Jack didn't want to tell her, but he finally admitted what the doctor reported, that any chemotherapy treatment wouldn't help him. He needed a bone marrow transplant to survive. That was when Lindsey begged Jack to contact his sons. He refused adamantly, saying he'd done enough damage in their lives, he couldn't ask anything from them.

Then Jack made Lindsey swear she wouldn't tell her mother. He didn't want to ruin the long Panama Canal cruise they'd planned for months. He promised to tell her before they got back.

Lindsey reluctantly agreed, hoping she could help convince him to contact his sons. Then she saw the ad for a temporary veterinarian position in San Angelo and the referral name of Travis Randell. She had to go. If only to meet one of Jack's sons. One of the boys he'd abandoned when he was sent off to prison.

Suddenly her cell phone rang and she dug into her purse to find it. "Hello."

"Well, I was wandering if you'd ever answer your phone." Jack Randell's voice came through loud and clear.

She tried to calm her panic. "Dad, you're back?"

"Not quite, your mother and I are spending another week away. We're in Los Angeles visiting friends."

She sighed in relief. "That's great, you two haven't had a vacation in so long."

"How about you, Lindy? How's the job hunting going?"

"Oh, I've had a few interviews, but I'm still looking for just the right position." She'd already found it, but knew that she'd never be able to stay here.

She changed the subject. "Have you had a chance to tell Mom?"

There was a long hesitation. "The right time hasn't come up, yet."

She closed her eyes. "Oh, Dad. I wish you'd think about what I suggested."

"Look, Lin, your mother wants to talk to you, so I'll say goodbye for now. I love you."

Tears filled her eyes. "I love you, too, Dad."

"Lindsey?" her mother said when she got on the phone. "How are you, honey?"

"Outside of missing you guys, pretty good. The job hunting is slow." She lied again and hated it. She and her mom had gone through a lot together before Jack came into their lives. She didn't like keeping this secret from her.

"I think you should hold out for what you want. And you know Jack and I would love to have you close to home."

That was her problem. Lindsey had already felt as if she'd come home, right here. "I've got my résumé out there, but I might just have to take something temporary until the good job comes around. I still have school loans to pay back."

"You know we want to help you."

"Thanks, Mom. I'm fine."

"My independent daughter." She heard her mother giggle, knowing Jack was probably distracting her. "Maybe you should take some time off. Go on a vacation and find yourself a man."

Lindsey's thoughts turned to Brady. She already had, but she couldn't compete with his lifestyle. Captain Randell was definitely off-limits. For more reasons than she could count.

The next morning Lindsey was awakened by pounding on her door. "Just a minute," she called as she threw on a robe over her pajamas, walked out of the bedroom and across the tiled floor through the main room.

Who could be here this early?

She tossed her mussed hair back as she opened the door to find Brady on her porch. He was in jeans and his flight jacket and the usual straw cowboy hat.

"Brady?"

"Morning, Doc." He walked inside with a sight limp.

"Uh, it's a little early to visit don't you think?" She glanced at the clock over the fireplace that read 6:30 a.m. and hugged her robe together.

He smiled. "This is the best part of the day. I loved those early-morning runs, the sun just coming up over the horizon." He released a breath. "Nothing like it, being all alone with the endless sky overhead and the desert floor below." Then he came out of his thoughts. "Or if I'm in a roll, the sky below and the ground above."

She watched the flicker of emotions play over his face and it tugged at her heart. "You miss it, don't you?"

He shrugged. "There's no rush like it." Then he straightened. "I'm sorry to bother you, but I was taking a ride in the golf cart this morning. That's when I saw the mustang. A mare. She's either lame or hurt."

Lindsey was on her way outside before Brady finished explaining. The cold weather had her hugging her robe together. "Where? Is she close by?"

Brady looked out. "She was. It's that little buckskin. Maybe she just picked up a rock."

"Or maybe worse. Hank told me he had some trouble a few months back when one of the mustangs was wounded. He said it looked like someone was shooting pellets."

"You think we should call Hank?" he asked.

"I'll have a look first."

"I'm going with you."

She didn't need to be anywhere around this man. But he could help her find the pony. She looked down at her pajamas. "Give me five minutes."

The golf cart wasn't easy to maneuver over the rough terrain, but it was all they had at the moment. A few hundred yards away Brady spotted the small herd of mustangs. Hanging back from the others was the mare.

So as not to disturb them, he drove the cart along the edge of the trees. "That's her," he said, his voice soft and even.

Stopping, he handed the binoculars to Lindsey. As she adjusted the focus to watch the herd, Brady couldn't help but watch her. She was pretty, though not in the traditional way. Her eyes were too large for her face, and very expressive. Her mouth was full, those lips… He swallowed, recalling her taste. She sure got his attention.

When she'd opened the door this morning, he'd lost all conscious thought as to why he was there. Her hair wild, her eyes with that sleepy quality, her mouth looking so kissable. Like yesterday, he found it hard to resist her and wanted nothing more than to carry her back to where she came from. Bed.

"Bingo," Lindsey said, still watching the mare. "I can spot a smear of blood high on her right forearm."

"How bad?" He took the binoculars from her and looked for himself.

"Bad enough that the wound should be treated." She got out of the cart and reached in the backseat for her bag. "I wonder if she'll let me get close to her."

"No need. I'll get her." Brady got out, went to the back of the cart, pulled up the seat and took a rope from the compartment.

She came after him. "You can't. Let me help."

He glared at her. "If I need your help I'll holler."

Lindsey had no doubt Brady could do this with or without a bad leg, or he'd die trying. And she had to let him.

"Fine." She went back to her seat.

For a big man, he moved quietly and swiftly in his athletic shoes, even with his walking cast. Most men would look clumsy. But not Brady.

After tying the end of the rope to a tree, he walked carefully behind the herd. One of the stallions whinnied and danced away, putting more distance between them. The mare looked up and began to shy away.

"It's okay, princess," Brady said, keeping his voice quiet and even. "I'm not going to hurt you, girl. I just want to help make you feel better."

The mare bobbed her head, but didn't move away from the intruder. Unlike the rest of the herd that had wandered farther down the meadow. Brady continued his journey as he crooned to the trembling buckskin. Surprisingly, he handled the rope expertly making the large loop. Mesmerized by his husky voice, Lindsey barely noticed when he slipped the lasso around the mare's neck, then led her back to the cart.

The docile pony followed without much resistance. Lindsey knew from Tess that the mare had been around for a long time. And by the look of the blood on her forearm, she was wounded.

"I guess my persistence as a kid learning to rope a steer paid off," he remarked as he held the mare steady.

"Hello, girl," Lindsey said softly. She moved slowly so she wouldn't spook the horse.

Brady shortened the rope so the animal couldn't move. "Come on, princess, Doc only wants to help you."

Lindsey tried to get a look, but the mare wouldn't let her too close. There was no doubt that there was blood and she saw the fresh entry wound of a bullet.

Lindsey stood. "She's been shot."

"Damn." Brady looked around. "Guess I should call Hank." He pulled out his phone. "He isn't going to be happy to learn someone's invaded Mustang Valley."

CHAPTER FOUR

IT TOOK nearly thirty minutes for Lindsey and Brady to lead the mustang to the Circle B Ranch. They could have transported her to the clinic, but Lindsey didn't want to take the time or traumatize the mare any more than necessary.

Lindsey had to anesthetize the animal to remove the .22 bullet embedded in the fleshy part of her forearm. The surgery went well, thanks to the help of Hank and Brady.

She went into Hank's house to clean up, then she returned to the barn to check the patient. The pony would be groggy from the anesthesia, and Lindsey wanted to keep a close watch on her for the next few days before they released her back out to the range.

When she entered the cool interior of the barn she paused at the sight of Brady leaning over the pony's stall, his injured leg rested on the lowest rail. Her attention went to his worn jeans pulled taut over his nicely shaped butt. She couldn't help but take the time to admire the view.

"How's my girl doing?" Brady crooned. Not surprisingly the little mare reacted to his voice. He didn't attempt to touch her, but waited until she came to him. She did, but only so close.

"Don't be afraid, sweetheart. I'm not gonna hurt you."

Lindsey closed her eyes as his deep voice reverberated through her. She didn't doubt that Captain Randell had spoken those words many times. To how many women? She also knew she couldn't be added to that list, but it was getting harder and harder to convince herself. Not even when she knew if she gave in it would be disastrous.

Suddenly Brady glanced over his shoulder, those dark eyes alert as he examined her closely. "Hi."

"Hi." She nodded toward the horse. "Looks like you've made a friend."

"What can I say? Females can't resist me."

She couldn't help but laugh. "And modest, too."

He walked toward her. "Haven't you heard? Viper pilots are a cocky bunch."

"How does that combination work for you?"

He shrugged. "Not bad." He leaned his forearms against the railing, his gaze zoned in on hers. "What works on you, Doc?"

Her heart pounded in her chest as she tried to come up with a believable lie. "I'm not interested in a fling, Captain. I'm too busy for one thing, and smart enough not to start something with a man who will be leaving soon."

He frowned. "You must know more than I do."

"Come on, Brady, we both know our careers come first. You're going to work like crazy to get back to flying your F-16, and I'm going to work just as hard to get my practice off the ground."

He took off his hat and ran his fingers through his short hair. "That doesn't mean we can't enjoy time with each other."

That would be a bad idea, she thought. "In the biblical sense, of course."

He gave her the once-over. "We don't have to jump into anything, but that could be…interesting."

"And like I said, that's dangerous."

"I would go for incredible. I seem to remember a kiss yesterday that nearly blew my socks off."

Hers, too. "So we just go for instant gratification?"

He shrugged. "Would it be so bad?"

She glared at him.

"Okay, okay. Then, how about we go for friends? You're just about the only person around here who isn't a Randell or related to one."

She tensed. Okay, technically she wasn't a Randell. But when her identity was discovered, Brady's loyalty would go to his family. That was the best reason she needed to put a stop to this. And now.

From the doorway of the barn, Hank watched Brady and Lindsey. Anyone who had any horse sense could see there was something brewing between those two.

The brooding captain's whole demeanor had changed since the pretty vet had shown up in town. Now, if they could just find a way to get Lindsey to give him a chance, then maybe they'd both stick around. Old Doc Hillman wanted to retire, or at least bring in another vet as a partner in the practice, and Lindsey Stafford would be perfect.

Stafford. He wished he could remember why that name sounded familiar.

"Hank?"

He turned around to see Ella. A rush of feelings stirred in him as he smiled at his wife.

"Is there trouble with the mare?"

"No, she seems to be coming along fine. I was just enjoying the scene." He nodded at the couple. "Mark my word, there's sparks between those two."

"Of course there is. They're young, good-looking and their hormones are on a rampage."

Ella had been the best thing that had happened to him in a long time. He'd been a fool to have taken years to realize his love for her. He drew her close to his side. "You don't have to be young to have those feelings."

She actually blushed and pushed him away. "Hank Barrett, stop talking like that. Someone might hear."

"So what if they do? We're not dead, woman. So don't put me out to pasture just yet." He took her hand. "Now, come on, let's go see how the mare is doing."

Hank and Ella reached the stall. "How she doin'?" he asked.

"She's coming along fine," Lindsey said. "But you should keep her a day or two longer. I'll give her another dose of antibiotics in the morning." She raised an eyebrow. "Did you report the shooting?"

Hank nodded. "Called the sheriff, but I'm sorry to say that it isn't a top priority. A lot of people don't care for the wild horses. That's the reason I wanted to make sure this land was a haven for them. I thought it would keep them safe." He turned to the pretty vet. "I appreciate all that you've done, Lindsey."

"I'm just glad Brady found the mare in time."

Brady shrugged. "I got lucky."

Hank grew serious. "Lucky or not, we appreciate it, Brady. Thank you, too. And you can bet I'm going to take the threat to heart. This has happened before and it's time I put a stop to it. I won't allow someone to trespass on my land and endanger my stock, or worse, my family."

Hank sighed. "And since the sheriff won't do much, I'm going to have to go out myself and find these good-for-nothin' cowards. Even if it's some crazy kids, we still have to stop them."

"I'd like to go along," Brady said.

Hank knew the captain had a lot to prove, mostly to himself. "And I welcome your help, son, but I don't want any heroics here."

Brady nodded. "You give the orders."

"I thought we'd do some investigating. Maybe the person or persons left behind some clues."

"I can help, too," Lindsey volunteered.

Hank wasn't sure about that. "I was thinking about sending the boys out on horseback. And we might not get back until after dark."

"I've ridden after dark," she added.

"Maybe it would be safer if you went by truck with Brady. You two seem to make a good team."

By late afternoon Lindsey was exhausted when she entered the cabin. After leaving the Circle B, she'd finished her scheduled appointments, and now only had twenty minutes before Brady was due to pick her up. Although she was eager to help, she had plenty of apprehension over being paired with the one man she'd been trying to avoid. But she cared enough about the mustangs to want to find the person or persons who were responsible for the shooting.

After a quick shower, Lindsey hurriedly dressed in clean jeans and a sweatshirt over a thermal T-shirt and slipped on her comfortable boots. She slapped together two ham sandwiches and was just finishing up when a knock sounded on the door. She opened it to find Brady. He, too, was dressed in a sweatshirt, jeans and his bomber jacket.

"Ready?"

"No, I'm running late." She handed him a sandwich and a bottle of water.

"Thanks."

"Are we going to meet at Hank's place?"

"No. He gave me a map of the area he wants us to cover. Chance and Hank are teamed together in a vehicle searching the other side of the ranch. Cade and Travis are on horseback, along with Jarred and Wyatt. You and I are teamed up to check this side of the property."

"Okay, let's go, Captain." She pulled on her all-weather nylon jacket, a scarf and stocking cap for warmth.

He held the door open for her, and she ducked under his arm. He suddenly looked big and intimidating, and deadly serious. She realized this situation could be the same, too. Whoever was shooting at defenseless animals was dangerous.

Outside, they made their way along the path that led up the rise. Even without his cane, Brady didn't seem to have any trouble making the climb up to the parking area. Next to her SUV was the Randell Guest Ranch four-by-four truck. He opened the door and slid into the driver's side. Why not? His right leg was fine.

She got in the passenger side as he bit into his sandwich. That's when his jacket opened and she saw a flash of metal. A gun was tucked into the waistband of his jeans.

"You brought a gun."

He stared the truck. "Yeah, Doc, I did." The floodlight overhead illuminated part of his face. "I hope I don't have to use it." He took another hearty bite and chewed. "But there's no way in hell I'm going out there unarmed." His voice took on a husky quality. "Let's just say it's a precaution."

Lindsey could see the determination in Brady's face and heard it in his voice. He made her feel safe. Besides, they needed to catch whoever was shooting at the mustangs.

She glanced out at the fading daylight. "Where are we supposed to go?"

He handed her the area map from the bench seat between them, then backed the truck out and headed for the highway. "Hank's marked the area he wants us to search."

She looked over the written directions. "Okay, at the

highway turn left and go down about a half mile to a service road."

Brady nodded and followed her navigation, trying to concentrate on his job and not think about Lindsey seated so close to him. How was he supposed to do that with her fresh lemon scent filling the small cab? It seemed to wrap around him, trying to distract him, reminding him how long it had been since he'd been with a woman. A long, long time.

With a groan, he shifted in his seat.

Lindsey turned to him. "You okay? Is your leg hurting you?"

Like hell. "No. I'm just trying to get into a comfortable position. If you can't see the directions, there's a flashlight on the floor."

"I can read just fine. If you'd rather I can drive."

"I said I can handle it," he told her, then finished the last of his sandwich.

"Okay, I'm just trying to help."

"Then read the map," he told her. "And get us to where we need to be."

"Then get ready." She pointed toward the driver's side of the road. "The turn-off should be coming up soon. There it is."

Brady pulled the truck onto the gravel road. After about twenty yards they came to a sign that read, Private Property. No Trespassing. But they soon discovered the gate was already open. "Maybe Hank left it open."

He threw the gearshift in park, reached for the cell phone and punched the buttons.

"This is Hank." Hank's voice came through laced with static. "Have you made it to your location?"

"Not quite. We're at the service road just off the highway. The gate's open. We weren't sure if you'd been here or not."

"Haven't been there in over a week, and none of the ranch hands would leave it open, either."

"Then we'll check it out."

"Call us if you see anything," Hank said. "We'll hightail it over there." There was a pause. "I know you won't walk into anything blindly, but be careful."

"Will do." Brady put the truck in four-wheel drive and moved cautiously down the road. He felt a rush of excitement. Besides bringing in the mare, this was the first useful thing he'd done in months.

When he came to a fork at the large tree, he slowed, then veered off to the right on the more-traveled road. They went along the uneven dirt path, passing through thick mesquite bushes that were so close they brushed the sides of the truck.

"Do you think this is the right way?" Lindsey asked.

He'd noticed the scratches on the truck when he'd gotten in. "I'd say this is a normal route. Besides, I have no choice but to keep going, even if it's just to turn around." He gave her a quick sideways glance, then returned his attention to the road. He slowed as they came out of the bushes into a grassy clearing. Right away he saw evidence that someone had been there recently.

"Bingo." Brady shut off the engine and got out. Lindsey followed after him. Together, they walked into the remnants of what was once a fire ring, a circle of rocks and some burnt wood.

"Well, someone sure as hell has been here," he said as he walked to the log and found scattered fast-food wrappers and several beer cans along with an empty whiskey bottle. "I'd bet there've been a few parties here."

"I'll call Hank," Lindsey said.

"Good idea." Brady went to the truck and returned with flashlights. He handed her one. "We're losing daylight fast. I'll search the area."

She punched in Hank's number and when he answered, she said, "We found a makeshift campsite about a half mile in. Looks like some kids have been here, and they've been drinking."

"Darn it, I was afraid of that. Is there any sign of anything else?"

"Brady's still looking around."

"Okay, we can be there as soon as we change a flat tire."

Lindsey hung up to see Brady wander off through the high grass. She caught up to him. "Hank will be here as fast he can. Maybe it would be better if you wait for Hank, and don't go out there alone."

He cocked an eyebrow. "Why, Doc, you're worried about me."

"I suspect you can handle yourself okay."

"Thanks for the credit. I've been able to get out of enemy territory, I think I can go look for some simple tracks." He pointed the flashlight down. "And in about ten minutes there'll be no light at all."

"Then I'm coming with you."

She followed after him, letting him lead the way.

He stopped and crouched down, motioning for Lindsey to do the same. "See how the grass is bent?"

She knelt down beside him. His hand pressed against her back, making it hard for her to concentrate on what he was saying.

"I don't think it was done by cattle. Hank doesn't have a herd even close to here. Could be the mustangs, but my guess is they're humans."

"So the shooter was probably here?"

He shrugged as his gaze met hers. "Or it could lead to a place one of the boys took his girl for some privacy." He raised an eyebrow. "A little private make-out place."

She felt the stirring in her stomach and she stood up. "We better keep looking."

Brady stood, too. He concentrated on finding some clues, anything that would prove a shooter was here. They continued to walk through the brush, then came to another clearing and more beer cans.

He aimed his flashlight along the perimeter and caught sight of a shiny object. He knelt down and picked up a brass shell casing, then another. He found a total of three.

"Well, I'll be damned."

Lindsey arrived at his side and looked at his hand. "Shell casings." She looked up at him. "So the shooter was here."

"He was, if these will match the bullet you removed from the mare." He noticed that she was shivering. "Come on, you're cold. Besides, it's too dark to find anything else. We'll wait for Hank." He pocketed the casings and guided her back to the truck.

Once inside, he started the truck and turned on the heater. "Sorry, I didn't notice the drop in temperature."

"It's okay, I'm fine." She smiled, but she was still shivering. "It was worth it. We found this place."

"And we might find who's responsible," he told her. He liked the fact that Lindsey Stafford wasn't afraid to get her hands dirty. He'd watched her yesterday with the mare. Saw firsthand her dedication.

He turned in his seat and leaned back against the door, stretching out his injured leg on the floor. Lindsey was huddled deep in her coat, trying to keep warm. He couldn't stand to watch her shivering.

"Lindsey." He spoke her name and she turned to him. Silently he held out his hands.

"Not a good idea, Brady."

"It's only to keep warm." He reached out and drew her into his arms. Once he opened his coat, she burrowed into his chest seeking warmth. He bit back a groan when her breasts pressed against him. Her hands were splayed against his ribs. He didn't dare take a breath. After a few minutes of heaven, he asked. "Have you gone to sleep on me?"

"No, but I could use some." She turned her head and shifted position slightly. "My beauty sleep was interrupted by someone pounding on my door at dawn."

He smiled, feeling her soft hair against his chin. "I'd say it was for a good reason. Besides, sleeping is highly overrated." He looked down at the woman in his arms. "I can think of more interesting ways to kill the time."

She didn't open her eyes. "Aren't you a little old to be trying to seduce a woman in the woods?"

It was her fault that he'd been thinking like a high school kid. "Hey, there was a time when I could do a lot with some moonlight, a little privacy and a bench seat."

She finally sat up and glared at him. "I bet."

"What can I say? Every teenage boy had one goal in mind."

"I wouldn't know. I didn't date much in school. I was focused on getting into college."

"I'm sure the boys in your school were disappointed."

The faint sound of a song on the radio filled the cab. Even in the darkness, he could feel her eyes on him.

"Hardly, they were more into blondes."

"They were fools." He leaned closer, but Lindsey put up her hand.

"Stop right there."

"Why, darlin', you seemed to like my kisses well enough the other day."

She breathed in a sharp breath. "Well, you didn't give me much of the chance to turn you down."

He studied her cute button nose and stubborn chin. Damn, she was pretty. "You're the one who showed up at my door. To me that said you were interested."

"To you, interested is if a woman breathes."

"I'm more selective than you think. Not just any woman, Doc." He leaned closer and gave in to temptation as he brushed a soft kiss against her lips.

She sucked in a breath, but didn't pull away. "Brady, don't start this. Neither one of us needs this kind of complication."

"You talk too much, Doc. It's cold outside and we need to generate some heat."

"Turn up the heater."

His hand cupped her face and turned her toward him. "How about this instead?" He captured her mouth just as a whimper escaped, but she didn't stop him. It took a few seconds to convince her but slowly her arms went around his neck and she allowed him to slide his tongue inside and taste her.

By the time he broke off the kiss, they both needed air. "Damn, woman, you're dangerous."

She started to pull away and he stopped her.

He leaned forward and nipped at her lower lip, drawing another moan from her. "And I'm a man who lives for danger."

She broke free and sat up. "Well, I don't. So back off fly boy."

He had to admit he wasn't used to this kind of resistance. He held up his hands. "Fine."

Irritated, Brady sat up. That's when he saw the headlights.

Still a little shaky from the kiss, Lindsey managed to get to the other side of the cab and pull herself together.

"Stay here," Brady told her. "It's cold out."

She could only nod when Brady grabbed his hat and climbed out of the truck. She could see he, too, had been affected by the kiss. That wasn't good.

"Hank," Brady called as they got out of the truck.

"What'd you find, son?"

"Over here." They walked to the campsite and shone the flashlights around the area. He handed Hank the casings. "Looks like whoever comes here has been doing it for a while."

Hank didn't look happy. "Well, I'm about to put a stop to it."

"Why not hold off on that for now? Instead, set a trap for them. That way you can let the law handle it. And hopefully stop the problem for good."

Chance stepped in. "What are you thinking of when you say trap?"

"Electronic surveillance." He glanced back at the truck, wanting to get back to Lindsey. "I could come by the ranch and discuss it with you." He glanced back and forth between the men.

"Sounds good," Hank said, but held up his hand. "I just don't want anyone to get hurt. Not us, or those kids. Nothing is worth that." He sighed. "So stop by tomorrow and we'll see if we can agree on a way to handle this."

Brady nodded. "Sounds good."

"Now, go and take Lindsey home. And thanks for the help."

They said their goodbyes, and Hank waved to Lindsey in the truck, then drove off with Chance.

Brady climbed into the warm cab, shifted into gear and followed the other truck out. "Looks like you got your wish, Lindsey. I can take you home and get you in bed."

"My, Captain, aren't you taking a lot for granted?"

He grinned and winked at her. Her heart tripped in her chest and she couldn't find any more words to say.

She was in big trouble.

Lindsey didn't talk on the drive back to the cabin. It had been a mistake going with Brady tonight, and letting him kiss her again was even more stupid. It was time to end any involvement with the man. Not give him encouragement, because in the end he'd walk away when he learned her connection to Jack Randell. The real reason she'd come here.

When they pulled into the parking area, Lindsey tried to get out of the truck before Brady could follow her. She wanted no repeat of what happened earlier. No more kissing Brady Randell was her recited mantra.

But the stubborn captain refused to take no for an answer and walked her to the well-lit porch. She unlocked the door but didn't go inside. Instead she turned around to face Brady. "Okay, I'm safely home. You can go now."

He leaned an arm against the doorjamb. "Look, Doc, I know you're ticked off at me right now, but if the truth be told, you were into that kiss just as much as I was."

"I'm not talking about this to you. So you need to go." She didn't want to admit how much she was drawn to him. "All I want is some sleep. My day starts early tomorrow."

Brady shifted his stance. He didn't have to get up at all, if he didn't want to. Even though his leg was throbbing like crazy, he didn't want to go back to the cottage and sit there alone watching some meaningless late-night television.

He raised a hand to argue when her cell phone went off. She pulled it from her coat pocket. "Dr. Stafford," she answered.

Brady watched her forehead wrinkle in a frown.

"I should be there in about twenty minutes," she said as she went inside and picked up a pen off the counter. "Give me the directions," she said, then began to jot down the instructions. "Yes, I know the road. Okay." She nodded. "I'm on my way." She flipped the phone closed.

"What's wrong?"

"The Carson's mare is having trouble birthing her foal. I've got to get out there." She hurried into the kitchen area, grabbed a bottle of water from the refrigerator and headed for the door.

"Need some help?" he called to her when he caught up with her on the driver's side of her SUV. "It's been a while, but I helped my dad a few times with calves."

She stopped. "It's a messy job and could take hours."

He smiled. "I'm your man, Doc."

That was what she was afraid of.

CHAPTER FIVE

THIS was getting to be a habit.

Brady was behind the wheel of her SUV, and Lindsey sat in the passenger seat, giving directions to the ranch. It took nearly twenty minutes to get to the Carson's place. A boy about ten stood by the road and flagged them down, then pointed toward the barn. That was where they found the boy's mother, Bonnie Carson, with her quarter horse.

In the oversize stall, the young mare was already down, her head cradled in her owner's lap, and visibly in distress. Lindsey knelt on the fresh straw floor.

"Mrs. Carson, I'm Dr. Stafford. This is Brady Randell."

"I can't tell you how glad I am to see you, Doctor, Mr. Randell."

Lindsey could hear the fatigue and fear in the woman's voice. "This here is Under the Mistletoe. We call her Missy."

Lindsey studied the laboring mare. "How long has Missy been down?"

"She's been up and down for the last few hours, but

this time it's been about ten to fifteen minutes. My husband would have been here, but he's stranded at the Denver Airport." There was a tremor in her voice. "Of course Missy chose now to go into labor." She nodded to her son. "Buddy has helped his dad, so I thought we could handle it. Then when Missy didn't seem to be getting anywhere, I called you."

Lindsey felt a strong contraction, and the horse's head came up and she let out a whinny. She soothed the animal until she calmed again. "It's okay, girl. We'll figure out what's taking so long." She looked at Bonnie. "I'll know more after I examine her."

Lindsey stood and went to her large case, not wanting to say out loud her suspicions that the foal might be breech.

Brady stood next to her. "What can I do?"

His voice was reassuring, and she was suddenly glad he was here with her. "You can bring me those clean towels and keep them handy." Stripping off her jacket, she nodded to the stack on a trunk outside the stall. She opened her medical bag and hung her stethoscope around her neck, then worked a waterless disinfectant over her hands and arms, took out a pair of latex gloves and slipped them on.

"I'll need you to go help Mrs. Carson, make sure that Missy stays down while I examine her."

"Done." Brady grabbed the towels and stacked them close by, then took his position to help the owner.

Lindsey knelt down and checked the horse's heart rate. Definitely fast. All the while she continued to talk softly as she slipped her hand inside the womb. She grimaced when she discovered the answer to the mare's long labor.

She sat back on her heels. "There's good news and bad," she said to Bonnie Carson. "The foal isn't a standard breech, but the legs are back. I need to bring them forward."

She looked at Brady. "Hold her still again." Their gaze met and he nodded, feeling a knot tighten his chest. He'd do his damnedest for her.

After another contraction, Lindsey reached back inside as far as her arm would allow and managed to get hold of one of the foal's legs. She pulled it forward. "Got one."

She looked at Brady and he sent her an encouraging wink. A little shiver rippled through her.

"Come on, Doc, one more to go," he whispered. "You can do it."

She had to glance away. That was when she spotted the preteen boy and a little girl peering between the stall railings. She didn't have to wonder what this horse meant to them.

Everyone went silent as if their concentration could help her search for the missing limb. It seemed to take forever, then she finally located it. "There you are." She maneuvered the leg in position as tears filled her eyes.

Entranced, Brady watched the intense focus on her face as she worked to help the mare. He soon discovered she was stronger than he could imagine. Beads of sweat popped on her forehead as she did her job. He could see her determination. With the next contraction, her efforts paid off when the mucus-covered hooves appeared.

"Come on, Missy." Tears filled Bonnie's eyes as she

coaxed the horse to continue the birthing. With Lindsey's assistance the foal slid out into the world. The kids cheered as Lindsey wiped the reddish-colored filly with a towel and nudged her to stand.

"Good job, Doc," Brady said. He was surprised to see Lindsey's blush, then her attention went back to her other patient.

"Missy did all the work." She patted the still-down mare. "Take a rest, girl, you deserve it."

Ten minutes later a mother's instinct took over and the horse stood to check out her baby.

"Thank you so much, Doctor," Bonnie said. "I was so afraid we were going to lose them both."

"I'm glad you called me." She turned to the kids. "Have you two come up with a name yet?"

They shrugged shyly, then the boy said, "Maybe we can call her Doc Lindsey."

Two hours later they finally got back in the truck, Lindsey didn't even bother fighting Brady for the keys. She closed her eyes and leaned back against the headrest, feeling exhausted and exhilarated at the same time.

"Was this your first?" Brady asked. "Your first breech, I mean."

"Did it show?"

"No. You did an incredible job."

"Until tonight, I've only assisted in breech deliveries. Not that I would have told Bonnie Carson that."

"Well, mama and baby are doing fine. That's all that counts," Brady said.

His compliment meant a lot to her. "Thanks. And thank you for your help, too."

"Why? You did all the work."

"Keeping a large horse calm is a big help, but especially with a first-time mother, it isn't easy."

He reached across the seat, took her hand and squeezed it. "Just glad I was there for you."

She found she liked his reassuring touch. She needed it right now; she needed him. How easy it would be to let go. Even though he had danger written all over him, she would eagerly welcome his attention, his strength…his heart-stopping kisses. She sighed deeply.

Who was she kidding? Brady Randell was already buried deep into her thoughts. A man any woman would desire, and she was no exception.

Even if she wasn't truly related to Jack Randell, it still wouldn't be safe to get involved with a man who would leave her when his time here was up.

He'd go back to his first love, flying.

Brady pulled into the parking lot. "Home, safe and sound." He looked at her from across the car, and she quickly climbed out to avoid temptation.

He came around the car and gave her the keys, then slipped his hands in the front pockets of his jeans. "It's been quite a night, Doc. Thanks for letting me tag along."

"I need to thank you again, Brady. You were a big help." Lindsey needed to get away from the man, before she made a big mistake. "You really don't have to walk me down to my door. I know your leg has to be hurting."

"It's not a problem."

Shaking her head, she started to back away, praying he wouldn't pursue her. "You can watch from here to see that I get inside safely."

He looked disappointed but nodded. "Well, Doc, it's been an interesting evening to say the least." He took a step closer, but Lindsey wasn't about to let him kiss her. Oh, no, she'd be a goner for sure.

"Good night." She turned and hurried down the slope, then tossed him a wave as she opened the cabin door. She sighed with relief when he saluted back and headed for Hank's truck.

Once inside, she shut the door with a final click. She was alone. Brady was gone. Maybe for good. Suddenly she felt the absolute loneliness rush over her.

In the past ten years, she'd concentrated on school and her career. There hadn't been time in her life for a man. Not that she missed it. She hadn't found anyone yet who made her heart race, made her breath catch. Until now.

Until Brady Randell.

He wasn't the answer, she told herself. He didn't want commitment, or a future with a woman. He was the love-'em-and-leave-'em type. He got his thrills from piloting a F-16 thousands of feet over the earth. He was just killing time, hanging around and flirting with her.

"So get any silly thoughts out of your head," she told herself as she headed to the bedroom, stripping off her dirty sweater. Removing her boots, she kicked free from her jeans and tossed them in the corner, deciding to deal with them in the morning. She looked longingly at the huge canopy bed with the thick satin comforter that was definitely made for two, as was the large sunken tub in the bathroom. She pushed aside any thoughts of sharing these amenities with a man.

Right now she needed sleep. Grabbing a pair of pajamas from the drawer, she slipped on the cotton bottoms and was tying the drawstring when she heard the knock on the door.

She glanced at the clock. It was after midnight. Far too late for anyone to come by. She slipped on her T-shirt and robe, then hurried to the door.

"Who is it?"

"Brady."

She closed her eyes. "Look, Brady, I'm tired."

"Believe me, I'd like to be home and in a warm bed, too. But the truck won't start."

She opened the door, and cool air hit her. Brady Randell was huddled in his coat. She could see his breath. "What's wrong with it?"

"As far as I can tell it's a dead battery. I think I left the dome light on."

Lindsey realized she'd been the one who turned it on in the first place. She stepped aside to let him in. "Come inside where it's warm."

"Look, I hate to bother you, but I can't call Hank this late. Could you loan me your car to get home, and I'll bring it back in the morning?"

"Could you get it back by six?" she asked. "I have an appointment at seven."

He groaned, then glanced at the sofa in front of the

fireplace. "Then I'll guess I'll just bunk down here for the night, okay?"

She saw the fatigue and pain etching his face and didn't have the heart—or the energy—to turn him away. "I'll get you some blankets."

He was in trouble.

Brady gripped the throttle hard, but he still couldn't control the vibration. In his head, he ran through the aircraft's checklist, reminding himself over and over that he was an experienced pilot. He'd been able to bring in crippled planes before, but his instincts told him this was different. For one, he wasn't over friendly territory.

Another warning light screamed. The jet was losing altitude. Fast. His heart pounded hard in his chest, he sucked in oxygen, fought the panic.

He was going down.

The only safety net he had was his communication with ground control. He made his Mayday call.

He was left with no choice but to eject. There wasn't any time left to think about it. He reached for the yellow-and-black-striped handle, said a quick prayer and yanked hard. He gasped at the powerful force that shot him upward. He cried out, and everything went black.

"Brady! Brady! Wake up!"

He gasped for air and jerked up. Oh, God. He blinked away sleep and saw Lindsey's face. He groaned.

"Are you okay?" she asked.

He worked to slow his breathing and lied with a nod.

"Sorry. I didn't mean to wake you." He tried to turn away. "Please, go back to bed."

She touched his arm, causing his gaze to meet hers. "Were you dreaming about the crash?"

"It's not a big deal." He lifted his shoulders. "It happens sometimes."

Brady watched her stand up. A part of him hoped she would leave him alone. Another part ached to pull her down and hold her.

She went into the dimly lit kitchen and returned with a bottle of water. She handed it to him, then sat down on the floor in front of the sofa.

He took a hearty drink, then blew out a breath. After finishing off the water, he dropped his head back on the pillow. "Please, Lindsey, go back to bed."

"I want to make sure you're okay."

"I'm fine." He closed his eyes.

"If you tell me about it, I might be able to help."

He released another sigh. "The way I'm feeling right now, Doc, I want a hellava lot more than just your sympathy. So if you know what's good for you, you better leave. Now."

Lindsey had been warned, so why didn't she go? She examined his solid and well-developed chest. He had the kind of six-pack abs most men only dream about.

Not only was he every woman's fantasy, he looked more than capable of taking care of himself. But there was something in those dark, brooding eyes that wouldn't let her leave him. His body might be healing quickly from his accident, but what about his soul?

"Lindsey, I said go…."

"Since when do you give the orders?" she tried to joke. "Besides, I'm awake now. So I guess you're stuck with me. You told me the other day you loved early mornings. So do I. To see the sun come up when everything is so fresh and new." She reached out a hand and touched his bare arm, not surprised to feel the sheen of sweat on his warm skin, the subtle tremble. He wasn't totally naked. He still had on his jeans.

Not much of a barrier, she warned herself, and she let her hand drop away. "There are times when we need to know that we're not alone, Brady."

"And sometimes we need to be by ourselves to think things through."

"And sometimes we *over*think things," she countered.

"Easy for you to say. I have to go through a Medical Review Board and let them decide if I'm fit to fly again. And nightmares don't help my cause."

She was surprised at his admission. "Brady, it's okay to be afraid sometimes." She'd been there so many times herself. "I used to have nightmares. I was scared all the time, but nighttime was the worst of all. I was so afraid to close my eyes."

Brady rolled on his side and propped his head in his hand. "Afraid monsters would get you?"

"Yeah. But this monster was very real. My father." She shivered, hating that she still held on to the memories. "He liked to drink. And when he drank, he got mean…and nasty."

This time Brady reached for her hand and he gently squeezed her fingers.

"He used to take it out on my mother mostly."

Brady cursed. "Tell me he didn't come after you."

She shrugged. "A few times he tried. My mom stopped him, then she paid a big price for it." She felt the tears in her voice.

He growled. "Man, that's rough, Doc."

She shook her head. "No, I didn't tell you so you'd feel sorry for me. Just to let you know that we all have nightmares, Brady. And it's always worse when we're alone." She wasn't sure if she was speaking for him or herself.

"I'm glad you're here." He tugged on her hand, bringing her closer as he leaned toward her. "What I'm going to do right now has nothing to do with my nightmare. I'm going to kiss you, Doc. So if you want me to stop, let me know right now."

She didn't say a word.

His mouth descended on hers before Lindsey could resist. Not that she wanted to, because kissing Brady Randell was like nothing she'd ever experienced before. The feelings he created in her were unbelievable.

He groaned and coaxed her up to lie down beside him on the sofa. He pulled her closer and deepened the kiss, tasting her thoroughly. She knew this wasn't wise, but she wanted this man so much, she refused to listen to common sense.

Her body quaked as he pulled her under him. She whimpered, feeling the wonderful weight of him. She sensed a new tension in his body as his hands went to work pleasuring her. He caressed her skin beneath her T-shirt, causing her to arch up, offering him her breasts. When he finally touched her, she gasped, bracing herself for the sensation he caused as he lifted her shirt and his lips drew a nipple into his eager mouth.

She cried out.

"Lindsey… I can't seem to keep away from you." His mouth returned to hers, the kisses became more and more intense.

Lindsey's hand moved over Brady's back, then bravely she slipped her fingers inside his jeans, finding his taut bottom.

With a groan, he raised his head and tugged her against his chest, skin to skin. "I've got to feel you against me, Doc." His gaze met hers reflecting his heated desire. "I want you."

Her heart drummed in her chest. She wanted him, too. "Brady…"

"We've been dancing around these feelings since we met. You want this, too, Doc."

She opened her mouth to speak, but her cell phone began to ring. "I've got to answer that."

With a groan he raised his arm, letting her get up.

Lindsey scrambled off the sofa, pulling her clothes back together as she grabbed the phone from the table. "Hello."

"Well good morning, Lin." At the sound of Jack's voice, Lindsey fought her panic but lost. She looked at the bare-chested Brady lying on the sofa and mouthed, "I need to take this call."

She nearly changed her mind on seeing the desire in his eyes, but common sense took over. She turned away and walked into the bedroom and closed the door.

"Jack, is something wrong?" A dozen things raced through her head, none good.

"No, but we're wondering about you. Your mother and I haven't heard from you."

"That's because you're on the trip of a lifetime. Who wants their kid calling all the time to check up on them?"

There was a long pause. "C'mon, Lin, we love hearing from you. And since you weren't answering at your apartment, we were kind of concerned."

She blew out a breath as she paced the bedroom. "I went to visit Kelly Grant," she said, which wasn't exactly a lie. She had gone to stay with her college friend nearly a month ago. "And I've been checking out some job prospects."

"That's good. Find anything interesting?"

"I'm not sure." She tried to change the subject. "How was your trip?"

"It was great. We got back yesterday. And if you come home this weekend we'll fill you in on everything and bore you with pictures."

Lindsey could hear the fatigue in her stepfather's voice. Had he told Mom the truth yet?

"We'd really love to see you."

"I can't this weekend, Jack. I've got a few interviews coming up. But I'll be home for Thanksgiving."

There was a hesitation, then Jack said, "I told your mother…everything. We talked most of the night and she finally fell asleep."

Tears filled her eyes. "Oh, Jack. How did she take it?"

"As well as can be expected. I know it would do her good to see you."

"And she'll get to. I promise I'll be there for her." She held her emotions in check. "You know I'll do anything I can to help you both."

"I know, Lin." There was another pause. "But there might not be any options this time. And you and your mother have to accept that."

"There are still some alternatives out there, Jack."

"Not as far as I'm concerned."

"How do you know if you don't try?"

"Please, Lin, don't push this. This is the way it has to be."

She knew the man was stubborn, but so was she. "Okay, I'll let it go for now. Tell Mom I love her and I'll call her later. I love you, Jack." She wiped the tears from her face.

"Love you, too, Lin."

She hung up the phone. Dear Lord, how was she going to convince him to come here? She turned and found Brady standing in the doorway.

She gasped. "I'm sorry the call took so long."

"Not a problem. Are you okay?" He came to her, and brushed a tear off her face. "I take it that wasn't a business call."

She shook her head. "It was my stepfather. My parents just got back from a cruise."

Lindsey was rambling, but if she stopped she'd end up back in his arms. Bury herself in his strength, but it would be fleeting. There couldn't be a repeat of that. Brady would be gone soon.

Lindsey stepped back from the temptation. "I should get ready for work."

Brady glanced at the clock. "You still have two hours. Are you sure you're just not afraid of what nearly happened between us."

She stiffened. "I need to get you home."

"I can call Hank or Luke." His eyebrows drew together. "Is everything okay with your family?"

Lindsey swallowed. "Yes. I'm going home for Thanksgiving."

She didn't want Brady Randell to be nice to her. She didn't want to like the man who just moments ago had been doing a good job of seducing her. The most important thing she needed to remember was that her step-father, Jack, was also Brady's uncle.

And when she finally came clean about her true reason for coming here, the entire Randell family might just band together and run her out of town. Brady was a Randell. His loyalty would lie with his family.

She nodded. "If you don't mind, I need to take a shower."

He studied her for a long moment, then turned and walked away.

Lindsey had to fight hard to keep from calling him back. Then she reminded herself that he was only around temporarily, just like she was. In the end, they'd both go back to their separate lives. She thought about the scene on the sofa. Of the hunger of Brady's kisses, the incredible touch of his hands on her body. She drew a breath and closed her eyes, vowing not to let things go any further.

She knew she couldn't keep that promise.

Thirty minutes later the sun was up, a pot of strong coffee was on. Brady probably should have called Hank and let him know about the truck, but he decided he wasn't ready to leave Lindsey Stafford. She presented herself as a tough, independent veterinarian, but he knew better. After she'd told him about her father's abuse, he had a feeling that her stepdad was the man who'd been there for her.

Damn. He shouldn't get involved in any one else's problems. Brady took another sip of coffee. He had enough to concentrate on with his career and adapting to a place in his new family. That was about all he could handle right now.

When the door to the bedroom opened, he turned to see Lindsey. She had on fresh jeans and a white blouse under a navy sweater. Her auburn hair was shiny and curled against her shoulders.

She glanced around the living room, then turned toward the kitchen. He smiled and held up a mug of coffee.

"You looking for this?"

She blinked in surprise. "I wouldn't mind a cup." She came toward him and took her mug. "I can't function without caffeine."

Brady agreed. "I need that extra kick in the morning, too. If you had more time I would have treated you to my famous cinnamon pancakes." He grinned. "Maybe next time."

She stopped her mug's journey to her mouth. "Sorry, Captain, there isn't going to be a next time."

He faced her. "Oh, Doc, that's the one thing I am sure about. Things aren't settled between us. So there's definitely going to be a next time."

CHAPTER SIX

ABOUT an hour later, Lindsey pulled up at the foreman's cottage to drop off Brady. What she didn't expect to find was his brother, Luke, Tess and another woman Lindsey didn't recognize standing on the porch.

"Please, tell me you called your brother to let him know what happened with Hank's truck."

"It was too late last night, and I guess I forgot about it this morning."

"You better think about answering some questions, because to them it's going to look like we spent the night together."

He looked at her and grinned. "We did. Technically."

"This isn't a game, Brady." She shifted the SUV into park not far from the porch. "I'm trying to build a reputation here."

His smile died. "So let's not tarnish it by letting people think you spent the night with a washed-up jet jockey." He pushed open the door.

Lindsey grabbed his arm. "Brady, you know that's not what I meant. I like to keep my private life private."

"Don't worry, Doc. I'll stay clear of you from now on." He slammed the door and started toward the porch.

With a frustrated sigh, Lindsey hit the steering wheel. She hadn't meant to hurt his feelings, but that's exactly what she'd done. At the very least she'd stepped on his ego. She climbed out of the car and leaned against the hood. "Oh, Brady," she called out. "Thank you for last night."

He stopped, but didn't turn around. She didn't miss the tension in his broad shoulders.

She poured it on. "I had a great time. Call me anytime." With a wave to Luke and Tess on the porch, she got back into the car and drove off, calling herself crazy. Why should she care what Brady Randell thought?

Darn it, she did.

Brady walked up the pathway to the porch, surprised to feel a heat climbing up his neck. Lindsey had just let people think there was something going on between them. He suddenly smiled. So he was getting to her.

"Good morning, Luke, Tess. Hi, Brenna." He arched an eyebrow. "Am I late for my session?"

The cute therapist smiled. "Not for an hour or so. I came by to visit with Tess."

"Good, I'd like a chance to shower and change."

"I'll be back, though." She nodded to his injured leg. "How's the leg doing since our last workout?"

"Okay."

"All right, see you later." She and Tess headed up to the main house.

Luke stayed back. "I don't want to track your every move, but it would nice if you answered your cell phone."

Brady pulled it out and saw that the battery was dead. "I guess I didn't think about it. We were too busy looking for the guys who shot the mustang. When I took Lindsey home, she had an emergency call and I went along to help deliver a foal. By the time we got back, the battery in Hank's truck had died. So I spent the night at the cabin."

His brother nodded. "So you're seeing Lindsey?"

"I spent yesterday with her, but that isn't exactly 'seeing.' Why? You have a problem with that?"

Luke shrugged. "It's not my business what you do. I was just trying to have a conversation with my brother. And I want to help see that you heal and get back to what you want to do, fly. Isn't that what you want, too?"

For the first time Brady hesitated. "That doesn't mean I can't enjoy a beautiful woman's company while I'm here."

"I just don't want to see anyone get hurt."

Brady headed for the door as his brother stepped off the porch. "Look, Lindsey was joking around when she said what she said. I spent the night on her sofa." Not that it was where he'd wanted to be. He recalled how good it had felt when she'd come to check on him. How good she felt to hold. "You don't have to worry about her."

His brother stared at him. "Who says Lindsey is the one I'm worried about?"

"Do five more…but take it slower, then hold it," Brenna said. "That's it."

Brady fought a groan. He lay on the workout table

in one of the cottage bedrooms, after taking off his removable booted cast from his leg, he'd strapped weights to his ankle as he did leg lifts.

Luke had made sure that there was enough equipment to help his younger brother stay in shape. And Brady had taken full advantage by working out the frustration of being confined to the house.

Although Brenna Gentry looked small and unassuming, she was strong as the dickens, working him through the isometric exercises and some light weight lifting. He wanted more. He wanted to get back to normal. And fast.

"Slow down," she told him, and grabbed hold of his leg as he pumped the weight. "You overdo and you could lose ground." She rolled those pretty brown eyes. "What am I saying? I normally have to prod my patients to work harder. But you I can't hold back."

"I want to get this over and be normal again."

"You'll get there, Brady," she told him. "You've made great progress."

"Not fast enough." He sat up and took the towel she offered. "It's been months since my accident."

"It's been three months. And you're coming along as scheduled."

"It's just not *my* schedule," he said.

"Then talk to your doctor at the next visit. Maybe he can give you a better idea."

"I plan to." He studied the pretty woman. "Thanks for all your help, Brenna. I couldn't have gotten this far without you."

"Don't you know I'm a sucker for Randell men?"

Brady hadn't had much of a chance to get to know his cousins. He'd heard a little about Dylan Gentry having been a bull rider. His career had ended after a bad spill off one mean bull. "You better not let your husband hear you say that. I don't need him coming after me."

She smiled. "Oh, I wouldn't worry so much. He's long past those wild days. He's practically a stay-at-home dad now."

His cousins and his brother all seemed content with their lives, happily married and with children. Brady had never stayed in one place long enough to want that. Growing up, family had been him and his mother. His dad was away too much.

"Well, I hope he realizes what he's got."

Her smile grew mischievous. "Oh, he knows, all right. But hey, feel free to tell him yourself if you come to Thanksgiving."

He frowned. "I don't do holidays." He thought about Lindsey being gone.

"You will now, Captain. But relax, it's not the entire family. This is the off year. Most wives around are going to the in-laws. Since my family will be gone, Tess invited us here along with a few others. So you aren't meeting everyone, yet. That will come a little later." She leaned back against the treadmill. "So Thanksgiving will only be about twenty or so."

"How many kids?"

Well, there's Livy. You know she's planning on marrying you."

"Very funny."

Brenna shook her head. "You're just like all the rest of your cousins, Brady Randell. No matter what age, the women flock to you."

The only woman Brady wanted was determined to hold him at an arm's length. "I prefer my ladies over the age of consent. Anyway, I'm married to the air force. And I like my women willing, but not long-term."

"I've heard that before," Brenna said. "Even a world-champion bull rider, Dylan 'Dare Devil' Gentry had succumbed to love of the right woman." With a knowing smile, she headed toward the door and called out, "See you later."

Whoa, just because his cousins and brother found marriage agreeable didn't mean the institution was for him. He'd never given much thought about a wife and kids. It had always been the military, his career. He'd known men who'd done it, handled a family and flying. His dad hadn't been one of them.

Georgia Randell had been on her own more often than with her husband during their marriage. Maybe that had been the reason Brady hadn't sought out a long-term relationship. Or was it the fact that he'd just never met a woman who made him want to change his priorities?

Surprisingly, his thoughts turned to Lindsey.

A week later Lindsey had returned from Thanksgiving with her parents. It had been the first time in memory she'd hadn't wanted to be home for a holiday. It was hard to see her mother's sadness. It was also hard to keep her secret from them. She'd managed to get through it and was now more determined than ever to talk with Jack's boys.

Her first call was at the Rocking R to check on Tess's stallion. In truth she hoped she'd run into Brady. She hadn't been able to get him out of her thoughts since she'd dropped him off after their night together. She kept playing it over in her head, the hungry kisses, the way he'd touched her. Brady had distracted her from thinking about everything else.

Lindsey climbed out of her SUV and headed toward the barn, forcing herself not to look toward the cottage. On her trek through the corral, she tried to stay focused on important things like the reason she'd come to San Angelo. The reason she still needed to talk about with the Randells. And she was running out of time. What was more important, Jack was running out of time.

Inside the barn she went toward Whiskey's stall and set down her case. The animal greeted her eagerly.

"Hi, boy," she crooned, thinking about her mother and what she'd been going through.

Gail Randell was strong and independent, and she loved Jack fiercely. For the past eighteen years, they'd been each other's salvation. After her mother's abusive relationship with her first husband finally ended, she'd been left with next to nothing and a ten-year-old daughter to raise.

One day Jack had shown up at the ranch. He'd just been released from prison and needed a job. With little money, her mom hired him. Over time, Jack told them about his past, his sons and all the mistakes he'd made in his lifetime.

It took years, but together they built a thriving horse-breeding business and—in the meantime—fell in love. And now Jack could possibly die. Tears threatened, and Lindsey quickly blinked them away. She wasn't ready to lose him. Not for a long, long time.

"Lindsey."

She swung around to see Brady walking toward her, his booted cast strapped around his lower leg. He still looked good dressed in jeans and his familiar flight jacket. That was when she realized she'd been attracted to him from the first time she laid eyes on the handsome pilot. She'd missed him.

"Oh, Brady. Hi."

He didn't smile back. "Is something wrong?"

She shook her head. "I needed to check Whiskey."

He frowned. "That's right, you've been gone."

"Just over Thanksgiving." She smiled. "My mom made a big fuss with a turkey, dressing and tons of pies. How about you?"

He shrugged. "I spent it with Luke and Tess and a few assorted cousins."

Had he missed her not being around? Probably not.

She glanced away from his stare. "It's nice to have family."

"Haven't decided that yet. I'm not into big crowds."

She knew he was still getting used to the Randells. If she'd learned anything since being here, it was that the Randells could be a little overwhelming. Not that she wouldn't love to be a part of their clan.

"Well, speaking for myself," she began, "I'd never

turn down all that turkey and dressing. And, oh, the pies." She sighed. "Pumpkin's my favorite, but I wouldn't say no to pecan or warm apple pie with tons of whipped cream."

Brady had trouble not reacting to Lindsey's enthusiasm, and he wasn't talking about the food. Well, maybe the whipped cream. He grabbed her by the hand and led her the short distance to the tack room.

"Brady, this isn't a good idea," she began as he shut the door behind them.

He looked into her gorgeous eyes, and a thrill shot through him as he drew her into his arms. "Hell, I know that. But I've wanted to do this since that night at your cabin. It's been too damn long." He bent his head and captured her mouth.

Lindsey made him forget everything, but she also made him feel things. Things he didn't have any business feeling, things that went beyond need, desire, gratification. Nothing had prepared him for Lindsey Stafford.

Brady broke off the kiss, willing himself to slow his breathing. "Just a little something to make sure you haven't forgotten about me." He stared into her incredible green eyes and nearly lost it again.

He didn't wait for a response, his mouth closed over hers again. Her soft moan stirred him as his hands went inside her jacket and began to move over her luscious curves. He had about enough brain power left to realize where this was leading. He pulled back and took a breath, seeing her mouth swollen from his kisses. His gaze moved to her blouse, the rise and fall of her breasts.

"Damn!" He backed away. He didn't need someone like Lindsey in his life, but that didn't stop him wanting her.

She blushed. "We seem to get in these situations…" she began.

"Situations!" he groaned. "Situation? Hell, woman, we practically go up in flames whenever we're together."

Lindsey glanced away. "Then it's better if we stay away from each other."

Before Brady could agree wholeheartedly, he heard his name called out. What now? He shot her one last look, then went out the door to find his sister-in-law coming down the aisle.

"Brady. I've been looking for you."

"What's up?"

"I wanted to remind you about the family dinner at Hank's place tonight."

Brady bit back a curse. "Look, Tess, I don't think I can handle—"

She rested her hand on her hips. "Brady, they're having this dinner for you. Come on, we weren't able to all get together at Thanksgiving and this is the best time. We're just family." Her gaze wandered toward the tack room door to see Lindsey walk out. "Oh…Lindsey. Hi. Sorry I wasn't here to meet you."

"That's okay. I was just starting to examine Whiskey."

Tess nodded, but she wasn't fooled over the story. "I'm glad you're here because I wanted to extend an invitation to you for tonight, too."

Lindsey shook her head. "No, no, I'm not intruding on family. But you need to go, Brady."

Brady liked Tess's idea. "Not without you."

Tess smiled. "Well, you two work it out. Just be at Hank's place about six." She disappeared down the aisle.

Once they were alone, Brady turned toward Lindsey. "Look, I'm not into family things. So if you go, some of the focus will be off me."

"And on me," she said. "And there's another problem, Brady, everyone will think we're a couple."

"Of course. It's only natural you'd be attracted to a devastatingly handsome fighter pilot."

She fought a smile. "Oh, really?"

He grinned. "They're going to speculate, anyway. Why not let them?"

He saw the doubt in those eyes. "Brady, you really think that settles it?"

"Oh, Doc, as far as I'm concerned, this is far from being settled."

Brady was a coward. He'd faced danger at 10,000 feet, but meeting the entire Randell clan terrified him. He'd met all the cousins at one time or the other, but never all together.

"Relax, Brady. This isn't a firing squad," Lindsey said, sitting in the passenger seat in his brother's BMW.

"That might be easier than the series of questions I'm going to get tonight."

That had been one of the reasons he'd wanted to bring Lindsey, hoping it would direct attention off him.

"Big tough guy like you can handle it," she said. "Besides, you're good-looking and charming, so the women will love you. You're a fighter pilot, so the men will be envious, and the kids will go crazy to hear your stories."

He couldn't help but grin. "You think I'm good-looking?"

She glared at him. "Like that's something you don't know. But maybe I did go a bit overboard when I used the word *charming*."

He drove under the Circle B Ranch archway. "Sorry, it's too late to take it back."

"The one thing you don't lack is ego," she told him.

He'd known a lot of women, but none like Lindsey. He knew that might not be a good thing. He parked next to the trucks that lined the new barnlike structure. He shut off the engine and turned to her.

"Hey, I know who I am." He thumbed his chest. "A damn good fighter pilot. Would you want anyone but the best defending your country?"

Her green eyes locked with his. "No. I only want the best."

He gave her his best cocky grin. "You got him, Doc." Brady climbed out of the car to help her. His gaze moved over her. She wore a pair of black slacks and a rust-colored sweater under a black leather jacket. Her hair was pulled up away from her face showing off hoop earrings.

"You look nice tonight."

"Thank you. I should have brought something."

"We brought wine." He pulled the bag out of the backseat. "I'm sure the ladies will like that."

Lindsey took a deep breath and released it. She shouldn't have come. Although technically she was a stepsister and stepcousin. As far as the Randells knew she was the new veterinarian. And there was a possibility that if the Randells discovered her deception, she wouldn't be invited back.

Hank walked toward them, smiling. "Hello, Lindsey."

"Hello, Hank," she said.

He turned to Brady. "And the guest of honor."

"If you keep saying that, I'm going to leave. There was no need for this get-together."

The older man laughed. "You don't know women very well. Come on, you two, let's go and see everyone."

They entered the large structure that had been built a few years back and used as the guest ranch's meeting hall with a cafeteria-style kitchen. In one section, there were linen-covered tables decorated for the party.

The noise level was nearly deafening as several kids ran around chasing each other, having a good time. Lindsey had already met several of the brothers, but not all the wives.

"Hey, cuz, it's nice you made it." Chance pulled a pretty blonde against his side. "You haven't had the pleasure of meeting my wife, Joy. Joy, this is Brady and Dr. Lindsey Stafford."

"Hello, Joy," Brady said.

"Brady, Lindsey, it's nice to finally meet you both."

She pointed to a name tag across her upper chest and then handed them theirs already filled in. "This should simplify things a little."

"I appreciate that," Lindsey said as she saw Brenna Gentry standing with Tess across the room. She smiled and sent a friendly wave toward them.

Lindsey took a breath and released it as she stole a glance at Jack's other sons. She'd gotten a big shock the other day when she learned about Jarred Trager and Wyatt and Dylan Gentry. Lindsey believed with all her heart that Jack deserved to know about them.

Chance's voice interrupted her thoughts. "We'll take a pass on giving all the children's names—"

"That's because you can't name them all," his brother Cade said as he handed Brady a beer.

Chance glared. "No, I just think their parents should handle it. This family can be a little much all at once."

"You think?" he murmured, and took a drink from his longneck bottle.

Hank and Ella stepped into the circle. "Welcome to the family, Brady."

Hank didn't forget her, either. "Welcome, too, Lindsey. Glad you could make it."

"Thank you for inviting me to share in your family dinner."

The older man frowned. "You'll always be welcome here. We have a saying, 'You don't have to be blood to be in this family.'" He nodded. "And our hope is that you'll want to be a permanent part of our community, too. We want you to stay on here."

She wanted that, too, but she couldn't, not until things were settled for her. "Honestly, I have been thinking about it." She couldn't make a decision yet. "Thank you so much for the offer." She saw Tess setting food on the table. "I think I'll go help the women." She walked off before anyone could stop her.

Brady's gaze followed Lindsey. He wondered why she was so evasive about Hank's offer.

Suddenly he saw the group of kids gathering. He had his own problems to worry about.

"Uncle Brady," Livy called as she ran to him.

He couldn't help but smile as the cute five-year-old came up to him along with another group of little girls. "Hi, Uncle Brady."

"Hello, princess." He bent over to her level.

"These are my cousins, Sarah Ann, Cassie and Kristin."

"Hello, ladies. My, aren't you all looking pretty."

His words drew girlish giggles.

Interest grew as more of the younger generation wandered over. The boys. "Who do we have here?"

Livy took over the introductions again. "This is Evan and he's nine years old." She pointed to a tall, lanky boy. "Jeff is fourteen." Another tall teenager. "Brandon is the oldest, and he's nineteen. His brother is James Henry and he's seven. All the rest are with their mommies."

"It's nice to meet you all." Brady held out his hand and shook the boys' hands.

It was Jeff who spoke first. "Are you really a captain in the air force?"

"Yes, sir. I am. I'm also a certified pilot on the F-15 and F-16."

"You got a call sign?" Brandon asked.

"They call me 'Rebel' Randell. But we won't get into the reasons why."

"That's so cool," another boy said.

Then a little girl stepped up. Her name tag read Cassie. "Does your leg hurt?"

He looked down at the boot cast strapped on his lower leg. "Sometimes." He backed up, found a chair and sat down. "But not right now."

Livy moved in closer to Brady as if staking her claim. "Uncle Brady is going to marry me," the five-year-old announced.

"Is that true?" Sarah Ann, belonging to Brenna and Dylan, asked.

He looked up just as Lindsey arrived. Their gazes met, causing his pulse to race. "Yes, she's my best girl. She's going to take care of me when I'm old."

He stood and leaned toward Lindsey and whispered, "At least, it's the best offer I've had so far."

By ten-thirty that night Brady was parking at Lindsey's cabin. She didn't argue when he climbed out and came around to her side. Silently they walked down the slope to her cabin.

"So tonight you're going to let me walk you to the door?"

She stopped. "Not if your leg is bothering you."

"My leg is fine," he assured her.

Lindsey was nervous, more than any other time she'd gone out with a man. And she couldn't deny any longer this had been a date. They showed up at a family function together. And since they hadn't been able to keep their hands off each other, it would be wise to say a quick good-night and lock the door.

Right. She knew that wasn't going to happen, especially after having seen a different side to Brady tonight. How he'd interacted with the cousins and shown a softer side with the kids, patiently answering all their questions. So he wasn't the total tough guy he'd led her to believe.

How was she supposed to distance herself from this man?

After unlocking the door, she turned to face Brady, meeting his heated gaze. It was impossible. Silently she led him inside.

The room was illuminated by the dim light she'd left on. She saw his handsome face, along with the need reflected in his dark eyes.

Lindsey just wanted to drink in the beauty of the man. An inner strength and gentleness was underneath the cocky attitude.

The corner of his mouth twitched, then he lowered his head and brushed his lips across hers. The touch was featherlight, causing her to want more. Ache for more.

Then his mouth found its way to her ear, and she shivered at the sensations he created. She gasped as he tugged on the hoop earring, causing other parts of her body to clench.

"You have to have the sexiest ears," he breathed. His

hand moved upward and cupped her face. "But they've got nothing on your mouth." He dipped and took a nibble.

She gasped and made a moaning sound. Oh, how she wanted more, so much more.

He didn't disappoint her as his mouth closed over hers, angling his lips just perfectly to hers. Then his tongue slipped along the seam of her mouth, and she opened for him, welcomed him inside.

She clutched at his shirt, then slipped her arms around his waist, wanting to get closer to him. Brady helped things move on as he slid her coat off her shoulders, letting it drop to the floor, followed quickly by his. Next, it was her sweater that hit the ground, then his shirt disappeared.

He finally released her but never took his gaze from her. "I want you, Lindsey. But whether I stay or go is up to you."

She could turn him away. That would be for the best, but the feelings she felt for this man wouldn't let her deny herself this night. "Please, Brady, stay with me."

Brady gave a slight tug and they walked together into the bedroom. Once beside the large bed, he kissed her again and again. Then he sat down on the mattress and took off one boot and the cast. Lindsey removed her shoes, but when she started to take off her slacks, he stopped her and did it for her.

Standing there in her panties and bra, she enjoyed the hungry look in his eyes.

"You're so beautiful," he whispered and closed his mouth over hers until they both slipped onto the bed. Next came her bra.

She gave a moan as he circled one nipple with his tongue, causing the peak to harden. She arched her body and he opened his lips to take what she offered.

His easy hands moved over her warm skin, touching and stroking. It wasn't long before the rest of their clothes disappeared, and he lifted his body over hers. He paused as their gazes locked. She could see how tightly he was holding on to his self-control.

When it came to Brady Randell, she soon discovered she had no control.

CHAPTER SEVEN

LINDSEY woke with a start. She blinked to clear the fog from her head as the bright sunlight came through the window. She also heard the sound of the shower running. That was when the picture of a naked Brady Randell climbing into her bed and making love to her, again and again, flashed through her mind.

With a groan she flopped back on the pillow, clutching the blanket against her own nakedness. She rolled onto her side and inhaled the man's intoxicating scent, causing her to relive the pleasure he'd given her during their night together. She'd never experienced anything like it. Ever.

And she never would again. Not with this man.

She sat up. Her only alternative to correct this big error in judgment was to tell Brady the truth.

The bathroom door opened and the man in question came into the room. Oh, my. He was naked except for a towel wrapped around his waist. Beads of water still clung to his broad chest, then found their way down to his washboard-hard stomach.

With the last of her resolve, she forced her attention back to his face. Darn the man, he was grinning.

"Good morning, darlin'," he said as he limped to the bed, leaned down and planted a lingering kiss on her surprised mouth. "Yep, it's definitely starting out to be a good one, too."

"It's a late one." She glanced away. With a death grip on her blanket, Lindsey looked at the clock. Seven-thirty. "Oh, no, I need to be at the clinic by eight-thirty."

His gaze moved over her as a slow cocky smile crossed his tempting lips. "So I can't talk you into calling in late?"

She opened her mouth to answer, but no response came out. Good Lord, she was thinking about it. Was she crazy? "No!" she croaked. "I have scheduled appointments."

He looked disappointed. "Maybe later. Tonight?"

This had gone way too far, and she needed to tell him everything. "Yes, tonight. Now, I've got to get into the shower."

He nodded. "While you're showering, I'll fix breakfast."

He walked to where he'd dropped his jeans last night. She looked away as he slipped on his pants, then fastened his leg brace under the slit pant leg.

He grabbed his shirt and boot and headed for the door. He stopped and looked over his shoulder. "I could bring you coffee while you're in the shower."

She forced a smile. "No, thanks, I can wait."

"Well, holler if you need anything."

"I won't." She continued to sit there. "Now, would you mind?"

Brady wanted to hang around, just to see her blush some more. Lindsey wasn't dealing well with the morning-after routine. Not that he was a pro at this, either, but he wouldn't turn down an invitation to join her in another shower. But he knew that wasn't going to happen, so he wouldn't push it.

"I'll get coffee started."

He heard a murmured "thank you" as he walked out and closed the door. She wanted privacy. Okay, he'd give her that, he thought as he put on his sock and boot. He knew last night that Lindsey Stafford wasn't the type who usually brought men home. He liked that about her. Hell, he just plain liked her. A lot.

He made his way into the small kitchen, opened the coffee canister and scooped the correct amount into the coffeemaker, added water and turned it on.

Why was he still hanging around? That wasn't like him. He never wanted to give a woman the impression that this would lead to anything permanent. Over the years he'd tried relationships, but his career always came first. He couldn't blame women for not wanting to wait around for him.

Brady thought back to his own dad. He knew his parents' marriage wasn't perfect, but they loved each other, and their limited time together had been special to them. He'd always wondered if he'd find someone that he could love that much.

So far, no woman had held his interest beyond the casual stage. He'd decided long ago that a personal life would have to wait until he was a civilian again. He glanced down at his leg with the cast. That might come sooner than he wanted it to.

It had been a long few months since his accident. He glanced toward the bedroom door. Last night he hadn't thought about anything but being with Lindsey. She was different than any woman he'd known in the past. He liked her independence. She was self-assured in her work, and he especially liked how she cared about her patients. No doubt she could handle almost anything.

He took orange juice out of the refrigerator, noticing the shelves were bare. Toast would have to do, for now, but he owed Lindsey some decent food. Maybe he should have her over to his place for a change.

Whoa, he stopped. Was he crazy? His future was so uncertain, he couldn't begin to figure anything else out in his life.

Did he want this to go further? Suddenly he pictured the pretty redhead in bed last night and this morning. Oh, yeah, he wanted to see where this could lead, at least for a little while.

A knock sounded on the cabin door. Brady hesitated but decided that the Randells knew he'd taken Lindsey home last night. Besides, he was a little old to sneak out the back.

He opened the door to find a stranger wearing a sheepskin jacket. A black Stetson sat on his head. He had his back to him. At first he thought it was someone from the construction crew, then the man turned around.

Brady's breath caught as his gaze moved over the man's face, the square jaw and deep-set brown eyes. He had thick, steel-gray hair and a broad forehead, partially covered with a cowboy hat.

Damn, if he wasn't a dead ringer for his dad.

The older man frowned. "I'm sorry, I must have gotten the wrong cabin."

"Well, it all depends on who you're looking for," Brady said. "If it's a Randell, I'm your man, Uncle Jack."

The man's eyes narrowed, then he examined Brady closer. "You're Sam's boy?"

Brady couldn't believe it. Jack Randell had come back. "I'm one of them—Brady. Luke is the one you probably know about." What was he doing here after all these years? "If you're looking for your boys—"

"No! I'm not." He shook his head. "Actually, I'm looking for Lindsey Stafford's cabin."

Okay, he was confused now. Why would his uncle be looking for the vet?

Just then the bedroom door opened and Lindsey came rushing out, pulling on a sweater over her blouse. "I sure could use that coffee," she began. "But that's all I have time for." She finally glanced up and saw the two men at the door. She paled, then managed to say, "Jack. What are you doing here?"

Jack moved past Brady and into the cabin. "Funny, I came to ask you the same question."

Lindsey swallowed and tried to slow her heart rate. It didn't help. She stole a glance at Brady's confused look. She hadn't wanted him to find out this way.

She went to Jack. "I told you I was job hunting."

"Except you purposely left out the part about coming

to San Angelo," Jack said. "If it wasn't for your friend, Kelly, I wouldn't have discovered what you're up to." He gave her a stern look. "Lin, we discussed this, and you agreed you'd stay out of it."

She took in his gaunt face. He'd lost weight. "I can't, Jack." She turned to Brady. "Brady, this is my step-father, Jack Randell."

"Isn't this a kick? Your stepfather is my uncle. How about that for a coincidence."

Her voice softened. "I was going to tell you, I just couldn't find the right time."

His dark gaze grew hard. "Then I guess Uncle Jack showing up solved your problem." He looked at the older man. "You're legendary in these parts. And after all these years you come back. I'm curious if that's how you're going to greet your sons. You gonna just knock on the door. Surprise, here I am."

Jack shook his head. "I'm not going to disturb their lives. Lin and I are going back to Ft. Worth."

"No, Jack, you can't leave. You're here now, you've got to tell them."

Jack straightened. "Lindsey, I told you I'm not going there."

Brady grabbed his coat off the chair. "I'll let you two fight this out," he said as he headed for the door.

Lindsey went after him. "Brady, please." She grabbed his arm when he reached the porch. "You've got to let me explain."

"Why, so you can make an excuse about why you lied to everyone?"

"No, I didn't lie, everything I told you was true." She blinked at tears, biting back the words her stepfather refused to share with his family.

His eyes flashed. "So he sent you here to scout for sympathy."

That hurt her. "No. He wasn't going to contact his sons at all. This was all my idea." She rubbed the chill from her arms. "When I saw the ad for the veterinarian's position, I told myself I just wanted to meet one of Jack's boys. He'd talked about them for years, and Travis was doing the interview. I couldn't believe how much he looked like Jack. Then when he offered me the job, I found myself taking it."

She looked out at the scene of the incredibly beautiful valley. "Who wouldn't, Brady? I've heard stories about the Randell boys since Jack came to work on our ranch when I was ten years old." She didn't reveal that she'd always wanted to be part of that large family.

Brady jammed his hat on his head. "Then if you think he's so great, go back home with him. Believe me, when the brothers find out, there will be hell to pay."

She stiffened. "Then I'll pay because I'm not leaving here, not until Jack sees his sons." She fought her anger and tears. "And I plan to do everything I can to help him, and I'm not letting him lose—" she hesitated "—this chance to resolve things, not without a fight. So if you're going to run and tell the cousins, fine. I'll be ready for them."

Before she could leave, Brady grabbed her. "Dammit, Lindsey. Do you realize what kind of position you've put me in? I have nothing against Jack, but I owe some loyalty to my cousins. We're business partners."

She nodded, knowing Jack had more at stake. He could lose everything. "I know. And I owe my loyalty to the man I think of as my father. The man who helped raise me, who believed in me when I didn't believe in myself." She folded her arms over her chest. "Jack might have made a lot of mistakes when he was younger, but he's paid a heck of a price. He spent years in prison, lost his boys, his family." She looked Brady in the eye. "Mom and I did, too. I didn't lie about my childhood. Jack made us a family. Deep down, he's a good man, Brady. For God's sake, he's a Randell, too."

Brady cursed and paced the porch. "Hell, Lindsey, you're asking me to be his cheering section. I can't do it. I don't know how I can help you without causing a big family upheaval. And I'm not crazy enough to go against six brothers."

"Six brothers?"

Lindsey and Brady turned around to see Jack right behind them. "What are you talking about?"

Lindsey sighed and went to Jack. "It was something I learned just a few weeks ago." She took a breath. "You have three other sons, Jack. Jarred Trager, and twins Wyatt and Dylan Gentry. They've come here to live, too."

Jack paled and his eyes closed momentarily. "No wonder I'm so hated. Dammit, Lindsey, we're leaving."

She shook her head. "No, Jack, you can't. You've got to see this through."

"Well, I'm out of here." Brady started up the steps to where his car was parked.

Lindsey went after him. "Brady, wait. What are you going to do?"

He shook his head. "You tell me, Lindsey. What should I do? Just pretend I didn't see Jack Randell here?"

"No. But I just want a little time."

"Why? No amount of time will make this situation better."

"I know that. But I wasn't expecting Jack on my doorstep this morning." She couldn't blame him for feeling this way, especially after last night. She should have told him. "I'd already invited you back tonight, and I was going to tell you then."

"For another seduction so I wouldn't care about any of this deception?"

That hurt more than she wanted to admit to him. "You pursued me. You kept showing up at my door. I didn't set out for anything to happen between us." She could see by his steely look he didn't believe her. "Fine, do whatever you need to do, Brady. But I'm going to do any and everything I can to help Jack."

Lindsey turned around and made her way down the steps, hating that she'd allowed Brady Randell to get close to her. Well, never again. Ignoring Jack, she marched inside the cabin to the phone. She punched the number to the clinic and asked the receptionist to re-schedule her morning appointments.

Jack had wandered back inside, too. "Give it up, Lindsey. Get packed and let's go home before anyone gets hurt."

"Stop it, Jack. I'm not letting you off the hook that easily. You're sick. Your sons are here." She released a breath. "You're the one who taught me never to give up, and now you want to. No. Forget it, I won't let you. I'm going to fight, Mom's going to fight, and you're going to fight, too." Tears filled her eyes. "We love you too much to let you go."

His eyes were sad. "You might just have to, Lin."

He came to her and hugged her close. She shut her eyes and allowed herself to feel his strength, his tenderness and the love she'd come to cherish. He'd saved her so many times over the years, she had to save him. She wasn't ready to let him go. No, not yet. She pulled back and wiped the tears away. "At the very least, Jack, you've got to see your sons."

He couldn't seem to say anything to that.

But she knew he wanted that, too. She punched out numbers on the phone.

"Lin, who are you calling?"

"I hope it's the one person who can help us. Hank Barrett."

About twenty minutes later Brady pulled up at the house. He parked the car and left the keys on the seat. He wasn't anxious to talk with Luke or Tess or anyone.

This way he didn't have to explain anything. Damn. The tranquil life he'd known since coming here was about to end. All hell was going to break loose, even if Jack Randell was smart enough to turn around and head for Ft. Worth. Brady knew he'd been here. He knew that Lindsey Stafford was Jack's stepdaughter.

Did Lindsey really come here on her own, or had Jack sent her to test out the waters? To see if his sons would be receptive to their father.

Brady shook his head. "It's none of my business." He didn't want it to be. He hadn't had Randells in his life growing up, but they'd gathered him into the fold even before he'd arrived here. He recalled waking up after surgery to see, not only Luke but Chance and Cade.

Brady thought back to Lindsey. Jack might have acted like a bastard to his sons, but he could see that father and daughter loved each other.

Brady climbed the single step to the porch. He sat down on the railing, recalling how Lindsey had responded to him last night. She'd held nothing back. After just a few weeks, he'd quickly learned she was that way about everything. She was fierce about her animals. He didn't doubt her love and loyalty for her family. For Jack.

"So you finally made it home."

Brady turned to see Luke coming up the path. "I didn't know I needed to check in."

"I'm not your keeper, Brady. I think it's great that you're getting along with Lindsey."

That was an understatement. "It's short-lived. We both know I'm going to be leaving soon."

Luke watched him. "You don't have to sound so

anxious to go. We've kind of gotten used to having you around."

"Hell, you've only known me a few months."

"And you're my brother." He stared out at the corral. "Even though you're a pain in the butt sometimes, there's a bond between us. You feel it, too. We're family. We should be able to depend on each other."

That was Brady's problem. For so long he only depended on himself. He wasn't sure he could change— he thought of Lindsey—for anyone.

It took Hank an hour before he could get away to go and see Lindsey. She sounded anxious on the phone. He hoped she wasn't going to tell him she was leaving the valley. Well, he was going to do his darnedest to change her mind.

He parked his truck and climbed out, and that was when he spotted the black Ford crew cab pickup with the gold lettering for Stafford Horse Farm, Ft. Worth, Texas. So Lindsey's parents had come to visit her.

A strange feeling gnawed at his gut as he made his way to the cabin door. Then suddenly the pieces fit together. But before he could knock, the door opened and a large man stepped into view.

Deep-set brown eyes stared back at him, examining him closely. About sixty, with thick gray hair, he was wide-shouldered with an imposing barrel chest. He'd looked a lot older than his years, but Hank still had no trouble recognizing him. He'd seen those features every time he looked at his boys.

"Hello, Jack. I wondered if this day would ever come."

"Yeah, the rotten bastard came back."

"No, I was gonna say, I didn't think you had the...*cojones* to face your past. What changed your mind?"

Jack blinked. "Nothing. I came to get Lindsey. I don't want her exposed to my mess."

So his hunch had been right. "I thought I'd recognized the name when Lindsey mentioned it." He studied the man closely. "I'd heard you settled in the Dallas/Ft. Worth area after your release, and got a job at the Stafford Horse Farm. I take it Lindsey is your stepdaughter."

Lindsey appeared. "And proud of it. Hello, Hank."

She stepped back to allow him inside. Removing his hat, Hank followed Jack to the seating area by the fireplace. He took a seat across from Jack, watching the man. So different from the young, cocky, know-it-all guy who couldn't seem to stay home for his wife and boys. When he did, he ran his daddy's ranch into bankruptcy. Yet worst of all was when he'd been arrested for cattle rustling and was sent off to prison, leaving his three sons alone.

That was decades ago, but some scars never fade, especially for the kids left behind.

Lindsey came in carrying a tray with coffee. She set it on the table. "Thank you, Lindsey." He picked up the steaming mug and took a sip. "Well, Jack. Tell me what this is all about."

Jack exchanged a look with Lindsey, but she spoke first. "Hank, Jack, didn't ever plan to come back here. My mom and I urged him many times, but he wouldn't do it."

"It was for the best," Jack said. "I knew the boys were

settled with you, and you gave them a good life. I thank you for that Hank."

Hank nodded. "If that's true, why now?"

"It was because I came here." Lindsey exchanged another look with Jack. "I saw the ad for a vet and that Travis Randell was doing the interview, and I got curious. By the end of it I found I was agreeing to come here. I never meant to deceive anyone, but there wasn't a good time to blurt out who I was."

Jack interrupted. "I want her to return home and forget about this. I don't want any trouble, Hank. The boys are settled." He glanced away. "Lindsey tells me that I have three other sons."

Hank nodded. "Jarred Trager. Do you remember an Audrey Trager?"

Hank had to admit he got satisfaction seeing Jack uncomfortable. "Yes, I do."

"Then there's the twins, Wyatt and Dylan Gentry. Wyatt ended up buying your half of the Rocking R."

Hank could see more recognition and pain flash across Jack's face. "The ranch was in pretty bad shape when Wyatt got it, but it's a showcase now. Dylan showed up a few months later. He'd been badly injured by a bull while on the rodeo circuit."

"Dylan Gentry. He was world champion a few years back," Jack said.

Hank nodded again. "All the boys live around here now, they all married, happily."

Jack nearly jumped from his chair. "Stop. I have no right to know these things. I gave up those rights long ago."

Lindsey could see the pain in her stepfather's eyes. She wished he'd let her tell Hank about his illness. "Jack, you've always wanted to know how the boys were doing."

He swung around to his daughter. "It's worse knowing. I'm never going to be a part of their lives, or their children's lives." He drew a breath and calmed down. "I need to get back home to your mother."

Her mother? "You didn't tell Mom you came here?"

He shook his head. "I thought I could bring you home before she found out. She'd just worry."

"Jack, she's going to worry, anyway," Lindsey said, then turned to Hank. "The reason I came here was I was hoping his sons could help."

"Lindsey…" Jack sent her a warning look. "We're going home. I'm not going to see the boys."

"They're not boys anymore, Jack," Hank told him. "They're men and can make their own choices."

"Please, Jack," Lindsey pleaded. "You'll regret not talking to them before you leave."

She could see the pain in his face. "I can't mess up their lives again," he said. "I just can't, nothing is worth that."

Lindsey turned to Hank, fighting tears. "Please, make him understand this might be his chance to settle things."

"But it's a chance I'm not taking," Jack argued.

Hank held up his hand to stop them. "I think it's not up to you, Jack. It's your sons' decision."

CHAPTER EIGHT

BY the end of the day, Lindsey was exhausted. After the confrontation with Brady and Jack, the last thing she wanted to do was to take a call at the Rocking R Ranch. But after hearing Tess's concern about her colicky mare, Lindsey got there as soon as she could.

She wasn't ready to see Brady again, so she entered the barn on the corral side. How immature was that? As if she should care, since her job here would be coming to an end shortly. Just as soon as Hank talked to the brothers, Travis would ask her to leave.

She didn't want to think about how much she wanted to stay on. And if she were lucky enough to buy into a practice, this one would be perfect. She loved the area.

But she wouldn't leave Jack, not when he had to start treatment again. She wanted to be there for him and her mother.

Tess met her at the barn door. "Oh, Lindsey, thanks for coming so soon."

"Not a problem. How's Lady doing?"

Before Tess could answer, the horse whinnied. "As

you can tell she's not good. She's been taking in a lot of water, and her respiration is rapid. We've had her off her feed all day." They headed out to the corral where Brandon and Luke were walking the animal.

Lindsey saw right away the animal was excited and thrashing as the teenager tried to keep her under control.

With a closer look, Lindsey was pretty sure what the problem was. "I think she's having intestinal spasms. Hear the gut noises?"

Both Luke and Tess nodded. "Yes."

"Spasmodic colic. Bring her into a stall," she told Luke.

Luke followed her orders, and led the mare inside. Once the examination was finished and an ailment was confirmed, Lindsey went to her bag, filled a syringe and injected the mare with an analgesic to relax the intestines. Slowly Lady began to calm.

She sent Brandon to her car for some supplies, mineral oil and lubricated tubing. With the others help, she administered a hearty dose of oil to the animal. Then they waited and let nature take its course. Soon after, the treatment began to take effect.

Nearly two hours later, a smelly and dirty Lindsey walked back to the car. Tess and Luke were still with Lady and Brandon had gone on home. The good thing about her fatigue was she hadn't had time to think about Jack waiting back at the cabin. She also knew he was going to try and convince her to come home with him.

Home. She wanted San Angelo to be her home, but knew that was pretty much impossible now.

Lindsey glanced up and paused, seeing a large figure

in the shadows. Brady was leaning against her car. A shiver went through her. Why this man? Why did this man have to cause her to feel, to want, to desire?

He spoke first. "Is Lady all right?"

Lindsey continued toward the back of the SUV. "She is now." She set her case on the ground and opened the hatch. Brady came back and lifted the case to set it inside. "That's quite a fragrance you're wearing, Doc."

She knew she smelled, but the mare was better, and that was all that mattered. "It's one of the hazards of the job. That's what happens when you work around animals. Not a big deal, it'll wash out." She snapped her fingers. "That's right, you jet jockeys go for another kind of horsepower."

She was pushing him, but she didn't care. It was her only defense. She'd needed his support this morning when Jack showed up, and it hurt when he walked out. "Just so you know, I called Hank, and he talked with Jack. They're deciding what do." She slammed the hatch. "So don't worry, you're off the hook, Captain." She started for the driver's side, but he grabbed her arm to stop her.

"All right, so I didn't handle things well this morning." His gaze bore into her. "I'm new at dealing with family situations."

"You didn't handle anything, Brady, you walked away." She'd needed him, too. "After last night…" She hesitated then tried to pull away but he held tight.

"Dammit, Lindsey. It was a shock to find out my uncle is your stepfather."

"Okay, I blew it," she admitted. "But I never dreamed things would go so far, either. Just believe me when I say I was planning to tell you everything tonight."

He held her hand tighter. "Now that I've had a chance to think about it, I promise to listen to the whole story."

She needed to believe he was on her side, but couldn't yet. "Brady, I can't do this. I'm tired and dirty and I need to get back to the cabin. Jack is waiting."

He straightened. "That's it? You're just walking away?"

She didn't want to, but there wasn't any choice. "I can't worry about anything but Jack right now. He needs to see his sons, Brady. If only to close that door on his past mistakes. It's not going to be easy for any of us. You might have to choose sides." She didn't wait for an answer as she climbed into the car.

She couldn't bear to lose another man she loved.

Lindsey drove back to the cabin, praying for some good news. So far, she'd messed up royally when she only wanted to help.

Her biggest mistake was falling for Captain Brady Randell. No matter how things turned out for her job here, or for Jack, Brady was still going back to the air force. And he wasn't going to worry about the girl he left behind.

Great, she'd finally trusted a man and it was someone who didn't want the same things she did.

After parking behind the cabin, Lindsey walked down the slope. She didn't want Jack to see her worried, so she put on a smile as she walked inside. On the sofa Jack and her mother were in a tight embrace.

"Mom, you're here?"

Gail Stafford Randell pulled out of her husband's arms and stood. She wasn't much taller than her daughter, but her short hair was brown and she had large hazel eyes. At fifty-five, she looked trim in her dark slacks and teal sweater.

"Since I can't believe anything anyone in this family tells me, I decided I'd better come myself."

Lindsey felt tears rush to the surface. "I'm sorry, Mom. I never meant to make such a mess of everything."

"I know you didn't, honey. I'm still upset with Jack, though. He should have told me right away that the leukemia returned." She gave him an irritated look. "But, Lindsey, you should have let me in on your plan. I would have helped you."

Jack came up next to his wife. "And if I'd have faced my responsibilities years ago, we wouldn't be in this mess." His eyes narrowed. "But I'm telling you both right now, I won't coerce my sons. They don't owe me a thing. So they're not to know about my condition. Ever. You both have to promise me that you won't tell them."

Lindsey didn't want to, but she agreed. "What is Hank going to do?"

"He's talking to the boys tonight." He sighed. "So we'll know tomorrow if they decide to meet with me. I have no idea what to say to Chance, Cade and Travis. But even worse is Jarred, Wyatt and Dylan."

"We'll deal with it together." Gail's arm slipped around her husband's waist. The exchange of love

Lindsey saw caused her chest to tighten. She couldn't help but envy what they shared.

Jack leaned down and kissed his wife. "That's because I have you, Gail. We'll get through this like we have everything else, as a family."

Her mother nodded. Tears filled her eyes as she rested her head against her husband's chest. Jack wrapped her in his strong arms.

Lindsey suddenly felt like a fifth wheel. She glanced at her watch. "I need to get out of these smelly clothes and shower. I have another appointment."

"I bet you haven't eaten," her mother said.

Lindsey started for the bedroom. "Don't worry about me, I'll get something while I'm out. I'll probably be gone for hours. So please, you two take the bed."

"Honey, no," her mother said. "We can go to a hotel."

"No, I want you here. I'll just crash on the sofa when and if I get home."

She disappeared into her bedroom, then into the shower. Under the warm spray, she cried for her parents, for the Randells, for the years she'd taken for granted. Mostly she cried for herself, and the family she might lose.

Hank had summoned all six brothers to the house that night, but told Chance, Cade and Travis to come earlier. The four of them sat around the large kitchen table. The pine surface had many scars from the kids who'd eaten here for years. It was also the place where there had been many family discussions, punishments had been handed out and big announcements made. But never once in over twenty years, had he been able to tell his boys that their father had come home. Until tonight.

"I called all the brothers, but I wanted to talk to you three first."

The trio exchanged looks. "Come on, Hank, just tell us," Cade said.

"Okay. Jack is back."

He kept an eye on the three men he'd called his sons for over the last two decades. Their expressions were controlled, but he could see their underlying anger.

"What the hell does he want?" Cade finally asked. He'd always been the one to anger the fastest.

"Well, from what I learned today, he wants to see you boys," Hank told them. "Jack has been living outside Ft. Worth. He's been remarried for about a dozen years, and he breeds horses with his wife. You might have heard of the Stafford Breeding Farm."

"Wait a minute," Travis began. "Stafford. You can't mean to tell me that Lindsey Stafford is related to Jack?"

Hank nodded. "His stepdaughter. Lindsey told me she's wanted to tell you all who she was from the beginning, but never found the right time."

Travis spoke up. "So, she's trying to cozy up to us so Jack can come back into our lives?"

Hank raised a hand. "I don't think that's it. Lindsey swears she came here because she's always wanted to meet Jack's sons, and she found the opportunity when Travis went looking for Dr. Hillman's replacement."

"Does she think we're just going to welcome him

back into the fold?" Chance said and shook his head. "I can't do it, Hank."

Travis and Cade murmured pretty much the same sentiment.

Hank hadn't hoped for much more. "Okay, but you know you're missing a good opportunity here. I mean, you always had questions you needed to ask him. If you refuse to see Jack, there might not be another chance."

Chance frowned. "I don't have much to say to him. When he got out of jail, he called and asked for money, which I gave him to stay out of our lives."

"And he's done that," Hank said. "I don't think he would be here if it weren't for Lindsey. She's the one who's campaigned for him to come back. She told me she was always curious about you three. Jack always talked about you."

"She should have told us who she was," Travis said.

"Would you have offered her the job?"

Travis folded his arms over his chest. "I'm not sure. Damn, she's a good vet. And everyone only has great things to say about her."

Cade spoke up. "How long would they, if they knew she was Jack's stepdaughter? People have long memories."

"And you boys have turned the name of Randell around to mean something good," Hank said. "There's a few old-timers who won't let go of what happened years ago, but you three have never listened to the talk. You've proven yourselves over and over again. You're your own men. And you're nothing like Jack. I'm so proud of you three, I can't even tell you."

The brothers sat up a little straighter.

"If it's any help," Hank went on, "Jack has turned his life around, too. The Stafford Horse Farm has a reputation as a top breeder in the area. Isn't it nice to know that he's doing well, too? That he's finally taken responsibility."

"I guess I wouldn't mind seeing him," Chance said, and looked at Hank.

The oldest of the three, Chance had been the one who'd tried to shield his brothers. He worked to keep them together, trying to be a man at fourteen. "I think I speak for all of us, that we haven't considered Jack our father for a long time," Chance said. "Not since we sat here that first time and you gave three scared kids a home."

Hank swallowed hard against the sudden emotion.

"Did we ever thank you?" Cade asked.

Hank nodded. "Every day when I watched you three grow into fine young men. A…a father couldn't be more proud."

Later that night a rainstorm moved into the area, dropping the temperature ten degrees. Brady was staying dry inside and fixing some soup. He'd planned his evening with supper and a strenuous workout, hoping to take the edge off his restlessness.

Now, if he could only stop the recurring thoughts of last night and Lindsey. How she'd felt in his arms, all soft and curvy. How her hands moved over his body, her mouth on his skin. He closed his eyes and his gut tightened as a renewed ache coursed through him.

A knock on the door brought him back to reality. He

wiped his hand over his face. "You've got to pull it together," he warned himself as he walked across the room. He hoped the late-night caller wasn't his brother, wanting to go over business. He definitely wasn't in the mood.

Brady pulled open the door to tell Luke just that when he found Lindsey on the porch. She looked cold and miserable.

His heart soared. "Well, this is a switch. I'm usually pounding on your door."

She shivered. "My mother is at the cabin with Jack. I think they need to be alone." Those sad green eyes met his, then glanced away. "I didn't have anywhere else to go," she whispered.

He felt another tug inside his chest. "You do now." In one swift motion he lifted her into his arms and over the threshold into the warm house.

"I know you're angry with me," she began, but he cut her off with a kiss so intense that when it finally ended they were both breathless.

"I'm getting over it." He brushed his mouth across hers again, loving the soft purring sounds she made.

"I didn't come here for this, Brady." She drew a breath. "Last night was a crazy mistake, for both of us. We don't need to repeat it."

"I'll go along with crazy, but what happened between us wasn't a mistake. It was damn incredible."

She pushed away from him. "Don't, Brady, I can't think straight when you say things like that. And I need to keep a clear head." She took another step back. "Along with a favor."

He shrugged. "Ask away."

"Let me hang out here for a while. Maybe sleep on your sofa."

His gaze searched her face. "You want to stay here?"

She nodded. "My mom and Jack need some time alone. I'm kind of the odd man out. I could go to a motel if it's a bother."

Lindsey Stafford definitely bothered him, in so many ways he'd lost count. He raised an eyebrow as the rain pounded against the roof. "How can I send you out in this? You hungry?"

She nodded and followed him into the kitchen. "I could eat."

"It's just tomato soup and grilled cheese."

"Some of my favorites," she said. "Let me help." She went to the hot griddle on the stove. A loaf of bread and cheese already sat on the counter. "How many sandwiches would you like?"

"Two, but you don't have to cook them."

"I think I owe you a little kitchen time."

"If you insist." He went to the refrigerator and took out a jug of milk. He held it up. "This okay?"

Lindsey nodded and placed the buttered bread on the grill. She shouldn't have come here to Brady. She glanced at the handsome jet jockey with the day's growth of beard across his square jaw. He was too sexy for comfort. Those dark, deep-set eyes could pierce right through her resolve. Oh, yeah, she was in trouble. But she still didn't want to go anywhere else.

"Hey, stop thinking about it," Brady said, calling her

back from her reverie. "Jack and the Randells will handle things."

"I can't help it," she told him. There was more riding on this visit than just patching up old times. "I never wanted to hurt anyone. They probably hate me now."

Brady came to her. "Stop. I've only known the Randells for a short time. If I've learned anything about them it's that they're fair. You didn't do anything to them. Their beef is with Jack. And from what I've heard they've got good reason." He kissed the end of her nose, then took the spatula from her and flipped the sandwiches. "Now go sit down before you burn the food."

She huffed, unable to stop her smile. "I wasn't burning anything. They taste better with a dark, almost burnt crust."

"No. Golden brown is the only way." He scooped the cheese sandwiches off the grill. She carried the soup bowl then she glanced at the wall to see the calendar with the big red X marked at the tenth of the month.

She nodded to it. "What's that? D-day?"

"It's my next doctor's visit. Dr. Pahl is going to be the one who gives me the okay to shed this cast."

That was just a few days away. She looked across the table at Brady. She'd trusted him enough to share herself with him last night, body and soul. And she quickly discovered she wanted more time. "And if your leg has healed properly, do you go back to flying?"

He took a spoonful of soup. "I wish it was that easy. No, even with my doctor's okay, I still need the okay from a board of review to see if I'm fit to fly fighters again."

"You mean physically fit?"

"And mentally." He took a hearty bite of his sandwich. "No one wants any unstable pilots out there flying military aircraft."

"You aren't unstable." To herself she added, *A little stubborn, cocky and, oh, yeah, arrogant.*

"Thanks for the vote of confidence, but it's standard procedure that has to be followed."

"Well, I'm sure you're going to do fine," she said halfheartedly, knowing it was what Brady wanted, what he loved to do. She suddenly wasn't hungry anymore. "I guess both our lives will be changing soon."

His dark eyes locked with hers. "Why? You going somewhere?"

She shrugged. "This was only temporary. I doubt that I'm going to be staying here much longer." And she had to be back in Ft. Worth to help her mother with Jack.

"Doc, I doubt the Randells are going to send you away. You're too good at your job. Besides, I like the idea of coming back here and seeing you."

God, she was pathetic. She was actually thinking about waiting around for a man who couldn't make her any promises.

"Dream on, fly boy, like I'll be holding my breath for your return," she lied.

Brady pinned her with a long, heated stare. She tried to draw in air, but it was difficult.

"Even as much as I might want to stay, Doc, I have a commitment to the air force."

"And I have a commitment to my career. I need to

set up practice. My family is important to me. So I should go back to the Dallas/Ft. Worth area."

He scooted back his chair, reached for her and pulled her toward him.

She put up token resistance. "Brady, this isn't helping the situation." She went to him, anyway, allowing him to sit her on his lap.

He kissed her below the ear. "You know what, Doc?"

She gasped as a shiver went through her, and she wrapped her hands around his neck. "No, what?"

His mouth worked its way along her jaw. "When I look into your big, green eyes, you knock me out, you make me forget everything," he murmured. He raised his head, but his hands continued to move over her body, her bottom, up her back, drawing her in a tight embrace. "And when you're in my arms and I feel your body against mine, you make me forget everything but making love to you."

She tried to ignore the feelings, too. She pulled away and stood. It would be so easy to take the pleasure he offered, use it to help make her forget.

He came up behind her. "Lindsey?"

She turned around and saw the concern on his face. "I'm sorry, Brady. I can't do this." She hesitated. "I should just leave." She tried to get past him, but he reached for her.

"The hell you are. Tell me what's going on."

"Just because I don't want to go to bed with you—"

"Hell, I've been shot down before, but I think there's something else going on here. Talk to me, Doc," he said in a husky voice as he reached for her.

She buried her face in his chest. God, it felt good just to lean on someone.

"It's Jack." She raised her head and looked him in the eye. "He's sick."

"How sick?"

"Very. That's the reason Mom and I tried to get him to come here and see his sons. He refused over and over. So when I saw the ad for the veterinarian…"

"You came here to try and pave the way for Jack," he finished for her.

She nodded. "He's not happy with me right now. And even though I'm here, he still made me swear not to tell Chance, Cade and Travis about it."

"Did he make you swear not to tell me?"

She looked at him. "No, but…"

He tugged her to the sofa and made her sit down beside him. "Come on, Lindsey, maybe I can help."

Brady might not love her, but she found she trusted him. She needed him to get through this. "Jack has leukemia."

He cursed and pulled her to him. It was like the flood-gates opened as she began to tell him the four-year story. She shed tears as he held her. She fell asleep with the sound of his words in her ear, "Don't worry, Lindsey. It's going to be all right."

CHAPTER NINE

THE next morning, the rain was gone and the sun was shining. Brady ached to move and get the circulation back in his arm. He glanced down at Lindsey. Just as she'd been all night, she was curled up against him.

A strange feeling tightened his chest. She'd been carrying quite a burden around on those small shoulders of hers. And he felt privileged and humbled that she'd trusted him enough to share it with him.

She stirred in her sleep, shifting closer, and her breasts brushed against his chest. He bit down on his lip, feeling his body stir. She was killing him in more ways than one. He wanted Lindsey. He had from the moment he'd opened his eyes and seen her that first day on his porch. Keeping his hands off her during their evening together had been difficult, especially since they'd made love just the night before. He knew what it felt like to touch her, to feel her body react to the pleasure he'd given her.

He also knew that his longing hadn't stopped, his desire hadn't been quenched. He still wanted her more than ever. But right now she needed a friend more than a lover.

He grimaced. Friends with a woman? It had never been his style, but this pretty redhead had changed his mind about a lot of things. She'd pushed her way into his solitary life, making him rethink all other commitments.

Lindsey stirred once again. This time she blinked, then finally opened those incredible green eyes.

"Good morning, Doc."

With a gasp Lindsey sat up as she tried to regain some brain function. She'd spent the night with this man. She glanced down in relief to see they were both dressed and sharing the sofa in Brady's house. Memories flooded back and she remembered it all, especially the things she'd told him.

She brushed her hair away from her face. "I should get back to the cabin." She started to stand, but Brady stopped her.

"What is it about mornings that you're always so fired up to leave?" he asked. "Or are you just running out on me?"

She didn't want to acknowledge the closeness they'd shared last night. It had been far more intimate than anything physical that had taken place between them before. Now she'd shared her heart with this man.

"I just need to check on my parents."

"Okay, go call, but you better tell them you have plans this morning."

She raised an eyebrow. "I do?"

He nodded. Even with his hair mussed and his beard heavy, he was sexy as all get-out. "It's Wednesday and the clinic is closed this morning," he reminded her. "So how about playing hooky with me?"

She didn't like where this was leading. "Brady, I told you last night—"

"Doc, I'd like nothing better than a repeat of our night together." His voice turned husky. "Making love with you was incredible. But you're not ready."

She found herself blushing. Would she ever be ready for someone like Captain Brady Randell?

A lazy smile appeared on his handsome face. "So get sex off your mind, along with everything else, for a little while anyway. We're going horseback riding."

"You can ride?"

"I've been able to most of my life."

She frowned. "You know what I mean. With your bad leg."

"My leg is fine. I'm sure I can handle Dusty. Come on. I've been cooped up too long. I need to see some sky."

She got up so he could stand, too. "I'll still need to check my messages to see if there are any emergencies." She quickly went through about a half-dozen voice mails. One was from her mom. Lindsey returned the call and relieved her mother's concerns. She also heard about the meeting this morning between Jack and his sons. Once Lindsey hung up, Brady handed her a cup of coffee.

"Here, I think you need this."

"Thanks." She took the mug. "I also need a shower."

"I could use one, too. You go first, and I'll get in a short workout."

She nodded. "I carry a change of clothes in my car."

"I'll get them. You hit the shower." He headed for the door, but she stopped him.

"Brady, thank you for last night. You could have taken advantage of the situation."

He nodded. "Just so you know, Doc, I'm not always going to be a nice guy. Not when I want something. And I want you."

Hank wasn't sure how he was going to handle this meeting with Jack. He'd expected it years ago. Now the boys were adults, he wasn't even needed here, except that Chance asked him to come along.

Although the three sons had turned into six in the past few years, Chance, Cade and Travis were going to talk with Jack first. Jarred, Wyatt and Dylan would be arriving a little later.

Hank and Chance drove from the Circle B, and they were to meet Cade and Travis along the creek. As they got out of the truck, they saw the tall figure of Jack Randell already waiting under the trees.

They made their way down the slope beside Lindsey's cabin where they saw an attractive woman on the porch. He knew she must be Jack's wife and Lindsey's mother, Gail Stafford Randell. Hank nodded in greeting, not wanting to stop and visit at this time.

"Damn," Chance hissed and stopped on the path. "I didn't think it would be this hard."

"It's time to face him," Hank said.

"I know, let's get it over with." Chance nodded at the two riders coming in. "Here come Cade and Travis."

They rode in from the direction of Travis and Josie's house. Hank's chest tightened at the thought of his own daughter, Josie Gutierrez. He hadn't learned about her existence until she came to find him. He'd welcomed her with open arms, then after her marriage to Travis, he'd gifted her with Circle B acreage to build a home. He'd divided the rest of the property between the boys he considered his sons, Chance, Cade and Travis.

They made their way to the edge of the creek, and to Jack. The two Randell men faced each other as if they were gunslingers from the Old West, instead of father and son. There was more silence as Cade and Travis dismounted and stood alongside their older brother. This was how it had been for years. You got one Randell brother, you got them all.

Chance spoke. "Well, we're here. What do you want?"

"Not a thing," Jack assured them, "except to see that y'all are doing okay."

"We're just fine. No thanks to you," Cade said.

Jack's gaze examined them all closely. "Yes, you boys have turned out fine." He took a breath. "I know this is a little late, but I want to apologize for not being around to raise you, and for causing you so many problems. I know it couldn't have been easy after I got sent away."

Hank could see the emotions all the men held in check.

"You're right," Travis said. "It wasn't easy, but as you can see, we survived. So it's a little late to be worrying about us now."

Jack nodded, looking pale under his tan, weathered skin. "Yes, you turned out fine. Thank you, Hank."

Hank nodded. "My pleasure."

Jack slipped off his hat and ran fingers through his hair. "There's one other thing I want to ask. You can be angry with me all you want, but don't take our problems out on Lindsey. She's innocent in all this. She only wanted to meet you all."

"She should have told us who she was," Travis said.

"Maybe, but I'm asking you to not hold that against her. She's a good veterinarian, and that's all that should matter."

Cade spoke up this time. "Or she might be a way for you to worm your way back into our lives."

Jack looked stricken. "If I'd wanted that I wouldn't have waited over twenty years." He put his hat on his head. "When a man gets to a certain age, he realizes he needs to make peace with his past. So I promise you that when I leave here today, it will be for the last time."

Brady had forgotten how good it felt to be in the saddle. The last time he'd ridden had been on his dad's ranch a few years back. He wasn't going to wait that long again.

He was on Dusty, and Lindsey was on Luke's roan gelding, Rebel. They were headed for the valley as the sun warmed up the early December air. Although they had worn jackets, he didn't doubt that they'd have them off before long.

"This was a great idea," Lindsey said.

"I come up with a few." He rested his hand against the saddle horn, giving his horse the lead.

"Your leg feeling okay?"

He grinned. "I told you, it's fine." In fact, he hadn't thought about it once. His concentration had been on Lindsey. She was smiling. He hadn't seen that in a while.

"I thought we'd head for the valley," Brady said. "It wouldn't hurt to check on the herd to see if they're okay."

"Good. It's been a few weeks since I've had the time to go by."

"You've had a few things going on, Doc." They rode side by side as they approached the rise. "Besides, there haven't been any incidents since the mare was shot. Maybe Hank's new security system is doing its job."

They started down toward the creek, looking for the mustangs. Instead, they saw a group of men.

Lindsey pulled up on the reins. "It's Jack. He's with Chance, Cade and Travis." She looked at Brady. "Maybe we should leave."

Brady watched the exchange between the men. His cousins were agitated. "They don't look happy."

"Oh, Brady, Jack's not as well as he's been pretending. And this stress isn't helping."

He reached for her hand and squeezed it. "Then tell his sons about their father's illness."

She shook her head. "Jack would never forgive me."

Brady wanted to shake them all. "Then the least we can do is even the odds. Come on, let's go stand with your father."

They made their way down and dismounted by the trees. Brady escorted Lindsey the rest of the way down to the group.

"Good morning, cousins," Brady said. "Hank, Uncle Jack."

"Lindsey, you shouldn't be here," Jack said.

"Maybe I should, since I'm the one who started all this." She looked at the three brothers. "It was never my intention to cause trouble."

"Jack's right, Lindsey," Cade said. "This doesn't concern you."

"Yes, it does," she corrected him. "Jack has been my father for the past dozen years. I love him." She fought tears. "Okay, he's made mistakes, but we all have."

"Lin, please." Jack went to her. "You don't need to defend me. We all know what took place all those years ago. I need to own up to it with my boys."

"Dammit, we're not your boys," Chance hissed.

Jack looked stricken. "I know. I gave up that privilege a long time ago."

There was only silence, until they heard the sound of the riders. It was Jarred, Wyatt and Dylan.

"We heard shots fired," Jarred called out.

Hank cursed. "Any ponies hit?"

Wyatt shook his head. "The herd scattered, but I think they're okay."

"Where did the shots come from?"

He pointed toward the west. "Same area as before."

"Well, this is going to stop today." Chance headed toward Lindsey. "You think I can borrow your horse?"

"Of course. I'll go to the cabin."

Chance went to Dusty and mounted up. His brothers did the same.

Brady was going to ride, too, but Hank stopped him. "Let's go in the truck. If the boys can't reach them, we'll be able to head them off."

Jack followed the group up toward the parking lot. "Mind if I go along?"

"I don't see why not," Hank told him.

Gail Stafford was waiting on the porch, but Jack only called to her that he'd be back soon.

"Take care of your mother," Jack said.

When Lindsey started to argue, Brady reached for her. "Look, it'll be better if you stay here. Then I don't have to worry about you, too."

She nodded. "Just watch out for Jack."

"Sure." He leaned down and gave her a quick kiss. "We'll be back soon." He tipped his hat to Gail, then hurried to Hank's truck.

"You drive, Brady," Hank insisted, then headed for the passenger side while Jack climbed in the back door.

Brady started the engine and headed toward the highway, all the time aware of the danger. "Maybe you should call the sheriff, Hank."

Hank pulled out his cell phone. "A lot of good it'll do us."

"It's a precaution. If anything happens today, we want it on record that we called the authorities."

Jack spoke up from the backseat. "I take it these guys have taken potshots at the ponies before."

"We've had two wounded in the past few months. Thanks to Lindsey, the little buckskin mare recovered."

"That's my girl," Jack said proudly.

Hank continued to fill him in as Brady turned off the highway. Jack climbed out to open the gate, then returned to the truck.

"The lock's been busted," he told them.

Hank's fist hit the dashboard. "I'll get these guys if it's the last thing I do. And I might just tan their hides before I turn them over to the sheriff."

"I might just hold them down for you." Brady drove along the bumpy dirt road, then turned at the fork. After another half mile, he pulled off and parked. They all climbed out, then Hank took two rifles off the rack in the back window of the truck.

"I'm not going in without backup," he said.

Brady called Chance to learn their location, then he silently walked toward the spot where he and Lindsey had found the camp once before. He heard voices, and used a hand signal to alert Hank and Jack that he was going closer.

The thick mesquite bushes were great cover so he could peer at the intruders. Four teenage boys were sitting on the downed logs, drinking.

Brady returned. "There's four of them," he said. "Teenagers. They have two rifles, but it gets worse. They're passing around a fifth of whiskey."

"Somebody raided their daddy's liquor cabinet," Jack said.

"Their parents aren't going to be happy to have to

bail them out of jail, either," Hank added. "I'm pressing charges."

Brady wasn't crazy about dealing with drunk kids, especially holding firearms. He pulled out his phone and called the sheriff again, telling him what they'd found.

Closing his phone, he reported, "A deputy is on his way."

"I'm not letting them get away. So it looks like we're on our own," Hank said.

Brady looked at Jack, noticing his rapid breathing and pale complexion. "Are you okay?"

Jack brushed off the concern. "Sure, I'm fine. I'll hang back in case one of them tries to run."

They circled the area, then Hank showed himself first. He cocked his rifle and pointed it. "Okay, boys, the party's over."

The teenagers jumped up, shouting curses. One tall, thin boy boldly stepped forward. "It's only an old man."

"Well this old man is going to make your life miserable." Hank waved the rifle. "Now, move away from the weapons. We don't want anyone to get hurt."

"We don't have to listen to you," the same kid mouthed off.

"Look, I'm the one holding the rifle on you. And you're trespassing on my land, shooting at defenseless animals. Wild mustangs. So I'd suggest you keep your mouth shut. Now, move." He waved the barrel of the rifle to show the direction.

Brady came into view. "I'd do as he says if I were you."

They reluctantly walked away from their whiskey

and rifles. "My daddy isn't gonna like what you done," one of the boys said as he swayed on his feet.

"If your daddy's smart, he'll whip your butt for this stunt."

The boy cursed. "Old man, you're gonna be sorry. My daddy is important in this town."

Brady could see one of the smaller kids looking panicky. Then suddenly the boy took off running. "Dammit." He looked at the other kids. "Don't even think about it."

Suddenly they heard the boy cry out. Brady went to see that Jack had tackled the kid. Brady smiled. "Hey, Jack, you need some help?"

"No, I got him."

Brady turned back to the other boys to see if they'd lost their attitudes.

"What are you going to do to us?" the kid asked.

"Nothing. We're turning you over to the sheriff."

Just then Chance came riding in. "Good, you got 'em." He climbed down as Jack brought in the other boy.

Chance took the rope off his saddle and began tying the boys' hands.

Brady gave his rifle to Cade when he arrived, then went to help Jack. The man was leaning against the kid's truck. They tied the teenager's hands with rope from the truck bed. Brady directed him toward Chance, then came back to Jack.

"You don't look so good," he said, seeing the blood drain from Jack's face. "I think we should head back."

"I wouldn't mind that." He pushed himself off the truck, swayed, then collapsed.

Jack Randell was unconscious before he hit the ground.

CHAPTER TEN

AN HOUR later, trying to control her panic, Lindsey and her mother hurried through the hospital doors and upstairs to the third floor. Brady had called about Jack's collapse and instructed her where to come, but she had no idea what condition her stepfather was in.

All the way up the elevator, she couldn't help but blame herself for this mess. If only she hadn't come here....

"Stop trying to second-guess yourself, Lindsey," her mother said. "Jack needed to come back here and see his boys."

"But I could have handled things differently." She bit back the tears. "And if Chance, Cade and Travis knew about Dad's condition, they could help him."

Her mother gripped her hand. "And we both know Jack would never ask them."

The doors opened and they went to the desk to get information. She looked around for Brady.

Not only Brady, but every one of Jack's sons were in the waiting area. Chance, Cade and Travis stood by the window, and talking with Brady were Jarred, Wyatt and Dylan. When Brady saw her, she felt her chest tighten. She needed him. He didn't disappoint her as he came to her.

He hugged her close. It felt so good, she never wanted to leave the safety of his arms. Finally she raised her head. "Where's my dad?"

"He's down the hall. Dr. Hartley is with him." He looked at her mother. "Mrs. Randell, I'm Brady Randell. I'm sorry about your husband. We got him here as soon as possible."

"Thank you." Gail nodded, fighting tears. "He's been really sick. We need to get him back home."

Before Brady could speak, the doctor came out of the room down the hall. Gail Randell went to him, and Lindsey followed her. "Dr. Hartley, I'm Gail Randell, how is my husband?"

The gray-haired specialist frowned. "He's a sick man, Mrs. Randell. Thanks to the information your daughter gave us over the phone, I've been in touch with his oncologist in Ft. Worth." He sighed. "I don't need to tell you Mr. Randell's condition is serious."

Gail shook her head.

"The recurrence of his leukemia and the failure of all aggressive treatments leaves a bone marrow transplant as his only option," the doctor stressed. "He's on the national donor list, so there isn't much else we can do for him."

"Is…is he going to die?" her mother asked.

Dr. Hartley paused, not needing to say the words. Then he glanced at the men in the waiting area. "Unless you can find a relative to be a donor."

Lindsey felt her mother's trembling hand. "Can I see him?"

With his nod, Gail released her daughter, then went with the doctor. Lindsey turned around to find Brady standing behind her. "Thank you for all your help."

"Hell, I didn't do anything. Not yet, anyway." He went down the hall to Jack's room. He caught Dr. Hartley just outside. "Doctor, I'm Jack Randell's nephew. Where do I go to be tested as a donor?"

Lindsey caught up to hear his words. Her chest tightened. Brady hadn't hesitated to give her father this chance for survive. At that moment she couldn't love him more. "Oh, Brady."

"It's okay, Lindsey." He pulled her close. "We're not giving up yet."

"Give up what?" Chance asked as he showed up, followed by his brothers. "What's wrong with Jack?"

With a reassuring glance from Brady, Lindsey announced, "Jack has acute lymphocytic leukemia. He needs a bone marrow transplant."

"I'm getting tested." Brady held Lindsey tighter as he watched his cousins absorb the information.

"So that's what he came back for?" Cade asked.

Brady stiffened. "Will you get rid of the attitude? This isn't the time to drag up the past. Whatever you think about your father, let it go. Jack could be dying."

He glanced at the group of Randell brothers who circled him and Lindsey. "Even with the good, the bad and the ugly, your stepsister loves that man in there." He pointed toward Jack's room. "The same man who made all those mistakes years ago. But I think he's redeemed himself a little because of how hard he's worked and the accomplishments he's made the past twenty years."

Brady started to walk away. "Oh, and the reason Jack came here was to bring his daughter back to Ft. Worth. He didn't want her involved in his mess. But Lindsey convinced him to at least see his sons. All he wanted from you boys was to make peace."

He turned away. "Okay, Doctor, show me where I need to go." He kissed Lindsey, promised to be back, then went off with the doctor. By the time he got to the elevators, he discovered the other Randells had followed him. "What now?"

"Maybe we want to be tested, too," Travis said. "We're probably a better match than you, anyway." His gaze narrowed. "You got a problem with that?"

"None whatsoever." Brady only prayed that someone was a match for Jack.

A few hours later, when Brady got back upstairs, he saw his brother, Luke, and suddenly he felt pretty lucky to have him there.

"Hey, I hear it's been a pretty busy morning."

"Yeah. Lindsey's having a tough time. We're all waiting to see if any of us are a match as a marrow donor."

"I hear you started things off."

Brady shrugged. "I couldn't just stand by and not do anything." He sighed. "I look at Lindsey and can see how much she loves him." He caught his brother's gaze. "The man had to do something right to gain her loyalty."

"Lindsey's pretty special. You care about her, too."

"Yeah, but that doesn't mean it's headed anywhere."

Luke smiled. "Not long ago I thought the same thing about Tess."

In the waiting room, Lindsey couldn't believe she was sitting with her stepbrothers. They were actually carrying on a conversation, wanting to know about the years with Jack.

"I wasn't exactly a model teenager," she told them.

"That makes me happy," Chance said, "knowing you gave Jack a rough time. I love payback."

"Oh, I did that and more. I ran away more times than I could count." She looked over at Jarred, Wyatt and Dylan. They had stayed in the background most of the day, although they volunteered to be tested as donors along with the other brothers. "About the age of fifteen I realized he wasn't going to give up on me."

"He never would, either."

Lindsey swung around to see her mother had joined them. When the men started to stand, she motioned for them to stay seated.

"How is Jack?" Lindsey asked.

"He's resting comfortably." She blew out a breath. "Jack asked to see Jarred, Wyatt and Dylan." She raised a hand. "But he'll understand if you don't want to see him."

The three glanced at each other. "I guess it's about time we met him," Jarred said as he stood. The others did the same and they all went off to the room.

Gail turned back to the group and sat down in one of

the vacant chairs. "I've wanted to meet you all for so long." She put on a smile. "Jack has spoken of you boys nearly every day since we met. When he first came to the ranch, he'd just been released from prison. He needed a job and I needed help with our rundown farm. The only place I had for him to stay was the barn."

She blinked rapidly. "He worked from sunup to sundown, doing needed repairs and working with the four horses that I was able to hang on to.

"When Jack finally began to talk, it all just poured out of him. That's how I learned about you boys. He had pictures, too. Of course, you were all a lot younger then." She scanned the row of large, strapping men. She nodded at Chance. "You're Chance. Your hair is the lightest sandy brown, and your eyes, too." She continued her search. "Cade, you're the tallest. And Travis, you're the baby of the family."

"Not any longer," he said. "Wyatt and Dylan are."

"If you take away nothing else, just know Jack was proud of all of you, although he knew he had nothing to do with it. He was just happy that you had someone like Mr. Barrett to take care of you."

"Yeah, we were lucky," Travis said. "Hank was the father that Jack never could be."

Gail nodded. "Just because he gave you up doesn't mean that you aren't in his heart."

Lindsey glanced around at the men, seeing the raw emotion in their eyes, and the way their throats worked as they swallowed back more feelings than they could admit.

"I can't thank you all enough for offering Jack this

chance." She brushed away a tear and smiled. "Even if it doesn't work out, Lindsey and I will never forget what you've done."

The room was silent. Then came sound of footsteps as Dr. Hartley made his way to the group.

"Mrs. Randell. It looks like we have a donor match."

There was a pause, then Cade said, "Don't keep us in suspense, Doctor. Who is it?"

The doctor scanned the three remaining Randell brothers. "It's Chance."

The following Monday, Brady sat in Dr. Pahl's office, waiting anxiously for the news as the orthopedic surgeon looked over the X rays and MRI again.

"Your fracture has healed nicely," he said. "And there's no permanent damage to the muscle or tendon." The young doctor sat down on the front edge of his desk. "In other words, Captain, I'm releasing you and sending you back to active duty."

Brady had wanted this for months, but now that it was actually happening, it seemed too soon. "That's great news."

The doctor gave a curt nod. "By this time next week you'll be back at your home base in Utah."

Brady wanted to be happy, but he knew he had a way to go before he was able to climb back into the cockpit. "Thank you, Doctor. You'll never know how much this means to me." He stood and shook the doctor's hand.

"You're welcome, Captain. I'll send all your medical records to your commanding officer. Good luck."

Brady walked out of the office, without his cast for the first time in months. A smile broke out as he took off in a near run through the parking lot. He started the car and pulled out into the street to go back to the ranch.

Suddenly it seemed a lifetime ago since he'd been at Hill AFB. It had been. A long four months since he'd been to his apartment just off the base. He'd been deployed overseas for a few weeks when the accident happened and they flew him back to the States.

To San Angelo. To his family. Although they had crowded him sometimes, he'd found he kind of liked being part of the craziness. The family get-togethers. It was the first time he'd spent Thanksgiving with relatives.

Then there was Lindsey. Being with her had been like nothing else he'd experienced with a woman. Yet, since that night in the hospital, he hadn't seen or heard from her. Mostly it was his fault. He knew he'd be leaving soon, and she needed to be with her family. He'd called her a few times, but got her voice mail. He'd never left any messages.

Lindsey had her family here, and she was busy with the vet practice. Now more than ever, their lives were starting to run in different directions.

In a few days she'd return to Ft. Worth for Jack's procedure. Since Chance had agreed to be the marrow donor, they were busy doing the final prep for the surgery. And by then Brady would be on his way to Utah and his squadron.

Brady decided not to push his attentions on Lindsey. He needed his own space, too. All he'd done was think, and it had only been about Lindsey. She'd become more important to him than he'd thought possible. She was the first person he wanted to share his news with. He passed the ranch and headed for the cabin. He didn't know what he was going to say, only that he needed to see her.

Lindsey stacked her suitcases by the door and glanced around the cabin that had been her home for the past few months. A tightness constricted her chest, and she fought tears. She'd come to think of the place as hers. She'd never forget the time she'd spent here with Brady. The night they'd made love. Never before had she given herself so completely to a man, body and soul…and heart.

She closed her eyes, reliving his touch, each caress and each kiss. How she prayed it would never end. During those hours in his arms, she'd fallen in love with him. Then she woke up the next morning knowing she had to let him go. He'd be returning to the air force, and she was headed back home with her parents.

No more delays, either. She opened the door and stepped out onto the porch, but stopped suddenly when she ran into a hard body.

"Oh," she gasped, and looked up. "Brady?"

He smiled, but his hands remained on her waist. "Hi, Doc. Catch you at a bad time?"

She wasn't sure she could answer. It had been four days since she'd seen him. She shook her head. "Do you need something?"

"I just wanted to see you." He kept coming toward her until she backed through the door. "I missed you."

I've missed you, too, she cried silently. "I pretty much stayed at the hospital. Mom needed me."

He played with the hat in his hand. "That's understandable. Is everything going okay with the upcoming marrow transplant?"

She nodded. "Chance is on his way to Ft. Worth." She stole a glance at him. "I never got to thank you for helping us, for being the first to volunteer to be a donor."

He shrugged. "Not a big deal. I knew my cousins would step up."

"Well, I'll never forget it," she told him.

He studied her for a long time. "Are you coming back here after the procedure? I hear there's a permanent position to fill."

It was hard to answer. She wanted to, but not when Brady would be coming back and forth, too. "Hank and Dr. Hillman have both talked to me about it." She shook her head, unable to tell him the real reason, that she didn't want to run into him. "I don't think it's such a good idea, especially with my relationship to Jack."

"I doubt the brothers are the type to hold a grudge against you."

"It's still best I stay close to home. Jack and Mom need me right now. At least for a few months."

"I'm sure they'll want you to go ahead with your own career."

"Whether that's true or not, my family will always come first. I should find a job around Ft. Worth." She glanced down to notice he was missing his cast. "Oh, Brady, you went to the doctor?"

He nodded. "He released me this morning. My leg is healed perfectly. You're the first person I've told."

She didn't want to read anything into his comment. "When do you go back?"

"I need to report to my base Monday morning."

Her heart ached, but she put on a smile. "That's wonderful news. You can fly again."

He raised an eyebrow. "That's not confirmed yet, Doc. But I'll know soon. They're reviewing my accident right now."

"You'll get back into the cockpit. I have complete confidence that "Rebel" will be flying once again. You'll be back to doing what you love."

He hesitated. "I'm not so sure anymore, Doc. A lot of things have changed in the past few months…since the accident. Since you." His gaze went to hers in a heated look. "I came to realize how my career was all I had."

"But you have a brother now and cousins." She smiled. "And a cute little niece who adores you."

He shrugged. "Yeah, and I ran headlong into a beautiful redheaded vet who put me in my place."

She shrugged. "I didn't want you to get bored while your leg was healing. It's a known fact fighter pilots are a cocky lot."

"I've heard more colorful words used to describe me. How did you manage to put up with me?"

It was easy, she whispered to herself. "By humbling you to do my dirty work."

"You have an incredible way with animals. Following you around was fascinating."

"There are easier ways to kill time."

At that he reached for her and pulled her into a tight embrace. "Doc, believe me, killing time was the last thing on my mind. Those nights I spent with you meant something. More than you'll ever know. At least if this is going to end, can't we be honest with each other?"

She didn't want honesty. "Why? What good would it do, Brady? Sorry. I'm a big girl. I've accepted that you're leaving." She was lying big-time.

He nodded. "Dammit, Lindsey. I have a commitment to the air force."

"And I respect you for that."

"Hell, Doc, I wish you didn't. You don't think I want more for us? I want you so bad, I want to kidnap you and steal you away with me." His mouth came down on hers in a bruising kiss, then it gentled as his arms cradled her against him.

His hard body pressed to hers, creating an unbearable need only Brady could fill. She whimpered softly and wrapped her hands around his neck, arching her body into his, wanting to grasp this moment and this feeling forever.

"Brady," she breathed, and pulled back. "We can't keep doing this." She loved him so much it was killing her.

He finally stepped back. His dark eyes narrowed, as his hands cupped her face. "I could get lost in you so easily. Your eyes mesmerize me, your body tempts me. Ah, hell, Doc, you make me forget everything."

"Problem is, Brady, we can't forget our obligations."

His gaze locked with hers. "I wish…I wish we had more time. Wish things could be different."

She stepped back, putting more space between them. "No, Brady. We always knew it could come to this point. You have a military career. You're a Fighting Falcon pilot. You have to be so proud of that. I am."

He nodded. "I'm proud of you, too, Doc. You have a pretty good career started yourself, wherever you decide to practice. But I have to say I wish you were coming back here. I like to think about you with the mustangs. That little buckskin mare wouldn't be here if you hadn't nursed her back."

"And you helped catch the guys who were shooting at them." She paused, her voice grew soft. This was goodbye and they both knew it. "I only wish the best for you, too, Captain." She turned away to catch her breath, then looked back at him. Big mistake. She straightened defensively. "Look, Brady, I have an appointment I have to get to. Then I'll be leaving tomorrow."

He continued to stare at her. "So this is it? We just go our separate ways?"

"There doesn't seem to be any choice."

The following twenty-four hours seemed endless. Lindsey was gone. Brady was leaving the next day, so he took advantage of the little time he had left. He ignored Luke's request to see the progress of the Golden Meadow project. He trusted his brother's expertise. Instead he took refuge in horseback riding. He'd only had one other opportunity, and that had been with Lindsey. Oh, God, he wished now he could have more time with her.

Brady pulled on Dusty's reins as they arrived at the creek that edged the valley. Maybe he'd come here to remember his time with Lindsey, or maybe it was to say goodbye to what they'd shared here. There was no telling when he'd be back.

His commanding officer had called earlier, telling him of the review board meeting. That they would have the results by the time he returned to the base. That would be 1600 hours on Monday when he was to report to the base.

Then his thoughts turned back to Lindsey. Their last kiss, their bad goodbye. The longing he'd felt since she'd left the valley. She just tore out his heart and walked away. He took a breath. Oh, damn. At this moment, never seeing her again seemed harder than anything. Now he realized how his parents must have felt whenever they were separated. How does a marriage survive when you're apart so much?

He glanced out at the herd of mustangs and saw the buckskin mare Lindsey had treated. She belonged here, working with the ponies, making sure they were healthy and safe.

Everything she loved was here.

When Brady heard his name called out, he turned around and saw his brother riding toward him in the golf cart.

"Hey, you're a hard guy to track down."

"I've been around. Something wrong?"

Luke smiled. "No, I'd say everything is going right. Joy called from Ft. Worth. The bone marrow transplant is scheduled for Tuesday morning. I thought you'd want to know."

Brady closed his eyes momentarily. Lindsey had to be happy, but scared, too. "Thanks."

"I was kind of surprised you didn't go to be with her."

"I don't think she needed me around."

Luke shrugged. "Funny, it didn't seem that way to me. You two seemed pretty tight these past few weeks."

"Things change," Brady said. "Doc decided to return to Ft. Worth, and I have to go back to my squadron."

His older brother frowned. "You're not worried about being cleared to fly again are you?"

"No. It's just a lot of things are different now."

Luke smiled. "A woman always changes things. If it's the right woman, it's all good."

"What if I'm not ready for *that* woman?"

Luke grinned this time. "Are we ever really ready? But take it from me, having Tess in my life makes it worthwhile. You can lose everything and it doesn't matter, not when you know she loves you."

Brady suddenly realized that he wanted Lindsey with him. "How can I ask Lindsey to give up everything she's worked for and follow me around from base to base?"

"I don't know." Luke shrugged. "But I think you need to give her the opportunity to decide."

Brady blew out a breath. "Doesn't seem fair."

Luke patted his brother on the back. "Cousin Chance

once told me that Randell men seem to fall hard for their women. And they love forever.

"So ask yourself, brother, do you want Lindsey forever?"

CHAPTER ELEVEN

THE next afternoon Lindsey stood in the hospital room watching Jack sleep. He wore a surgical mask over the lower half of his face, to keep him as germ free as possible. It was worth the inconvenience before and after the procedure. The important thing was after the marrow transplant, she knew Jack was going to get better. Tomorrow would be a long day for all of them. Her mother was back at the hotel resting, too.

Lindsey looked out the window at the cold December day. So many times in the last week she'd thanked God for this miracle. Not only for the bone marrow, but the chance Jack had gotten to see his sons again. She doubted the Randell brothers would ever take him back as their father, but they'd all moved on enough from the past to want to help.

She felt the raw emotions surface again and fought them. She needed to be strong to handle the next few days. But not everything was so easy to put aside or forget. She thought about Brady. He'd probably gone back to Utah by now. Over the past few days, Tess had called several times to keep her informed, but she hadn't heard anything about Brady's review board. Not that Lindsey had asked.

"You're looking awfully worried." Jack's voice broke through her reverie. "Is there something else the doctor's told you?"

"No. Just that you're going to be around a long time." She kept a safe distance. "You should be resting."

"Seems that's all I've been doing," he told her. "Speaking of which, aren't you tired of hanging around my room?"

"Someone has to make sure you behave yourself."

He ran a hand over his gray hair. "I've been too weak to do anything else." He glanced around. "Please, tell me your mother left to get some rest."

"Yes, about an hour ago."

"Then I want you to go, too." He raised a hand when she started to argue. "Please, Lin, you need to get out of here for a while."

She bit down on her lip. "Are you trying to get rid of me."

"Oh, no, darlin'." He held out a hand and she came to him. "I know this has been hard on you and your mother, but it's going to be okay."

"We don't want to lose you."

"You won't. We have our miracle. A second chance." He hugged her close as her tears fell freely. Finally he spoke again. "I have a feeling this might be about something else entirely. Maybe a certain air force captain."

She pulled herself together and stood. "It doesn't

matter. He's gone back to the base. I'm not going to run after him, either. Not when he didn't have a problem leaving me."

Jack pulled the surgical mask down to make a point. "He's in the air force, Lin. He doesn't have a choice."

She raised a hand. "I know, I know. The military comes first. I just wanted him to care enough about me to ask if I want to share that part of his life."

"There's no doubt Brady cares for you, Lin, but he has commitments. You've got to give him time to work through them." Jack smiled. "You're a lot like your mother. Believe me, you won't be easy for him to forget."

She wanted to believe him, but Brady was still gone. And she was here…alone.

"You're tired, honey. You need to get some rest, too. You've spent all your time helping me." He gripped her hand. "How can I thank you for bringing me together with my boys? Starting tomorrow, I'm going to take charge of this family again. What can I do to help you?"

She loved him so much. "Just stay around a long, long time."

He grinned. "I'll do my darnedest."

"Good." She smiled.

Suddenly a familiar figure appeared at the glass partition. It was Brady, looking tall and handsome in his air force blue dress uniform, his cap tucked under his arm. His once-shaggy black hair was now cut military short.

Her heart accelerated more as she glanced up at the man's face, and familiar brown eyes stared back at her.

"Hi, Doc," he said from the doorway. "Your mother

told me you were visiting your dad." He turned to the bed. "Hello, sir. I hope I'm not disturbing you."

Jack sat straighter in the bed and replaced his mask. "No, of course not. I wish I could invite you in, but there are rules."

Brady smiled. "Not a problem, sir. Wouldn't want to do anything to upset tomorrow's procedure."

"That might not be taking place if you hadn't started things. I'm grateful to you for offering to be a donor."

"I'm glad everything worked out."

Lindsey couldn't believe he'd shown up here. "Brady, I thought you were going back to your base."

He checked his watch. "I am. I just took a detour. My connecting flight leaves in a few hours. But I wanted to see how Jack and you were doing."

She felt herself blush.

Her father spoke. "I'm doing fine, Brady, even better after tomorrow."

"I wish you only the best, sir."

"And I appreciate you coming by," Jack said. "We never got much of a chance to talk. Sam and I were close growing up, but things changed over the years. I believe your father would be happy his sons are back at the Rocking R." He smiled. "I hope if you ever get back to Ft. Worth, you'll stop in and see us. I'll tell you some great stories about your daddy."

Brady nodded. "I'd like that, sir. Right now, I have some things to straighten out with my career." He turned to Lindsey. "And lately things have gotten more complicated."

Lindsey could feel the heat of his gaze, making her uncomfortable. "Dad, I think I will go back to the hotel."

Brady stepped in. "Lindsey, could I talk with you?"

She sighed. "I don't think there's anything to say."

He blocked the doorway. "Please, let me walk you out."

She nodded, then glanced at her stepfather. "Now, you better get some rest, too. Bye, Jack."

Brady said his goodbye, too, and allowed Lindsey out into the corridor, then they walked to the elevators.

Her chest tightened at the thought of talking with him. "What are you really doing here, Brady? We already said everything."

"You think we could find somewhere to talk?" He checked his watch. "Maybe I can walk you to your car. You look dead on your feet."

"Just what every woman wants to hear."

He took a step closer. "I didn't mean it that way. You're a beautiful woman, Lindsey. Missing some sleep could never take that away." He took her by the arm and walked her to the elevator. Silently they rode down to the first floor, then out the front doors and across to the parking structure.

Lindsey walked fast, aching to get this over. Soon they were next to her SUV.

She drew a calming breath. "Why are you really here, Brady?"

"I wanted to make sure you were okay. I couldn't leave things the way they were, Doc. Without letting you know what you mean to me."

Before she could speak, his mouth closed over hers

in a tender kiss that only made her want more. More than he could give her.

He pulled back. "I told myself I wouldn't do that." Frowning, he cursed. "But I can't help remembering how you felt in my arms." He paced back and forth. The sound of his shoes echoed in the deserted structure. Then suddenly he stopped in front of her. "I never expected to find someone like you. Someone who made it so damn hard to walk away." He drew a long breath. "And as much as I want to make you promises, Lindsey, I can't right now."

She loved this man, and right now nothing else mattered but that. "I'm not asking you to, Brady."

"You deserve more. I don't want to leave you, but I committed time to the air force. I could be deployed again."

She hated the fact that she understood. Yet she was afraid for him, too. "That's an excuse, Brady. We all have commitments, but that doesn't mean we can't work out some sort of compromise."

He rested his forehead against hers. "I've got some ghosts to face—obligations." He checked his watch. "I have to go. My flight leaves…"

Lindsey nodded. It took every bit of strength inside her to step back. The air force was his life. Flying was his passion. She'd known that from the start.

With tears blurring her vision, she watched him walk out of her life.

CHAPTER TWELVE

It was more than a week later, just days before Christmas, when Lindsey found herself back in San Angelo. Hank had called and convinced her to stay on as the veterinarian, if only temporarily. Since Brady was gone and she hadn't heard from him, there wasn't any reason she couldn't return to what she loved to do. And with Jack on the mend from his successful transplant, she could leave Ft. Worth.

She walked out onto the porch of the same cabin she'd stayed in before. It was hard to push aside the memories, all the time she and Brady had shared here.

She wanted to forget him, but she loved this man who put duty and love of his country at top priority. She only wanted a small part of his life and for him to let her go with him. Had he been deployed overseas? No matter where he'd gone, there was no denying she loved him.

Lindsey glanced up into the cloudless sky. She hoped he was happy now. She hugged her jacket closer for warmth as she wandered down the path toward the creek. The small herd of mustangs grazed in the golden meadow grass.

She was doing what she loved, too. In a place she'd come to love like a home. Even if she didn't stay on after Dr. Hillman's practice was sold, Hank had invited her to come back periodically and check the ponies.

Hank Barrett hadn't been subtle in trying to convince her to stay permanently. She wanted so much to live here and be around the Randells. To keep that one link between Jack and his sons.

Still she missed Brady, wanted the best for him. "I hope you've banished your ghosts," she whispered into the cool breeze.

"I have, Doc," a familiar voice answered.

She turned around to see Brady on Dusty. He wore his same bomber jacket and cowboy hat. And a silly grin.

She blinked several times, wondering if she'd wanted to see him so badly that she dreamed him up. "Brady? How? You're here?"

He swung his leg over the horse's rump and jumped down. "Surprised?"

"Well, you seem to pop up everywhere." She didn't like this. "Are you home for the holidays?"

"You could say that." He walked toward her. "But mostly I'm here to see you."

"I thought you'd gone back on active duty. Tess said you aced the review board."

"I did. I've even been up in an F-16, and everything went fine. Great, in fact. No more nightmares about the crash. I only dream of you these days."

She refused to get excited. "I'm happy for you."

Brady had been hoping for a friendlier welcome.

"I'm glad you came back here, Lindsey. It's where you belong." He moved closer. "I'm selfish, since I like having you around."

She stiffened. "So you think I'm going to be around for your convenience whenever you come home on leave? Well, think again, fly boy. You can just turn around and ride off."

Brady couldn't help but smile. God, he'd missed her. "Never again, Doc. I care too much for you." He tried to reach for her, but she stepped back.

"If you do, then why do you keep coming after me, then leaving me again?" She clenched her fists. "How many times do you expect me to say goodbye to you?"

He sobered. "I'm not saying goodbye, Lindsey. I came by your cabin because I wanted to see you, tell you how I feel."

She bit her lower lip. "We both know how it will turn out," she said, then started up the hill toward the cabin.

Brady tied Dusty's reins to a nearby tree and strode after her. "You aren't even going to hear me out?"

"Why? So you can tell me again how much the military means to you? I know how much, Brady."

"No, Lindsey, you mean more."

She turned around and shouted. "Prove it. Ask me to go with you."

Brady was taken aback by her request. "Okay. Lindsey Stafford, will you go with me?"

She looked shocked, then said, "Yes, Brady. I'll go wherever you go."

He continued up the hill until he stood before her.

"You'd do that, Doc? You'd go off with me without knowing what the future holds?"

She nodded slowly. "We'd be together."

"What if I go as close as Laughlin Air Force in Del Rio." He raised an eyebrow. "Or say we only have to go as far as the Rocking R's foreman's cottage? That's where we'll live until I build us a bigger house."

Her pretty green eyes narrowed suspiciously.

He let out a long breath. "In two and a half months I'm resigning from active duty."

She gasped. "No, Brady, you can't do that. You love to fly. And I'd never ask you to give it up."

Fighting his own emotions, he reached for her and pulled her close. "I know you wouldn't. God, that's one of the reasons I love you so much."

She searched his face. "I love you, too. But I can't let you do this."

He placed a finger over her lips. "Listen to me first. I'm not resigning my commission. If I decide to take a flight instructor job at Laughlin we'd be close by in Del Rio. The other choice is that I go into the air force reserves. I still get to fly." He smiled. "I hope you can put up with me being gone one weekend a month and two weeks in the summer."

She finally smiled. "I want you to be happy, Brady."

"I've discovered I'm happy when I'm with you. So I'm leaning toward going into the reserves."

"Then I'm happy, too…as long as I get you the rest of the time, fly boy."

His hold tightened. "If I get you, too." His head

lowered and his mouth captured hers. The kiss was tender yet hungry, letting Lindsey know how much he cared and wanted a life with her.

When he broke off the kiss, Brady stepped back and reached into his inside jacket pocket, finding his hands were shaking. "I'd planned to do this tonight over a candlelight dinner, but I can't wait any longer. I want everything settled between us." He kissed her again. "I've asked you to wait too many times." He pulled out a black velvet box and opened it, showing off the pear-shaped diamond in a platinum setting.

Lindsey gasped as Brady got down on one knee.

"God, Lindsey, I love you so much. You've become my heart, my soul. I want us to build a life together. Have kids and raise them here in this valley." He swallowed hard. "Will you marry me?"

"Oh, Brady. Yes, I'll marry you."

He stood and slipped the ring on her finger, then she went into his arms. He kissed her again and again. "It's all going to be so good for us, Doc. I've talked with the other Randells. They want me to be the pilot for a flight service to bring guests to the valley. And if you still want it, you can tell Dr. Hillman that you want to buy his practice."

"Whoa, Brady. Do you have any idea what a veterinarian clinic and practice cost?"

"No, but I have money saved, plus my half of the sale of the valley land to Hank. And besides, you're a wonderful vet, Doc. And it's what you always wanted."

She smiled and touched his face. "You are what I

always wanted. A good man who loves me. And a big family to share everything with."

He grinned. "Be careful what you ask for. We've got more family than we know what to do with."

"Oh, no," Lindsey gasped. "Including your niece, Livy. How are you going to tell her that you aren't going to marry her?"

He pulled Lindsey against him. "I'll let her down gently. I'll tell her how much I love you, and she'll understand. And I do love you, Doc."

It was true. Lindsey was the only thing he needed in his life. She was his family. Well, maybe a few Randells thrown in the mix wouldn't hurt.

EPILOGUE

Six months later, spring had come to the valley. Lindsey looked at her parents seated on the cabin porch. They'd rented it during their visit here. The Randells had had to adjust to her parents being around after Lindsey's marriage to Brady. And thanks to the bone marrow from Chance, Jack's leukemia was in remission.

They were all learning that life was fragile.

Jack had been grateful for every day, and for the opportunity to come back to see his sons. Of course, he could never take the place of Hank, but he had never planned to. Lindsey knew Jack had been given a second chance in many things, and he wasn't about to mess it up.

She would never forget her wedding day, having Jack there to give her away, and all the Randells showing up to celebrate their special day.

She'd been Mrs. Brady Randell for only a month, and never realized how much she could love another person. Now they were trying to adjust to their new life together. For the time being, Brady had declined the instructor's job at Laughlin. He'd chosen to resign from active duty and make a permanent home here in the valley.

He had just finished up his two weeks of reserve duty and only returned home yesterday. Lindsey felt the heat rise to her face, recalling how Brady spent most of the night, showing her how much he'd missed her.

She sighed. Marriage was wonderful.

Today they planned to ride with the Randell cousins and Hank to check the mustangs. He'd heard one of the mares had dropped a foal. She wanted to make sure everything was all right. Besides, she enjoyed riding with Brady. It wasn't an F-16, but he'd told her riding around his own ranch with his wife was thrill enough.

As a wedding gift, Brady had bought them two quarter horse yearlings from Chance's breeding stables. His cousin had named the large black stallion Wild Blue Yonder. For Lindsey, a sweet roan filly named Captain's Doc. They'd gotten a reduced family price with the promise that Chance got their first foal, and a discount on Lindsey's veterinarian services.

Right now Dusty and Lady were tied to the post, waiting for everyone. Brady had to go with Luke to the construction site for some final details for this next weekend. They were expecting a large crowd at the Golden Meadow Estates open house.

She glanced up the hill to see Brady's truck pulling up, and a rush of feelings raced through her. He came down the steps toward the cabin, stopping briefly to say hello to her parents. Then he continued toward her.

Brady's excitement grew as he neared, picked her up

in his arms and kissed her soundly. "God, I missed you," he groaned.

"We've only been separated an hour."

He kissed her again. "I'm talking about the last two weeks."

"I thought you made up for that last night…and this morning." She smiled. "And again after breakfast."

"Never enough."

Lindsey stepped back. "Well, you're going to have to postpone showing me your undying love, because right now we're supposed to go round up some mustangs."

He reluctantly released her. "Okay, but remember where I left off."

"Not a problem." She looked up toward the cabin and waved at Jack and her mom.

He gripped her hand. "I'm glad your parents could come for a visit. It's good for the cousins, too."

"Were you surprised when Chance asked them here?"

He shook his head. "No. It's time to heal."

"And I think there's a place for all of us here in the valley." She looked at her husband. "I also think your dad would be happy that you and Luke are back here now."

Brady found he had a lot to be grateful for, starting with the day he woke up in the hospital and found his family…and love.

Up on the hill, Hank sat on his horse, his wife, Ella, next to him on the bay gelding he'd given her on her birthday a few years back.

He rested his arm on the saddle horn and looked

down at the valley. A herd of wild ponies were grazing in the serene meadow, unaware that anything was going on. Just as he wanted everything to be. Undisturbed.

"Well, are you happy now?" Ella asked.

He tipped his hat back and grinned. "Yes, I am. It's pretty amazing that I can keep enjoying this place." He glanced toward the cabin and saw Jack and Gail. He never thought he'd see the day that that man would come back here. And Hank couldn't be happier. Chance, Cade and Travis needed this closure to their past. Jarred, Wyatt and Dylan had needed to know their roots, too.

"You've done good, Hank Barrett. Not only did you manage to raise some fine sons, but you've seen to it that these ponies are protected from any harm."

Hank's horse shifted as he looked out over the acres of untouched land. He felt a little selfish to have all this beauty, but it wasn't only for him. "It's just the way it should be. We never should forget our past, and the mustangs were a big part of it."

Several riders began to appear. Chance came from one direction along with Cade and Travis. From the west rode Jarred, Wyatt and Dylan. They met and rode up the rise together. They were a formidable group of men on horseback. Hank glanced back over his shoulder and saw Luke and Tess coming from the direction of the Rocking R. He was touched that they all wanted to help with the mustangs. But he knew his boys loved the ponies.

Something caught his eye, and he turned to the creek to see Brady and Lindsey. "Our family keeps growing."

"With more weddings comes more babies," Ella said excitedly. "I wonder who'll be first among the cousins."

Hank Barrett grinned. "Doesn't matter. I say, bring 'em on. There's plenty of love to go around."

He would teach them about the history of this valley. How family was the most important thing. And how the Randells and the mustangs could live together in harmony in this special valley for many generations to come.

THE MOST
EXPENSIVE LIE
OF ALL

MICHELLE CONDER

This book is dedicated to Amber and Corin for opening up the world of polo for me and doing it with such warmth and generosity.
You guys are great.

To a formidable squash champ, Juan Marcos, who promptly responded to my queries about his game.

And also, to my lifelong friend Pam Austin who wrote down every memory she ever had of her visits to Mexico which could have been a novel in itself.

Thank you!

CHAPTER ONE

'EIGHT-THREE. MY SERVE.'

Cruz Rodriguez Sanchez, self-made billionaire and one of the most formidable sportsmen ever to grace the polo field, let his squash racquet drop to his side and stared at his opponent incredulously. 'Rubbish! That was a let. And it's eight-three *my* way.'

'No way, *compadre*! That was my point.'

Cruz eyeballed his brother as Ricardo prepared to serve. They might only be playing a friendly game of squash but 'friendly' was a relative term between competing brothers. 'Cheats always get their just desserts, you know,' Cruz drawled, moving to the opposite square.

Ricardo grinned. 'You can't win every time, *mi amigo.*'

Maybe not, Cruz thought, but he couldn't remember the last time he'd lost. Oh, yeah, actually he could—because his lawyer was in the process of righting that particular wrong while he blew off steam with his brother at their regular catch-up session.

Feeling pumped, he correctly anticipated Ricardo's attempted 'kill shot' and slashed back a return that his brother had no chance of reaching. Not that he didn't try. His running shoes squeaked across the resin-coated floor as he lunged for the ball and missed.

'*Chingada madre!*'

'Now, now,' Cruz mocked. 'That would be nine-three. My serve.'

'That's just showing off,' Ricardo grumbled, picking himself up and swiping at the sweat on his brow with his sweatband.

Cruz shook his head. 'You know what they say? If you can't stand the heat…'

'Too much talking, *la figura*.'

'Good to see you know your place.' He flashed his brother a lazy smile as he prepared to serve. '*El pequeño*.'

Ricardo rolled his eyes, flipped him the bird and bunkered down, determination etched all over his face. But Cruz was in his zone, and when Ricardo flicked his wrist and sent the ball barrelling on a collision course with Cruz's right cheekbone he adjusted his body with graceful agility and sent the ball ricocheting around the court.

Not bothering to pick himself up off the floor this time, Ricardo lay there, mentally tracking the trajectory of the ball, and shook his head. 'That's just unfair. Squash isn't even your game.'

'True.'

Polo had been his game. Years ago.

Wiping sweat from his face, Cruz reached into his gym bag and tossed his brother a bottle of water. Ricardo sat on his haunches and guzzled it.

'You know I let you win these little contests between us because you're unbearable to be around when you lose,' he advised.

Cruz grinned down at him. He couldn't dispute him. It was a celebrated fact that professional sportsmen were very poor losers, and while he hadn't played professional polo for eight years he'd never lost his competitive edge.

On top of that he was in an exceptionally good mood, which made beating him almost impossible. Remembering the reason for that, he pulled his cell phone from his kit-bag to see if the text he was waiting for had come through, frowning slightly when he saw it hadn't.

'Why are you checking that thing so much?' Ricardo queried. 'Don't tell me some *chica* is finally playing hard to get?'

'You wish,' Cruz murmured. 'But, no, it's just a business deal.'

'Ah, don't sweat it. One day you'll meet the *chica* of your dreams.'

Cruz threw him a banal look. 'Unlike you, I'm not looking for the woman of my dreams.'

'Then you'll probably meet her first,' Ricardo lamented.

Cruz laughed. 'Don't hold your breath,' he replied. 'You might meet an early grave.' He tossed the ball in the air and sent it spinning around the court, his concentration a little spoiled by Ricardo's untimely premonition.

Because there *was* a woman. A woman who had been occupying his thoughts just a little too often lately. A woman he hadn't seen for a long time and hoped to keep it that way. Of course he knew why she was jumping into his head at the most inopportune times of late, but after eight years of systematically forcing her out of it that didn't make it any more tolerable.

Not that he allowed himself to get bent out of shape about it. He'd learned early on that the things you were most attached to had the power to cause you the most pain, and since then he'd lived his life very much like a high-rolling gambler—easy come, easy go.

Nothing stuck to him and he stuck to nothing in return—which had, much to everyone's surprise, made him a phenomenally wealthy man.

An 'uneducated maverick', they'd called him. One who had swapped the polo field for the boardroom and invested in deals and stock market bonds more learned businessmen had shied away from. But then Cruz had been trading in the tumultuous early days of the global financial crisis and he'd already lost the one thing he had cared about the most. Defying expectations and market trends seemed inconsequential after that.

What had really fascinated him in the early days was how people had been so ready to write him off because of his Latino blood and his lack of a formal education. What they hadn't realised was that the game of polo had perfectly set him up to achieve in the business world. Killer instincts combined with a tireless work ethic and the ability to think on his feet were all attributes to make you succeed in polo and in business, and Cruz had them in spades. What he didn't have right now—what he *wanted*—was a text from his lawyer advising him that he was the proud owner of one of East Hampton's most prestigious horse studs: Ocean Haven Farm.

Resisting another urge to check his phone, he prowled around the squash court, using the bottom of his sweat-soaked T-shirt to swipe at the perspiration dripping down his face.

'Nice abs,' a feline voice quipped appreciatively through the glass window overlooking the court.

Ah, there she was now.

Lauren Burnside, one of the Boston lawyers he sometimes used for deals he didn't want made public knowledge before the fact, her hip cocked, her expression a smooth combination of professional savvy and sexual knowhow.

'I always thought you were packing a punch beneath all those business suits, Señor Rodriguez. Now I know you are.'

'Lauren.' Cruz let his T-shirt drop and waited for her hot eyes to trail back up to his. She was curvy, elegant and sophisticated, and he had nearly slept with her about a year ago but had baulked at the last minute. He still couldn't figure out why. 'Long way to come to make a house call, counsellor. A text would have sufficed.'

'Not quite. We have a hitch.' She smiled nonchalantly. 'And since I was in California, just a hop, skip and a jump away from Acapulco, I thought I'd deliver the news *mano-a-mano*.' She smiled. 'So to speak.'

Cruz scowled, for once completely unmoved by the flick of her tongue across her glossy mouth.

He knew women found him attractive. He was tall, fit, with straight teeth and nose, a full head of black hair, and he was moneyed-up and uninterested in love. It appeared to be the perfect combination. '*Untameable*,' as one date had purred. He'd smiled, told her he planned to stay that way and she'd come on even stronger. Women, in his experience, were rarely satisfied and usually out for what they could get. If they had money they wanted love. If they had love they wanted money. If they had twenty pairs of shoes they wanted twenty-one. It was tedious in the extreme.

So he ignored his lawyer's honey trap and kept his mind sharp. 'That's not what I want to hear on a deal that was meant to be completed two hours ago, Ms Burnside.' He kept his voice carefully blank, even though his heart rate had sped up faster than during the whole squash game.

'Let me come down.'

For all the provocation behind those words Cruz could tell she had picked up his *not interested* vibe and was smart enough to let it drop.

'She your latest?'

'No.'

Cruz's curt response raised his brother's eyebrows.

'She wants to be.'

Cruz folded his arms as Lauren pushed open the clear door and stepped onto the court, her power suit doing little to disguise the killer body beneath. She inhaled deeply, the smell of male sweat clearly pleasing to her senses.

'You boys have been playing hard,' she murmured provocatively, looking at them from beneath dark lashes.

Okay, so maybe she wasn't that smart. 'What's the hitch?' Cruz prompted.

She raised a well-tended brow at his curtness. 'You don't want to go somewhere more private?'

'This is Ricardo, my brother, and vice-president of Rodriguez Polo Club. I repeat: what's the hitch?'

Lauren's forehead remained wrinkle-free in the face of his growing agitation and he didn't know if that was due to nerves of steel or Botox. Maybe both.

'The hitch,' she said calmly, 'is the granddaughter. Aspen Carmichael.'

Cruz felt his shoulders bunch at the unexpectedness of hearing the name of the female he was doing his best to forget. The last time he'd laid eyes on her she'd been seventeen, dressed in nothing but a nightie and putting on an act worthy of Marilyn Monroe.

The little scheme she and her preppy fiancé had concocted had done Cruz out of a fortune in money and, more importantly, lost him the respect of his family and peers.

Aspen Carmichael had bested him once before and he'd walked away. He'd be damned if he walked away again.

'How?'

'She wants to keep Ocean Haven for herself and her uncle has magnanimously agreed to sell it to her at a reduced cost. The information has only just come to light, but apparently if she can raise the money in the next five days the property is hers.'

Cruz stilled. 'How much of a reduced cost?'

When Lauren named a figure half that which he had offered he cursed loudly. 'Joe Carmichael is not the sharpest tool in the shed, but why the hell would he do that?'

'Family, darling.' Lauren shrugged. 'Don't you know that blood is thicker than water?'

Yes, he did, but what he also knew was that everyone was ultimately out for themselves and if you let your guard down you'd be left with nothing more than egg on your face.

He ran a hand through his damp hair and sweat drops sprayed around his head.

Lauren jumped back as if he'd nearly drenched her designer suit in sulphuric acid and threw an embarrassed glance towards Ricardo, who was busy surveying her charms.

Cruz snapped his attention away from both of them and concentrated on the blank wall covered in streaks of rubber from years of use.

Eight years ago Ocean Haven had been his home. For eleven years he had lived above the main stable and worked diligently with the horses—first as a groom, then as head trainer and finally as manager and captain of Charles Carmichael's star polo team. He'd been lifted from poverty and obscurity in a two-dog town because of his horsemanship by the wealthy American who had spotted him on the *hacienda* where Cruz had been working at the time.

Cruz gritted his teeth.

He'd been thirteen and trying to keep his family from going under after the sudden and pointless death of his father.

Charles Carmichael, he'd later learned, had ambitious plans to one day build a polo 'dream team' to rival all others, and he'd seen in Cruz his future protégé. His mother had seen in him an unmanageable boy she could use to keep the rest of his siblings together. She'd said sending him off with the American would be the best for him. What she'd meant was that it would be the best for all of them, because Old Man Carmichael was paying her a small fortune to take him. Cruz had known it at the time—and hated it—but because he'd loved his family more than anything he'd acquiesced.

And, hell, in the end his mother had been right. By the age of seventeen Cruz had become the youngest player ever to achieve a ten handicap—the highest ranking any player could achieve and one that only a handful ever did. By the age of twenty he'd been touted as possibly the best polo player who had ever lived.

By twenty-three the dream was over and he'd become the joke of the very society who had kissed his backside more times than he cared to remember.

All thanks to the devious Aspen Carmichael. The devious and extraordinarily beautiful Aspen Carmichael. And what shocked Cruz the most was that he hadn't expected it of her. She'd blindsided him and that had made him feel even more foolish.

She had come to Ocean Haven as a lonely, sweet-natured ten-year-old who had just lost her mother in a horrible accident some had whispered was suicide. He'd hardly seen her during those years. His summers had been spent playing polo in England and she had attended some posh boarding school the rest of the year. To him she'd always been a gawky kid with wild blonde hair that looked as if it could use a good pair of scissors. Then one year he'd injured his shoulder and had to spend the summer—her summer break—at Ocean Haven, and *bam!* She had been about sixteen and she had turned into an absolute stunner.

All the boys had noticed and wanted her attention.

So had Cruz, but he hadn't done anything about it. Okay, maybe he'd thought about it a number of times, especially when she had thrown him those hot little glances from beneath those long eyelashes when she assumed he wasn't looking, and, okay, possibly he could remember one or two dreams that she had starred in, but he never would have touched her if she hadn't come on to him first. She'd been too young, too beautiful, too *pure*.

He found himself running his tongue along the edge of

his mouth and the taste of her exploded inside his head. She sure as hell hadn't been pure *that* night.

Gritting his teeth, he shoved her out of his mind. Memory could be as fickle as a woman's nature and his aviator glasses were definitely not rose coloured where she was concerned.

'You okay, *hermano*?'

Cruz swung around and stared at Ricardo without really seeing him. He liked to think he was a fair man who played by the rules. A forgive-and-forget kind of man. He'd stayed away from Ocean Haven and anything related to it after Charles Carmichael had given him the boot. Now his property had come up for sale and objectively speaking it was a prime piece of real estate. The fact that he'd have to raze it to the ground to build a hotel on it was just par for the course.

Of course his kid brother wouldn't understand that, and he wasn't in the mood to explain it. He'd left Mexico when Ricardo had been young. Ricardo had cried. Cruz had not. Surprisingly, after he'd returned home with his tail between his legs eight years ago, he and his brother had picked up from where they'd left off, their bond intact. It was the only bond that was.

'I'm fine.' He swung his gaze to Lauren. 'And I'm not concerned about Aspen Carmichael. Old man Carmichael died owing more money than he had, thanks to the GFC, so there's no way she can have that sort of cash lying around.'

'No, she doesn't,' Lauren agreed. 'She's borrowing it.'

Cruz stilled. Now, that was just plain stupid. He knew Ocean Haven agisted horses and raised good-quality polo ponies, but no way would either of those bring in the type of money they were talking about.

'She'll never get it.'

Lauren looked as if she knew better. 'My sources tell me she's actually pretty close.'

Cruz ignored Ricardo's interested gaze and kept his face visibly relaxed. 'How close?'

'Two-thirds close.'

'Twenty million! Who would be stupid enough to lend her twenty million US dollars in this economic climate?' And, more importantly, what was she using for collateral?

Lauren raised her eyebrows at his uncharacteristic outburst, but wisely stayed silent.

'Hell!' The burst of adrenaline he used to feel when he mounted one of his ponies before a major event winged through his blood. How on earth had she managed to raise that much money and what could he do about it?

'Do you want me to start negotiating with her?' Lauren queried.

'No.' He turned his ordinarily agile mind to come up with a solution, but all it produced was an image of a radiant teenager decked out in figure-hugging jodhpurs and a fitted shirt leaning against a white fencepost, laughing and chatting while the sun turned her wheat-blonde curls to gold. His jaw clenched and his body hardened. Great. A hard-on in gym shorts. 'You focus on Joe Carmichael and any other offers lurking in the wings,' he instructed his lawyer. 'I'll handle Aspen Carmichael.'

'Of course,' Lauren concurred with a brief smile.

'In the meantime find out who Aspen is borrowing from and what exactly she's offering as collateral—' although as to that he had his ideas '—and meet me in my Acapulco office in an hour.'

Ricardo waited until Lauren had disappeared before tossing the rubber ball into the air. 'You didn't tell me you were buying the Carmichael place.'

'Why would I? It's just business.'

Ricardo's eyebrows lifted. 'And *handling* the lovely Aspen Carmichael will be part of that business?'

People said Cruz had a certain look that he got just before a major event which told his opponents they might as well pack up and go home. He gave it to his brother now. 'This is not your concern.'

His brother, unfortunately, was one of the few people who ignored it.

'Maybe not, but you once swore you'd never set foot on Ocean Haven again. So, what gives?'

What gave, Cruz thought, was that old Charlie had kicked the bucket and his son, Aspen's uncle, Joseph Carmichael, couldn't afford to run the estate and keep his English bride in diamonds and champagne so was moving to England. Cruz had assumed Aspen would be going with them—to sponge off him now that her grandfather was out of the picture.

It seemed he had assumed wrong.

But he had no intention of talking about his plans with his overly sentimental brother, who would no doubt assume there was more to it than a simple opportunity to make a lot of money. 'I don't have time to talk about it now,' he said, making a split-second decision. 'I need to organise the jet.'

'You're flying to East Hampton?'

'And if I am?' Cruz growled.

Ricardo held his hands up as if he was placating an angry bear. 'Miama's surprise birthday party is tomorrow.'

Cruz strode towards the changing rooms, his mind already in Hampton—or more specifically in Ocean Haven. 'Don't count on me being there.'

'Given your track record, the only person who still has enough hope to do that is Miama herself.'

Cruz stopped. Ricardo's blunt words stabbed him in the heart. His family still meant everything to him, and he'd help any of them out in a heartbeat, but things just weren't the same any more. With the exception of Ricardo, none of his family knew how to treat him, and his mother constantly threw him guilty looks that were a persistent

reminder of the darker days of his youth after he'd gone
to the farm.

Charles Carmichael had been a difficult man with a formidable temper who'd liked to get his own way, and Cruz
had never been one to back down from a fight until *that*
night. No, it had not been an easy transition for a proud
thirteen-year-old to make, and if there was one thing Cruz
hated more than the capricious nature of the human race
it was dwelling on the past.

He glanced back at Ricardo. 'You're going to be stubborn about this, aren't you?'

Ricardo laughed. 'You've cornered the market in stubborn, *mi amigo*. I'm just persistent.'

'Persistently painful. You know, bro, you don't need a
wife. You *are* a wife.'

Aspen decided that she had a new-found respect for tele-
marketers. It wasn't easy being told no time after time
and then picking yourself up and continuing on. But like
anyone trying to make a living she had to toughen up and
stay positive. Stay on track. Especially when she was so
close to achieving her goal. To choke now or, worse, give
up, would mean failing in her attempt to keep her beloved
home and that was inconceivable.

Smiling up at the beef of a man in front of her as if she
didn't have a head full of doubts and fears, Aspen surreptitiously pulled at the waist of the silk dress she'd worn to
impress the polo patrons attending the midweek chukkas
they held at Ocean Haven throughout the summer months.

In the searing sunshine the dress had taken on the texture of a wet dishrag and it did little to improve her mood
as she listened to Billy Smyth the Third, son of one of her
late grandfather's arch enemies, wax lyrical about the game
of polo he had—thankfully—just won.

'Oh, yes,' she murmured. 'I heard it was the goal of

the afternoon.' Fed to him, she had no doubt, by his well-paid polo star, who knew very well which side his bread was buttered on.

Billy Smyth was a rich waste of space who sponged off his father's cardboard packaging empire and loved every minute of it—not unlike many others in their circle. Her ex-husband still continued unashamedly to live off his own family's wealth, but thankfully he'd been out of her life for a long time, and she wasn't going to ruin an already difficult day by thinking about him as well.

Instead she concentrated on the wealthy man in front of her, with his polished boots and his pot belly propped over the top of his starchy white polo jeans. Years ago she had tried to like Billy, but he was very much a part of the 'women should keep silent and look beautiful' brigade, and the fact that she was pandering to his unhealthy ego at all was testament to just how desperate she had become.

When he'd asked her to meet him after the game she had jumped at the chance, knowing she'd dance on the sun in a bear suit if it would mean he'd lend her the last ten million she needed to keep Ocean Haven. Though by the gleam in his eyes he'd probably want her naked—and she wasn't so desperate that she'd actually hawk herself.

Yet.

Ever, she amended.

So she continued to smile and present her plan to turn 'The Farm', as Ocean Haven was lovingly referred to, into a viable commercial entity that any savvy businessman would feel remiss for not investing in. So far two of her grandfather's old friends had come on board, but she was fast feeling as if she was running out of options to find the rest. Ten million was small change to Billy and, she thought, ignoring the way his eyes made her skin crawl as if she was covered in live ants, he seemed genuinely interested.

'Your grandpop would be rolling in his grave at the thought of the Smyths investing in The Farm,' he announced.

True—but only because her grandfather had been an unforgiving, hard-headed traditionalist. 'He's not here anymore.' Aspen reminded him. 'And without the money Uncle Joe is going to sell to the highest bidder.'

Billy cocked his head and considered his way slowly down to her feet and just as slowly back up. 'Word is he already has a winner.'

Aspen took a minute to relax her shoulders, telling herself that Billy really didn't mean to be offensive. 'Yes. Some super-rich consortium that will no doubt want to put a hotel on it. But I'm determined to keep The Farm in the family. I'm sure you understand how important that is, being such a devoted family man yourself.'

A slow smile crept over Billy's face and Aspen inwardly groaned. She was trying too hard and they both knew it.

'Yes, indeed I do.'

Billy leered. His smile grew wider. And when he rocked back on his heels Aspen sent up a silent prayer to save her from having to deal with arrogant men ever again.

Because that was exactly why she was in this situation in the first place. Her grandfather had believed in three things: testosterone, power, and tradition. In other words men should inherit the earth while women should be grateful that they had. And he had used his fearsome iron will to control everyone who dared to disagree with him.

When her mother had died suddenly just before Aspen's tenth birthday and—surprise surprise—her errant father couldn't be located, Aspen had been sent to live with her grandfather and her uncle. Her grandmother had passed away a long time before. Aspen had liked Uncle Joe immediately, but he'd never been much of an advocate for her during her grandfather's attempts to turn her into the perfect debutante.

So far she had been at the mercy of her controlling grandfather, then her controlling ex, and now her misguided, henpecked uncle.

'I'm sorry Aspen,' her Uncle Joe had said when she'd managed to pin him down in the library a month ago. 'Father left the property in my hands to do with as I saw fit.'

'Yes, but he wouldn't have expected you to *sell it*,' Aspen had beseeched him.

'He shouldn't have expected Joe to sort out the mess of his finances either,' Joe's determined wife Tammy had whined.

'He wasn't well these last few years.' Aspen had appealed to her aunt, but, knowing that wouldn't do any good, had turned back to her uncle. 'Don't sell Ocean Haven, Uncle Joe. Please. It's been in our family for one hundred and fifty years. Your blood is in this land.'

Her mother's heart was here in this land.

But her uncle had shaken his head. 'I'm sorry, Aspen, I need the money. But unlike Father I'm not a greedy man. If you can raise the price I need in time for my Russian investment, with a little left over for the house Tammy wants in Knightsbridge, then you can have Ocean Haven and all the problems that go with it.'

'*What?*'

'*What?*'

Aspen and her Aunt Tammy had cried in unison.

'Joseph Carmichael, that is preposterous,' Tammy had said.

But for once Uncle Joe had stood up to his wife. 'I'd always planned to provide for Aspen, so this is a way to do it. But I think you're crazy for wanting to keep this place.' He'd shaken his head at her.

Aspen had been so happy she had all but floated out of

the room. Then reality at what exactly her uncle had offered had set in and she'd got the shakes. It was an enormous amount of money to pay back but she *knew* if she
got the chance she could do it.

The horn signifying the end of the last chukka blew
and Aspen pushed aside her fear that maybe she *was* just
a little crazy.

'Listen, Billy, it's a great deal,' she snapped, forgetting
all about the proper manners her grandfather had drummed
into her as a child, and also forgetting that Billy was probably her last great hope of controlling her own future.
'Take it or leave it.'

*Oh, yes and losing that firecracker temper of yours is
sure to sway him*, she berated herself.

A tiny dust cloud rose between them as Billy made a
figure eight with his boots in the dirt. 'The thing is, Aspen,
we're busy enough over at Oaks Place, and even though
you've done a good job of hiding it The Farm needs a lot
of work.'

'It needs some,' Aspen agreed with forced calm, thinking she hadn't done a good job at all if he'd seen through
her patchwork maintenance attempts. 'But I've factored
all that into the plan.' *Sort of.*

'I just think I need a bit more of a persuasive argument
if I'm to take this to my daddy,' he suggested, a certain
look crossing his pampered face.

'Like…?' A tight band had formed around Aspen's chest
because, really, it was hard to miss what he meant.

'Well, hell, Aspen, you're not that naïve. You *have* been
married.'

Yes, unfortunately she had. But all that had done was
make her determined that she would never be at any man's
mercy again. Which was exactly where arrogant, controlling men like this one wanted their women to be. 'For just
you, Billy?' she simpered. 'Or for your daddy as well?'

It took Mr Cocksure a second or two to realise she was yanking his chain and when he did his big head reared back and his eyes narrowed. 'I ain't no pimp, lady.'

'No,' she said calmly, flicking her riot of honey-coloured spiral curls back over her shoulder. 'What you are is a dirty, rotten rat and I can see why Grandpa Charles said your kind were just slime.' *Who gave a damn about proper manners anyway?*

Instead of getting angry Billy threw back his head and hooted with laughter. 'You know. I can't believe the rumours that you're a cold one in the sack. Not with all that fire shooting out of those pretty green eyes of yours.' He reached out and ran a finger down the side of her cheek and grinned when she raised her hand to rub at it. 'Let me know when you change your mind. I like a woman with attitude.'

Before she could open her mouth to tell him she'd mention that to his wife he sauntered off, leaving her spitting mad. She watched him pick up a glass of champagne from a table before joining a group of sweaty riders and willed someone to grab it and throw it all over him.

Of course no one did. Fate wasn't that kind.

Turning away in disgust, she cursed under her breath when a gust of hot wind whipped her hair across her face. Too angry to stop and clear her vision, she would have walked straight into a wall if it hadn't reached out and grabbed her by her upper arms.

With a soft gasp she looked up, about to thank whoever had saved her. But the words never came and the quick smile froze on her face as she found herself staring into the hard eyes of a man she had thought she would never see in the flesh again.

The air between them split apart and reformed, vibrating with emotion as Cruz Rodriquez stared down at her with such cold detachment she nearly shivered.

Eight years dissolved into dust. Guilt, shame and a host of other emotions all sparked for dominance inside her.

'I…' Aspen blinked, her mind scrambling for poise… words…*something*.

'Hello, Aspen. Nice to see you again.'

Aspen blinked at the incongruity of those words. He might as well have said *Off with her head*.

'I…'

CHAPTER TWO

CRUZ STARED DOWN at the slender woman whose smooth arms he held and wished he hadn't left his sunglasses in the car. At seventeen Aspen Carmichael had been full of sexual promise. Eight years later, with her golden mane flowing down past her shoulders and the top button of her dress artfully popped open to reveal the upper swell of her creamy assets, she had well and truly delivered. And he was finding it hard not to take her all in at once.

'You…?' he prompted casually, dropping his hands and raising his eyes from her cleavage.

She glanced down and quickly closed the top of her dress. Clearly only men offering part of their vast fortunes were allowed to view the merchandise. The realisation of his earlier assumption as to what she might be using as leverage to raise her cash was for some reason profoundly disappointing.

'I…' She shook her head as if to clear it. 'What are you doing here?'

'Old Charlie would roll over in his grave if he heard you greeting a polo patron like that,' Cruz drawled. *Even one he didn't think would ever be good enough for his perfect little granddaughter,* he added silently.

Cruz's velveteen voice, with no hint at all of his Mexican heritage, scraped over Aspen's already raw nerves and she didn't manage to contain the shiver this time.

She couldn't tell his frame of mind but she knew hers and it was definitely disturbed. 'My grandfather probably feels like he's on a spit roast at the moment.' She smiled, trying for light amusement to ease the tension that lay as thick as the issues of the past between them.

'Are you implying he's in hell, Aspen?'

He probably was, Aspen thought, but that wasn't what she'd meant. 'No. I just…you're right.' She shook her head, wondering what had happened to her manners. Her composure. Her *brain*. 'That was a terrible greeting. Shall we start again?'

Without waiting for him to reply she stuck out her hand, ignoring the racing memories causing her heart to beat double time.

'Hello, Cruz, welcome back to Ocean Haven. You're looking well.' Which was a half-truth if ever she'd uttered one.

The man didn't look well. He looked superb.

His thick black hair that sat just fashionably shy of his expensive suit jacket and his piercing black eyes and square-cut jaw were even more beautiful than she remembered. He'd always had a strong, angular face and powerful body, but eight years had done him a load of favours in the looks department, settling a handsome maturity over the youthful virility he'd always worn like a cloak.

The apology she'd never got to voice for her part in the acrimonious accusations that had no doubt contributed to him leaving Ocean Haven eight years ago hovered behind her closed lips, but it seemed awkward to just blurt it out.

How could she tell him that a couple of months after that night she had written him a letter explaining everything but hadn't had the wherewithal to send it without feeling a deep sense of shame at her ineptitude? It was little comfort knowing she'd been distracted by her grandfather's stroke at the time, because she knew her behaviour that night had probably brought that on too. After he had recovered sending Cruz a letter had seemed like too little too late, and she'd pushed out of her mind the man who had fascinated her during most of her teenage years.

And maybe he was here now to let bygones be bygones. She didn't know, but why pre-empt anything with her own guilt-riddled memories?

Because it would make you feel better, that's why.

'As are you.'

As she was what? Oh, looking well. 'Thank you.' She ran a nervous hand down the side of her dress and then pretended she was flicking off horse dust. 'So…ah…are you here for the polo? The last chukka just finished, but—'

'I'm not here for the polo.'

Aspen hated the anxious feeling that had settled over her and raised her chin. 'Well, there's champagne in the central marquee. Just tell Judy that I sent—'

'I'm not here for the champagne either.'

Even more perturbed by the way he regarded her with such cool detachment she felt as if she was frying under the blasted summer sun. 'Well, it would be great if you could tell me what you *are* here for because I have a few more people to schmooze before they leave. You know how these things go.'

He looked at her as if he was seeing right inside her. As if he knew all her secrets. As if he could see how desperately uncomfortable she was. *Impossible*, she thought, telling herself to get a grip.

Cruz could almost see the sweat breaking out over Aspen's body and noted the way her cat-green eyes wouldn't quite meet his. He didn't know if that was because he was keeping her from an assignation with Billy Smyth, or someone else, or because she could feel the chemistry that lay between them like a grenade with the pin pulled.

Whatever it was, she wasn't leaving his side until he

had won over her confidence and figured out a way to handle the situation.

His brother's silky question about 'handling the lovely Aspen Carmichael' came into his head. He knew what Ricardo had meant and looking at Aspen now, in her svelte designer dress and 'come take me' heels, her wild hair curling down around her shoulders as if she'd just rolled out of her latest lover's bed, he had no doubt many men had 'handled' her that way before. But not him. Never him.

So far he'd drawn a blank as to how to contain her money-grabbing endeavours without alerting her to his own interest in Ocean Haven. Until he did he'd just have to rein himself in and keep his eyes away from her sexy mouth.

'I'm here to buy a horse, Aspen. What else?'

'A horse?'

Aspen blinked. That was the last thing she had expected him to say, though what she *had* expected she couldn't say.

'You do have one for sale, don't you?' he continued silkily.

Aspen cleared her throat. 'Gypsy Blue. She's a thoroughbred. Ex-racing stock and she's gorgeous.'

'I have no doubt.'

Aspen frowned at his tone, wondering why he seemed so tense. Not that he *looked* tense. In his bespoke suit with his hands in his pockets, his hair casually ruffled by the warm breeze, he looked like a man who didn't have a care in the world. But the vibe she was picking up from him was making her feel edgy—and surely that wasn't just because of her sense of guilt.

'Are you hoping the horse will materialise in front of us, Aspen, or are you going to take me to see her?'

'I…' Aspen felt stupid, and not a little perturbed to be standing there trying not to look at his chiselled mouth. Which was nearly impossible when the memory of the kiss they had shared on that awful night was swirling inside her head. 'Of course.' She glanced around, hoping to see Donny, but knew that was cowardly. It was really *her* responsibility to show him the mare, not her chief groom's.

'She played earlier today, so she should be in the south stables.' It was just rotten luck that she happened to be in the building where she had kissed Cruz on that fateful night. 'Hey, why don't I take you past the east paddock?' she said, using anything as a possible distraction. 'Trigger is out there, and I know he'd remember you and—'

'I'm not here on a social visit, Aspen.'

And don't mistake it for one, his tone implied.

No polo, no champagne, no socialising. Got it.

Still, she hesitated at his sharp tone. Then decided to let it drop and listened to the sound of their feet crunching the gravel as they walked away from the busy sounds of horse-owners loading tired horses into their respective trucks. It was all very normal and busy at the end of the afternoon's practice, and yet Aspen felt as if she was wading through quicksand with Cruz beside her.

She cast a curious glance at him and wondered if he felt the same way. Or maybe he didn't feel anything at all and just wanted to do his business and head out like everyone else. In a way she hoped that was the case, because the shock of seeing him again had worn off and his tension was raising her stress levels to dangerous proportions.

But then he had a reason for being tense, she reminded herself, and her skin flushed hotly as the weight of the past bore down on her. Years ago she had promised herself that she would never let pride interfere with the decisions she made in her life, but in avoiding the elephant walking alongside them wasn't that exactly what she was doing now?

Taking a deep breath, she stopped just short of the stable

doors and turned to Cruz, determined to rectify the situation as best she could *before* they made it inside.

Shading her eyes with one hand, she looked up into his face. Had he always been this tall? This broad? This good-looking?

'Cruz, listen. This feels really awkward, but you took me by surprise before when I ran into you—*literally.*' She released a shaky breath. 'I want you to know that I feel terrible about the way you left The Farm all those years ago, and I'm truly sorry for the role I played in that.'

'Are you?' he asked coolly.

'Yes, of course. I never meant for you to get into trouble.'

Cruz didn't move a muscle.

'I didn't!' Aspen felt her temper flare at his dubious look, hating how defensive she sounded.

She'd gone down to the stables that night because Chad—now thankfully her ex—had stayed for dinner so he could present his idea to her grandfather that he would marry her as soon as she turned eighteen. Aspen remembered how overwhelmed she had felt when neither man would consider her desire to study before she even thought about the prospect of marriage.

She'd known it was what her grandfather wanted, and at the time pleasing him had been more important than pleasing herself. So she'd done what she'd always done when she was stressed and gone down to be with the horses and to reconnect with her mother in her special place in the main stable.

Gone to try and make sense of her feelings.

Of course in hindsight letting her frustration get to her and kicking the side of the stable wall in steel-capped boots hadn't been all that clever, because it had brought Cruz down from his apartment over the garage to investigate.

She remembered that he had looked gorgeous and lean

and bad in dirty jeans and a half-buttoned shirt, as if he had just climbed out of bed.

'What's got you in a snit, *chiquita*?' he'd said, the intensity of his heavy-lidded gaze in the dim light belying the relaxed humour in his voice.

'Wouldn't you like to know?' she'd thrown back at him challengingly.

Inwardly grimacing, she remembered how she had flicked her hair back over her shoulder in an unconscious gesture to get his full attention. She hadn't known what she was inviting—not really—but she hadn't wanted him to go. For some reason she had remembered the time she had come across him kissing a girlfriend in the outer barn, and the soft, pleasure-filled moans the girl had made had filled her ears that night.

Acting purely on instinct she had wandered from horse stall to horse stall, eventually coming to a stop directly in front of him. The warm glow of his torch had seemed to make the world contract, so that it had felt as if they were the only two people in it. Aspen was pretty sure she'd reached for him first, but seconds later she had been bent over his arm and he had been kissing her.

Her first kiss.

She felt her breathing grow shallow at the memory.

Something had fired in her system that night—desperation, lust, need—whatever it had been she'd never felt anything like it before or since.

Looking back, it was obvious that a feeling of entrapment—a feeling of having no say over her future—had driven her into the stables that night, but it had been Cruz's sheer animal magnetism that had driven her into his arms.

Not that she really wanted to admit any of that to him right now. Not when he looked so...*bored*.

'This is old news, Aspen, and I'm not in the mood to reminisce.'

'That's your prerogative. But I want you to know that I told my grandfather the next day that he'd got it wrong.'

'Really?'

'Yes, really.' But her grandfather had cut her off with a look of disgust she hadn't wanted to face. She looked up at Cruz now, more sorry than she could say. 'I'm—'

'Truly sorry? So you said. Have you become prone to repeating yourself?'

Aspen blinked up at him. Was it her imagination or did he hate her? 'No, but I don't think you believe me,' she said carefully.

'Does it matter if I do?'

'Well, we used to be friends.'

'We were never *friends*, Aspen. But I was glad to see your little indiscretion didn't stop Anderson from marrying you.'

Aspen moistened her parched lips. 'Grandfather thought it best if I didn't tell him.'

Cruz barked out a laugh. 'Well, now I almost feel sorry for the fool. If he'd known what a disloyal little cheat you were from the start he might have saved himself the heartache at the end.'

Oh, yes, he hated her all right. 'Look, I'm sorry I brought it up. I just wanted to clear the air between us.'

'There's nothing to clear as far as I'm concerned.'

Aspen studied him warily. He wasn't moving but she felt as if she was being circled by a predator. A very angry predator. She didn't believe that he was at all okay with what had transpired between them but who was she to push it?

'I made a mistake, but as you said you're not here to reminisce.' And nor was she. Particularly not about a time in her life she would much rather forget had ever happened.

She turned sharply towards the stables and kept up a brisk pace until she reached the doors, only starting to feel herself relax as she entered the cooler interior, her high heels clicking loudly on the bluestone floor. Her nose was filled with the sweet scent of horse and hay.

Cruz followed and Aspen glanced around at the worn tack hanging from metal bars and the various frayed blankets and dirty buckets that waited for Donny and her to come and finish them off for the day. The high beams of the hayloft needed a fresh coat of paint, and if you looked closely there were tiny pinpricks of sunlight streaming in through the tin roof where there shouldn't be. She hoped Cruz didn't look up.

A pigeon created dust motes as it swooped past them and interested horses poked their noses over the stall doors. A couple whinnied when they recognised her.

Aspen automatically reached into her pocket for a treat, forgetting that she wasn't in her normal jeans and shirt. Instead she brushed one of the horses' noses. 'Sorry, hon. I don't have anything. I'll bring you something later.'

Cruz stopped beside her but he didn't try to stroke the horse as she remembered he might once have done.

'This is Cougar. Named because he has the heart of a mountain lion, although he can be a bit sulky when he gets pushed around out on the field. Can't you, big guy?' She gave him an affectionate pat before moving to the next stall. 'This one is Delta. She's—'

'Just show me the horse you're selling, Aspen.'

Aspen read the flash of annoyance in his gaze—and something else she couldn't place. But his annoyance fed hers and once again she stalked away from him and stopped at Gypsy Blue's stall. If she'd been able to afford it she would have kept her beloved mare, and that only increased her aggravation.

'Here she is,' she rapped out. 'Her sire was Blue Rise, her dam Lady Belington. You might remember she won the Kentucky Derby twice running a few years back.' She sucked in a breath, trying not to babble as she had done over her apology before. If Cruz was happy with the way things were between them then so was she. 'I have someone else interested, so if you want her you'll have to decide quickly.'

Quite a backpedal, Cruz thought. From uncomfortable, apologetic innocent to stiff Upper East Side princess. He wondered what other roles she had up her sleeve and then cut the thought in half before it could fully form. Because he already knew, didn't he? Cheating temptress being one of them. Not that she was married now. Or engaged as far as he knew.

'I've made you angry,' he said, backpedalling himself.

This wasn't at all the way he needed her to be if he was going to get information out of her. It was just this damned place. It felt as if it was full of ghosts, with memories around every corner that he had no wish to revisit. He'd closed the door on that part of his life the minute he'd carried his duffel bag off the property. On foot. Taking nothing from Old Man Carmichael except the clothes on his back and the money he'd already earned.

Of its own accord his gaze shifted to the other end of the long walkway to the place where Aspen had approached him that night, wearing a cotton nightie she must have known was see-through in the glow of his torch. He hadn't been wearing much either, having only thrown on a pair of jeans and a shirt he hadn't even bothered to button properly when he'd heard something banging on the wall and gone to investigate.

He'd presumed it was one of the horses and had been absolutely thunderstruck to find Aspen in that nightie and a pair of riding boots. She'd looked hotter than Hades and when she'd strolled past the stalls, lightly trailing her slender fingers along the wood, he couldn't have moved if someone had planted a bomb under him.

It had all been a ploy. He knew that now. He'd kissed her because he'd been a man overcome with lust. She'd kissed him because she'd been setting him up. It had been like a bad rendition of Samson and Delilah and she'd deserved an acting award for wardrobe choice alone.

His muscles grew taut as he remembered how he had held himself in check. How he hadn't wanted to overwhelm her with the desperate hunger that had surged through him and urged him to pull her down onto the hay and rip the flimsy nightie from her body. How he hadn't wanted to take her *innocence*. What a joke. She'd played him like a finely tuned instrument and, like a fool, he'd let her.

'Like I said before.' She cleared her throat. 'This feels a little awkward.'

She must have noticed the direction of his gaze because her voice sounded breathless; almost as if her memories of that night mirrored his own. Of course he knew better now.

About to placate her by pretending he had forgotten all about it, he found the words dying in his throat as she raised both hands and twisted her flyaway curls into a rope and let it drop down her back. The middle button on her dress strained and he found himself willing it to pop open.

Surprised to find his libido running away without his consent, he quickly ducked inside the stall and feigned avid interest in a horse he had no wish to buy.

He went through the motions, though, studying the lines of the mare's back, running his hands over her glossy coat, stroking down over her foreleg and checking the straightness of her pasterns. Fortunately he was on autopilot, because his undisciplined mind was comparing the shapeliness of the thoroughbred with Aspen's lissom figure and imagining how she would feel under his rough hands.

Silky, smooth, and oh, so soft.

Memories of the little sounds she'd made as he'd lost

himself in her eight years ago exploded through his system and turned his breathing rough.

'She's an exceptional polo pony. Really relaxed on the field and fast as a whip.'

Aspen's commentary dragged his mind back to his game plan and he kept on stroking the horse as he spoke. 'Why are you selling her?'

'We run a horse stud, not a bed and breakfast,' she said with mock sternness, her eyes tinged with dark humour as she repeated one of Charles Carmichael's favourite sayings.

'Or an old persons' home.' He joined in with Charles's second favourite saying before he could stop himself.

'No.' Her small smile was tinged with emotion.

Her reaction surprised him.

'You miss him?'

She shifted and leant her elbows on the door. 'I really don't know.' Her eyes trailed over the horse. 'He had moments of such kindness, and he gave me a home when Mum died, but he was impossible to be around if he didn't get his own way.'

'He certainly had high hopes of you marrying well and providing blue stock heirs for Ocean Haven.' And he'd made it more than clear to him after Aspen had returned to the house that night that Cruz wouldn't be the one to provide them under any circumstances.

'Yes.'

Her troubled eyes briefly met his and for a moment he wanted to shake her for not being a different kind of woman. A more sincere and genuine woman.

'So what do you think?'

It took him a minute to realise she was talking about the mare and not herself. 'She's perfect. I'll take her.'

'Oh.' She gave a self-conscious laugh. 'You don't want to ride her first?'

Oh, yes, he certainly did want to do that!

'No.'

'Well, I did tell you to be quick. I'll have Donny run the paperwork.'

'Send it to my lawyer.' Cruz rubbed the mare's nose and let her nudge him. 'I hear Joe is planning to sell the farm.'

She grimaced. 'Good news travels fast.'

'Polo's a small community.'

'Too small sometimes.' She gestured towards the mare. 'She'll ruin your nice suit if you let her do that.'

'I have others.'

So nice not to have to worry about money, Aspen thought, a touch enviously. After the abject poverty she and her mother had lived in after her father's desertion, the wealth of Ocean Haven had been staggering. It was something she'd never take for granted again.

'Where are you planning to go once it's sold?'

'It's not going to be sold,' she said with a touch of asperity, stepping back as Cruz joined her outside the stall. 'At least not to someone else.'

He raised an eyebrow. 'You're going to buy it?'

'Yes.' She had always been a believer in the power of positive thinking, and she had never needed that more than she did now.

Gypsy Blue whickered and stuck her head over the door and Aspen realised her water trough was nearly empty. Unhooking it, she walked the short distance to a tap and filled it.

'Let me do that.'

Cruz took the bucket from her before she could stop him and stepped inside the stall. Aspen grabbed the feed bucket Donny had left outside and followed him in and hooked it into place.

'It's a big property to run by yourself,' he said.

'For a girl?' she replied curtly.

'I didn't say that.'

'Sorry. I'm a bit touchy because so many people have implied more than once that I won't be able to do it. It's like they think I'm completely incompetent, and that really gets my—' She gave a small laugh realising she was about to unload her biggest gripe onto him and he was virtually a stranger to her now. Why would he even care? 'The fact is…' She looked at him carefully.

He had money. She'd heard of his business acumen. Of the companies he bought and sold. Of his innovative and brilliant new polo-inspired hotel in Mexico. He was the epitome of a man at the top of his game. Right now, as he leant his wide shoulders against the stall door and blocked out all sources of light from behind, he also looked the epitome of adult male perfection.

'But the fact is…?' he prompted.

Aspen's eyes darted to his as she registered the subtle amusement lacing his voice. Did he know what she had just been thinking? 'Sorry, I was just…' *Just a bit distracted by your incredible face? Your powerful body? Way to go, Aspen. Really. Super effort.* 'The fact is—' she squared her shoulders '—I need ten million dollars to keep it.'

She forced a bright smile onto her face.

'You're not looking for an investment opportunity, are you?'

CHAPTER THREE

SHE COULDN'T BELIEVE she'd actually voiced the question that had just formed in her mind but she knew that she had when Cruz's dark gaze sharpened on hers. But frankly, with only five days left to raise the rest of the money and Billy Smyth firmly out of the picture, she really was that desperate.

'Give you ten million dollars? That's a big ask.'

Her heart thumped loudly in her chest and her mouth felt dust dry. 'Lend,' she corrected. 'But you know what they say…' She stopped as he straightened to his full height and she lost her train of thought.

He shoved both hands into his pockets. '*They* say a lot of things, Aspen. What is it exactly you're referring to?'

'If you don't ask you never know,' she said, moistening her lips. 'And I'm desperate.'

Cruz's eyes glittered as he looked down at her. 'A good negotiator never shows that particular hand. It puts their opponent in the dominant position.'

Heat bloomed anew on her face as his tone seemed to take on a sensual edge. 'I don't see you as my opponent, Cruz.'

'Then you're a fool,' he returned, almost too mildly.

Aspen felt her hopes shrivel to nothing. What had she been thinking, approaching a business situation like that? Where was her professionalism? Her polish?

But maybe she'd known he'd never agree to it. Not with the way he obviously felt about her.

'What would I get out of it, anyway?'

The unexpected question surprised her and once again her eyes darted to his. Had she been wrong in thinking he wouldn't be interested? 'A lot, actually. I've drawn up a business plan.'

'Really?'

She didn't like his sceptical tone but decided to ignore it. 'Yes. It outlines the horses due to foal, and how much we expect to make from each one, and our plans to purchase a top-of-the-line stallion to keep improving the breed. We also have a couple of wonderful horses we're about to start training—and I don't know if you've heard of our riding school, but I teach adults and children, and— well… There's more, but if you're truly interested we can run through the logistics of it all later.' Out of breath, she stopped, and then added, 'It has merit. I promise.'

'If it has so much merit why haven't any of the financial institutions bankrolled you?'

'Because I'm young—that is usually the first excuse. But really I think it's because unbeknownst to any of us Grandfather hadn't been running his business properly the last few years and—' Realising that yet again she was about to divulge every one of her issues, she stopped. 'The banks just don't believe I have enough experience to pull it off.'

'Perhaps you should have thought about furthering your education instead of marrying to secure your future.'

Aspen nearly gasped at his snide tone of voice. 'I didn't marry to secure anything,' she said sharply. Except perhaps her grandfather's love and affection. Something that had always been in short supply.

Upset with herself for even being in this position, and with him for his nasty comment, Aspen thought about telling him that she was one semester out from completing a degree in veterinary science—and that she'd achieved that while working full-time running Ocean Haven. But she knew that in her current state she would no doubt come across as defensive or whiney, and that only made her angry.

'If you have such a low opinion of me why pretend any interest in my plans for The Farm?' she demanded hotly, slapping her hands either side of her waist. 'Are you planning to steal our ideas?'

That got an abrupt bark of laughter from him that did nothing to improve her temper. 'I don't need to steal your ideas, *gatita*. I have plenty of my own.'

'Then why get my hopes up like that?'

'Is that what I did?'

Aspen stared him down. 'You know that's exactly what you did.'

He stepped closer to her. 'But maybe I *am* interested.'

His tone sent a splinter of unease down her spine but she was too annoyed to pay attention to it. 'Don't patronise me, Cruz. I have five days before The Farm will be sold to some big-shot investment consortium. I don't have time to bandy around with this.'

'Ocean Haven really means that much to you?'

'Yes, it does.'

'I suppose it *is* the easiest option for a woman in your position,' he conceded, with such arrogance that Aspen nearly choked.

Easy? Easy! He clearly had no idea how hard she worked on the property—tending horses, mending fences, keeping the books—nor how important Ocean Haven was to her. How it was the one link she had left with her mother. How it was the one place that had made her feel happy and secure after she'd been orphaned. After her marriage had fallen apart.

She was incredibly proud of her work and her future plans to open up a school camp for kids who'd had a tough start in life. Horses had a way of grounding troubled adolescents and she wanted to provide a place they could come to and feel safe. Just as she had. And she hated that Cruz was judging her—*mocking her*—like every other obnoxious male she had ever come across. That she hadn't expected it from him only made her feel worse.

Hopping mad, she had a mind to order him off her property, but she couldn't quite kill off this avenue of hope just yet. He was supposed to be a savvy businessman after all, and she had a good plan. Well, she hoped she did. 'Ocean Haven has been in my family for centuries,' she began, striving for calm.

'I think the violinist has packed up for the day...'

Aspen blinked. 'God, you're cold. I don't remember that about you.'

'Don't you, *gatita*? Tell me...'

His voice dropped an octave and her heartbeat faltered. 'What *do* you remember?'

Aspen's gaze fell to his mouth. 'I remember that you were...' *Tall. That your hair glints almost blue-black in the sun. That your face looks like it belongs in a magazine. That your mouth is firm and yet soft.* She forced her eyes to meet his and ignored the fact that her face felt as if it was on fire. 'Good with the horses.' She swallowed. 'That you were smart, and that you used to keep to yourself a lot. But I remember when you laughed.' *It used to make me smile.* 'It sounded happy. And I remember that when you were mad at something not even my grandfather was brave enough to face you. I rem—'

'Enough.' He sliced his hand through the air with sharp finality. 'There's only one thing I want to know right now,' he said softly.

If she remembered his kisses? Yes—yes, she did. Sometimes even when she didn't want to. 'What?' she asked, hating the breathless quality of her voice.

'Just how desperate *are* you?'

His dark voice was so dangerously male it sent her brain into overdrive. 'What kind of a question is that?' She shook her head, trying to ward off the jittery feelings he so effortlessly conjured up inside her.

He reached forward and captured a strand of her hair between his fingertips, his eyes burning into hers. 'If I were to lend you this money I'd want more than a share in the profits.'

Aspen felt her chest rising and falling too quickly and hoped to hell he wasn't going to suggest the very thing Billy Smyth had done not an hour earlier.

Reaching up, she tugged her hair out of his hold. 'Such as…?'

His eyes looked black as pitch as they pinned her like a dart on a wall. 'Oh, save us both the Victorian naïveté. You're no retiring virgin after the life you lived with Chad Anderson—and before that, even. You're a sensual woman who no doubt looks very good gracing a man's bed.' He paused, his gaze caressing her face. 'If the terms were right I might want you to grace mine.'

Was he kidding?

Aspen felt her mouth drop open before she could stop it. Rage welled up inside her like a living beast. Rage at the injustice of her grandfather's will, rage at the way men viewed her as little more than a sexual object, rage at her mother's death and her father's abandonment.

Maybe Cruz had a reason for being upset with her after she had failed to correct her grandfather's assumption that they were sleeping together years ago, but that didn't give him the right to treat her like a—like a whore.

'Get out of my way,' she ordered.

His eyes lingered on her tight lips. 'Make sure you don't

burn your bridges unnecessarily, Aspen. Pride can be a
nasty thing when it's used rashly.'

She knew all about pride going before a fall. 'It's not
rash pride making me reject your offer, Cruz. It's simple
self-respect.'

'Whatever you want to call it, I'm offering you a
straightforward business deal. You have something I've
decided I want. I have something you need. Why complicate it?'

'Because it's disgusting.'

'What an interesting way to put it,' he sneered. 'Tell
me, Aspen, would it have been less *disgusting* if I'd first
said that you were beautiful before taking you to bed? If
I'd first invited you out for a drink? Taken you to dinner, perhaps?' He took a step towards her and lowered his
voice. 'If I had gone down that path would you have said
yes?' His lips twisted with mocking superiority. 'If I had
romanced you, Aspen, I could have had you naked and
beneath me in a matter of hours and saved myself a hell
of a lot of money.'

Aspen threw him a withering look, ignoring the sudden
mental picture of them both naked and tangled together.
'You can save yourself a hell of a lot of money *and* skin
right now and get off my property,' she said tightly.

His nostrils flared as he breathed deeply and she suddenly realised how close he was, how far she had to tilt
her head back to look up at him. 'And for your information,' she began, wanting to stamp all over his supersized
ego, 'I would *never* have said yes to you.'

'Really?'

He stepped even closer and Aspen felt the harsh bite
of wood at her back. Caged, she could only stare as Cruz
lifted one of her spiral curls again; this time carrying it to
his nose. Her hands rose to shove him back but he didn't
budge, and almost immediately her senses tuned in to the

warm packed muscle beneath the thin cotton of his shirt, to the fast beat of his heart that seemed to mirror her own racing pulse.

A flash of memory took her back eight years to the feel of his mouth on hers. The feel of his tongue rubbing hers. The feel of his hands spanning her waist. Heat pooled inside her and made her breasts heavy, her legs unsteady. She remembered that after they'd been caught she had been so shocked by her physical reaction to him and so scared of her grandfather's wrath she'd fallen utterly silent—ashamed of herself for considering one man's marriage proposal while losing herself in the arms of another. Cruz hadn't raised one word of denial the whole time and she still wondered why.

Not that she had time to consider that now… He leant forward as if her staying hands were nothing more than crepe paper. His breath brushed her ear.

'Let me tell you what I remember, *gatita*. I remember the way your curvy backside filled out those tight jodhpurs. I remember the purple bikini top you used to wear riding your horse along the beach. And I remember the way you used to watch me. A bit like the way you were watching me stroke the mare before.' His hand tightened in her hair. 'You were thinking about how it would feel if I put my hands on you again, weren't you? How it would feel if I kissed you?'

Aspen made a half coughing noise in instant denial and tried to catch her breath. There was no way he could have known she'd been thinking exactly that.

'Have you turned into a dreamer, Cruz?' she mocked with false bravado, frightened beyond belief at how vulnerable she suddenly felt. 'Because really a dream would be the only place I would ever want something like that from you.'

Dreamer?

Cruz felt his jaw knot at her insolent tone. How dared she accuse him of being a dreamer when *she* was clearly the dreamer here if she thought she could buy and hold onto the rundown estate Ocean Haven had become?

Memories of the past swirled around him and bit deep. Memories of how she had felt in his arms. How she had tasted. Memories of how she had stood there, all dazed innocence, and listened to her grandfather rail at him. He'd been accused of ruining her that night but it was her—her and that slimy fiancé of hers, Chad Anderson—who had tried to ruin him. She and her lover who had set him up for a fall to clear the way for Chad to take over as captain of Charles Carmichael's dream team.

There'd been no other explanation for it, and he'd always wondered how far she would have taken things if her grandfather had turned up five minutes later. Because that was all it would have taken for him to twist her nightie up past her hips and thrust deep into her velveteen warmth.

His eyes took her in now. Her defiant expression and flushed face. Her rapidly beating pulse and her moist lips where her pink tongue had just lashed them. Her hands were burning a hole in his shirt and he was already as hard as stone—and, by God, he'd had enough of her holier-than-thou attitude.

'You would have loved it.' Cruz twisted her hair into a knot at the back of her head and pulled her roughly up against him. '*Will* love it,' he promised thickly, wrapping his other arm around her waist and staunching her shocked cry with his mouth.

Her lips immediately clamped together and she pushed against him, but that only brought her body more fully up against his as her hands slipped over his shoulders. She stilled, as if the added contact affected her as much as it affected him, and with a deep groan he ran his tongue across the seam of her lips. He felt a shiver run through her and then she shoved harder to dislodge him. He told himself he wasn't doing his plan any favours by forcing himself on her, but the plan paled into insignificance when compared to the feel of her warm and wriggling in his arms. He wanted her to surrender to him. To admit that the chemistry that had exploded through him like a haze of bloodlust as soon as he had seen her again wasn't just one-sided.

But some inner instinct warned him that this wasn't the way to get her to acquiesce, and years of experience in gentling horses rushed through him. He marshalled some of that strength and patience now and gentled her. Sucking at her lips, nipping, soothing her with his tongue. She made a tiny whimper in the back of her throat and he felt a sense of primal victory as she tentatively opened her mouth under his, aligning her body so that her soft curves were no longer resisting his hardness but melting against him until he could feel every sweet, feminine inch of her.

With a low growl of approval he gentled his hold on her and angled her head so that he could take her mouth more fully. When her lips opened wider and her arms urged him closer he couldn't stop himself from plundering her, couldn't resist drawing her tongue out so that she could taste him in return.

An unexpected sense of completeness settled over him—a sense of finding something he'd been searching for his whole life—and he didn't want the kiss to end. He didn't want this maddening arousal to end.

If he'd had any idea that it would be like this again he wasn't sure that he would have started it. But now that he had he didn't want to stop. *Ever.* She tasted so sweet. So silky. So *good.*

He made a sound low in his throat when she circled her pelvis against his in an age-old request and he couldn't think after that. Could only grab her hips and smooth his hands over her firm backside to mould her against him.

'Yes,' he whispered roughly against her mouth. 'Kiss me, *chiquita*. Give me everything.'

And she did. Without reservation. Her mouth devouring his as if she too had dreamed of this over and over and over. As if she too couldn't live without—

'Ow!'

Her sharp cry of pain echoed his deeper one as something pushed the back of his head and bumped his forehead into hers. He pulled back and glared over his shoulder to where the horse he had just agreed to purchase snorted in disgust.

Aspen blinked dazedly, rubbing at her head. Then the stunned look on her face cleared and he knew their impromptu little make out session had well and truly finished.

'You bastard.'

She raised her arm and slapped his face. The sound echoed in the cavernous stall and he worked his jaw as heat bloomed where her palm had connected.

About to tell her that she had a good arm, he was shocked to see that she had turned white and looked as if she might pass out.

'Aspen?'

She looked at him as if *he* had hit *her*. 'Now look what you made me do!' she cried.

Well, wasn't that typical of her—to blame him?

'I didn't *make* you do anything. You hit me. And if I'm not mistaken all because you enjoyed my kisses just a little too much.'

'Oh!'

She pushed against him with all her might and he was only too glad to step away from her.

'I've already turned down one slimy rat today and now I'm turning down another.' Her glare alone could have buried him. 'Now, get off my property before I have every man available throw you off.'

'I'm flattered you think it would take that many.'

'Oh, I bet you are.' Every inch of her trembled with feminine outrage. 'But I'm not prepared to take chances with a bully like you.'

'I didn't bully you, *chiquita*. You were asking for it.'

'Don't call me that.'

Cruz rubbed his jaw and scowled. 'What?'

'You know what.'

His brain must still have been on a go-slow because he couldn't recall what he'd called her. The thought irked him enough that he said, 'Maybe you should think about the way you act and dress if you don't want men thinking you're free and easy in bed.'

'Oh, my God. Are you serious?'

'Silky dresses that outline every curve, killer heels and just-out-of-bed hair all tell a man what's what.'

Fascinated, he watched her pull herself up to her full five feet and four inches—six in the heels.

'Any man who judges me on the way I look isn't worth a dime. You and Billy—'

Cruz raised his hand, cutting short her dramatic tirade. 'I am not like him,' he snarled.

'Keep telling yourself that, Cruz.' She tossed her head at him. 'It might help you sleep better at night.'

'I sleep just fine,' he grated. 'But if you should decide to change your high and mighty little mind about my offer I'll be staying at the Boston International until tomorrow morning.'

'Don't hold your breath.' She reefed open the stall door and stomped past him. 'I'd have to be crazy to accept an offer like that.'

Cruz ran a shaky hand through his hair and listened to the staccato sound of her high heels hammering her ire against the stone floor.

Her words, 'don't hold your breath' rang out in his head. Hadn't he told his brother the same thing a few hours ago? *Hell*. If he had, he couldn't remember why.

CHAPTER FOUR

'DAMMIT.' ASPEN CURSED as her hair caught around the button she had just wrenched open on the front of her dress. 'Stupid, idiotic hair.'

She yanked at it and winced when she heard the telltale crackle that indicated that she'd left a chunk behind. Then the pain set in and she rubbed her scalp.

God, she was angry. Furious. She pulled at the rest of her buttons and stopped when she caught sight of herself in the free-standing mirror that stood in the corner of her bedroom. Slowly she walked towards it.

An ordinary female figure stared back. An ordinary female figure with a flushed face and a wild mane of horrible hair. And tender lips. She put her fingers to them. They *looked* the same as they always did, but they *felt* softer. Swollen. And there was a slight graze on her chin where Cruz's stubble had scraped her skin.

Her pelvis clenched at the remembered pleasure of his mouth on hers. He hadn't even kissed her like that eight years ago. Then he'd been softer, almost tender. Today he'd kissed her as if he hadn't been able to help himself. As if he'd wanted to devour her. And never before had she kissed someone like that in return. Thank God Gypsy Blue had tried to knock some sense into them.

She had no idea why she'd acted like that with a man who had insulted her so badly. Maybe it was the fact that seeing him again had knocked her sideways. Somehow he had dazzled her the way he'd used to dazzle the women at polo matches. He was so attractive the crowds had always doubled when he had played, because all the wives and girlfriends had insisted that they simply *loved* polo and had to spend the *whole* day watching it. Really, they'd just mooned over him when he'd been on the field and drunk champagne and chatted the rest of the time. He'd dazzled her friends too.

Unconsciously she licked her tender lips and felt his imprint on them. Really she felt his imprint everywhere—and especially in the space between her thighs.

Heaven help her! She would have had sex with him. Had inadvertently *wanted* to have sex with him. The realisation of that alone was enough to shock her. She hated sex!

So why was she currently reliving Cruz's wicked kisses over and over like a hopeless teenager? He hadn't kissed her out of any real passion—he'd kissed her to make a point and to put her in her place and by God she had let him! Putting up a token resistance like the Victorian virgin he had accused her of acting like and then melting all over him like hot syrup.

She scratched the hair at her temples and made her curls frizz. Grabbing the offending matter, she quickly braided it, pulled on her jeans and shirt and stomped down to the stables.

Donny raised a startled eyebrow as she muttered a few terse words in his direction and started work at the other end. The rhythmical physical labour of putting away tack and shifting hay, of bantering with the horses and going through the motions of bedding them down for the night, was doing nothing to eradicate the feeling of all that hard male muscle pressed up against her.

'Make sure you don't burn your bridges unnecessarily, Aspen. Pride can be a nasty thing when it's used rashly.'

Pride? What pride. She had none. Well, she'd had enough to say no to both him and Billy Smyth.

'Oh, Billy Smyth! There's no way I would have slept with him even if he wasn't married,' she told Delta as she brushed her down vigorously.

But you would have with Cruz Rodriguez. Even without the money.

'I would not,' she promised Delta, knowing that if she had sex again with any man it would be too soon.

She stopped and leant her forehead against the mare. She breathed in her comforting scent and stared out over the stall door, looking up when something—a rat, maybe—disturbed a sleeping pigeon.

Her eye was immediately drawn to a rusty horseshoe lodged firmly between two supporting beams. Her mother had told her the story about how it had got there when she was little and it was the first thing Aspen had looked for when she had come to Ocean Haven, missing her mother desperately. Since then, whenever she was in a tricky situation she came out here and sought her mother's advice.

'And, boy, do I need it right now,' she muttered.

Delta nudged her side, as if to tell her to get on with it.

'Yes, I know.' She patted her neck. 'I'm thinking.'

Thinking about how much this place meant to her. Thinking about the dreams she had that would never materialise if she lost it. And she would lose it. To some faceless consortium in five days. Her stomach felt as if it had a rock in it.

Cruz's offer crept back into her mind for the thousandth time. He was right; it was pride making her say no.

So what if she said yes?

No, she couldn't. Cruz was big and overpowering and arrogant. Exactly the type of man she'd vowed to keep well away from.

But you're not marrying him.

No, but she would have to sleep with him. Which was just as unpalatable.

Sighing, she contemplated the peeling paint on the stall door. Her mother's face swam into her mind. Her tired smile. The day she had died she had been so exhausted after working two jobs and caring for Aspen, who had been sick at the time, that she'd simply forgotten that cars drove on the left-hand side of the road in England and she'd stepped out onto a busy road. It had been horrific. Devastating.

Aspen felt a pang of remorse and a deep longing. She had to keep Ocean Haven if only to preserve her mother's memory.

Feeling weighted down by memories, she continued brushing Delta. She had eked out a life here. She felt whole here. Protected. And, dammit, if she could keep it she would. She hadn't worked this hard to lose everything now.

Rash pride.

Rash pride had stopped her grandfather and her mother from reaching out to each other and maybe changing their lives for the better. Rash pride had made her grandfather refuse to listen to her own concerns about Chad after she had mentioned her doubts to him right before the wedding.

Rash pride wasn't going to get in the way of her life decisions any more. If Cruz Rodriguez wanted her body he could damned well have it. She didn't care. She hadn't cared about that side of things for years. And, anyway, once he found out what a dud she was in bed he'd change his mind pretty quickly.

Familiar fingers of distaste crawled up her spine as she recalled her wedding night before she could prevent herself doing it. She swallowed. What surprised her most was that being in Cruz's arms had been nothing like being in Chad's. But then Chad had often been drunk during their brief marriage and the alcohol had changed him. After that first night Aspen had frozen so much on the rare occasions he had approached her that he'd sought solace elsewhere. And made sure she knew about it. Always being deeply apologetic the following day when the alcoholic haze had retreated.

She'd stayed with him for six months and tried to be a better wife, but then he'd unfairly accused her of sleeping with his patron. It had been the final straw and she'd fled to Ocean Haven and never looked back.

She shivered.

'If you should happen to change your high and mighty little mind I'll be staying at the Boston International until tomorrow morning.'

Had she changed her mind?

There was no doubt that Cruz hated her after what had happened eight years ago, but he must also want her to make such an extreme offer. Could she put her concerns aside and sleep with him? She already knew she responded differently with him, felt differently with him, but what if she froze at the last minute as she had with Chad? What if he laughed at her when he learned about her embarrassing problem?

Rash pride, Aspen...

She groaned. To find out was to experiment, and to experiment meant opening herself up to knowing once and for all that *she* had been the problem in the bedroom and not Chad—as she sometimes liked to pretend when she was feeling particularly low.

'Coward,' she said softly.

Delta whickered.

'Oh, not you, beauty.' Aspen fished inside her pocket for a sugar cube. 'You're brave and courageous and would probably not bat an eyelid if I told you that Ranger's Apprentice had paid money to mount you if it meant saving The Farm.'

Aspen unwound Delta's tail from the tight bundle it had been wrapped in for the polo and wondered what would become of her beloved horses if she had to leave. Wondered if they'd be well cared for.

She felt she should warn the unsuspecting mare. 'If I keep The Farm I probably will be putting you in with him next season. I hope you don't mind. He's quite handsome.'

Not that looks had anything to do with the price of eggs.

She sighed as Donny stopped by Delta's stall and said that his lot were all set for the night and he would help out with some of the others if Aspen needed it.

At the rate she was going Aspen would need an army to get the horses done before the week was out.

She smiled at him. He had worked on the farm for six years now and she'd be lost without him. 'You're a gem, but I'm good. You go home to Glenda and the kids.'

'You're sure?' He shifted his gum around in his mouth. 'You seem a little wound up.'

Oh, she was. Ten million dollars wound up.

'Donny, what would you do if everything you loved was being threatened?' she asked suddenly.

He stuck a finger through his belt buckle and considered his shoes. 'You mean like Glenda and Sasha and Lela? Like my home?'

'Yeah,' Aspen said softly. 'Like your home.'

Donny nodded. 'I'd fight if I could.'

Aspen smiled. 'That's what I thought.'

Donny turned to go and then looked back over his shoulder. 'You sure you're all right, boss?'

'Fine. See you Monday.'

Cruz was going crazy. When a man let his ego get in the way of common sense that was the only conclusion to make. And the only one that made sense.

What other explanation could there possibly be when

he had just offered a woman he didn't even like ten million dollars to sleep with him?

And what would he have done if she'd said yes? Because he'd had no intention of going through with it. The very idea was ludicrous. He'd never paid for sex in his life.

So he wanted her? Big deal. It was because she was even more alluring than he remembered. And more stuck-up. Her hair was longer too, her cheekbones more defined, her breasts fuller, her mouth— He laughed. What was he doing? A full inventory? Why? There were plenty of women in his sea. Plenty more beautiful than this one when it came down to it.

And, yes, he liked to pit himself against an opponent for the sheer thrill of it, but making that offer to Aspen Carmichael had felt a bit like riding a nag into the middle of a forty-goal polo game without a bridle or a saddle and telling his opponents to have at him.

He certainly hadn't come anywhere close to finding a way to ensure that she wouldn't be able to raise the money to buy Ocean Haven herself—which had been his original goal.

Cruz poked at the half-eaten steak sandwich on his plate and stuffed an overcooked chip into his mouth. All he'd done instead was lump himself in with the likes of Billy Smyth and he was nothing like his lot.

No, you're worse, his conscience happily informed him. *You'd like to screw her* and *steal her family home out from under her as well.*

Yeah, whatever.

Unused to having a back and forth commentary inside his head about a woman—or about his decisions—he shoved himself to his feet and headed outside to see if the answer to his problem was written in the stars.

Of course it wasn't, but he stood there and let the warm evening air wash over him until memories of the past sailed in on the scent of jasmine and lilac. The sickening ball that had settled in his gut as he'd driven through the stone archway to Ocean Haven returned full force.

Focusing on something else, he listened to the distant murmurs of the light-hearted partying he could hear coming up off the darkened beach. Probably teenagers enjoying yet another stunning summer evening. Light flickered and wisps of smoke trailed in the moonlight. He imagined that many of them would be pairing off before long and snuggling down beside a campfire.

Unbidden, his mind conjured up an image of Aspen flirting with Billy Smyth earlier that day. He'd watched them for a couple of minutes before approaching her, not really wanting anyone to recognise him and start fawning all over him.

Aspen had used all her feminine wiles so the unhappily married Billy would notice her, but it hadn't been until she had let him run his finger down the side of her face and held his cheek afterwards, as if preserving his touch, that real bitterness and anger had rolled through Cruz like an incoming thunderstorm. Would she have let Smyth kiss her and shove her up against the wall of the stable as she had done with him earlier? Had she *planned* to later on?

'Damn her anyway.' He slammed the palm of his hand against the bronze railing and told himself to forget about her. Forget about the way she had caught fire in his arms once again. Forget about the way he had done the same in hers. Unfortunately his body was more than happy to relive it, and he was once again uncomfortably hard as he headed inside and downed the rest of his tequila.

As far as Cruz was concerned the Aspen Carmichaels of the world deserved everything they got. So why was he hanging around his hotel room feeling like the worst kind of male alive?

No reason.

No reason at all.

The hotel phone rang and he crossed to the hall table and picked it up, almost disappointed to find that the number on the display was a local one. Because he knew who it was even before he answered it. And now was the time to tell her that he had no intention of giving her the money in exchange for her delectable body. No intention at all.

But he didn't say that. Instead he threw his conscience to the wind and said, 'I'll pick you up at seven in the morning.'

There was enough of a silence on the other end of the line for him to wonder if he hadn't been mistaken, but then Aspen's husky tones sounded in his ear.

'Why?'

'Because I'm flying back to Mexico first thing in the morning.'

She cleared her throat. 'I can wait until you're next in Boston.'

She might be able to. He couldn't.

'You need that money by Monday, don't you?'

Again there was a pause long enough to fill the Grand Canyon. He waited for her to tell him to go to hell.

'Yes,' she said as if she was grinding nails.

'I'll see you tomorrow, then.'

He hung up before she could say anything else and stood staring at the telephone. He didn't know what shocked him more: the fact that he hadn't rescinded his ludicrous offer or the fact that he had made it in the first place. What didn't shock him was the fact that she had accepted.

He waited for a sense of satisfaction to kick in because he had finally come up with a way to stop her going after anyone else for the money. Instead he felt a sense of impending doom. Like a man who had bitten off more than he could chew. Because he had no intention of lending her the money and he didn't like what that said about him.

Maybe that he needed more tequila.

'Just have a shower, *imbecil,* and get some sleep,' he told himself.

Come Saturday The Rodriquez Polo Club would run the biggest polo tournament in Mexico for the second year and he had a Chinese delegation coming over to view the proceedings. They had some notion that he could form a partnership with them to introduce polo into China via a specialised hotel in Beijing. So he had to be on site for the next three days and be at his charming best.

'Better get rid of the *chica*, then,' he told his reflection grimly as he stripped off and stepped into the shower. Because watching Aspen flick her hair and flirt with everything in pants was not, he already knew, conducive to putting him in a good mood.

Ah, hell, maybe he should just forget the whole thing. Forget buying Ocean Haven. Yes, it was an exceptional piece of land, with those rolling hills and the bluff that looked out over the North Atlantic Ocean. But there were plenty of beautiful spots in the world. What did he really want it for anyway?

He squirted shampoo over his head and rubbed vigorously.

The fact was eight years ago Aspen Carmichael had set him up so that her over-indulged fiancé could take his place on the dream team without batting a pretty eyelash. She'd walked up to him and shyly put her arms around his neck and, like a fool who had fantasised about her for too long, he'd lost control. He would have done anything for her back then because, if he was honest, he'd liked her a little bit himself. Liked her a lot, in fact, and he hated knowing that she'd so easily fooled him.

But not this time. This time he would be the one holding all the cards. He relaxed for the first time that night. And why not? Why not take what she had offered him eight years ago? She was older now, and obviously still prepared to use her delectable body to get what she wanted. *So, okay—game on, Ms Carmichael. Game on.*

And if a small voice in his head said that he was wrong about her—well, he couldn't see how.

So what that she had loved the horses and been kind to everyone she came into contact with? So what if her apology earlier had seemed genuine? She knew how to play the game, that was all *that* said about her, but in the end she'd used him for her own ends just like everyone else in his life had done.

So, no, he didn't owe Aspen-damned-Carmichael any-damned-thing. And if this was fate's way of evening the score between them then, hell, who was he to argue?

CHAPTER FIVE

ASPEN WAS PACKED and ready by six the following morning. She'd told Mrs Randall, their long-time housekeeper, that she was going to Mexico to look over Cruz's horses for future growth opportunities. It was the best explanation she could come up with at short notice, especially when Mrs Randall had looked so pleased at the mention of Cruz's name.

'He missed his family terribly, that boy. Of course he was too proud to show it, but I suppose that was why he left so suddenly when he was a young man. He wanted to get back to them.'

Aspen would have liked to believe that homesickness had contributed to Cruz leaving The Farm eight years ago, but she suspected it was more because she had put him in an untenable situation.

Guilt ate at her, and all the confusing emotions she'd experienced at that time came rushing back. Her desperate need for approval from her grandfather, her fear of the future, her confusing feelings for Chad and the amazing pull she'd always felt towards Cruz.

Fortunately Mrs Randall was doing her Thursday morning market shopping when Cruz drove up in a mean black sports car, because Aspen was sure her confused state would have been on display for the wily older woman to see and that would have only added to her anxiety. Especially when she had decided that the best way to approach the situation was to be optimistic and positive. Treat it as the business transaction it was.

Shielded by the velvet drapes in the living room, she watched as Cruz climbed out of the car and literally prowled towards the front steps of the house, breathtakingly handsome in worn jeans that clung to his muscular thighs and a fitted latte-coloured T-shirt that set off his olive skin tone and black hair to perfection.

Not wanting him to think she was nervous at the prospect of seeing him, Aspen waited a few minutes after he'd pressed the bell before opening the door; glad that just last week she had given the front door a fresh lick of white paint and cleaned down the stone façade of the portico with an industrial hose.

'Good morning.' She hoped he hadn't heard her voice quaver and told herself that if she was really going to go through with this she needed to do better than she was now. 'Did you want coffee or tea?'

His gaze swept over her face and lingered on her chin, and when he unconsciously rubbed his jaw she knew he had noticed the mark—*his* mark—that she had made a futile effort to cover with concealer. Involuntarily her own eyes dropped to his mouth and heat coursed through her; she was mortified and embarrassed when his lips tightened with dismissal and he turned abruptly to scan the rest of the hallway.

'No. My plane's on standby. Let's go.'

Great. She wasn't even going to have the benefit of other commuters to ease the journey.

Turning to pick up her keys from the hallway table, she spotted the document she had spent half the night drafting. She couldn't believe she'd forgotten it. But then rational thinking and Cruz Rodriguez didn't seem to go together for her very well.

'I'd like you to sign this first.'

He looked at it dubiously. 'What is it?'

It was a document stipulating a condition she hoped he'd agree to and also preventing him from reneging on their deal if he found himself dissatisfied with the outcome of their temporary liaison. Which he undoubtedly would. But since this was a business arrangement Aspen wanted to make sure that when their physical relationship failed he was still bound to invest in Ocean Haven.

'Read it. I think it's clear enough.'

He took it from her and the paper snapped in the quiet room. The antique grandfather clock gauged time like a marksman.

It wasn't long before he glanced back at her, and Aspen swallowed as he laughed out loud.

Her mouth tightened as she waited for him to collect himself. She'd had an idea that he might have some objections to her demands but she hadn't expected that he find them comical.

'Once?' His eyes were full of amusement. 'Are you're kidding me?'

She wasn't. *Once*, she was sure, was going to be more than enough for both of them.

'No.'

When he looked as if he might start laughing again Aspen felt her nerves give way to temper.

'I don't see what's so funny?'

'That's because you're not paying the money.'

He circled behind her as if she was some slave girl on an auction block and he was checking her over.

She swung around to face him. 'If you read the whole document it says that I'm planning to pay you back the money anyway, so technically it's free.'

'With what?'

He unnerved her by circling her again, but this time she stood stock-still. 'I don't know what you mean.'

'What are you intending to pay me back with?' he murmured from behind her.

'The profits from The Farm.'

He scoffed, facing her. 'This place will be lucky to break even in a booming market.'

His eyes held hers and the chemistry that was as strong as carbon links every time they got within two feet of each other flared hotly. Aspen took a careful breath in. He was pure Alpha male right now, and his self-satisfied smile let her know that *he* knew the effect he was having on her.

Not that it would help either one of them in the long run. But she had to concentrate. If she didn't there was a chance she'd end up with nothing. Less than nothing. Because she'd lose the only tie she had left to her mother.

'That's your opinion. It's not mine.'

He studied her and she didn't know how she managed not to squirm under that penetrating gaze.

'It would want to be a damned good once, *gatita*.'

Aspen raised her chin. It was going to be horrible.

'It's a good deal.' She repeated what she'd said to Billy Smyth and so many others before him. 'Take it or leave it.'

He regarded her steadily, his eyes hooded. 'I tell you what. You make it one night and I'll agree.'

One night?

'As in the *whole* night?'

His slow smile sent a burst of electrical activity straight to her core. 'What a good idea, *gatita*. Yes, the whole night.'

Bastard.

'What *is* that you're calling me?' she fumed.

His smile was full of sex. '*Kitten.* You remind me of a spitting kitten who needs to be stroked.'

'Fine.' Aspen picked up the pen but didn't see a thing in front of her.

'Wait. Before you make your changes I want to know what this is.' Cruz stabbed his finger at her second point— the one that said he had to pay no matter what happened or didn't happen between them. 'Is this your way of telling me you're going to welsh on me?'

She frowned. 'Welsh on you?'

'Renege. Back out. Break your word.'

'I know what it means,' she snapped, wondering if he wasn't having a go at her character. 'And rest assured I am fully prepared to uphold my end of the bargain. I just want to make sure you do as well.'

Her throat bobbed as he continued to watch her and Cruz wondered if she had guessed that he was stringing her along.

Once!

He nearly laughed again. But he had to hand it to her. The document she had crafted was legally sound and would probably hold up well enough in a court of law.

Something about the way she stood before him, all innocently defiant, like a lamb to the slaughter, snagged on his conscience like an annoying burr in a sock, which you'd thought you'd removed only to have it poke at you again.

He couldn't do it. He couldn't let her go into this blind. 'There's something you should know.'

Her eyes turned wary. 'Like what?'

'I own Trimex Holdings.'

Aspen frowned. 'If that's supposed to mean something to me it doesn't.'

'Trimex Holdings is currently the highest bidder for Ocean Haven.'

He watched a myriad of emotions flit across her expressive face as the information set in. Shock. Disbelief. Anger. Uncertainty.

'So…' She frowned harder. 'This isn't real?'

How much he wanted her? Unfortunately, yes.

He tried not to let his gaze drop once again to the spot on her chin. He'd obviously grazed her with his stubble the day before and, although he'd hate to think that he'd hurt her, there was a part of him that was pretty pleased to see her wearing his mark. The moronic part.

Oh, yeah, it was real enough. But he knew that wasn't what she was referring to.

'My offer?'

'Yes.'

'It's real.'

'That doesn't make sense. Why would you lend me money to buy a property you are trying to buy for yourself?'

'Because I believe I'll win.' And he had just decided to instruct Lauren to keep upping his offer until it was so ludicrously tempting Joe Carmichael would see stars.

Aspen shook her head. 'You won't. Joe is very loyal to me.'

All families were loyal until money was involved. 'Care to back yourself?'

She looked at him as one might a maggot on a pork chop. 'I never realised how absolutely ruthless you are.'

'I'm absolutely successful. For a reason.'

She shook her head. 'You're not going to be this time. But can I trust you?'

The fact that she questioned his integrity annoyed him. 'I didn't have to tell you this, did I?'

'Fine,' she snapped, pacing away from him to the other side of the neat sitting room. She glared at him. Shook her head. Then paced back. Picked up the pen. 'It's not like I have a better option right now.'

Her fingers shook ever so slightly as she put pen to paper and something squeezed inside his chest.

'I'll do it.'

Impatient for this to be finalised, he grabbed the pen and replaced 'once' with 'one night'. Then he scrawled the date and his signature on the bottom of the page.

His gaze drifted down over her neat summer tunic which showed the delicate hollows either side of her collarbones and hinted at her firm breasts before it skimmed the tops of her feminine thighs. She'd been soft and firm pressed up against him yesterday. Svelte, he decided, glancing at her fitted jeans and ankle boots.

His body reacted predictably and he told himself it was past time to stop looking at her.

The flight from East Hampton to Acapulco took five hours. It might as well have been five days. Cruz had barely uttered a word to her since leaving The Farm—not much more than 'This way', 'Mind your step' and 'Buckle up; we're about to take off'. And Aspen was glad. She didn't think she'd be able to hold a decent conversation with the man right now. He wasn't a rat, she decided. He was a shark. A great white that hunted and killed without compunction.

And she was playing the game of her life against him.

Thank heavens she had her uncle on her side. But could she trust Cruz to give her the money? He'd looked startled and not a little angry when she had questioned his integrity. Yes, she was pretty sure she could trust him. His pride alone would mean that he upheld his end of the deal.

The deal. She had just made a bargain to sleep with the devil. She shuddered, glancing across the aisle to where Cruz was seated in a matching plush leather chair and buried in paperwork. It was beyond her comprehension that she should still want him. Which was scary in itself when she considered that she didn't even like sex. And, yes, she'd enjoyed kissing him, but that wasn't sex. She knew if they'd been anywhere near a bed she would have clammed up.

Urgh... She hated the thought of embarrassing herself in front of him. He was so confident. So *arrogant*. She hated that he just had to look at her and she had to concentrate extra hard to think logically. His touching her made her want to do stupid things. Things she couldn't trust.

And she particularly hated the thought of being vulnerable to him. Especially now. Now when he had made it clear that he'd win anyway. That she was doing this for nothing. It just made her more determined that he wouldn't.

Aspen pulled out her textbook. Questioning whether she had done the right thing in coming with him wouldn't change anything now. She'd signed the document she herself had drafted and she'd assured him that she wouldn't 'welsh' on him.

It would mean that her beloved home was hers. It would mean she would have the chance to put all the naysayers who didn't believe that a girl on her own could run a property the size of Ocean Haven in their places. And it would mean that for the first time in her life she would be free and clear of a dominating man controlling her future. That alone would be worth a little embarrassment with the Latin bad boy she had once fantasised about.

It was a thought that wasn't easy to hold onto when the plane landed on a private airstrip and a blast of hot, humid air swept across her face.

Cruz's long, loose-limbed strides ate up the tarmac as if the humid air hadn't just hit him like a furnace. He stopped by a waiting four-by-four and Aspen kept her eyes anywhere but on him as she climbed inside, doing her best to ease the kinks out of shoulders aching with tension.

Still, she noticed when he put on a pair of aviator sunglasses and clasped another man's hands in a display of macho camaraderie before taking the keys from him.

He was just so self-assured, she thought enviously, and she hated him. Hated him and everything he represented. Yesterday she'd been willing to greet him as a friend, had felt sorry for the part she had played in his leaving The Farm. Now she wished her grandfather had horsewhipped him. It was the least he deserved.

But did he?

Just because he wanted to buy her farm it didn't make him a bad guy, did it? No, not necessarily bad—but ruthless. And arrogant. And so handsome it hurt to look at him.

'You know I hate you, don't you?' she said without thinking.

Not bothering to look at her, he paused infinitesimally, his hands on the key in the ignition.

'Probably,' he said, with so little concern it made her teeth grind together.

He turned the key and the car purred to life. Then his eyes drifted lazily over her from head to toe and she felt her heart-rate kick up. He was studying her again. Looking at her as if he was imagining what she looked like without her clothes on.

'But it won't make a difference.'

His lack of empathy, or any real emotion, drove her wild. 'To what?'

'To this.'

Quick as a flash he reached for her, grabbed the back of her neck before she'd realised his intention and hauled her mouth across to his. Aspen stiffened, determined to resist the force of his hungry assault. And she did. For a moment. A brief moment before her senses took over and shut down her brain. A brief moment before his mouth softened. A brief moment before he pulled back and looked at her with lazy amusement. As if he was already the victor.

'He won't sell to you,' she blazed at him.

His smile kicked up one corner of his mouth. 'He'll sell to me.'

Aspen cut her gaze from his. She hated his insolent confidence because she wished she had just a smidgeon of it herself. 'How long till we get there?' she griped.

He laughed softly. 'So eager, *gatita*?'

'Yes,' she fumed. 'Eager to get out of your horrible company. In fact I don't know why we didn't just do this on the plane. Or at The Farm, come to think of it.'

His head tilted as he regarded her. 'Maybe I want to woo you.'

Aspen blew out a breath. 'I wonder what your mother would have to say about your behaviour?'

'Damn.' Cruz forked a hand through his hair, his lazy amusement at her expense turning to disgust.

He cursed again and gunned the engine.

'Problem?' she asked, hoping beyond hope that there was one.

'You could say that.' His words came out as a snarl.

She waited for him to elaborate and sighed when he didn't. This situation was impossible. There was no way she would be able to relax with this man enough to have sex with him. Which was fine, she thought. It would serve him right, all things considered.

Switching her mind off, she turned her attention outside the window. From the air Mexico was an amazing contrast of stark brown mountains and stretches of dried-up desert against the brilliant blue of the Pacific Ocean. On the ground the theme continued, with pockets of abject beauty mixed with states of disrepair. A bit like her own mind, she mused in a moment of black humour.

But gradually, as Cruz drove them through small towns and along broken cobblestoned streets alive with pedestrians and tourists fortified against the amazing heat with wide-brimmed hats, Aspen felt herself start to relax.

She snuck a glance at Cruz's beautiful profile. His expression was so serious he looked as if he belonged on a penny. The silence stretched out like the bitumen in front of them and finally Aspen couldn't take it any longer. 'So you went back to Mexico after you left The Farm?'

He cut her a brief glance. 'You want the low-down on my life story, *gatita*?'

No, she wanted to know if it would take a silver bullet to end his life, or whether an ordinary one would do the trick.

One night, Aspen.

'I was making polite conversation.'

'Choose another topic.'

Okay.

'Why do you want my farm?'

'It's a great location for a hotel. Why else?'

Aspen glared at him. 'You're going to tear it down, aren't you?' Tear down the only home she'd ever loved. Tear down the stables.

'Perhaps.'

'You can't do that.'

'Actually, I can.'

'Why? Revenge?'

She saw a muscle tick in his jaw. 'Not revenge. Money.'

Aspen blew out a breath, more determined than ever that he shouldn't get his hands on her property. 'How much further is it to the hotel?' she asked completely exasperated.

Cruz smiled. 'You sound like you're not expecting to enjoy yourself, *gatita*.'

She didn't answer, and she felt his curious gaze on her as she stared sightlessly out of the window.

'It will be a while,' he said abruptly. 'We have a small detour to make.'

Aspen glanced back at his austere expression. 'What sort of detour?'

'I have to stop at my mother's house.'

'Your mother's house?' She frowned. 'Why would you take me to meet your mother?'

'Believe me, I'm not happy about it either,' he said. 'Unfortunately my brother has arranged her surprise birthday party for today and I promised I'd show up.'

'Your mother's...' She cleared her throat as if she had something stuck in it. 'You could have warned me.'

'I just did.'

She blew out a frustrated breath.

'Don't make a big deal out of it,' he cautioned. 'I'm not.'

'Well, that's obvious. But how can I not? What will she think of me?'

'That you're my latest mistress. What else?'

Cruz saw a flash of hurt cross her face and hated how she made him feel subtly guilty about the situation between them. He had nothing to feel guilty about. She had asked him for money, he had laid down his terms, and she'd accepted. And now that she knew he was in direct competition with her his conscience was clear. Or should have been. Still, it picked at him that he might be making a decision he would later regret. His body said the opposite and he ran his eyes over her feminine, but demure outfit. All that wild hair caught back in a low ponytail just begging to be set free.

'I don't have anything for her,' she said in a small voice.

Cruz forced himself to concentrate on a particularly dilapidated section of road before he had an accident. 'I've got it covered.'

She fell blessedly silent after that as he navigated through the centre of town and he was just exhaling when she spoke again.

'What did you get her?'

'Excuse me?'

'Your present. I would know what it was if I was really your mistress.'

'You *are* my mistress,' he reminded her. 'For one night anyway.'

If possible even more colour drained from her face, and it irritated him to think that she saw sleeping with him as such a chore. By the time he was finished with her she would be screaming with pleasure and begging for more than one night.

'Money,' he said, pulling his thoughts out of his pants.

'Sorry?'

'I'm giving her money.'

'Oh.'

Her nose twitched as if she'd just smelt something foul.

'What's wrong with that?' he snapped.

'Nothing.'

Her tone implied *everything*.

'Money makes the world go round, *gatita*,' he grated.

'Actually, I think the saying is that love makes the world go round.'

'Love couldn't make a tennis ball go round,' he said, knowing from her tight expression that she didn't approve or agree. Well, he didn't give a damn. *She* hadn't been given up as a child. 'Look, my mother sold me to your grandfather when I was thirteen. I think I know what she likes.'

Aspen looked aghast. 'I had heard that rumour but I never actually believed it.'

'Believe it,' he said, hating the note of bitterness that tinged his words.

'I'm sure she didn't *want* to send you away.'

Cruz didn't say anything. She sighed and eventually said, 'I know how you feel.'

'How could you possibly know how I feel?' he mocked.

'You grew up on a hundred-acre property and went to a private school.'

'I wasn't born into that, Cruz. My father left my mother when I was three and she struggled for years to keep our heads above water while she was alive. What I was getting at was that my grandfather paid my father to stay away.'

Cruz frowned. He'd assumed her mother had lived off some sort of trust fund and her father had died. 'Your father was a ski instructor, wasn't he?'

'Yes.'

'Probably better that you didn't have anything to do with him.'

'Because of his profession?'

'No, because he accepted being paid off. A parent should never give up a child, no matter what.'

'I'm sorry that happened to you,' she said quietly.

Cruz didn't want her compassion. Especially not when he understood why his mother had done it. Hell, wasn't that one of the reasons he worked so hard? So that if he did ever marry no wife of his would ever have to face the same decision?

He shrugged it off, as he always did. 'I had a lot of opportunities from it. And worse things happen to kids than that.'

'True, but when a child feels abandoned it's—'

He cut off her sympathetic response. 'You move on and you don't look back.'

Aspen registered the pain in his voice, the deep hurt he must have felt. She experienced a strange desire to make him feel better—and then reminded herself that he was a wealthy man who was determined to steal her home away from her and was so arrogant he was lending her money to challenge him.

'I'd like to stop for flowers,' she said stiffly.

Cruz turned down a side street and cursed when the

traffic came to a standstill along a busy ocean-facing bou-
levard, completely oblivious to the cosmopolitan coastline
that sparkled in the sun.

'What?'

'I'd like to stop for flowers.'

'What for?'

She looked pained—and stiff. 'Your mother's birthday,
for one, and the fact that I'm visiting someone's home and
don't have a gift.'

'I told you I have it covered.'

'And given your attitude to money I'm sure it's very
generous, but I would prefer to give something more personal.'

Cruz ground his teeth together, praying for patience.

Five minutes later he swung the big car onto the side of
the road in front of a group of shops. When she made to
get out of the car, he stopped her. 'I'll get them. You wait
here and keep the door locked.'

'But they're supposed to be from me.'

'Believe me, my mother will know who they're from.'
The last time he'd given her flowers he'd picked wild dahl-
ias by the side of the road when he'd been about twelve.

Not long after that Aspen was relieved when Cruz pulled
into the circular driveway of a large *hacienda,* with fat
terracotta pots either side of a wide entrance filled with
colourful blooms.

She stepped out of the car before Cruz reached her side
and saw his scowl grow fiercer as he unloaded a box of
brightly wrapped presents from the back.

'You told me you were giving your mother money,' she
said, confused.

'I am. These are for my nieces and nephews.'

That surprised her, and she wondered if maybe he had
a heart beating somewhere inside his body after all. The

thought lasted for as long as it took for his eager nieces and nephews to descend on him in a wild flurry.

It was as if Santa had arrived and, like that mythical person, Cruz was treated with deference and a little trepidation. As if he wasn't quite real. Aspen saw genuine affection for him on the faces of his family, but it was clear when no one touched or hugged him that all was not quite right between them.

For his part, Cruz didn't seem to notice. His cool gaze was completely tuned in to the delighted squeals of his six nieces and nephews as they unearthed remote-controlled cars, sporting equipment and several dolls. That was when Aspen realised that the gifts were either an ice-breaker or possibly a replacement for any real affection between them.

'This is Aspen,' he said once the furore had died down. 'Aspen, this is my family.'

Succinct, she thought as each one of his family members warily introduced themselves, clearly unsure how to take her. Deciding to ignore the way that made her feel and make the best of the situation, she smiled at them as if there was nothing amiss about her being by Cruz's side.

'These are from both of us,' she said, handing Cruz's mother the elaborate posy he had purchased and watching as her gentle face lit up with pleasure. She must once have been a great beauty, Aspen thought, but time and life had wearied her, lining her face and sprinkling her thick dark hair with silvery streaks. She gazed up at her son with open adoration and Aspen could have kicked Cruz when he barely mustered a stiff smile in return.

An awkward silence fell over his sisters until his brother, Ricardo, took charge and led them all out to the rear patio, where the scent of a heavenly barbecue filled the air.

Cruz's youngest sister, Gabriella, who looked to be about nineteen, hooked her arm through Aspen's and took it upon herself to introduce her two brothers-in-law, who each had a pair of tongs in one hand and a beer in the other.

Gabriella pointed out the small vineyard her mother still tended, and the lush veggie patch in raised wooden boxes. Three well-fed dogs lazed beneath the shade of a lemon-coloured magnolia tree and the view of the ocean from the house was truly spectacular.

'Cruz has never brought a girlfriend here before,' Gabriella whispered.

Aspen smiled enigmatically. She knew the label hadn't come from Cruz but she wasn't about to correct his sister and embarrass them both. And, anyway, 'girlfriend' sounded much better than mistress to her ears, even if it did mean that she had terrible taste in men.

Returning to the patio, she found Cruz sprawled in a deckchair at the head of the large outdoor table, with his sisters and his mother crowded around him like celebrity minders who were worried about losing their jobs. One after the other they asked if he was okay or if he needed anything with embarrassing regularity, offering him food and drink like the Wise Men bestowing gifts on the baby Jesus.

The two brothers-in-law had cleverly retreated to tend the state-of-the-art barbecue, and Aspen tried her best to appreciate the amazing view of grapevines tripping down the hillside towards the azure sea below.

The conversation was like listening to an uninterested child practising the violin: one minute flowing and easy, the next halting and grating. Nobody seemed to know which topic of conversation to stick to.

Even worse, Cruz's mother kept throwing guilty glances his way, while treating him like a king. Cruz either didn't notice, or pretended that he didn't, conversing mainly with his brother about work issues.

It made her think about what Mrs Randall had said the day before. *He missed his family terribly, that boy.*

Ironically, Cruz didn't look as if he had missed them at all, and yet Aspen sensed from his intermittent glances along the table that Mrs Randall had been right.

What had it been like for him? she wondered. On The Farm, all alone and cut off from his family? And how did one reconnect after that?

Bizarrely, she started to feel sorry for him, and found herself wanting to break through the solid barrier he seemed to have erected around himself.

Thankfully one of the older boys brought out the new basketball Cruz had bought and called for everyone to play Four Square. Gabriella jumped up and mercifully asked Aspen to join in. It was the only time Cruz wasn't asked if he wanted to partake.

One of the children quickly drew out four squares and Aspen patiently waited for a cherubic-looking boy with a mop of curly black hair to explain the rules while his ten-year-old sister tapped her foot impatiently and said, 'We know…we *know.*'

Before long there was a mixed line of adults and kids and Aspen found she was enjoying herself for the first time that day, laughing with the children and jockeying for position as king of the game.

When one of the older children tried a shifty manoeuvre the ball went spinning off towards the stone table. Cruz deftly caught it and threw it back to Aspen.

Some devil on Aspen's shoulder made her toss the ball straight back at him. 'Come and play.'

'No, thanks.'

'He never plays games when he comes,' Gabriella whispered.

Aspen gave her a half-smile, knowing exactly how it felt to hanker after the affection of someone who wouldn't give it. She remembered that her grandfather and her uncle had been far too serious to play games with her and she'd very quickly learned not to ask.

Sensing that Cruz was far too serious as well, and that if he just lightened up a little everyone else could start to as well, she bounced the ball back in his direction.

'Are you afraid you'll lose?' she challenged lightly.

He stood up from the table and placed his beer bottle down with deliberate restraint.

Every member of his family seemed to hold their collective breath—even the two men tending the sizzling barbecue—waiting to see what he would do. If a tree had fallen in Africa they would have heard it.

Aspen saw the moment Cruz became conscious of the same thing and the smile on her lips died as he stared at her with a dangerous glint in his eyes. He came towards her slowly, like a hungry panther, his black hair glinting in the sunlight just as she remembered.

A shiver of awareness skittered over her skin. Her mind told her to run, but her body was on another frequency because it remained rooted to the spot.

Towering over her, Cruz took her hand and carefully placed the ball in it, as if he was handing back a newborn baby—or a bomb about to go off. He leant closer, and Aspen forgot about their audience as his gaze shifted to her mouth.

'I said no.'

When his gaze lifted to hers there was an implicit warning for her to behave deep within his cold regard. Then without a word he spun on his heels and stalked towards the garden.

Aspen released a shaky breath and heard Gabriella do the same.

'Doesn't he scare you when he frowns at you like that?'

His sister was right. His anger should have scared her. Terrified her, in fact. Her grandfather had wielded his temper like a weapon and when Chad had been drunk he had been volatile and moody. But Cruz didn't scare her in that way. Other ways, yes. Like the way he made her feel shivery and out of control of her senses. As if when he touched her he consumed her, controlled her.

That scared her.

Pushing her troubled thoughts aside, she sought to reassure Gabriella. 'No, he doesn't scare me that way. I think his bark—or his look—is more ferocious than his bite.'

The sound of the back door opening drew Aspen's gaze from Cruz's retreating figure and she watched Ricardo back out of the doorway, an elaborate birthday cake resplendent with pink icing and brightly coloured flowers held gingerly in his arms.

'Where's Cruz?' he asked, casting a quick glance at the now vacant chair.

There was a bit of low murmuring that Aspen understood, despite not speaking Spanish, and she felt a guilty flush highlight her cheekbones. It was her fault that Cruz had stalked off.

'I'll go and get him.'

Ricardo looked as if he was about to argue with her but then changed his mind. 'Thank you.'

Following the path Cruz had taken, she found him out by the small vineyard, his head bent towards a leafy vine laden with bunches of purple grapes. The bright sun darkened his olive skin as he stood there, which was extremely unfair, Aspen thought, when her skin was more likely to turn pink and blister.

A bee buzzed lazily past her face and she stepped out of its way.

Cruz must have heard the sound of her steps on the dirt

but he gave no indication of it, putting his hands in his pockets and staring out across the ocean like a god from the days of old. Strong. Formidable. *Impenetrable.*

'I was hoping for a moment's peace,' he said without turning around, his deep voice a master of creation.

'They're about to serve the birthday cake,' Aspen informed him softly.

'So they sent you to find me?'

'No.' She stood beside him and watched tiny waves break further out to sea. 'I volunteered.'

He made a noise that seemed to say she was an idiot. And she was—because she had an overpowering urge to reach out to him.

'They don't know how to treat you, you know.' She glanced up at him, no longer able to ignore what had been going on since they arrived. 'Your mother seems to be suffering. From guilt? Remorse? It's not clear, but it *is* clear that she loves you. They all do.'

Cruz tensed and dug his hands further into his pockets. Aspen had inadvertently picked a scab off an old wound. He knew his mother felt guilty. He'd told her she shouldn't but it hadn't worked. He had no idea what to do about that and it made being around his family almost impossible, because he knew that without him around they would be up singing and dancing and having a great time.

'Don't start talking about what you can't possibly understand,' he grated harshly.

'I understand that you're upset…maybe a little angry about what happened to you,' she offered gently.

He swung around to face her. 'I'm not angry about that. When my father died it was my job as the eldest boy to take care of my family while the girls ran the house. It's what we did. Rallied around each other and banded together.'

'Oh, dear, that must have made it even harder for you to leave them.'

Cruz scowled down at her. 'It's not like I had a say in it. Old Man Carmichael offered my mother money and she preferred to send me away than to let me provide for the family my way.'

'Which was…?'

Mostly he'd worked at a nearby *hacienda* and tended rich people's gardens. Sometimes he'd done odd jobs for the men his father had become involved with, but he hadn't been stupid enough to do anything illegal. Anything criminal.

'Boring stuff.'

'And your mother didn't work herself?'

'She cleaned houses when she could, but I have one brother and four sisters. All were under ten at the time. My father's family were what you would politely term dysfunctional, and my mother had been an only child to elderly parents. If I hadn't stepped up, nobody else would have.'

'I'm sorry, Cruz. That's a lot for a child to have heaped on his shoulders. You must have really struggled.' She grimaced. 'I guess that's why they treat you like you're a king now.'

He looked at her sharply. 'They don't treat me like a king. They act like it didn't happen. They tiptoe around me as if I'm about to go off at them.'

She paused and Cruz caught the concern in her gaze. Something tightened in his chest. What was he doing, spilling his childhood stories to this woman? A person he didn't even *like*.

As if sensing his volatile thoughts she murmured half to herself and he had to strain to capture the words. '…not real.'

'Excuse me?' He glanced at her sharply. 'Are you saying my feelings for my family are not real?'

'Of course not. Though it might help them relax a bit if you scowled a little less.' She shot him a half-smile. 'I can see that you love your family. Which is strangely reassuring though I don't know why. But there's no hugging. No touching.' Her pause was laden with unwanted empathy. 'Truthfully, you remind me of my grandfather. He found it tough to let anyone get close to him as well.'

His eyes narrowed. Nobody in his family talked about the past—not even Ricardo. Cruz had come back from Ocean Haven eight years ago angry—yes, by God, *angry*—and he'd stayed that way. And he liked it. Anger drove him and defined him. Made him hungry and kept him on his guard.

He looked at Aspen. Unfortunately for her he was *really* angry now. 'I don't remember reading anywhere in that makeshift document of yours that pop psychology was part of our deal.'

Her eyes flashed up at him. 'I was only trying to help. Though I don't know why,' she muttered, half under her breath, inflaming his anger even more.

'Helping wasn't part of it either. There's only one thing I want from you. Conversation before or after is not only superfluous, it's irrelevant.'

She gave him that hurt look again, before masking it with cool hauteur, and he felt his teeth grind together.

Dammit, why couldn't he look at her without feeling so…so *much*?

All the time.

Lust, anger, disappointment, hunger. A deep hunger for more—and not just of that sweet body which had haunted more dreams than he cared to remember.

He reminded himself of the type of woman she was. The type who would use that body to further her own interests.

She'd used it to good effect to deceive him years ago and hadn't cared a damn for his feelings. That was real. That was who she was. And once he'd had her in his bed, had slaked his lust for her—*used* her in return—then she'd be out of his life and his head.

Hell, he couldn't wait.

CHAPTER SIX

IT WAS EARLY evening by the time Cruz turned onto the long stretch of driveway that led to the Rodriquez Polo Club. A hotel, Aspen had heard it said, that was a hotel to end all hotels.

She didn't care. She was too keyed-up to be impressed. And, anyway, it was just a hotel.

Only it wasn't *just* anything. It was magnificent.

A palatial honey-coloured building that looked about ten storeys high, it curved like a giant horseshoe around a network of manicured gardens with a central fountain that resembled an inverted chandelier.

As soon as their SUV stopped a uniformed concierge jumped to attention and treated Cruz with the deference one usually expected only around royalty.

Expensively clad men and women wandered languidly in and out of the glassed entrance as if all their cares in the world had disappeared and Aspen glanced down at her old top and jeans. Despite the fact that her grandfather had once been seriously wealthy, Ocean Haven hadn't done well for so long that Aspen couldn't remember the last personal item she'd bought other than deodorant. Now she felt like Cinderella *before* the makeover, and it only seemed to widen the gulf between her and the brooding man beside her.

'Well, I can see why it's rated as seven stars and I

haven't even seen inside yet,' she said with reluctant admiration. 'And, oh…wow…' she added softly. A row of bronzed life-sized horses that looked as if they were racing each other in a shallow pool with shots of water trickling around them glowed under strategically placed lights, adding both pizazz and majesty to the entrance. 'There's so much to see. I almost don't want to go inside.'

'Unfortunately we're not allowed to serve meals on the kerb so you'll have to.'

Aspen switched her gaze to Cruz at his unexpected humour and her pulse skittered. He was just so handsome and charismatic. What would it feel like, she wondered, to be with him at the hotel because she *wanted* to be there and he *wanted* her to be there with him?

The unexpected thought had her nearly stumbling over her own feet.

Why was she even thinking like that?

The last thing she needed was to become involved with a man again. And Cruz had told her in no uncertain terms that he expected sex and nothing else. No need to pretty it up with unwanted emotion.

How had she convinced herself that she'd be able to do this? Not only because of her own inherent dislike of sex but because it was so cold. What would happen once they got upstairs? Did they go straight to the bedroom? Undress? Would he undress her? No. Probably not.

Fortunately she didn't have much time to contemplate the sick feeling in the pit of her stomach as the doorman swept open the chrome and glass doors and inclined his head as Cruz strode inside. Aspen scurried to keep up and couldn't help but notice the lingering attention Cruz garnered with effortless ease.

Another deferential staff member in a severely cut suit descended on him and Aspen left them to stroll towards a circular platform with a large wood carving of a polo player on horseback.

'Aspen?'

Having finished up with his employee, Cruz waited impatiently for her to come to him but Aspen couldn't help returning her gaze to the intricate carving.

'Did you do this?'

He looked startled. 'Why would you think that?'

'I just saw some smaller versions in your mother's house and they reminded me of the wood carvings you used to do in your spare time. Were they yours?'

He paused and Aspen felt a little foolish.

'I haven't done one of those in years.'

It was the most he'd said to her since leaving his mother's and her curiosity got the better of her. 'You don't play polo any more either. Why is that?'

For a minute she didn't think he had heard her.

'Other things to do.'

'Do you miss it?' she asked, imagining that he couldn't not, considering how good he was.

'Mind your step when you come down,' he said, turning away from her.

Right. That would be the end of yet another conversation, she thought, wondering why she'd even bothered to try and engage him. Her natural curiosity and desire to help others was clearly wasted on this man.

She thought back to his angry response to her gentle prodding at his mother's house and shook her head at her own gumption. What did she really know, anyway? Her own relationship history wasn't exactly the healthiest on the planet.

Following Cruz to the bank of elevators, she decided to keep her mouth shut. It was hard enough contemplating what she was about to do without adding to it by trying to come up with superfluous conversation.

When the lift opened directly into Cruz's private suite Aspen gasped at the opulence of the living area, but Cruz ignored it all, striding into the room and throwing his wallet and keys onto a large mahogany table with an elaborate floral arrangement in the centre. With barely a pause he pushed open a set of concertina glass doors that led to a long balcony. Beyond the doors Aspen could just make out a jewel-green polo field.

Stepping closer, she saw that beyond the field there was an enormous stone stable with an orange tiled roof and beyond that white-fenced paddocks holding, she knew, some of the finest polo ponies in the world.

'Wow....' She breathed hot evening air that carried the scent of freshly mown grass and the lemony scent of magnolia with it. 'Is that a swimming pool out there to the right?'

'Yes.' Cruz had his hands wedged firmly in his pockets as he stood behind her. 'It's a saltwater pool the horses use to cool off in.'

'Lucky horses.'

'If you take ten steps to your left and look around the corner you'll see a pool and spa *you* can use.'

Happy to move out of his commanding orbit, Aspen followed his directions.

'Oh...' She stared at a sapphire-blue lap pool which had a large spa at the end of it. The pool was shielded on one side by a thick hedge and from above by a strategically placed cloth sail that would block both the sun and any paparazzi snooping around. 'You don't do things by halves, do you?'

'Mexico is a hot place.'

Then why did she feel so cold?

Shivering, she glanced back at him, her attention caught by piercing black eyes and the dark stubble that highlighted his square jaw. Those broad shoulders...

She shivered again, and tossed her head to cover her reaction. 'Time to get this party started, I'd say.'

'Party?' He raised a cool eyebrow at her. 'In the pool?'

Aspen cast a quick glance at the inviting water, alarmed as an image of both of them naked and entwined popped into her head. It was so clear she could almost see them there—his larger, tanned body holding her up, the silky feel of the water lapping at her skin as it rippled with their movements, her arms curved over his smooth shoulders as she steadied herself, his hands stroking her heavy breasts....

She felt her face flame. She had the romantic—the *fantasy*—version of sex in her mind. The real version, she knew from experience, could never live up to it.

'Of course not.'

'Have you ever made love in the water, Aspen?'

Had he moved closer to her? She glanced at him with alarm but he hadn't moved. Or hadn't appeared to.

She inhaled and steeled her spine. 'The pool doesn't appeal to me.'

'Pity. It's a nice night for it.'

Aspen didn't want to complicate this. A bed was more than adequate for what was about to happen between them. And she could close her eyes more easily in a bed.

'A bed is fine.'

She wondered if Cruz would put a towel down, the way Chad had done.

A muscle ticked in Cruz's jaw and he stared at her as if trying to discern all her deepest thoughts. Then he turned abruptly away. 'Actually, I find I don't enjoy making love on an empty stomach.'

'This has nothing to do with love,' Aspen reminded him assertively.

Halfway to returning indoors, Cruz stopped and his

black eyes smouldered. 'When I touch your body, Aspen, you'll think it does.'

Oh, how arrogant was *that*? If only he knew that all his Latin charm was wasted on her.

Aspen hurled mental daggers at his broad back and wondered why he didn't want to get this over with as soon as possible. By all accounts he seemed to want her—but then so had Chad in the beginning. Oh, this was beyond awful. She hated second-guessing Cruz's desire. Hated hoping that with him it would be different. She knew better than to count on hope. It hadn't brought her mother or her father back into her life. It hadn't made her grandfather love her for herself in the end.

This time when she looked around the vast living area she noticed a bottle of champagne in a silver ice bucket on the main dining table. Maybe that was what she should do. Get drunk.

As if reading her mind, Cruz tightened his mouth. 'Come—I'll show you to your room.'

Aspen felt her heart bump inside her chest. *He's just showing you the room, you fool, not asking you to use it.*

Yet.

Standing back to let her pass, Cruz indicated towards a closed door. 'The bathroom, which should be stocked with everything you'll need, is through there.'

Aspen nodded, feeling completely overwhelmed.

When it became obvious she wasn't going to say anything Cruz turned to go. 'I'll leave you to freshen up.'

She noticed a book on the bedside table. 'This is your room,' she blurted out.

'You were expecting someone else's?'

'No. I...' She spared him a tart look. 'I thought you might like your own space.'

'I like my bed warm more.'

Right.

'Dinner should be served in twenty minutes.'

After he closed the door behind him Aspen sagged against the silk-covered king bed and wondered how long it would be before he realised she was a dud.

Feeling completely despondent, she picked up the novel beside the bed and noticed it was one of her favourites. Surprised, she flicked through it. Could he really be reading it or was it just for show? Just to impress the plethora of mistresses who wandered in and out of his life?

An hour later she was wound so tight all she could do was pick at the delicious Mexican dinner that for once didn't include *tacos* and *enchiladas*.

'Something wrong?'

Her eyes slid across Cruz's powerful forearms, exposed by his rolled shirtsleeves.

Was he serious? She was about to embarrass herself with a man who didn't even like her in order to save her home. Of *course* there was something wrong.

'Of course not,' she replied, feigning relaxed confidence.

He frowned down at her plate. 'Is it the *birria*? If it's too hot for you I can order something else.'

Oh, he'd meant the food. 'No, no, the food's lovely.'

He put down his fork and brought his wine glass to his lips. Now, *there* was relaxed confidence, she thought a little resentfully.

'Then why is most of it still on your plate?'

He licked a drop of red wine from his lower lip and Aspen couldn't look away. Remembered pleasure at the way his mouth had taken hers in the most wonderful kiss vied with sheer terror for supremacy. Unfortunately sheer terror was winning out, because he looked like a man who would expect everything and the kitchen sink as well.

'I…um…I ate a lot at the party.'

'No, you didn't. You barely touched a thing.'

'I'm not a big eater at the best of times.'

'And these are far from the best of times—is that it, Aspen?'

It was more of a statement than a question and Aspen wondered if perhaps he felt the same way. 'You could say that,' she said carefully.

'Is that because you're still in love with Anderson?'

'Sorry?' She knew her mouth was hanging open and she snapped it closed. '*No.* No, that was a disaster from the start.'

'So you're not still pining for him?'

'No.'

His eyes narrowed thoughtfully. 'Why was it a disaster?'

Had she really just told him being married to Chad had been a disaster? 'Don't ask.'

'I just did.'

'Yes, well, I'd rather not talk about it, if it's all the same to you.'

He sat staring at her and Aspen wished she knew what to say next. His unexpected question about Chad had completely derailed her.

'Come here.'

The soft command made her senses leap and she felt her breath quicken with rising panic. He was trying to control her, and she knew she couldn't let him do that.

She tossed her hair back behind one shoulder. 'You come here.'

Despite the fact that he hadn't moved she could sense the tightly coiled tension within him. It radiated outward across the table and stole the breath from her lungs. And for all her dismissive tone she still felt like a puppet on his string—despite her resolve not to be.

He watched her with heavy-lidded eyes and she was

totally unprepared for the scrape of his chair on the terracotta tiles as he stood up.

Aspen's heart jumped as if she'd been startled out of a trance.

Determined to remain neutral—outwardly at least—she didn't move. Couldn't, if the truth be told. Her limbs were completely paralysed—by his laconic sensuality as much as her own blinding insecurities.

'You have amazing hair.'

She snatched in a quick breath to feed her starving lungs. She could feel the heat emanating from his strong thighs beside her shoulders and even though he hadn't touched her she started to tremble. Her only saving grace was that he couldn't possibly be aware of her inner turmoil, and she stared straight ahead as she felt him roll a strand of her hair between his fingers as if it were the finest silk.

She couldn't do this. Already she was freezing up, and to put herself at another man's mercy was truly frightening.

Chad's roughness crowded her mind and permeated her soul, and it was as if Cruz ceased to exist in that moment.

'Dammit, Aspen. What is wrong with you?'

Cruz's dark, annoyed voice only added fuel to the raging fire of Aspen's insecurities. Panic enveloped her and galvanised her into action.

Gouging the floor tiles with her chair, she forced it back and moved in the opposite direction from the one Cruz was in. Unfortunately that only brought her to the balustrade. She gripped the iron railing, enjoying the coolness of the metal against her overheated palms, and pretended rapt attention in the glowing lights that outlined the low boards around the darkened polo field.

'What bothers you the most about this?' he grated. 'The money aspect or the fact that it's me you'll be sleeping with?'

Aspen knew he stood close behind her—every fibre of

her being felt as if it was attuned to every fibre of his—but she didn't turn around. Honestly, she should have known that when it came to the crunch she would fall at the first hurdle. But of course she needed to do this—her mind was so fogged that she couldn't comprehend any other way to save her farm.

'It's not the money.' She tilted her gaze to take in the starry sky. She was planning to pay him back every cent he loaned her, plus interest, so she'd reconciled that in her mind before he'd even picked her up. No, it was... 'It's—'

'Me?' The single word sounded like a pistol-shot.

Interesting, she thought, holding a conversation with someone you couldn't see. It made her other senses come alive. Her sense of hearing that was so in love with the deep timbre of his voice, the feel of the heat of his body that seemed to reach out like a beckoning light, his smell... Unconsciously she rubbed at the railing and felt the smooth texture of the iron beneath her sensitive fingertips.

'It's more the fact that you don't like me,' she said on a rush.

She hadn't realised how true that was until the words left her mouth. A beat passed and then she felt his hands on her shoulders, gently turning her. Embarrassed by the admission, she forced herself to meet his gaze. Because she knew she was right.

He stared at her, not saying anything, his large hands burning into the tops of her shoulders, his thumbs almost absently caressing her collarbones. It was hard to read his expression with only a candle flickering on the table and a crescent moon ducking behind darkened clouds. It was even harder when he lowered his gaze to his hands, his inky lashes shielding them.

He gently slid those large hands up her neck to the line of her jaw, setting off a whole host of sensations in their wake. Aspen stiffened as she felt the pad of one of his thumbs slowly graze her closed mouth. His eyes locked on her lips as he pressed into the soft flesh, making them feel gloriously sensitised.

They were both utterly still. The only movement came from his thumb as it swept back and forth, back and forth, across her hyper-sensitive flesh. Back and forth until her lips started to buzz and gave beneath the persuasive pressure, allowing him to reach the moisture within. Aspen trembled as he spread her own wetness along her bottom lip and then opened her lips wider, until he was touching her teeth. He traced their shape just as thoroughly, only they weren't as malleable as her lips and stayed firmly closed.

She should have known that he wouldn't stop there. Unfairly he was bringing his fingers into play, to knead the side of her neck, pressing firmly into her nape. On a rush of heat her senses were overloaded and her teeth parted, giving him greater liberties.

Only he didn't immediately take them, and without even realising it Aspen tilted her head, seeking to capture his thumb between her teeth, silently inviting him inside. Still he hung back, and with a small sound in the back of her throat she couldn't stop her mouth from closing around his thumb and sucking on his flesh, couldn't stop her tongue from wrapping itself around it as she sought to taste him.

Cruz didn't know if he'd ever experienced anything as erotic as Aspen drawing his thumb into her wide mouth, her cheeks hollowing as she sucked firmly and then softening as she used her tongue to drive him wild. With every stroke his erection jerked painfully behind his zipper and, unable to hold back any longer, he pulled his thumb from her mouth and replaced it with his own.

She immediately latched onto his mouth as if she was just as desperate as he was, and he backed her against the cast iron balustrading and didn't stop until he was hard up against her.

Incapable of thought, he let his instincts take over and hooked one of her legs up over his hip so he could settle into the cradle of her thighs, all the time ravaging her mouth until she fed him more of those hot little moans.

The deep neckline of her otherwise demure dress, which had tantalised him all night, was no barrier to his wandering hands and he deftly moved the soft jersey aside and cupped her, squeezing her full breasts together. He strummed his thumbs over her lace-covered nipples and felt exalted when she arched into him, moaning more keenly as he slowly increased the pressure.

He groaned, licked his way to her ear, bit it, and then trailed tiny kisses down over her neck, sucking on her soft skin. She smelled like flowers and tasted like honey and he knew he'd never experienced anything so sweet. So heady.

Her leg shifted higher as she sought a deeper contact, and her fingers dug into his shoulders as if she was trying to hold herself upright.

'Cruz, please....'

Needing no further invitation, he pushed her bra aside and leant back so that he could look at her.

'Perfect. You fit perfectly into my hands.'

He moulded her fullness, watching her beautiful raspberry-coloured nipples tighten even more as they anticipated his mouth on them. His body throbbed as it anticipated the same thing, and he tested the weight of each breast before drawing his thumb and fingertips together until he held just the tips of each nipple between his fingers, his touch too light to fully satisfy.

She cried out and arched impossibly higher, as if in pain, and he bent his head and gave her what he knew she needed, soldering his lips to one peak and pulling her turgid flesh deeply into his mouth while rubbing firmly over the other.

'Cruz! Oh, my God!'

She buried her hands in his hair and clung—and thank goodness she did. The taste of her made his knees feel weak and his hunger to be buried deep inside her impossibly urgent.

Wrapping one arm around her waist, he lifted her and ground his hardness against her core, his self-control shredded by her wild response. 'I want you, Aspen.' He smoothed his hand down the silky skin of her thigh and rode her skirt all the way up. 'Tell me you want me, *mi gatita*. Tell me this has nothing to do with money.'

He registered the rigidity in her body at the same time as his rough words reverberated inside his head, and both acted like a bucket of cold water on his libido.

What was he saying? More importantly, what was he *asking*?

'I...'

She looked up at him, flushed with passion. Dazed. Beautiful. The breeze whispered over her hair.

'I'm sorry,' she whispered breathlessly.

Sorry?

So was he.

The last time he had wanted something this badly he had lost everything. And he couldn't take her like this.

Couldn't take her because he was paying her.

Once again the image of a lustful Billy Smyth with his hand stroking her face clouded his vision. Up to yesterday Cruz would have said that he wasn't a violent man, but just the thought of her sleeping with anyone else curdled his blood. If he hadn't offered her this deal where else might she be tonight—and who with?

The question just added ice to the bucket and he unwound her arms from around his neck.

'Cruz…?'

Was he crazy? He had a hot woman in his arms so why was he hesitating? He couldn't explain it; he just knew it didn't feel right.

His hard-on pressed insistently against his fly, as if to say it had felt very right ten seconds ago, and he stepped away from her so he wouldn't be tempted to pull her back into his arms.

Something of his inner turmoil must have shown on his face, because she blanched and he thought she might throw up.

'Steady.'

He went to grab her but she pulled back sharply and quickly righted her dress as best she could before wrapping her arms around herself.

'I can't believe it. I've ruined it,' she muttered, more to herself than him.

On one level he registered the comment as strange, but part of him had already agreed with her—because, yes, she *had* ruined it. She was ruining everything.

His desire to buy Ocean Haven.

His peace of mind.

'That sounds like revenge,' she'd said earlier.

'Go to bed, Aspen,' he said wearily, upset with himself and his unwelcome conscience.

Her eyes were uncertain pools of dark green when she looked at him. 'But what about—?'

'I'm not in the mood.'

He turned sharply and tracked back into the penthouse before he threw his aggravating conscience over the balcony and did what his body was all but demanding he do.

Aspen stood on the balcony, the night air cooling her overheated skin as the realisation that he was rejecting her sank in. She swallowed heavily, her mind spinning back to those last few moments. She felt like an inept fool as memories of Chad's hurtful rejection of her years ago tumbled into her mind like an avalanche. His repulsed expression when he'd told her to go out and buy a bottle of lube.

At the time she'd been so naïve about sex she hadn't even known what he was talking about. So he'd clarified. *'Lubrication. You're too dry. It's off-putting.'*

Completely mortified, she'd searched the internet and learned that some women suffered dryness due to low oestrogen levels. She hadn't investigated any further. She'd shame-facedly done what he'd asked, but they'd never got round to using it. He hadn't wanted to touch her after that.

And no matter how many times she told herself that Chad's harsh words were more to do with his own inadequacies in the bedroom than hers it didn't matter. She didn't believe it. Not entirely. There was always a niggle that he was right.

Don't go there, she warned herself, only half aware that she had pressed her hand to her stomach. *Chad's long gone and you* knew *this was going to happen with Cruz so, okay, deal with it. And quickly. Then you can go home to Ocean Haven and be safe again.*

Fortifying her resolve, she moved inside and found Cruz pouring a drink, his back to her.

'You still have to lend me the money,' she said, glad that her voice sounded so strong.

Cruz felt his shoulders tense and turned slowly to face her.

She was a cool one, all right. Haughty. Dismissive. *Way too good for him.*

Slowly he folded himself into one of the deep-seated sofas. 'No, I don't,' he said, wanting to annoy her.

'Yes, you do. You signed—'

'I know what I signed.' He swirled his drink and ice clinked in the glass as he watched her. Her eyes were cool to the point of being detached. Damn her. That was usually *his* stock in trade.

'Then you know that if it turns out you don't want…' She stopped whatever it was she was about to say and raised her chin. 'I trusted you.'

He ignored the way those words twisted his gut. Her soft declaration was making his conscience spike again. 'The agreement didn't stipulate which night.' He waited for his words to sink in and it didn't take long. 'Consider yourself off the hook for tonight. As I told you, I'm not in the mood.'

She frowned. 'When *will* you be in the mood?'

Right now, as it happens.

'I don't know,' he said roughly, annoyed with his inability to control his physical response to her.

Of course that answer wasn't good enough for her.

'And if *I'm* not in the mood when you decide you are?'

This wasn't going to work. If he stayed here he'd damned well finish what he had started outside.

He sprang to his feet and those green eyes widened warily. And well they might. He stalked towards her and wrapped one hand around that glorious mane of hair. He tilted her face up so that she was forced to meet his steely gaze, unsure if he was angry with her or himself or just in general.

'When I decide to take you, Aspen, rest assured you'll be in the mood.'

Then he kissed her. Long and deep and hard.

Aspen held the back of her hand against her throbbing mouth as Cruz marched out through the main door to the lift.

And good riddance, she wanted to call out to his arrogant back. Except she didn't. She felt too shattered. Lack of sleep last night, the roller coaster of a day today. It all crashed in on her.

Not wanting to wait around in case he suddenly reappeared, she fled to the bedroom, hoping sleep would transport her back to East Hampton. Literally.

Only it wasn't her room she was in, and she quickly snatched her things together and headed to one of the spare bedrooms.

Ha—she would show him who wasn't 'in the mood'.

She let out a low groan as those words he had flung at her came rushing back. The embarrassing thing was she couldn't have been more in the mood if he had lit scented candles and told her he loved her.

And he had seemed to be totally in the mood.

When she found herself trying to analyse the exact moment it had all gone wrong she pulled herself up. That was a one-way street to anxiety and sleeplessness and she wouldn't go there again. Not for any man.

By the time Cruz let himself back into the penthouse his frame of mind had not improved. He'd gone down to the stables—something he'd always done when he felt troubled—but it hadn't made him feel any better.

In fact it had made him feel worse, because now that Aspen had walked back into his life—or rather he had walked back into hers—he couldn't get her out of his head.

Worse, he couldn't get the game he was playing with her out of his head. He'd had a lot of time to think about things since he'd picked her up, and although he'd like to be able to say that it had started out as an underhand way of getting what he wanted the truth was it hadn't even been that logical. He'd taken one look at her and wanted her. Then he'd made the mistake of touching her. Kissing her. He'd never felt so out of control. Something he hadn't anticipated at all.

He'd convinced himself that he could sleep with her for one night and send her home.

So much for that.

The reality was that right now he wanted her in his bed—and not because he was paying her a pit full of money but because she wanted to be there. And didn't that make his head spin? The last time he'd wanted something from a Carmichael he'd been kicked in the teeth, and he was about as likely to let that happen again as the sun rising in the west.

He thought about her comment about his family treating him like a king. He'd been so caught up in his own sense of betrayal and, yes, his anger at missing out on *knowing* them that he hadn't considered his own involvement in continuing that state of affairs. Now he saw it through Aspen's eyes and it made him want to cringe. Yes, he held himself back. But distance made things easier to manage.

But she had understood that as well, hadn't she? *'That's a lot for a child to have heaped on his shoulders. You must have really struggled.'*

Yes, it had been a lot. Particularly when Charles Carmichael had been such an exacting and forbidding taskmaster. Maybe others understood what he had gone through but no one had dared say it to his face.

And her suggestion that he could scowl a little less...?

He scowled now. Maybe he should just go and find her, have sex with her and be done with her. But something about that snagged in his unconscious. Something wasn't right about her hot and cold responses but he couldn't put his finger on what it was.

'I can't believe it. I've ruined it.'

Why would she have said that? If anything he'd ruined it by stopping. But she hadn't questioned that, had she? She'd had a look on her face that was one of resigned acceptance and moved on.

And hard on the heels of that thought was her comment about her marriage to Anderson being a disaster. He'd wanted to push her on that but had decided not to. Now he wished he had. There was something about the lack of defiance in her eyes when she had mentioned her ex that bothered him. Almost as if she'd been terribly hurt by the whole thing.

He frowned. The truth was he shouldn't give a damn about Aspen Carmichael, or her feelings, or her comments, and he didn't know why he did.

Throwing off his tangled thoughts, he tentatively pushed open his bedroom door and stopped short when he found the room empty. His wardrobe door lay open and a stream of feminine clothing crossed his room like a trail of breadcrumbs where she had obviously dropped them as she'd carried her things out.

Gingerly he picked them up and placed them on the corner chair. She'd no doubt be upset to realise she'd dropped them. Especially the silky peach-coloured panties. He rubbed the fabric between his thumb and forefinger and his body reacted like a devoted dog that had just seen its master return after a year-long absence.

'Not tonight, Josephine,' he muttered, heading for the shower.

A cold one.

Cruz rubbed his rough jaw and picked up his razor. Unbidden, Charles Carmichael's rangy features came to his mind. Initially he had admired his determination and objectivity. His loyalty. Only those traits hadn't stacked up in the end. The man had been ruthless more than determined, cold rather than objective, and his loyalty had been prejudiced towards his own kind.

Had *he* degenerated into that person? Had *he* become a hollow version of the man he'd thought he was? He stopped shaving and stared at the remaining cream on his face. Why did his life suddenly feel so empty? So superficial?

Hold on. His life wasn't empty or superficial. He barked out a short laugh. He had everything a man could want. Money. Power. Women. Respect.

His razor nicked the delicate skin just under his jaw. *Respect.*

He didn't have everyone's respect. He didn't have Aspen's. And he didn't have his own right now, either.

He thought again about the night Aspen had set him up. He supposed he could have defended himself against Carmichael's prejudiced accusations and changed the course of his life, but something in Aspen's eyes that night had stayed him. Fear? Devastation? Embarrassment? He'd never asked. He'd just felt angry and bitter that she had stolen his future.

Only she hadn't, had she? He'd disowned it. He'd thrown it all in. Nobody made a fool of a Rodriguez—wasn't that what his *padre* would have said?

He took a deep steadying breath, flexed his shoulders and heard his neck crack back into place.

So, okay, in the morning he would tell Aspen to go home. He wouldn't sleep with her in exchange for the money. She could have it. But she still wasn't getting The Farm. He wanted it, and what he wanted he got.

End of story.

CHAPTER SEVEN

WHEN SHE WOKE the next morning and decided she really couldn't hang out in her room all day Aspen ventured out into the living area of Cruz's luxury penthouse and breathed a sigh of relief to find it empty. Empty bar the lingering traces of his mouth-watering aftershave, that was.

After making sure that he really had gone she sucked in a grateful breath, so on edge she nearly jumped out of her skin when the phone in her hand buzzed with an incoming text.

Make yourself comfortable and charge whatever you want to the room. We'll talk tonight.

'About a ticket home?' she mused aloud.

The disaster of the previous night winged into her thoughts like a homing pigeon.

In the back of her mind Aspen had imagined that they would try to have sex, she would freeze, Cruz might or might not laugh, and Aspen would return home. Then she would get on with her life and never think of him again.

Only nothing was normal with Cruz. Not her inability to hate him for his ruthlessness or her physical reaction to him. Because while she had been in his arms last night she had forgotten to be worried. She'd been unable to do anything but feel, and his touch had felt amazing. So amazing that she'd mistakenly believed it might work. That this time she would be okay. Then she'd panicked and he'd stopped. And she really didn't want to analyse why that was.

'Urgh.' She blew out a breath. 'You weren't going to replay that train wreck again, remember?'

Right.

Determinedly she dropped her phone into her handbag and poured herself a steaming cup of coffee from the silver tray set on the mahogany dining table.

There was an array of gleaming dome-covered plates, and as she lifted each one in turn she wondered if Cruz had ordered the entire menu for breakfast and then realised that he wasn't hungry. Her own stomach signalled that she was ravenous and Aspen placed scrambled eggs and bacon on a plate and tucked in.

Unsure what do with herself, she checked in with Donny and Mrs Randall and then decided to do some studying. She was doing a double load at university next semester, so she could qualify by the end of the year, and she needed to get her head around the coursework before assignments started rolling in.

But she couldn't concentrate.

A horse whinnied in the distance and another answered.

The call of the wild, she mused with a faint smile. She walked out onto the balcony and leant on the railing. The grooms in the distance were leading a group of horses through their morning exercises and the sight made her feel homesick.

It was probably a mistake to go looking for her, but after three hours locked in a business meeting with his executive team, who had flown in from all over the States for a strategy session, Cruz's brain was fried. Distracted by a curly-haired blonde. He told his team to take an early lunch, because he knew better than to push something when it wasn't working. Once he'd found Aspen and organised for her to return to Ocean Haven he'd be able to think again. Until then at least the members of his team could find something more productive to do than repeat every point back to him for the rest of the day.

But, annoyingly, Aspen wasn't anywhere he had expected her to be. Not in his penthouse, nor the hotel boutiques, not one of the five hotel restaurants, nor the day spa. When he described her to his staff they all looked at him as if he was describing some fantasy woman.

Yeah, your fantasy woman.

Feeling more and more agitated, he stopped by the concierge's desk in case she had taken a taxi into town on her own. It would be just like her to do something monumentally stupid and cause him even more problems. Of course the concierge on duty knew immediately who he was talking about and that just turned his mood blacker.

'The strawberry blonde babe with the pre-Raphaelite curls all the way down to her—?'

'Yes, that one,' Cruz snapped, realising that someone— him—had neglected to inform his staff that she was off-limits.

Oblivious to his mounting tension, the concierge continued blithely, 'She's in the stables. At least she was a couple of hours ago.'

And how, he wanted to ask the hapless youth, *do you know that?* His mind conjured up all sorts of clandestine meetings between her and his college-age employee.

Growling under his breath, Cruz stalked across the wide expanse of green lawn that had nothing on her eyes towards the main stable. He reminded himself that if he'd waited around for her to wake up he would now know where she was and what she was up to.

Survival tactics? his conscience proposed.

Busy, Cruz amended.

He heard the lovely sound of her laughter before he saw her, and then the sight of her long legs encased in snug jeans came into view. He couldn't see the rest of her; bent as she was over the stall door, but frankly he couldn't take his eyes off her wiggling hips and the mouthwatering curve of her backside.

Another giggle brought his eyes up and he had to clear his throat twice before she reared back and stood in front of him. Cruz glanced inside the stall in time to see one of his men stuffing his wallet into his back pocket, a guilty flush suffusing his neck.

Unused to such testy feelings of jealousy, and on the verge of grabbing his very married assistant trainer by the throat and hauling him off the premises, Cruz clenched his jaw. 'I believe your services are required elsewhere, Señor Martin.'

'Of course, sir.' His trainer swallowed hard as he opened the stall door and ducked around Aspen. 'Excuse me, *señorita*.'

'Oh, we were just—' Aspen stopped speaking as Luis turned worried eyes her way, and she glanced at Cruz to find his icy stare on the man. He might have been wearing another expensive suit, but he looked anything but civilised, she noted. In fact he looked breathtakingly *un*-civilised—as if he had a band of warriors waiting outside to raid the place.

Irritated both by his overbearing attitude and the way her heart did a little dance behind her breastbone at the sight of him, Aspen went on the attack. 'Don't tell me.' She arched a brow. 'You've suddenly decided you're in the mood?'

'No.'

His expression grew stormier and he stepped into her space until Aspen found herself inside the stall with the almost sleeping horse Luis had been tending to.

'What are you up to, Aspen?' he rasped harshly, blocking the doorway.

Wanting to put space between them, Aspen stepped lightly around the mare and picked up the discarded brush Luis had been using to groom her.

'I feel bad that Luis didn't get to finish in here because of our conversation so I thought I'd brush Bandit down for him.'

'I meant *with* him?'

She paused, not liking the tone of his voice. 'If you're implying what I think you are then, yes, I did offer to sleep with Luis—but unfortunately he only has a spare nine million lying around.' She shrugged as if to say, *What can you do?*

'Don't be smart.'

Aspen glared at him. 'Then don't be insulting.'

He looked at her as if he was contemplating throttling her, but even that wasn't enough to stop the thrilling buzz coursing through her body at his closeness.

Aspen shook her head as much at herself as him. 'You really have a low opinion of me, don't you, Cruz?'

'Look at it from my point of view.' He balled his hands on his hips. 'I come out here to find you giggling like a schoolgirl and one of my best trainers stuffing his wallet back into his pocket. What am I supposed to think?'

Aspen's gaze was icily steady on his. 'That he was showing me pictures of his children being dragged along by the family goat.'

A beat passed in which she wouldn't have been surprised if Cruz had turned and walked away as he had the night before. It seemed to be his *modus operandi* when confronted with anything remotely emotional. Only he didn't.

'I'm sorry,' he said abruptly, raking a hand through his hair. 'I might have overreacted.'

Aspen had never had a man apologise to her before and it completely took the wind out of her sails. 'Well, okay...'

For the first time in her dealings with him he looked a tad uncomfortable. 'I didn't come here to quarrel with you.'

'What *did* you come here for? If you're checking on Bandit's cankers I had a look at the affected hoof before and it's completely healed.'

Cruz frowned. 'That's for the vet to decide, not you.'

'The vet was busy and I know what I'm doing. I'm one semester away from becoming a fully qualified vet. Plus, I've treated a couple of our horses for the disease. So,' she couldn't resist adding, 'not just marrying to secure my future, then.'

A muscle ticked in his jaw. 'You enjoyed telling me that, didn't you?'

'It did feel rather good, yes.'

They stared at each other and then his mouth kicked up at the corners. 'I suppose you want another apology?'

What she wanted was for him to stop smiling and scowl again so she could catch her breath. 'Would it be too much to hope for, do you think?'

'Probably.'

Aspen couldn't hold back a grin and quickly ducked down to pick up Bandit's rear hoof and clean it.

'You've changed,' he said softly.

She looked up and he nodded to the tool in her hand.

'You used to be much more of a princess type.'

'Really?' Her green eyes sparkled with amusement. 'That's how you saw me?'

'That's how all the boys saw you.' He shrugged. 'We got your horse ready and you rode it and then we brushed it down at the end. Back then you wouldn't have even known how to use one of those.'

Aspen grimaced and went back to work on the horse. 'That was because my grandfather wouldn't let me work with the horses. He had very clear ideas on a woman's place in the world. It was why my mother left. She didn't really talk to me about him, but I remember overhearing her talking to a friend and saying that he didn't understand anyone else's opinion but his own.'

Satisfied that the horse's feet were clean, Aspen patted her rump and collected the wooden toolbox. 'You're done for the day, girl.'

She glanced up as Cruz continued to block the doorway. The sound of someone moving tack around further along the stable rattled between them.

'Why did you set me up that night?'

The suddenness of the question and the harshness of his tone jolted her.

'What are you talking about?' She couldn't think how she had set him up, but—

'Eight years ago. You and your *fiancé*.'

'Fiancé?'

She frowned and then realised that he was talking about the night her grandfather had found them. She had no idea what he meant by setting him up, but it shocked her that he thought she'd been engaged to Chad at the time. Then she recalled her grandfather's vitriolic outburst. Something she'd shoved into the deepest recess of her mind.

She grimaced as it all came rushing back. 'Chad and I weren't actually engaged that night,' she said slowly.

'Your grandfather certainly thought you were.'

'That's because I later learned that he had accepted Chad's proposal on my behalf.'

Cruz swore. 'You're saying he forced you to go along with it?'

Aspen hesitated. 'No. I could have turned him down.'

'But you didn't?'

'No, but I certainly didn't consider myself engaged when I walked into the stables and saw you there.'

'How about when you kissed me?'

Aspen shifted uncomfortably. 'No, not then either.'

'That still doesn't answer my question.'

Aspen couldn't remember his question, her mind so full of memories and guilt. 'What question?'

'Why you set me up.'

She shook her head. 'I don't really understand what you mean by that.'

Cruz took in her wary gaze, frustration and desire biting into him like an annoying insect. 'You're saying it was a coincidence that your grandfather just *happened* to come across us and then just *happened* to kick me off the property, thereby paving the way for Anderson to take over as captain of the dream team?'

Her eyes widened with what appeared to be genuine shock. 'I would never...' She blinked as if she was trying to clear her thoughts. 'Grandfather said it was your decision to leave Ocean Haven.'

Cruz scoffed at the absurdity of her statement. 'It was one of those "you can go under your own steam or mine" type of offers,' he said bitterly.

But he could admit to a little resentment, couldn't he? He'd given Charles Carmichael eleven years of abject devotion that had been repaid with anger and accusations and the revocation of every promise the old man had ever made him.

Memories he'd rather obliterate than verbalise turned his tone harsh. 'He accused me of *deflowering* his precious *engaged* granddaughter and you let him believe it.'

'I don't remember that,' she said softly. 'I told him afterwards that we hadn't been together.'

Cruz wasn't interested in another apology. 'So you said.'

'But you still don't believe me?'

'It's irrelevant.'

'I don't think it is. I can hear in your voice that it still pains you and I don't blame you. I should never have let him think what he did. Not even for a second.'

'What you can hear in my voice is not pain but absolute disgust.'

He stepped closer to her, noting how small and fragile she looked, her shoulders narrow, her limbs slender and fine. He knew the taste of her skin, as well as her scent.

'When it happened...' He forced himself to focus. '*Then* I was upset. Devastated, if you want to know the truth. I thought your grandfather and I were equals. I thought he respected me. Maybe even cared for me.' He snorted out a breath and thrust his hand through his hair. 'I thought wrong. Do you know what he told me?'

Cruz had no idea why he was telling her something so deeply private but somehow the words kept coming.

'He told me I wasn't good enough for his granddaughter. He didn't want your lily-white blood mixing with that of a second-class *Mexicano*.'

'But my blood isn't lily-white. My mother saw to that in a fit of rebellion. My grandfather could never get past her decision and because they were both stubborn neither one could offer the other an olive branch. My mother wanted to go home to The Farm *so* many times.'

Aspen swallowed past the lump in her throat.

'But my grandfather had kicked her out. It was the same with you. Two days after you left he had a stroke and I'm sure it was because he had lost you. Of course no one outside the family knew about it, but I knew it had to do with what happened and I felt terrible. Ashamed of myself. But I was scared, Cruz.'

She looked at him with remorseful eyes and no matter what he thought of her it was impossible to doubt her sincerity.

'You know my grandfather's temper. I didn't know what he'd do to me.'

'Nothing,' Cruz bit out. 'He was angry at me, not you. He thought the world of you.'

'As long as I did what he wanted.' She shivered. 'I was so frightened when I arrived at Ocean Haven. I'd heard about the place from my mother and I'd loved it from a small child. I'd never met my grandfather before and I was determined that he wouldn't hate me. And he didn't. But nor did he like me questioning him or going against his wishes. At first that was okay, because I was little, but as I got older it became harder to always be agreeable. That night...' She stopped and looked at him curiously. 'Why didn't you defend yourself against him? Why didn't you tell him that it was *me* who had kissed *you*?'

'It hadn't exactly been one-way.' He ran a hand through his hair. 'And you looked...frightened.'

Aspen gave him a small smile. 'I was that, all right. I'd never seen him in such a rage. I didn't know what to do and I froze. It's a horrible reaction I've never been able to shake when I'm truly petrified. That night, if he had found out that I instigated things with you after he'd told me I was expected to marry Chad, I thought...I thought...'

Cruz briefly closed his eyes. 'You thought he'd disown you like he had your mother.'

The truth of what had happened that night was like a slap in the face.

'It seems silly now, but...'

'It was like history repeating itself. Your mother with the ski instructor...you with the lowly polo player.'

'*I* didn't think that, but he was so angry.' She shuddered at the memory. 'And I never wanted to leave the one place my mother loved so much. She used to talk about it all the time. Do you know that skewed horseshoe wedged between two roof beams in the stable?'

Cruz knew it. Old Charlie had grumbled about it whenever he was in a bad mood.

'Apparently years ago Mum and Uncle Joe were playing hooky with a bunch of them and when she was losing she got in a terrible snit and aimed one at his head.' Aspen laughed softly, as if she were remembering her mother recounting the story. 'Unfortunately she was a terrible shot and released it too soon. It went shooting up towards the roof and somehow it got stuck. Which was lucky for my uncle because she obviously put her back into it.' She smiled. 'Every time I see it, it's as if she's still here with me.'

She looked at him.

'That night I was so angry with my grandfather for ignoring my wishes that I went to the stable to talk to her. When you showed up and you weren't dressed properly I… I can't explain it rationally.'

Her eyes flitted away and then she seemed to force them back to his.

'I had wanted to kiss you for so long and I wasn't thinking clearly. I know you don't want to hear this but I am sorry, Cruz. I should have stood up for you. But I was selfishly worried about myself and—'

Cruz cupped her face in his hands and kissed her. Lightly. 'It's okay. I remember his temper.'

Aspen gave him a wobbly smile. 'I think I inherited that from him.'

He shook his head, his thumbs stroking her cheekbones. 'You're not scary when you're angry. You're beautiful.'

She made a noise somewhere between a snort and a cough and he couldn't resist kissing her again, his lips lingering and sipping at hers.

This time the noise she made was one of pleasure, and Cruz slid his hand into her hair to hold her head steady, nudging the toolbox out of his way with his knee so that he could shift closer. She pressed into him and he wrapped his other hand around her waist, deepening the kiss. Slowly.

Deliberately drawing out the sweet anticipation of it for both of them.

Aspen's arms rose, linked around his neck and time passed. How much, he couldn't have said.

Slowly she drew back, lifting her long lashes to reveal eyes glazed with passion. 'Wow...' she whispered.

Wow was right.

She moistened her lower lip, her eyes flitting from his, and he frowned. He could have sworn he saw a touch of apprehension in them. He nipped at her lower lip, kissed her again.

With a thousand questions pounding through his head—not least why she seemed nervous when it came to intimacy—he reluctantly ended the searing kiss and leant his forehead against hers. Their breaths mingled, hot and heavy.

'I don't hate you, Aspen,' he said, answering her question of the previous night. Her bewitching green eyes returned to his and he found himself saying, 'I have a formal dinner at the hotel tonight. Come with me.'

Aspen felt dazzled. By the conversation. By his sweet, tender kisses. By the piercing ache in her pelvis that made a mockery of her previous experiences with Chad. 'I'd like that...'

And she did—right up until she found an emerald-green gown laid out on her bed next to black stiletto sandals still inside their box.

Standing stock-still in the centre of the spare room Aspen stared at the exquisite gown.

'Don't wear that. You look awful in it. Here. Put this on.'

Aspen shivered. Chad's voice was so clear in her head he might as well have been standing beside her.

Cruz wasn't Chad. She knew that. But somehow her stomach still felt cramped. Because the dress symbolised some sort of ownership. Some sort of control. And she knew she couldn't give him that—not over her.

It made her realise just what she'd been thinking when he had invited her to the dinner. She'd been thinking it was a date. That it was real.

But this wasn't real. She wouldn't even be here if it wasn't for the deal he had offered her. A deal she had accepted and still hadn't fulfilled. Which she needed to do to keep Ocean Haven. How had she forgotten that? How had she forgotten that he was trying to steal it away from her?

But she knew how. He'd kissed her so tenderly, so reverently, it had been as if eight years had fallen away between them. And she couldn't think like that. Because as much as she hated the coldness of the deal they had struck she also knew that she couldn't afford to feel anything. She couldn't afford to want anything from him other than money. That way was fraught with disaster. It would turn her from an independent woman in charge of her own destiny back into the people-pleaser she had tried to be for her grandfather. For Chad.

She stared at the dress. Cruz was an extraordinarily wealthy man who was used to getting what he wanted. For some reason he had decided that he wanted her. For a night. But that didn't mean she had to wear clothes he'd chosen as well.

Before she could think too much about it she strode out into the living room. The sun was hanging low in the sky and it illuminated his fit body as he stood in front of the window, talking into his cell phone.

As if sensing her presence he turned, scanned her face and the dress she was holding, and told whomever he was talking to that he had to go.

She held the dress out to him. 'I can't wear this.'

He frowned. 'It doesn't fit?'

'No. Yes. Actually, I don't know. I haven't tried it on.'

He smiled. 'Then what's the problem?'

'The problem is—' She dropped her hand and paced away from him. 'The problem is that I'm not a possession you can dress up whenever you like. The problem is I'm an independent woman who has some idea about how to dress herself and doesn't need to be told what to wear by some high-powered male who has to own everything.'

A heavy silence fell over the room as soon as her spiel had finished but somehow her words hung between them like a hideously long banner dragged through the sky by a biplane.

'I take it your grandfather didn't like your choice in outfits?' He dropped into a plush sofa. 'Or was it Anderson?'

For a minute his astute questions floored her. 'Chad has *nothing* to do with this,' she bit out.

His beautiful black eyes glittered with confidence and Aspen was suddenly embarrassed to realise that she had just exposed a part of herself she hadn't intended to.

'At some point we need to talk about him.'

Aspen felt her heart hammer inside her chest. 'We so do not.'

His eyes became hooded. 'We will, but not now. As to the other.' He waved his hand at the emerald silk crushed in her hand. 'It's just a dress, Aspen. I assume you didn't pack anything formal?'

'No.' Deciding to ignore her embarrassment, she forged on. 'But I can buy my own clothes if I need to.'

Clearly exasperated, he looked at her from under long thick lashes. 'Fine. I'll forward you the bill.'

Aspen could tell he had no intention of doing that. 'You may have bought a night with me, Cruz, but that doesn't mean you own me.'

'I don't want to own you.' He laid his arm along the back of the sofa. 'Wear it. Don't wear it. It's irrelevant to me.'

'What *is* relevant to you?' she asked, goaded by his

nonchalant attitude. 'Because it seems to me that you've cut yourself off from everything that could have meaning in your life other than work. Your family. Your polo playing—' Aspen stopped, breathlessly aware that he had risen during her tirade and that he was nowhere near as relaxed as he had appeared.

'The dress was a peace offering.' He grabbed his suit jacket from the back of the nearby chair. 'But you can bin it for all I care.'

Feeling all at sea as he stalked out of the penthouse, Aspen returned to her room and leant against the closed door.

A peace offering?

She felt stupid and knew that she had acted like a drama queen. And she knew why. She was tense. The thought of sex with Cruz was hanging over her head like a stalactite. And felt just as deadly.

Glancing at the bed, she ignored the tight feeling in her chest and tossed the dress onto it. Then she stripped off and scalded herself with a hot shower, all the while knowing that as she plucked and preened and soaped herself with the delicious vanilla-scented soap that she was doing so with Cruz in mind. Which made her feel worse. This wasn't a romance. It was a deal.

A deal that would end as soon as they'd slept together.

A deal that could still go wrong if her uncle decided that he needed the money Cruz was willing to part with to turn Ocean Haven into a horrible hotel.

Trying not to dwell on that, she rolled her eyes at herself when she realised she'd changed her hairstyle five times. She looked at the spiralling mess. All her fiddling had turned her hair to frizz. *Great*.

Salvaging it as best she could, she stomped back into the bedroom and spied the offending gown she had flung onto the bed. Even skewed it rippled, and dared any woman not to want to wear it.

And given the contents of her suitcase what choice did she really have? None. And she hated that because she'd had so little choice in what had happened to her growing up on Ocean Haven. After Chad she had vowed she'd never be beholden to anyone again—especially not a man. But one night with Cruz didn't make her beholden to him, did it?

Once he'd lent her the money and she'd paid him back, as she would the other investors, they would be back on an equal footing. She exhaled. One night, straight up, and then she was home free.

Why did that leave her feeling so empty?

She looked again at the dress. Grimaced. Trust him to have such superb taste.

CHAPTER EIGHT

'ARE YOU EVEN listening to what I'm saying?'

Cruz glanced at Ricardo, who was debriefing him on who was attending the formal dinner that night and how impressed the Chinese delegation were with the facilities. The Sunset Bar, where they had decided to catch up for a drink before the evening proceedings, was full to bursting with excited players and polo experts from all over the globe.

'Of course,' he lied. 'Go on.'

Ricardo frowned, but thankfully continued working his way through the list.

Cruz studied it also, but his mind was elsewhere. More specifically his mind was weighing up how he was going to steal The Farm out from under Aspen's gorgeous fingertips when he now knew the truth about that fateful night.

He took a healthy swig of his tequila. He'd been *so* sure she had done him wrong eight years ago he'd been blind to any other possibility. *Tainted*, he realised belatedly. Tainted by his own deep-seated feelings of inferiority and hurt pride.

Hell.

He couldn't escape the knowledge that seeing Aspen again had unearthed a wealth of bitterness he hadn't even realised he'd buried deep inside himself—resentments he'd let fester but that no longer seemed relevant.

What is *relevant to you?*

Hell, that woman had a way of working her way inside his head. But as much as he hated that he knew in good conscience he couldn't take Ocean Haven away from her. He'd never be able to face himself in the mirror again if he did. But what to do? Because if he also let her continue with her foolhardy plan to borrow thirty million dollars to keep it she'd be bankrupt within a year.

Of course that wasn't his problem. She was an adult and could take care of herself. But some of that old protectiveness he had always felt towards her was seeping back in and refused to go away. He wanted to fix everything for her, but she was so fiercely guarded, so intent on doing everything herself. It was madness. But so was the fact that he couldn't stop thinking about her. That he even *wanted* to fix things for her in the first place.

Realising that Ricardo was waiting for him to say something, Cruz nodded thoughtfully. 'Sam Harris is playing tomorrow. Got it.'

'Actually,' Ricardo said patiently, 'Sam Harris is sick. Tommy Hassenberger is taking his place.'

'Send Sam a bottle of tequila.'

'I already sent flowers.'

Cruz shook his head at his brother. 'And you think you need a *wife*?'

Normally his brother would have returned his light ribbing, but to Cruz's chagrin he didn't this time.

'What's up?' he said instead.

Cruz rubbed his jaw and realised he should have shaved again. 'Nothing.'

'You're a million miles away. It wouldn't have anything to do with Aspen Carmichael, would it?'

Bingo.

'If I say no, you'll assume I'm lying, and if I say yes, you'll want to know why.'

Ricardo shook his head and laughed. '*Dios mio*, you've got it bad.'

Cruz dismissed Ricardo's comment. He *wanted* her badly, yes, and he was happy to admit that, but he didn't *have* it bad in the way his brother was implying.

A hush fell over the bar at the same time as the skin on the back of his neck started to prickle. Then Ricardo let out a low whistle under his breath.

'*Mi, oh, mi....*'

Slowly Cruz turned his head to find Aspen framed in the open double glass doorway of the bar like something out of a 1950s Hollywood extravaganza, the silky green gown he'd bought her flowing around her slender figure like coloured water. His mouth went dry. The halterneck dress was deceptively simple at the front but so beautifully crafted it lovingly moulded to her shape exactly as it was supposed to. She'd pinned her hair up in a soft, timeless bun—which must mean she had a fair amount of skin showing, as he was pretty sure the dress dipped quite low at the back.

Okay, make that completely backless, he corrected, fighting a primitive urge to bundle her up in his arms and return her to his room. His bed.

She hadn't spotted him yet, and when a male voice called out her name Cruz watched her turn her head, the wispy tendrils of hair she had left to frame her face dancing golden beneath the halogen lighting. Her expression softened as she spied a few of his polo players lounging in the club chairs that circled a small wooden table.

She walked towards them and Cruz tried not to react, but it was impossible to stop his gut from tightening as the men watched her with unrestrained lust in their eyes.

She looked so delicate.

So sensual.

So *his*.

The need to stamp his ownership all over her took hold and he didn't bother to contain it. For right now, for tonight, she was his—and he didn't care who knew it. In fact, the more who did the better. It would save him from having to keep tabs on her during dinner, and the four European jocks already halfway to being tanked would, he knew, be the best candidates to spread the news.

As conversation once again resumed in the bar he ignored Ricardo's keen gaze and went to her.

She had her back to him and he felt her jump as his thigh lightly grazed her hip. She looked up and he bent his head, let his eyes linger on her mouth, gratified by her quick intake of breath.

If it were possible, the more time he spent with her the more time he *wanted* to spend with her. It was a sobering thought, if he'd been in the mood to care.

He cupped Aspen's elbow in his palm. 'Gentlemen, if you'll excuse us?'

Slowly each man registered Cruz's proprietorial manner, but only Tommy Hassenberger had the nerve to look disgruntled. 'Looks like I'm too late,' he complained.

'You were too late when you were born, Tommy,' one of his friends joked, making the others laugh.

Aspen grinned, said she'd catch up with them at the formal dinner, and then felt intoxicated as Cruz placed his hand on the small of her back to guide her from the room, the heat of his palm scorching her bare skin.

She hadn't known what to expect when she had entered the bar but she had decided to try and relax. To try and forget about their deal and her fears and just brave it out. Cruz had invited her to dinner—a formal event, not a date—and for all she knew that was a peace offering as well.

'You wore the dress,' he said, his gravelly voice stroking her already heightened senses.

'Yes. I couldn't not in the end. Thank you.'

'You look stunning in it.'

The look he gave her made her burn.

Aspen took in his superbly cut tuxedo. 'You look—'
Simply divine. 'Nice too,' she croaked.

He gave her a small smile. 'Aspen, I need to tell you
something.'

Cruz gazed down at the utterly stunning woman at his
side and a ball of emotion rushed through him. Seeing her
like this…having her beside him…all the animosity of the
past fell away and he just wanted to take her upstairs and
make love to her with a need that floored him.

'What is it?'

Aspen tilted her head and Cruz heard a roaring in his
ears as their eyes connected. Reality seemed suspended
and—

'Señor Rodriguez, sir, the first lot of guests are assem-
bled in the Rosa Room.'

Cruz turned towards his head waiter. 'Thank you, Paco.
I'll be along in a minute.'

'Certainly.'

The waiter inclined his head and left and Cruz lifted
Aspen's fingers to his lips. He could see her pulse racing
and his did the same.

'I wish I'd never planned this idiotic dinner.'

'It's not idiotic.' She smiled up at him, her eyes almost
on a level with his chin because she was wearing the stilettos. 'It's to welcome honoured guests to your flagship
hotel for tomorrow's tournament. It's important.'

Not half as important as what he wanted to be doing
with her upstairs right now.

His nostrils flared as he fought to control the urge to
drag her into the nearest darkened corner. On one level
he thought he should be concerned about the intensity of
his hunger for her, but on another he just couldn't bring

himself to examine it. There was something about her that sent his baser instincts off the scale.

Nothing a night of straightforward, short-term hot sex wouldn't cure.

He smiled at the thought and, with the situation once again under his control, he tucked her elegant hand in the crook of his elbow and prayed for the evening formalities to fly by.

The dinner took all night. As it was supposed to.

The first course had been Mushroom-something. Aspen couldn't remember and Cruz, possibly noticing her picking at it dubiously, had swapped it for his goat's cheese soufflé. Then there'd been the main course. Beef or chicken. This time Aspen had swapped with him when she'd seen him eyeing her steak.

He'd smiled, grazed her chin with his knuckles and then resumed talking to two well-dressed Asian men, who'd nodded with polite restraint. Now and then he'd twined his fingers with hers when she'd left her hand on the tabletop while he talked, as if it was the most natural thing in the world for him to do. As if this really was a date.

Aspen had chatted to the wife of the Mayor, who was very down to earth and full of Latin passion, and their daughter who was studying to be a doctor. They'd swapped war stories of bad essay topics, boring lecturers and horror exams and then it had been time for dessert.

She was full. Even though she'd hardly eaten a thing.

Her dinner companions excused themselves, and Aspen was just contemplating whether she should move to the other side of the table to speak with an older woman who sat on her own when Cruz slid his fingers through hers again. His hand was so much bigger than hers, his skin tone darker, the hairs on the back of his wrists absurdly attractive.

He stroked his thumb over her palm and goosebumps raced themselves up her arm.

He glanced in her direction, brought her hand briefly to his lips and then answered one of the Asian men's questions.

The Mayor's daughter returned and Cruz dropped Aspen's hand as the girl produced a photo of her horse on her phone. Aspen made polite responses, all the time disturbingly aware of the man beside her.

Something had changed between them since she'd come downstairs. He was behaving as she imagined a man in love would behave. Little intimate glances, tucking her hair behind her ear, pouring her water, holding her hand...

Chad had seemed nice in the beginning too. Wooing her. Treating her lovingly. Somehow it had all come unstuck the year Cruz had left and her grandfather had been too sick to send the team to England. Chad had been unable to get a permanent ride that year and had started drinking more. By the time their wedding had rolled around she'd barely recognised him as the man who had courted her and treated her so deferentially. He'd moved back home when his father had threatened to halve his trust fund, and his father had used the opportunity to encourage Chad to get a real job. Aspen had tried to smooth things over but that had only seemed to make him resentful.

On their wedding night— No, she didn't want to remember that.

She glanced at Cruz to find him deep in conversation. Would he be rough? She swallowed, her gaze drawn to his hands, wrapped around a wine glass. He stroked the slender stem with the pad of his thumb. Aspen recalled how he had stroked her lips the same way and heat erupted low in her belly. For a man with such size and strength he had been gentle. Suddenly his thumb stopped moving and Aspen felt the air between them shift even before her eyes connected with his.

Her mouth dried and her heart thumped. Fear and desire commingled until she felt emotionally wrung out.

'Aspen?'

She glanced up but didn't really see him.

'Everything okay?'

Oh, God, that deep, sensual voice so close to her ear. She couldn't help it. She trembled. Then pulled herself together.

'Fine.' *Just me being a nincompoop.*

Nincompoop? Her mother had used that word when she'd been laughing at herself.

A wave of sadness overtook her and immediately made her think of Ocean Haven. Her horses. Her mother. Aspen had gained wealth by moving in with her grandfather but not love, and certainly not security.

Cruz moved his hand to the back of her chair. 'You look miles away.'

A wave of panic washed through her and she made the mistake of glancing up at him.

As soon as their eyes met his sharpened with concern. 'Hey, what's wrong?'

'Nothing.' She forced a smile. 'I just need to go to the bathroom.'

He scanned her face but thankfully didn't push her. 'Don't be long. We'll go when you get back.'

Oh, help.

She got up, stumbled and snagged the tablecloth with her leg. Cruz leaned over and held it while she straightened up. The deliciously sexy gown he had bought her swayed around her body and settled. She felt his eyes on her as she started to walk away, the dress floating around her legs as light as butterfly wings. Of course that was nothing compared to the butterflies using her belly as a trampoline.

Once in the bathroom she told herself to calm down and splashed cold water on her wrists, dabbed it on her cheeks. She checked her make-up, shocked to see her face so flushed. It was because every time he touched her she thought of sex.

A woman smiled at her in the mirror and Aspen dropped her gaze lest the woman accurately read her mind. Then she realised how rude that was and raised her eyes only to find the person had gone.

She let out a shaky laugh at her absurd behaviour. She felt like… She felt like… She frowned. She couldn't remember ever feeling this nervous.

Well, maybe she could. On her wedding day. She'd had a similar fluttering feeling in her stomach then that had turned out to be a bad omen.

She stared at herself. Fear knotted her insides. She couldn't do this. Her eyes looked like two huge dots in her face. She just couldn't do it. She was so anxious she'd probably throw up all over him.

An older woman entered the bathroom and Aspen pretended to be wiping her hands.

She'd have to tell Cruz.

Would it mean she'd still get the money if she backed out?

Oh, who cares about the money? This was no longer about the money. This was now about self-preservation. This was about going back to the wonderful, predictable life that she loved.

Yes, but there won't be that life if you don't go through with this.

She'd backed herself into a corner and the only way out was through Cruz. A man who, for all his surface arrogance, genuinely cared about his family and was smart. And also ruthless. He would chew her up and spit her out without a backward glance if she let him.

'Let's not forget why you're here, Aspen,' she told her reflection softly.

He was pitting himself against her for Ocean Haven. Her farm. She should hate him for that alone but she didn't, she realised. She didn't hate him at all. Because she had come to understand him a little better. Understand what he had thought of her. What had shaped him as a boy. What had shaped him as a man.

How did you hate someone you instinctively sensed was good underneath? And what did that even matter?

Shaking her head at her reflection, she refastened a few loosened strands of hair and wondered where all her positive self-talk had run off to.

Maybe down the toilet.

She smiled at her lame attempt at humour and nearly walked straight into Cruz where he leant against the wall opposite the ladies' room.

'You were taking so long I got worried. I was just about to go in but I didn't want to surprise you.'

'I would have been okay.' She let out a shaky breath. 'It's the old lady in the cubicle you might have had some trouble with.'

Cruz laughed and it broke the tension. He held out his hand. 'Shall we go?'

She looked at his perfect, handsome face. Then his hand, palm up. He was strong, maybe stronger than Chad, but he wasn't nasty. Even when he'd thought she had done him wrong he still hadn't picked on her the way Chad would have done. No, Cruz was arrogant and controlling, but he was honest and straight down the line. A straight arrow. Black and white. No shades of grey.

'Aspen?'

She saw hunger and desire in his eyes and it made her feel hot all over. Maybe she could do this. *Maybe.*

She glanced at his hand, wondered if she was as crazy as her uncle had suggested and placed hers in it.

He smiled.

She swallowed.

It wasn't until they were halfway across the foyer that she saw a familiar figure—a man—leaning against the reception desk. He had his back to her, so she couldn't see his face, but he was average height with blond hair and a slightly stocky bodybuilder's physique.

Chad?

Cruz pressed the lift button and Aspen's attention was momentarily snagged by their reflection in the gold-finished doors. They looked good together, she thought. He was tall and broad, and she looked feminine and almost otherworldly in the beautiful green dress.

His eyes met hers and she couldn't look away.

Then the lift doors opened. Aspen snuck another quick glance over her shoulder but the man she had spotted wasn't there. She let out a relieved breath. After their last acrimonious argument Chad had kept to his own part of the world and she to hers.

Still, she stabbed repeatedly at the penthouse button and only realised how questionable her behaviour looked when she noticed Cruz's bemused expression and realised he hadn't swiped his security tag across the electronic panel.

His eyebrows rose and Aspen's gaze dropped to the space between their feet, her heart beating too fast. Seeing the man who might or might not have been her ex-husband had been terrible timing. Just when she'd begun to think maybe her night with Cruz would be all right it was as if the powers that be had sent her a message to take care.

To remind her that being in a man's control was when a woman was at her most vulnerable.

As the lift ascended Cruz pushed away from the mirror-panelled wall and invaded her space, startling her out of her dark reverie when he placed his warm hands either side of her waist.

'Okay, talk to me. You're as nervous as a pony facing the bridle for the first time. The same as you were last night.'

Aspen gave a low laugh at his analogy and jumped when his thumbs stroked her hip bones through the dress. She couldn't tell him she thought she'd just seen Chad. That would raise a whole host of questions that she did not want to answer. And what if she was wrong? Then she'd just look stupid. Or paranoid.

'I'm fine.'

'You're shaking.'

Was she?

He gave her a look. 'Is it the deal? Because—'

'It's not the deal. Actually I'd forgotten all about that again.'

Her answer seemed to please him but she didn't have time to consider his satisfied—'Good.'—because the lift doors opened.

When he'd released her he placed his hand on the small of her back as he ushered her through to the living room. The housekeeper had been and the room was cast with shadows by the floor lamps that had been switched on for their convenience.

'Do you want a drink?'

'Yes, please.'

She'd said that too loudly and his eyes narrowed.

'Of…?'

Aspen forced a smile. 'Gin and tonic.' She winced. She hated gin and tonic.

She wandered over to the wall to study one of the paintings she'd admired the evening before but never taken the time to look at. An overhead light outlined it perfectly and she gasped.

'That's a Renoir.'

'I know.'

He was right behind her and she heard the tinkle of ice as he handed her the drink she didn't want.

'You're not having one?'

'No.' He perched on the arm of a nearby sofa, watching her. 'Something wrong with it?'

'What?'

He motioned patiently towards the highball in her hand. 'Your drink?'

'No. It's fine. At least, I'm sure it's fine.' It was all about maintaining control. If she did that she could get through this. 'Look, maybe we should just…start.'

'Start?'

Aspen could have kicked herself, and she moved towards a side table so she could let out a discreet breath and put the drink down. She knew he hadn't taken his eyes off her and she told herself that he wanted her. She'd felt how aroused he had been last night, and again in the stable that day. He had felt huge!

So why had he stopped? Was he struggling to maintain an erection with her as Chad had done? She shuddered. On those occasions Chad had been particularly vile.

Cruz tilted his head and looked as if he was about to say something, and then he changed his mind. Instead he uncurled his large frame and came towards her until he practically loomed over her. Then he reached for her hair.

She didn't mean to do it, of course, but she flinched and his hand stilled. 'I'm just going to take your hair down.'

She stared at his chest and tried to slow her heartbeat.

'Is that okay?'

She nodded, not trusting herself to speak.

'Turn around.'

It took all of her willpower to give him that modicum of control, but when she did turn around he stroked her shoulders.

'You have a beautiful back. Lean and supple. Strong.'

He kneaded the bunched muscles either side of her neck and her involuntary sigh of pleasure filled the quiet room.

'That feels so good. I know I must be really tight.'

Cruz groaned inwardly, knowing she hadn't meant that comment the way his depraved mind had interpreted it. Yes, she did feel tight. Too tight. Too nervous.

He wanted to ask her what was wrong, but she moaned softly and her head lolled on the graceful stem of her neck and the question died in his throat.

All through dinner he'd imagined doing this. Touching her, tasting her. He'd been harder than stone all night and he wasn't sure if he'd committed to five hotels in China or fifty. Nor did he care. Right now he'd put a hundred on Mars if someone asked him to.

Aspen moaned again and shifted beneath his pressing thumbs.

'Harder or softer?' he asked, the rough timbre of his voice reflecting his deep arousal.

He heard her breath catch, and then his did as well as her gorgeous bottom brushed his fly.

'Harder,' she whispered, and a shudder ripped through him.

The musky perfume of her skin was ambrosia to his senses and he trailed soft kisses across her shoulders. Her head fell forward and she braced her hands on the side table in front of her. Cruz registered her position on a purely primal level and knew all he'd have to do was lift that long silk skirt, tear whatever excuse for a pair of panties she was hiding underneath, bend her a little more forward and slide right into her—and he very nearly did.

But he wanted more of her taste in his mouth first, and with unsteady hands he gripped the side of her waist and trailed tiny moist kisses down the column of her spine until he reached the small of her back.

She undulated for him, arching backwards, and unable to hold himself back any longer he rose, spun her around to face him and slanted his mouth across hers. Not softly, as he had done earlier in the stables—he was too far gone for that—but hard, with barely leashed power and a deep driving hunger to be inside her.

She opened for him instantly, her fingers impatient as they delved into his hair to anchor him to her. That was okay with him. He barely noticed the bite of her short nails, concentrating instead on the throbbing sense of satisfaction as his tongue filled her mouth. He tasted coffee and cream and couldn't suppress a groan.

Somehow some of her earlier hesitation seeped into the minute part of his brain that still functioned on an intellectual level and he attempted to steady himself—before he just dragged her to the floor and had done with it.

Then her tongue stroked his and his mind gave out. Sensation hot and strong coursed through him, just as it had every other time he'd kissed her, and he couldn't help curving her closer so that they touched everywhere.

The silky fabric of her dress slid against his jacket in an erotic parody of skin on skin. Which was what he wanted. What he needed. And, keeping his mouth firmly on hers, he shucked out of it and then lashed at the buttons on his shirt.

She moaned, her warm hands pushing the fabric off his body as she shaped his arms and his shoulders before clinging once more around his neck.

Cruz reached behind her neck. His fingers felt clumsy in his desperation as he finally managed to undo the two pearl-like buttons that held the top of the dress together.

Aroused to an unbearable pitch, he smoothed a hand down to the small of her back, his lips cruising along her jawline until he could tug on the lobe of her ear. She was wearing tiny gold studs and he tongued one as he bit down gently on her flesh and brought his hands around to cradle both breasts in the palms of his hands. She trembled delightfully and her responsiveness rocked him to his core.

His thumb caught her nipple and she cried out, gripping him tighter. Cruz knew that neither of them was going to make it to the bedroom so he didn't even try. Instead he lifted her onto the side table and hoped it would hold.

It did, and he pulled back and looked down at her.

Her nipples pebbled enticingly beneath his lingering gaze and he plumped one breast up. 'You're so beautiful,' he breathed, taking the rosy tip into his mouth.

Arousal beat through his body, hot and insistent, and he urged her thighs wider so that he could settle his erection between her legs. Unfortunately the table wasn't high enough for him to take her on it and he knew he'd have to lift her onto him when the time came.

'Thank heavens you're wearing a dress,' he growled around her tight, wet nipple, his impatient hands delving beneath the reams of fabric to find her.

Moments later he felt her panic in the stiffening of her thighs and the press of her fingernails on his shoulders.

'Wait!'

His blurred mind tried to take in the change and he mentally pulled back.

'We might need some lubricant,' she blurted out against his neck.

Lubricant?

Cruz stilled, and was struck by how slight and vulnerable her body felt compared to his much larger frame curved over her. Instantly his libido cooled as he recalled those times she had flinched away from him when he'd reached for her. He frowned. Had she *never* experienced pleasure during sex?

He brought one hand up between them to cup her jaw and brought her eyes to his. 'Aspen, what's wrong?'

'I'm just…' She licked her lips, her mortified gaze flitting sideways. 'I don't have much natural lubrication. I should have told you earlier.'

Stunned, Cruz could only stare at her. He could tell she was serious but he had briefly felt her moist heat through her panties and knew she needed extra lubrication the way Ireland needed rain.

As if taking his prolonged silence as a rejection, she shoved his chest hard enough to dislodge him and desperately scooted off the table.

Only her stilettos must have come off when he'd lifted her because her feet tangled in the fabric of her dress and she pitched forward.

Cursing, Cruz grabbed hold of her before she fell. 'Aspen, wait.'

'No. Let me go.'

Ignoring her attempts to break free, he gently tugged her back into his embrace. She immediately buried her head against his neck and he brought one hand up to stroke her hair. His heart thundered in his chest as his dazed mind tried to process what was happening.

He waited until he felt her breathing start to even out and then he leaned back so he could look at her face.

'Who told you that you didn't have any natural lubrication?'

She groaned and burrowed even more fully against him.

Cruz cupped her nape soothingly. 'I know you're embarrassed. Was it Anderson?'

'It happens to some women.'

Cruz had no doubt she was correct, but he had already felt how damp she was through her lace panties and, whatever problems she had, he very much doubted this was one of them.

'I'm sure it does *chiquita*, but it hasn't happened to you.'

She pulled back. 'You're wrong. Chad and I... Can we not talk about this?'

He was going to kill the moron.

Cruz nudged her chin up until her baleful glare met his. He nearly smiled at her thorny gaze but this was too serious. 'Did he hurt you?'

She wet her lips, dropped her eyes.

'Aspen?'

'Oh, all right.' She sighed. 'On our wedding night Chad was... I was anxious. Chad had been drinking heavily and I knew I had made a mistake. Actually, I knew I'd made a mistake even before the wedding, but it became bigger than I was and I didn't know how to stop it. And Chad could be charming.' She gave an empty laugh. 'You might not know that, being a man, but my friends thought he was wonderful. But the alcohol changed him and that night...' She swallowed. 'That night...'

'He raped you,' he said flatly.

'No. It was my fault. I was nervous.'

Cruz barely held himself in check. 'Do *not* blame yourself.' He guided her eyes back up to look at him. 'He would have known that you were nervous.' He cursed under his breath. 'Hell, Aspen. You were all of eighteen.'

She gave him a wobbly smile and Cruz enfolded her in his arms. He held her until he felt her trembling subside.

'He didn't mean to, Cruz. It just wasn't easy.'

Uh-huh. When he did kill him he'd do it slowly.

'It's fine. I knew this would happen anyway. You can let me go.'

Let her go?

She tried to pull away, and when he looked at her she had that same resigned look on her face that she'd had the previous night.

'When I first arrived at Ocean Haven to work for your grandfather,' he began tentatively, 'I missed my family so much I cried myself to sleep every night for a month and I felt pathetic. You were right yesterday when you said it was a lot for a kid to take on. At the time, though, I thought I just needed to man up.'

'Oh, Cruz.'

Her hand curled around his forearm, and even though he knew he was sharing the memory with her to take her mind off her own past part of him still soaked up the comfort of her touch.

'I thought my mother was turning her back on me. That I was an embarrassment to the family.'

'No.' Aspen shook her head fiercely. 'I only met her yesterday but I *know* that can't be true.'

'Probably not. And what Anderson told you isn't true either.' When her eyes fell to the side Cruz tipped her chin up. 'Aspen, you're a beautiful, sensual woman and I want to prove that to you if you'll let me.'

She frowned. 'I don't see how.'

He cupped her face in his hands, halting her words. 'I want you, Aspen. I want to kiss you and touch you and make love to you until all you can think about is how good you feel. The question is, do *you* want that to happen?'

The question might also be what the hell was he talking about? It was one thing to make a woman feel good in bed. It was quite another to want to slay her demons for her.

Ignoring the fact that he had never donned the white knight suit before, and what that meant, Cruz waited for her answer.

And waited.

Finally, still clutching her dress to her chest, her eyes wide and luminous in the over-bright room, she nodded. 'I think so.'

'Then relax and let me take care of you. And, Aspen…?' He waited for her to look at him from beneath the fringe of her dark lashes. 'If you want me to stop at any time, then we'll stop. Understand?'

She paused and her green eyes opened a little wider. 'You'd really do that, wouldn't you?'

For a brief moment Cruz savoured all the ways he would break every bone in Chad Anderson's body, starting with his pompous head and working his way down.

'In a heartbeat, *mi chiquita*. No questions asked.'

CHAPTER NINE

ASPEN BREATHED IN Cruz's warm, musky scent as he carried her to his bedroom and told herself to relax. But it was impossible. She was too embarrassed. Her old panic had returned full force when she'd felt Cruz's warm hand slide between her thighs and now she clung to his neck like a spider monkey as he laid her on the bed.

'Aspen?'

The bedcover was cool at her back and his naked chest was hot at her front as he tried to prise her hands from around his neck. In her earlier fantasies about sex it was romantic and sensual. Dreamy and wonderful. Hot and desperate. This felt awkward and tense.

She didn't look at him as he turned onto his side, visualising how gauche she must appear, with her hair spread out around her and her body partially exposed, with the bodice of her dress undone and metres of silk twisted up around her waist. Keeping her eyes scrunched tight, she adjusted the skirt down her legs.

'Can you turn out the light?' She could feel it burning holes in her retinas even though her eyes were clamped shut.

'I will if it makes you more comfortable, but I won't be able to see you if I do that.'

'That would be the general idea.'

'Open your eyes, *gatita*.'

'Is it a prerequisite?'

His low chuckle had her squinting up at him. He looked lazy and indolent with his head propped in his hands, his gaze extremely male and hot as it met hers. Well, clearly only one of them was feeling awkward and tense.

'You're very comfortable with this, aren't you?'

'You will be too, very soon,' he promised. 'More than comfortable.'

He brought his hand up to her face and started drawing lazy patterns with his finger over her cheeks and nose and down the side of her neck to her collarbone. It wasn't easy for her to give him control, but Aspen lay as still as a stone, slowly recognising that her skin was tingling with a pleasant sensation and that goosebumps had risen up along her upper arms.

'How much pleasure have you actually had during sex, *mi chiquita*?'

She swallowed and would have turned from him then, but his magical finger edged along the loose side of her dress and feathered across her nipple. She sucked in a shallow breath, letting it out on a rush. 'Not much,' she answered honestly. *None* seemed too big an admission to make.

'Mmm...' Cruz ducked his head to her shoulder and trailed a line of kisses to the sensitive curve of her neck. 'Then we'll have to change all that. I am now taking it as my personal mission to teach you about pleasure.'

He shifted closer so that she could feel the heat of his body burn into the side of hers.

'Nothing but pleasure.'

He looked at her as if he wanted to devour her. As if he couldn't think of anything else but her. The thought frightened her, because her desire for him had grown exponentially over the course of a couple of days and she didn't know how that had happened.

He had invaded her thoughts and her dreams and seemed to make a mockery of her declaration that she would never again be at any man's mercy. Because here she was, lying nearly naked on his bed and feeling way out of her depth. And yet as scary as that thought was, as she looked at him like this, his face half in shadow from the bedside lamp, he looked amazing. His strong features and wide shoulders promised to fulfil all of her hidden desires and she felt utterly and completely safe with him, she realised with astonishment. Something she would have said she would never feel again in a man's arms.

Warmth returned deep inside her. Warmth and a sense of wonder that made her feel hot and restless. Her gaze fell to where her hands rested on his gorgeous chest and then she slowly returned her eyes to his. The look in his was both tender and hungry and it made her insides melt.

Reaching up, she stroked the sexy stubble already lining his jaw. 'Make love to me, Cruz. Please.'

As if he'd been waiting for her to say those exact words he took one of her hands and brought her palm to his lips. His answer, 'It will be my pleasure...' rumbled through his chest and arrowed straight into her heart.

His next kiss was hot and deep and sensation swamped her, sending sparks of excitement everywhere, cutting off her ability to think. Her inhibitions and worries seemed to be caught up with some primal desire and this time desire won out.

There was just no room to consider anything other than Cruz's big hands on her body, stroking her, adoring her. His whispered words of encouragement as he discarded her dress and moved her tiny thong down her thighs raised her level of anticipation to an unbearable pitch.

Within seconds she was naked beneath him and his mouth was tracking a path to her breast. Aspen held still, already anticipating the heady pleasure his mouth would bring. And she wasn't disappointed. Cruz drew the tight bud gently into his mouth, licked, circled, nipped and did things to her nipple that were surely illegal. Aspen felt dizzy and her hazy mind didn't even register when his hand slid over the outside of her thighs. Then every neuron in her brain tightened and focused as she felt his hand drift inwards.

'Still with me, *chiquita*?' he asked, blowing warm air across her moist breast.

'Yes, oh, yes.' She curled her hands around the defined muscles in his shoulders. 'But you're still partially dressed.'

'Not for long,' he assured her. 'But let's take care of something first.' He gently pressed her upper body back down on the bed. 'Lie back, *gatita*. This is all for you.'

Aspen complied, but she still tensed when his hand returned to her closed thighs. She half expected him to open them and maybe move over the top of her, to push himself inside her. What she didn't expect was that he would bend one of her knees up and start stroking her leg as one might a domestic cat. Or a startled horse.

And then she couldn't think at all, because he brought his mouth back to her breast and laved the tip with his tongue. She pressed closer, husky little sounds urging him on, and her lower body clenched unbearably with every tug of his lips on her nipple. Then his hand started circling higher on her leg. Slowly. So slowly it was sheer torture. She couldn't stop herself from restlessly trying to turn towards him. She needed weight, she realised, and pressure.

'Patience, *chiquita*,' he implored, his breathing heavy.

'I don't have any,' she groaned, and then gasped as his fingers lightly grazed over the curls between her legs before circling her belly and dipping down again, this time lingering a little longer and pressing a little lower.

Unbelievably Aspen shifted her legs a little wider of her

own accord and knew in that moment that she truly wanted this to happen. That she wanted more. That she wanted all of him. Inside her. Her fear of disappointing him, of failing, of him hurting her was completely eradicated as need spiralled through her and drove everything else out of her mind. If it didn't work out she no longer cared. She just needed *something*. Him!

She waited breathlessly as his finger ran along the seam between her legs again, only to exhale as it continued moving up to link with one of hers.

'Cruz, please...' She curled her free hand around his neck and dragged his mouth back to hers.

'You want me to touch you, *chiquita*?' he said against her lips.

'You know I do.' Then she had a horrid thought. 'Don't you want to?'

He stilled and held her gaze as he brought the hand he held down to the front of his pants. He was huge. That was Aspen's first thought. And her second was that she wanted to see him, touch him.

'Never doubt it,' he said fiercely. 'Never.'

His kiss was hard and hungry and then he wrenched his mouth from hers.

'But I'm trying to go slow. Make sure you're totally ready for me.' He took her hand in his again, linking his fingers over the back of hers. 'And I have something to show you.'

He laid her hand palm-down on her belly and then slowly guided her hand over her silky curls.

'Open your legs wider, *chiquita*,' he murmured beside her ear. 'No. More. Yes, like that...'

And then he directed her hand even lower until, with a gasp, Aspen felt herself as she never had before.

'Oh, my God—that feels...'

'Wet?'

Cruz ran the tip of his tongue around the whorl of her ear and she nearly came off the bed.

He pressed her hand downwards. 'Silky? Sexy?'

Yes!

Lost in a maelstrom of sensation, Aspen closed her eyes and let her feelings take over. She didn't know what to focus on as her fingers slipped over her body, making her want to press upwards.

'And now…' Cruz shifted until he lay on his stomach between her splayed legs, his olive skin dark against the cream bedcovers. 'Now I'm going to taste you.'

Aspen tried to close her legs in a hurry. 'Cruz, you can't.'

He looked up, the skin on his face tight as he held his hands still on her open thighs.

'Let me, Aspen. Remember? I promised you nothing but pleasure.'

Tensing just a little, she let him move her legs wider again and closed her eyes as he dipped down and opened her with his skilled tongue.

She'd heard of men doing this, of course. She had been to an all-girls school, and she knew that some girls liked it and some didn't. She had always put herself in the latter camp. Cruz's low groans of pleasure as he licked and lapped at her sensitive flesh shifted her firmly to the former.

She thought maybe he asked if she was okay, but by that stage he had brought his fingers into play and Aspen couldn't breathe, let alone answer. Her whole body was burning and intensely focused on something that seemed just out of reach. She writhed and twisted beneath him, delighting in the scrape of his stubble against her tender skin, not even registering that she was calling his name until he moved over her.

'It's okay, *chiquita*. Let go.'

Let go? Of what?

And then it happened. Somehow the gentle stroking of his fingers sped up and they moved in such a way that she felt something inside her shift. Within seconds her body had exploded into a thousand tiny pieces.

Distantly she was aware that he had moved down her body again, but she was in such a blissful state of completion she felt as if she was floating.

'Aspen, open your eyes.'

Were her eyes closed again?

Opening them, she saw Cruz watching her.

'How was that?'

She smiled. 'That was the most exquisitely pleasurable experience of my whole life.'

'And I'm just getting started,' he drawled arrogantly.

Aspen laughed, and then her breath caught as he rose over her with latent male grace; his powerful biceps bunched as he completely covered her and took her mouth with his again.

She felt the heavy weight of his erection against her stomach and unbelievably her lower body clenched, needing pressure again. She squirmed upwards, opening her legs automatically.

Groaning, Cruz rolled off her, yanked his pants off in a rustle of fabric and reached into the side drawer for a condom. She watched, completely motionless, as he tore the wrapper apart with his teeth and then held his hard length with one hand while he applied it.

'You keep looking at me like that, *mi gatita*, and I'll have no need for protection,' he husked, his gravelly voice rolling straight to her pelvis.

Aspen felt herself blush, but she didn't look away. He was too mesmerising. Too…

'Beautiful,' she said. 'You're beautiful.'

She ran her hand over his tanned back, briefly marvelling at the smooth heated texture of his skin and the way he trembled beneath her touch. Had *she* done that? Her eyes flew to his and she noticed the sheen of perspiration lining his forehead.

A smile of abject female joy slowly crossed her face. He saw it and groaned. Captured her mouth with his and pushed her onto her back, coming over the top of her in a position of pure male dominance. For once it didn't scare her. Because in that moment she felt a sense of feminine power she'd never known she had. And it was exhilarating. Drugging. *Freeing*.

'Hook your legs around my waist,' he instructed gruffly.

She did, and immediately felt the smooth rounded head of his penis at her entrance. Totally caught up in the wonder of it, she dug her hands into the small of his back as she pulled him closer.

He hesitated and for a moment her old fear returned, her nerves tightening in anticipation of possible pain, and then he nudged her so sweetly her breath rushed out on a sob. She clasped his head and brought his mouth down to hers, tears burning the backs of her eyes as he slowly eased inside her body.

She easily accommodated him at first, but then she did feel too full. Too stretched.

'Relax, *amada*,' he crooned against her lips. 'I've got you.'

He kissed her hungrily and withdrew almost all the way, before slowly pushing forward again, his tongue filling her mouth and mimicking his lower body's movements until Aspen felt as if she was melting into the bed.

He raised his face above hers and he looked intense. Focused. 'You feel amazing.'

He adjusted his weight and Aspen moaned, arching towards him.

'But you're so tight. I feel like I'm hurting you.'

'No.' She flexed her hips and rubbed against him, gasping as she felt him lodge deeper. 'It feels sensational. *You* feel sensational.'

Cruz groaned and seemed to praise God as he started moving inside her, his strokes smooth and slow before gradually picking up pace. Every time his big body pushed into hers Aspen clung harder to his damp shoulders, her body growing tighter and tighter until with a sudden pause she felt another rush of liquid heat, right before her body convulsed into a paroxysm of pleasure.

Dimly she was aware of Cruz still moving inside her, of her pleasure being completely controlled by the powerful movements of his. And it was endless as he drove into her, over and over and over, until with a pause of his own he tilted her bottom and surged into her with controlled power. Once, twice more, until she cried out and felt him rear his head back and fall over the edge with her.

Again time seemed endless as Aspen stared at the ceiling, slowly coming back into her body. She felt wonderful. Blissfully, sinfully wonderful. Her body was a sweaty, sensual mass of completion. Her hand lifted to Cruz's hair and she caressed the silky strands, enjoying his harsh breaths sawing in and out against her neck.

A smile curved her mouth as she recalled the moment Cruz had guided her hand between her legs so she could feel how wet she was. And she had been. Unbelievably wet—and soft. It had been like touching somebody else's body.

Unbidden, Chad's drunken taunts came to mind and she realised that it had been he who was unable to perform, not her. Deep down, and in moments of total confidence, she had told herself that exact thing, but believing it to be true was something else entirely. Especially when he was such a gregarious and charming person when he wasn't drinking. He was like a Jekyll and Hyde character, she realised, but after tonight what had happened in the bedroom with him would never haunt her again. She wouldn't let it.

Hours later Cruz woke and used the remote console beside his bed to open the curtains. The sky was pale blue outside so he knew it wasn't much after dawn.

Slightly disturbed by the whirring sound of the drapes, Aspen snuggled deeper beneath the covers he'd pulled over them both some time during the night.

Cruz's arm tightened around her shoulders. Last night had blown his mind. First finding out that Aspen had clearly had a poor excuse of a sex-life before him, and second, realising that *he* had had a poor excuse of a sex-life before her. Hell, he'd never come so hard or so often as he had last night, and he was half expecting to be rubbed raw.

He glanced at her delicate features softened by sleep. Her rosy cheeks and the dark sweep of her lashes. He grew hard just thinking about last night.

One night.

He frowned as their deal slid back into his mind like an insidious serpent. Her damned document. At the time one night had seemed like more than enough. He'd thought she was a vacuous princess type he had once lusted after and needed to get out of his system. He'd thought he'd take her to bed, slake his lust for her and move on.

Of course he'd still move on, but...

He thought about the hotel he'd planned to build on Ocean Haven. Last night he'd given up on that plan and, surprisingly, he didn't care. Aspen had been as much a victim of Charles Carmichael's warped ideas about what was right and wrong as he had been—maybe more so.

And the truth was he didn't need Ocean Haven and she did. Ergo, she should have it. Which seemed to be what her uncle thought as well, because he was still obstinately refusing Lauren's increasing offers on Cruz's behalf. He smiled. Stubborn old goat—he might not be as sanctimonious as his old man, but he'd inherited that attribute from him, all right.

And good for him—because as soon as Cruz got up he would tell Lauren to pull out of that particular race. Aspen had won and for once he didn't mind losing. One day he'd share that with Ricardo. Have a laugh. One day when he understood it better.

But for now he had to face facts.

Fact one: Aspen would want to return to Ocean Haven some time soon. Fact two: he was supposed to be flying to China to check out the site of the first of his—what was it?—fifty new hotels first thing tomorrow. Fact three…

Fact three was that he wanted neither of those things to happen. Fact four was that he didn't know why that was, and fact five was that she felt divine curled up against his side. Fact six was that he was definitely going crazy because he was yapping to himself again.

His throat felt as if he had a collar and tie around it.

Previously, making sure that he was rolling in money had been all that he could think about. He'd put his polo career on hold indefinitely to achieve it. After he'd left Ocean Haven he could have picked up any number of wealthy patrons who would have happily paid any fee to have him play for them, but he would still have been at their beck and call. Still disposable. Still an outsider in a world of rank and privilege. So he'd worked hard to change that. And, although many might say he had now achieved his goal, pride—or maybe that old sense of being vulnerable—drove him onwards.

But was it enough now? Hadn't he started to question how much satisfaction he actually derived from pushing himself so hard? Hadn't that old feeling of wanting a family started poking into his mind again? Wasn't that one of the reasons he'd tried not to visit his own family? And here was fact seven: he hated that feeling of being the one left out. Maybe Aspen was right about that. Maybe if he became more human around his family they might be the same with him.

Madre de Dio.

He was doing it again.

Cruz closed his eyes and let himself absorb the slender length of the woman who was pleasantly draped over his side like a human rug. Gently, so as not to disturb her, he stroked her hair. She shifted and the rustle of the sheets carried her scent to his nose. She smelled good. Superb.

His mind conjured up how she had looked last night, spread out beneath him while he made her come with his mouth. His body hardened and he had to bite back a groan. He wasn't sure he could do it again, and he was damned sure she was probably too sore, but his body had other ideas.

Trying to stanch the completely normal reaction of his body to the closeness of a naked woman, Cruz carefully extricated himself from under Aspen's warm body. Better he get up now, have a shower and start the day. It was going to be a busy one. First a round of meetings to finalise what he hadn't done yesterday, and then the polo matches would start just before lunch and run till the afternoon.

He would have made it too—except Aspen chose that moment to move again and attached herself to him like scaffolding on a building site. She moaned and smoothed her hand over his chest.

Cruz had closed his eyes, his senses completely focused on the southerly trajectory of her hand, when she suddenly snatched it back.

'I'm sorry. I…' She sat up and pushed the tangled mass of curls back from her face.

Fact eight: she looked adorable when she woke up. All

soft and pink, with her lips still swollen from where they had ravaged each other.

Unable to help himself, he dropped his eyes to her chest and she gave a small squeak, quickly dragging the sheet up over her nakedness. But not before he'd had a good glimpse of creamy breasts that wore grazes from his beard growth.

For some reason her obvious distress eradicated his own desire to put as much distance between them as possible. Which was surprising when he recalled how he had opened up about his childhood last night. That alone should have had him eating dust. But her loser ex had done her a disservice when it came to intimacy, and Cruz wasn't about to make that worse because he had itchy feet.

'Good morning.'

She turned wild eyes up at him. Dampened her lips. 'Good morning.'

Silence lengthened between them and Cruz realised he had no idea what to say. This was the equivalent of a one-night stand and, while he'd never had what could be considered a long-term relationship, he didn't indulge in one-night stands either.

'This is—'

'Awkward?'

She let out a shaky breath. 'Yes, but last night was…'

'Wonderful.'

She pulled a pained face. 'You don't have to say that. I mean yes, it was good, great for me but…oh, never mind.'

Cruz felt a well of rage at Anderson for hurting her. He wanted to reassure her that he was actually being honest, but he suspected she'd see his words as hollow.

'Spend the day,' he found himself saying instead.

'Why?' Her shocked eyes flew to his and he made sure his own surprise at his invitation didn't show on his face. But why shouldn't she spend the day? He had a first-rate polo tournament starting in a few hours. She loved polo. She ran a horse stud.

'I thought you were busy today?' she said.

'I am.' Her reserved response had him putting the brakes on the surge of pleasure he'd experienced at the thought of her staying with him. 'But there's plenty for you to stay for. The polo, for one. It's going to be an incredible event.'

She gave him a wan smile that made his teeth want to grind together. 'I don't want to complicate things.'

Confused by his own reaction to her reticence, he took refuge in annoyance. 'And how is watching a polo tournament complicating things?'

'Our deal—'

'Forget the deal.' He got out of bed. 'Stay because you want to. Stay because the sun is shining and because there's going to be a world-class polo tournament here that's sold out to the general public. Stay because you work too hard and you need a break.'

'Well, when you put it like that...'

Torn between wanting to kiss her and sending her home, Cruz nearly rescinded his offer when the cell phone on his bedside table rang.

They both looked at it.

'What's your decision?'

She dampened her lips. 'Yes, okay, I'd like to watch the polo.'

Aspen stood on the penthouse balcony and stared out over the shiny green polo field. Horse floats, white marquees, riders, grooms, horse-owners and hotel employees scurried about as they readied themselves for the day ahead.

Yet despite the heady anticipation in the air that preceded a major event all Aspen could think about was what she was still doing here.

Replaying their awkward morning-after conversation in her head, she cringed. When Cruz had first asked her to stay Aspen had felt her heart jump in her chest at the thought of spending the day with him. Then he'd confirmed that he'd be busy and she'd felt like an idiot. Of course he was busy. He had invited her to watch the polo, not to spend the day with *him*.

When his phone had rung she had automatically said yes because he'd looked beautiful and sleep-tousled and she hadn't wanted to leave.

Now she didn't think she could leave fast enough.

Because last night had changed her. She felt it deep within her bones. Last night had been everything she'd ever dreamed making love could be, because Cruz had taken the time to make it that way for her and she could already feel herself wanting to make more out of it than it was. Wanting to make it special, somehow. But what woman *wouldn't* want to do that when she'd just been so completely loved by a man like Cruz Rodriguez?

No, not loved, she quickly amended. Pleasured.

God.

She buried her forehead against her arms, which were resting on the balustrading.

It was beyond clear that Cruz had asked her to stay out of politeness or—worse—pity. She, of course, had said yes out of desire. Desire to spend more time with him. Desire to experience his lovemaking again. Desire to re-experience the pleasure she felt sure only he could give her.

But he was as much of a Jekyll and Hyde character as Chad when it came down to it, because he had come to Ocean Haven specifically to try and take her farm.

She had forgotten that. *Again.*

Was she a glutton for punishment? Was she so used to having men control her that she'd gladly fall in with the plans of another self-interested, power-hungry male?

Because while Cruz might have shown her the best night of her life, it didn't change the reality of why she was even here.

'Forget the deal,' he'd all but snarled.

Last night she had. This morning it was impossible to do so in the cold light of day.

Or course last night she had been in the grip of a wonderful sense of feminine power with Cruz that could easily become addictive if she let it. A smile curved her lips, only to fade away just as quickly. Cruz had freed her from years of feeling as if there was something wrong with her and she'd be forever indebted to him for that. He was also trying to buy her home out from under her, and that was like a sore that wouldn't heal. If she stayed today it would be for the wrong reasons. It would be because she was hoping for more from him. Something she didn't want from any man. Did she?

Aspen groaned. How could she even think about staying longer under the shade of such conflicting emotions?

The simple answer was that she couldn't. And dwelling on it wasn't going to make it any different.

Decision made, she spun on her heel and went to pack her suitcase.

Cruz looked up, annoyed, as his PA opened the door to his meeting. It was taking him all that he had to concentrate as it was, without yet another irritating interruption.

'What is it, Maria?'

He frowned as he heard Aspen's hasty, 'It's okay…don't interrupt…' in the background.

Maria glanced over her shoulder. 'Ah, Señorita Carmichael wishes to speak with you.'

'Send her in.'

Aspen materialised in the doorway and Cruz saw her suitcase by the side of the door.

He frowned harder. 'What's going on?'

'I can see you're busy.' She threw a quick glance around the room at his executive team. 'It can wait.'

'No, it can't.' He pinned her with a hard look, unaccountably agitated as he registered her intention to leave him. 'Is something wrong?'

'No, no. I just came to say goodbye. I didn't want to leave without letting you know I was going.'

'I thought you had decided to stay?'

She swallowed. 'Our deal was concluded this morning and—'

Cruz swore. 'I thought I'd already told you to forget the deal. It's not relevant. I'm not going to buy Ocean Haven any more. It's yours free and clear.'

A myriad of emotions crossed her lovely face, not completely unlike the morning when he had first told her that he *was* going to challenge her for The Farm.

Disbelief, shock, wariness, a tentative joy…

Three days ago he wouldn't have conceived of giving up something he wanted as much as he had wanted Ocean Haven, but a lot had changed in three days. He'd found out the truth about the night he'd left The Farm and he'd made love to Aspen. Held her in his arms all night. Woken with her still in his arms in the morning. When he looked at her he felt things he'd never felt for any woman before her. Feelings he was still unable to categorize.

'Really?' She took a hesitant step towards him. 'You're serious? It's mine?'

'Yes,' he said gruffly, wondering why it was that he couldn't look at her without wanting to strip her clothes off.

'Oh, Cruz…'

She looked as if she might cry, and just when he was about to back away she gave a gurgle of laughter and rushed over to him, jumping up to wind her arms around his neck. Instinctively Cruz grasped the backs of her thighs, and it seemed completely natural to raise her legs and lock them around his hips.

In an instant the chemistry between them ignited and he filled his hands with her taut curves as he sought to steady them both.

'Thank you, thank you… This means so much to me. You have no idea.'

Before he could formulate a sane response she leant forward and kissed him, her silky tongue sneaking out to wrap around his. Cruz held in a groan and took charge of the kiss. This was what he'd wanted from the minute he'd woken up this morning.

Then he'd held himself back. Now, with her honeyed taste on his tongue, he didn't bother. Her mouth was the greatest aphrodisiac he'd ever known.

She moved her hips and Cruz pressed himself more snugly against the seam of her jeans. She murmured something and he almost ignored it, but the words 'We're not alone…' and 'Everyone is watching…' somehow permeated his addled brain.

He glanced around at his stunned executive team. She was right. Not one of them had looked away and he couldn't say he blamed them. He was just as shocked that he'd forgotten they were still in the room as they were at seeing him with a woman locked in his arms.

He released a careful breath.

'Excuse me, everyone. I'm going to have to adjourn this meeting. Again.'

He held Aspen as still as a statue until the door snicked closed. Then he devoured her, pulling at her clothes and unzipping his jeans. He shoved aside the laptop on the mahogany table and laid her down. Her shirt was open around her and her breasts were heaving against the delicate cups of her plain white bra. She looked wild and wanton, her hair spilling out of the French braid she had secured it in.

His hands skimmed her, claimed her, and she arched up off the table towards him.

'That door isn't locked,' she got out between gasps of pleasure.

'No one will come through it unless they want to start looking for a new job.'

'This is…'

'Madness?' His hands felt clumsy as he yanked her jeans down her legs. 'You need to start wearing skirts more,' he complained.

She let out a husky laugh, and then her breath hitched as he ripped her panties aside and parted her legs. She was already slick and ready and he growled his appreciation.

'I've never wanted a woman as much as I want you.'

He ducked his head down and bathed her silky wetness with his tongue. Her legs fell further apart and he saw her watching him as he licked and sucked on her sweetness. The picture of his dark head nestled between her creamy thighs nearly unmanned him, and when he felt her inner walls start to tremble with her imminent release he rose up and pulled her towards the edge of the table.

'Not without me, *mi gatita*. I want to feel you come around me.'

Quickly applying a condom, Cruz hooked her legs over his forearms and drove into her. Her gasp was raw and shocked and, given everything she had revealed to him last night, he tried to check himself.

'No, don't stop. Please.'

Her hands clutched his forearms, urging him closer, and Cruz closed his eyes and pumped himself into her, grazing her clitoris with his thumb to maximise her pleasure. She came hard and fast at exactly the moment he did. Pleasure turned him inside out. The world might have ended at that moment and he wouldn't have had a clue.

CHAPTER TEN

'YOU DO MISS IT.'

'What?'

'Playing polo.'

'What makes you say that?'

'Oh, I don't know.' Aspen smiled up at Cruz. 'The wistful look on your face right now, perhaps.'

They were leaning on the fence post of one of the stable yards, watching the grooms and riders put the finishing touches to their horses before the main tournament got under way.

'I'm assessing the state of the horses.'

Aspen cocked her head and studied his profile, shadowed from the sun by a baseball cap. His hair curled sexily at the sides. 'Why did you give it up?'

He turned his head, his black eyes piercing. 'Money.'

'Ah. I'm sensing there's a theme here.' She laughed.

'No theme,' Cruz growled without heat. 'I didn't have much when I left Ocean Haven and I knew that polo wasn't going to give me what I needed.'

Aspen nodded. 'Money gives you the security that Ocean Haven gives me, but it's our loss. Watching you play polo was like watching poetry in motion.'

He looked at her strangely and then gave her a small smile. 'Those days are long gone now. And, while I did miss it, my life is full enough as it is. By the way...' His tone turned serious. 'Anderson is here. He was injured last month in Argentina so he wasn't expected to turn up. I told him to keep away from you.'

Aspen reeled. So it *had* been Chad she had glimpsed last night in the hotel foyer. She sucked in a deep breath and let it out slowly. She hadn't seen him in years, and while she really didn't want to she didn't want Cruz feeling as if he had to defend her just because she had unexpectedly opened up to him.

'You don't have to fight my battles for me, Cruz.'

He shook his head as if he knew better and tapped the tip of her nose affectionately. 'Somebody has to.' He took off his cap and fitted it to her head. 'You need a hat if you're going to stay out in the sun, *mi gatita*. Excuse me for a minute.'

He headed off inside the stable, his long stride and two-metre frame seeming to strike sparks in the air as he moved. Aspen tried to feel annoyed at his high-hand-edness, but after last night and then this morning on his conference table it was hard to stay irritated with him over anything. It had been so long since she had felt this good.

So long since she had just enjoyed herself without the pressure of work and bills getting in the way.

So long since she had felt the freedom of truly being in charge of her own destiny.

And it was exhilarating. She grinned to herself. Al-most—but not quite—as exhilarating as feeling Cruz move inside her body. She smiled again. Almost as exhilarat-ing as feeling his mouth on her breasts, between her legs.

As soon as she had *that* thought liquid heat turned her insides soft and her smile widened, because now that she recognised the sensation she could actually feel herself growing moist. She glanced around surreptitiously, just to make sure no one else could see that she was turning herself on.

Her newly awakened desire was like a runaway train. And while part of her knew she should probably try and put the brakes on it, another part of her wanted to roll around in it like a cat in the sun.

Mi gatita. His kitten.

Aspen rolled her eyes. She shouldn't get so much joy out of the pet name but she did.

Her cell phone beeped an incoming message and she snatched it out of her pocket, hoping it was her uncle returning her call. Earlier she had left an excited message on his answering machine, informing him that she had raised the money they had agreed upon for her to buy The Farm. She wondered if he had got it yet and whether he was surprised, wishing she could have told him in person. Unfortunately a trip to England was not in the cards for her in the next twenty-five hours. Although, seventy-two hours ago she would have said a trip to Mexico wasn't, either.

Checking her phone, she saw it was just Donny, informing her that he'd organised for Matty, one of the local teenagers who attended her riding school, to relieve him for the day. Aspen quickly texted back to tell him to have a great day off with his family.

Family...

That sounded so nice.

'Catch.'

Cruz's voice broke her reverie and Aspen looked up just in time to grab the bundle of clothes he had tossed at her and to see a smirk on his handsome face. 'What's this?'

'You're my new groom. How soon can you change?'

Aspen didn't miss a beat. 'Five minutes.'

'See Luis over there?' Cruz pointed with his free hand towards the players' area.

'Yes.'

'Meet me there in two.'

Aspen felt deliriously happy. She reached out and grabbed

his arm as he made to walk past, a thrill of excitement racing through her. 'You're really going to play?'

He paused, cocked his head. 'You wanted to see poetry in motion, didn't you?'

Aspen shook her head, smiling at his cockiness.

It was dangerous to feel this much happiness because of a pair of jeans and a shirt, but it wasn't that. It was the man.

She'd fallen in love with him, she realised with a sinking feeling.

He must have sensed her regard because he turned and met her gaze.

'One minute left,' he drawled.

Totally in love, she thought, and she had no idea what to do about it.

He was in love.

The thought gripped him by the throat in the middle of the game just as he was about to make a nearside forehand shot and he nearly fell off his horse and landed on his behind. Fortunately years of training and a horse that could play blind saw him come out of the offensive strike still in the saddle.

He pulled up and let one of his team members carry the ball to the goalposts.

He couldn't be in love with her. It was impossible. He didn't want to be in love with anyone. Not yet. It wasn't part of his plan.

Surely it was just the exhilaration of being out on the polo field again that was sending weird magnetic pulses to his brain? The sense of fun he hadn't felt in far too long?

He glanced towards the players' area and his eyes effortlessly zeroed in on Aspen standing beside one of his players. She wore his Rodriquez Polo cap and her flyaway blond curls billowed out at the sides. She'd put on his team colours and she looked curvy and edible as she clapped her hands wildly.

The horn went, signalling the end of the game, and Cruz trotted towards her almost hesitantly.

Unaware of his thoughts, she beamed up at him. 'You are such a show-off. Congratulations on the win.'

He returned her smile. She was gorgeous. Gorgeous and smart and funny and hot-headed. And, yes, he was in love with her.

Other players thumped him on the back and congratulated him and he could hear the commentators waxing lyrical about his statistics and his comeback—not that this *was* a comeback, more a hiatus in his normal working life—but he wasn't really paying attention to anything other than Aspen.

He hadn't had any idea that he was falling in love with her but now that he had acknowledged it, it made perfect sense. Probably he had always loved her.

And he couldn't wait to tell her because last night and earlier, when he should have been concentrating on work, she had looked at him in such a way that he was confident she felt the same as he did.

Not that he would tell her here. He'd do it in private. Maybe over an elaborate dinner. He smiled, already anticipating the moment.

Aspen took Bandit's reins and he dismounted. 'That last goal was simply brilliant.'

'I thought so.'

He readjusted his helmet and Aspen automatically pushed some of his hair out of his eyes. 'You need a haircut,' she admonished.

He stilled, his gaze holding hers. 'I have something I need to tell you.'

'What is it?'

'Not here.' He shook his head. 'I promised Ricardo I'd

check in with the Chinese delegation I have apparently neglected all day. How about we meet back in the suite in thirty minutes?'

'This sounds serious.'

'It is. Here, let me take Bandit back to the stables for Luis to get her cleaned up.' He mounted and reached down for the mallet Aspen was holding for him. Instead of taking it he gripped her elbow, raised her onto her toes and kissed her soundly. 'Very serious.'

Aspen watched Cruz canter back towards the stables, her fingers pressed to her throbbing lips.

'Now, that was really touching.'

Aspen swung around at the sound of a mocking voice behind her. For a moment all she could do was stare blankly, her mind frozen as if she'd just been zapped.

'Chad,' she finally managed to croak out.

His smile was charming and boyish. 'One and the same, babe, one and the same.'

CHAPTER ELEVEN

HOPING CHAD WAS just an apparition, Aspen blinked rapidly and then gave a sharp gasp as her vision cleared and she saw him properly. 'What happened to your eye?'

He fingered the puffy purple skin of his eye socket. 'I ran into your *boyfriend*. Didn't he tell you?'

Yes, he had, but he'd neglected to say that he'd done anything but talk to him. A warm glow spread through Aspen's torso. As much as she abhorred violence, the fact that Cruz had reacted on her behalf did make her feel good. Special.

'Are you okay?'

'Do you care?' he sneered.

'Of course.' Memories flooded in, preventing her from saying anything else. The unexpectedness of seeing him causing her heart to beat heavily in her chest.

He stood before her, the typical urban male, with his designer haircut, stubble and trendy sportswear. She knew it took him hours to achieve that casually dishevelled appearance, and that he'd always hated the fact that she didn't pay more attention to her own appearance.

'Can't you straighten your hair sometimes? It's a mess.'

'I didn't expect to see you so far from Ocean Haven.'

His words snapped her attention back to him and slowly she started breathing properly again.

'I'm...here on...business.' She stumbled over the words

and furtively looked around for Cruz. Then she felt angry with herself. She was no longer the naïve eighteen-year-old girl who had mistaken friendship for love and had thought that wealth was synonymous with decency. She didn't *need* Cruz to protect her. She didn't need any man to do that.

'Some digs,' Chad continued, looking back at the hotel. 'The stable boy has come a long way.'

'What do you want, Chad?'

'To say hello.'

'Well, now you've said it, so…'

'What?' He held his hands wide as if in surprise. 'That's all you're going to say?'

'We haven't spoken for a long time. I don't see any point in changing that.'

'What if I do?'

Aspen felt her mouth tighten. 'I believe Cruz told you not to come near me.' And she hated pulling that card.

Chad's lip curled. 'See, Boy Wonder would like to think he controls everything, but he doesn't control me. Does he control you, Assie?'

Aspen's mouth tightened. There was no way she was playing mind games with her ex-husband again. She'd done that enough when they had been married.

'Goodbye, Chad.'

She turned on her heel, intent on walking away from him. but it seemed he had other ideas.

'Aspen, wait.' He jogged after her. 'I didn't mean to upset you.'

'No?'

'No. I wanted to apologise to you, actually.'

Aspen stopped. 'For…?'

'For being such an idiot when we got married. I was in a bad way and—'

Aspen held up her hand like a stop sign. 'Don't, Chad.' She knew his game. She had heard his apologies a thousand times before. Usually they amounted to nothing. 'It doesn't matter anymore.' And amazingly it didn't. Cruz had seen to that.

Cruz who was *nothing* like Chad. Cruz who was proud, but gentle. Cruz who was smart and masterful and possessive. And it thrilled her. *He* thrilled her. And she couldn't wait to see him. Maybe even to tell him that she loved him if she had the courage.

She looked at Chad now. Really looked at him. He couldn't hurt her anymore and it made her feel a little giddy.

'Chad, I'm sorry, but I don't want to see you or talk to you. Whatever you have to say is irrelevant.' She smiled inwardly as she borrowed one of Cruz's favourite expressions.

'I just want to be friends, Aspen, put things behind us.'

Aspen felt petty in refusing him, but he had hurt her too much for her ever to consider him as a friend. 'I'd like to put things behind us too, but we can't ever be friends, Chad.'

'Because of *Rodriguez*?' Chad sneered. 'He won't want you for long. His heart belongs to his horses and nothing else.'

Aspen shook her head. This was the Chad she knew too well.

'Is it serious between you?'

'That's none of your business.'

'You're in love with him.' Chad spat on the ground. 'You always were.'

'I wasn't. I thought I loved you.'

'But you didn't, did you? It was him all along. I told your grandfather. That night.'

Aspen frowned. 'It was you who sent him out after me?'

'I watched you chase him like one of his fawning groupies. Did you have sex with him? Your grandfather would never say.'

God, this was awful, but Aspen wasn't sure if she was more appalled that he had talked to her grandfather so intimately about her or that he was talking to her about it now.

'Why do you hate Cruz so much?' She couldn't help asking.

Chad shrugged and stared at her mulishly. 'He was an arrogant SOB who never saw me as competition. He never took me seriously except where you were concerned.'

Aspen gave a sharp, self-conscious laugh. 'And there I was, thinking that you wanted Ocean Haven.'

Chad shook his head. 'I didn't. But he did. And he's won that too, I hear.'

An uneasy sensation slipped down Aspen's spine and she told herself to ignore him. To walk away. 'What is that supposed to mean?'

He looked at her like a hyena scenting a wounded animal. 'Boy Wonder bought The Farm. Not literally—unfortunately—but… You didn't know?'

Aspen knew better than most not to listen to anything Chad said, not to place any importance on his words, but she couldn't make herself leave. Not with her mother's cautionary advice that if something looked too good to be true it usually was ringing loudly in her ears.

'How would you know anything about the sale of The Farm?'

'My daddy wanted to buy it. He had high hopes of swooping in at the last minute and picking it up for a song.'

Aspen's head started to hurt. 'Well, it's not true. Cruz hasn't bought Ocean Haven. Your father has his facts wrong.'

Chad shrugged. 'I guess the guy brokering the deal is the one who has it wrong. My father did wonder when he heard Rodriguez had paid more than double the value of the property.'

More than double?

Aspen felt a burning sensation in the back of her throat. 'Yes, I'd say he's wrong. Excuse me.'

She pushed past Chad, only to have him grab her arm.

'He's not worth it, you know. You can't see it, but he won't hang around for long.'

Hardly in the mood for any more of Chad's snide comments, Aspen turned on him sharply. 'That's not your business, is it?'

Chad reeled back and covered the movement with a disbelieving laugh. 'You've changed.'

'So I've been told.'

She said the words automatically but Aspen knew that if there was any truth to Chad's words then she hadn't changed at all. Because if Cruz had bought The Farm out from under her it would mean that she had fallen into the same trap she had in the past—wanting the love and affection of a man who wouldn't think twice before walking all over her.

Telling herself to calm down, she stabbed the button on the lift to the penthouse and used the temporary access card Cruz had given her.

Chad had admitted that he hated Cruz, so this could just be trouble he was stirring up between them. But how would he know it would cause trouble? He couldn't. No one knew about the private deal she had struck with Cruz. No one but her knew that this morning Cruz had promised her he had decided not to buy Ocean Haven.

Calm, Aspen, she reminded herself, desperately trying to check her temper.

When the lift doors opened her eyes immediately fell on an immaculately dressed woman who looked like a supermodel.

For a minute she thought she was in the wrong suite, but deep down she knew she wasn't.

'I'm sorry...' She frowned. 'I'm looking for Cruz.'

'He's in the shower,' the woman said.

Was he, now?

Aspen swallowed down the sudden feeling of jealousy. The woman was dressed, for heaven's sake. 'And you are...?'

The woman held out her hand. 'I'm Lauren Burnside. Cruz's lawyer. Would I be right in assuming that you're Aspen Carmichael?'

The fact that his lawyer knew of her wasn't a good sign in Aspen's mind. 'Yes. Would *I* be right in assuming you're here about the sale of Ocean Haven?'

The lawyer's eyes flickered at the corners and an awkward silence prevailed over the room. 'You would have to ask Cruz about that.'

Cruz, not Mr Rodriguez, Aspen noted sourly. How well did this woman know him? And why did the thought of this woman running her hands all over Cruz's naked body hurt her so much?

Because you love him, you nincompoop.

Aspen moved to the side table beside the Renoir and placed her hands lightly on the wood-grained surface. Memories of the last time she had stood in this exact position, with Cruz behind her, kissing her neck, murmuring tender words of encouragement to her, lanced her very soul. Yes, she loved him—and that just took this situation from bad to completely hideous.

'His heart belongs to his horses and nothing else.'

Chad getting inside her head did nothing to stave off her temper either. But still she tried to convince herself that she didn't know the facts. That she wouldn't jump to conclusions as Cruz had done about her eight years ago.

'Lauren. Aspen!'

Aspen turned as Cruz entered the room. Pleasure shot through her at the sight of him fresh from the shower in worn jeans and a body-hugging white T-shirt.

He smiled at her.

She looked away, but he had already transferred his attention to the other woman.

'You have the contracts?'

'Right here.'

Aspen turned and leant against the side table, blocking all memories of the intimacies they had shared, blocking the pain of his betrayal, her foolish feelings for him.

'They would be the contracts to finalise the sale of my farm?' she said lightly.

Cruz's eyes narrowed and Aspen knew. She *knew*!

'When were you going to tell me?'

Her casual tone must have alerted him to her state of mind because he didn't take his eyes off her. 'Can you excuse us, please, Lauren?'

'Of course. I'll leave the contracts on the table.'

She threw Cruz an intimate glance and Aspen felt her cheeks heat at having witnessed it.

'So, here we are, then...' Aspen strolled across the room and stopped beside the urn of flowers on the dining table. She stroked the soft rose petals and thought how impervious they were to the fact that she felt like hoisting them up and hurling them across the room.

'Yes. And to answer your earlier question I was going to surprise you over dinner.'

Surprise her? Aspen's mouth hit the floor and her temper shot through the roof. *Surprise her!*

'Dinner? *Dinner?*' She laughed harshly. 'You filthy, gloating bastard.'

'Aspen—'

'Don't.' Disappointment coalesced into rage and she just needed to get away from him. 'Don't say a word. I don't want to hear it. I don't want to hear anything from you. I hate you.'

She whirled away and would have walked out of the room—no, run out of the room—but he was on her in a second.

'Aspen, let me explain.'

'No.' She shoved against him and beat her fists against his chest in her anger. 'You tricked me. You lied to me. You told me you weren't trying to buy Ocean Haven any more but you were.'

'Dammit, Aspen.' He bound her wrists in one of his hands but she broke loose and tried to slap him. 'Stop it, you little hellcat. Dammit. *Ow!* Listen to me. I left a message for Lauren to pull the pin on the sale but she didn't get it,' he said, breathing hard.

As suddenly as her rage had swept over her it left her, and Aspen felt deflated and appalled that she had hit him. She *hated* violence. 'Let me go, Cruz,' she said flatly.

He frowned down at her. 'It's the truth.'

Aspen sighed and pushed away from him, feeling shivery and cold when he released her. 'It doesn't matter.'

'Of course it matters.' Cruz moved to the table and picked up the wad of paper Lauren had left behind. 'Look at this.'

Aspen glanced at it warily. 'What is it?'

'As soon as I found out that your uncle had accepted my offer I had Lauren organise the immediate transfer of the deeds into your name. It's all here in this contract.'

'What?'

'That was what I was going to tell you over dinner.'

Aspen frowned. 'So you're saying our deal is still on?'

Cruz glowered at her. 'Of *course* the deal is not still on. I don't expect you to pay me back. I'm giving you the property.'

'You're giving…' She shook her head. 'You mean lending me the money to buy it?'

'No, I mean giving it to you.'

'Why would you do that?'

'Because this way you have security.'

'Security?'

'You would have been bankrupt within the year if you'd borrowed all that money.'

Scowling, she moved away from him. 'That's not true. I have a great business plan to get Ocean Haven out of trouble and—' She stopped as he shook his head at her as if she didn't have a clue.

'Aspen, there's no way you can carry that kind of debt and survive,' he said softly.

His words registered in her brain as if she was sitting at the back of a large lecture theatre and trying to read off a tiny whiteboard. 'So you're just giving it to me?'

'It's just a property, Aspen.'

It's just a dress.

It's just her self-worth.

Just her *heart*.

'I don't want you to give it to me,' she said.

'Why are you being so stubborn about this?'

Why? She didn't know. And then she did. For years she'd thought that all she wanted was security, but really— really what she wanted was validation. Trust in her judgement. What she wanted was to know that she could direct her own future. Her way. But somewhere in the last couple of days Cruz had become the centre of her world. Just as both her grandfather and Chad had been at one stage.

Hadn't she once pinned her hopes and dreams for the future on both of them and been let down?

She shook her head. 'I don't want it that way.'

'What way? *Hell!*' Cruz raked a hand through his hair. 'I don't see what the problem is.'

'I want to do it my way.'

'So do it your way,' he almost roared in frustration. 'Debt-free.'

'I would have thought you of all people would understand,' she said, completely exasperated. 'You hated that your mother didn't trust you to do things your way when you were a teenager.'

'This is not that same thing.'

'It is to me.'

'You're being stupid now.'

Aspen rounded on him. 'Do not call me stupid. I had one man put me down. I won't take it from another.'

'*Dios mio*, I didn't mean it like that.' He turned his back on her and then swung back just as quickly. 'Aspen, I'm in love with you.'

Aspen wrapped her arms around her chest as if she was trying to hold her heart in. Was this some backhanded way for him to get Ocean Haven? She stared at him, her emotions in turmoil, a terrible numbness invading her limbs.

'You're not.'

Cruz swore. 'I've just spent over two hundred million dollars on a property I'm prepared to give you. What would you call it?'

'Crazy.'

'Well, it is that…'

'What would you buy me for my birthday?' she asked suddenly.

Cruz frowned. 'Your birthday is…two months away.'

'You have no idea, do you?'

'How is that relevant?'

It was relevant because she knew if he presented her with an envelope full of cash it would break her heart. It was relevant because if he really loved her for who she was he *would* have some idea.

His eyes narrowed on her face. 'What is this? Some kind of test?'

'And if it is?'

A calmness seemed to pervade his limbs. 'You're being ridiculously stubborn about this. I'm giving you everything that you want. Most women would be on their knees with gratitude right now.'

Aspen wasn't sure if he meant sexually, but the fact that she thought it startled her. She wanted to be on her knees in front of him. She wanted to do all sorts of things to his body until he was as out of control as she was. But that wasn't right. His power over her was so much stronger than Chad's. Or her grandfather's. If she stayed, if she accepted his *gift*, she knew she would do anything for him. Would accept anything from him. And that scared her to death. She would be completely at his mercy and a shadow of herself. A woman seeking the approval of a man who didn't listen to her. It wasn't how she wanted to live her life. Nor was he the type of person she wanted to share her life with. Not again.

'I don't play those games, Aspen,' he warned.

'And I don't play yours. Not anymore. Goodbye, Cruz. I hope you never run out of money. You'll be awfully lost if you do.'

Thankfully the lift doors opened just as she pressed the button, but it wasn't divine intervention finally looking out for her. Ricardo was inside. His wide smile of greeting faltered when he glimpsed her expression and a stilted silence filled the space between them as she waited for the lift doors to close.

Once they had, Ricardo turned to his brother. 'What was that all about?'

Cruz let out a harsh laugh. 'That was Aspen Carmichael making me feel like a fool. Again.'

CHAPTER TWELVE

EXACTLY ONE WEEK to the day later Cruz sat on the squash court beside his brother after a particularly gruelling game. Both of them were sweat-soaked and exhausted and Cruz relished the feeling of complete burnout that had turned his muscles to rubber.

His phone beeped an incoming message and since he was right there he checked it.

Frustration warred with disappointment when he saw that it was from Lauren Burnside. Well, what had he expected? Aspen Carmichael to send him a message telling him how much she missed him?

Right. She'd rejected him. How many ways did he need to be kicked before he got the message?

'Now the woman sends me a text,' he muttered.

'Who?'

'My lawyer.'

Maybe if she'd dropped in he would have taken her up on her offer to get up close and personal with his abs. He wouldn't mind losing himself in a woman right now. Smelling her sweet floral scent with a touch of vanilla. Winding his hands through her tumble of wild curls. Hearing her laugh.

'You're muttering,' Ricardo said unhelpfully.

That was because he needed to visit a loony bin so that he could undergo electroshock therapy and once and for all convince his body that Aspen Carmichael was *not* the woman to end all women. Bad enough that he'd thought he had been in love with her. That he'd told her.

He clamped down on the unwanted memory. It had been a foolish thought that had died as soon as she'd walked out through the door. A foolish thought brought on by an adrenaline rush after the polo match.

Feeling spent, he scrolled through Lauren's text. 'Idiot woman.'

'I thought she looked quite smart.'

'Not Lauren. Aspen.'

'Ah.'

Cruz scowled. 'This is not a dentist, *amigo*. Close your mouth.'

Ricardo smiled. 'Are you going to tell me what she'd done now?'

'According to Lauren, she's signed Ocean Haven over to me.'

'Shouldn't you be happy about that? I mean, isn't that what you wanted?'

'No.' He ignored the interested expression on his brother's face. 'I don't want anything to do with that property ever again.' Scowling, he punched a number into his phone. 'Maria, get the jet fuelled up and cancel any meetings I have later today.'

'I thought you just said you didn't want anything to do with that property ever again?'

'I won't after I handle this.'

'Ah, *hermano*, I hate to point out the obvious, but this didn't end so well for you last week.'

Cruz picked up his bag and shoved his racquet inside. 'Last week I was too attached to the outcome. I'm not now.'

Aspen was in a wonderful mood. Super, in fact. Her chores were almost done for the day and all that was left was to bed Delta down in her stall. Now that the polo season was over there was less pressure on her and Donny to have the place ready for Wednesday night chukkas and there were fewer students. That was a slight downside, but Aspen found that as winter rolled around the lessons veered more towards dressage, with her students preferring to practise in the indoor arena rather than get frostbite in the snow.

Pity about the leak.

'Or not,' she said, to no one in particular. Roofs and their holes, walls and their peeling paint, fences and their rusted nails were no longer her problem. And she couldn't be happier.

'Ow!' Aspen glanced down at her thumb and winced. 'Damn thing.'

She looked at her other fingers with their newly bitten nails. When had that happened? When had she started biting her nails again? She hadn't since she was about thirteen and her grandfather had painted that horrible-tasting liquid on the ends of them.

Rubbing at the small wound, she picked up the horse rug she planned to throw over Delta and headed for her stall.

Delta whickered.

'Hello, beauty,' Aspen crooned. 'I see you've finished dinner. Me? I'm not hungry.'

Which was surprising, really, because she couldn't remember if she'd even eaten that day.

'Who needs food anyway?' She laughed. Who needed food when you didn't have any will to live? 'Now, that's not true,' she told Delta. 'I have plenty to live for. Becoming a vet, a new beginning, adventure, never having to see Cruz Rodriguez ever again.'

She leant against the weathered blanket she'd tossed over Delta's back. He'd told her he loved her but how could you love someone you didn't know? And she'd nearly convinced herself that she had loved him too.

'It's called desire,' she informed the uninterested mare. 'Lust that is so powerful it fries your brain.'

But she wasn't going to think about that. Had forbidden herself to think about it all week. And it had worked. Sort of.

Aspen took in a deep breath and revelled in the smell of horse and hay and Ocean Haven. Her throat constricted and tears pricked at the back of her eyes, her energy suddenly leaving her. She would miss this. Miss her horses. Her school. But things changed. That was the only certainty in life, wasn't it?

'The man who now owns you is big and strong and he'll take care of you.' Delta tossed her head. 'I'm serious. He loves horses more than anything else.'

'Is that right?'

Aspen spun around. Stared. Then swallowed. Cruz stood before her, wearing a striking grey suit and a crisp white shirt. 'What are you doing here?'

'I think you know why I'm here this time.'

She straightened her spine. 'Boy, that lawyer of yours works fast.'

'She should. She's paid enough. Now, answer my question.'

Aspen straightened Delta's already straight blanket over her rump. Better that than looking at Cruz and losing her train of thought. 'I would have thought it was obvious. You bought Ocean Haven so it's yours, not mine.'

'I told you that was a mistake,' he bit out. 'The whole thing happened while I was playing polo.'

Aspen shook her head. 'You really expect me to believe that?' she scoffed. 'That supermodel of yours wouldn't blink without your say-so.'

'Supermodel?'

'We *are* talking about the brunette who happened to know you were in the shower, aren't we?'

Cruz narrowed his gaze and Aspen stared him down. Then he smiled. A full-on toothpaste-commercial-worthy smile. 'I've never slept with Lauren.'

'Like I would care.' She jerked her head. 'Mind moving? I'm tired of you blocking my way. No pun intended.'

Cruz continued to smile. 'None taken.'

But he didn't move.

'You're right about Lauren acting under my instructions,' he began. 'Unfortunately they were my *old* instructions. My *new* ones were caught up somewhere in cyberspace when her firm's e-mail system went down.'

'I don't care. I'm moving on.'

'Where to?'

'I don't know.' She shrugged. 'Somewhere exciting.'

'And what about your mother's horseshoe?'

'It's gone.' She'd cried over that enough when she'd returned last week. 'And before you ask I don't know where and nor does Donny. When I came back last week it wasn't here.' She sniffed. 'I'm taking it as a sign.'

'A sign of what?'

His voice was soft. As gentle as it had been the night she had told him about Chad. It made a horrible pain well up inside her chest. 'A sign that I've put too much store in The Farm for too long. I thought I needed it, but it turns out I needed something else more.'

He stepped closer to her. 'What?'

'It's irrelevant. You know what *that* means, don't you, Cruz?'

Unfortunately he ignored her blatant dig. Blast him.

'Try me.'

'No.' She moved away from him and fossicked with Delta's feed bucket. 'I've discovered that I do have some pride after all, so...no.'

Cruz grabbed the feed bucket and took it out of her numb fingers. Aspen accidentally took a deep breath and it was all him. When he took her hands she closed her eyes to try and ward off how good it felt to have him touch her. She swallowed. Yanked her hands out of his.

'I'm going to finish my vet course and take an internship somewhere, start over,' she said quickly.

Not taking the hint that she didn't want him to touch her, he slid his hand beneath her chin and raised her eyes to his. 'Start over with me?'

Aspen jerked back. 'I didn't know you were looking for a new vet?'

'I don't mean professionally and you know it,' he growled. Then his voice softened. 'I've missed you, *mi gatita*. I love you.'

'I—'

'You don't believe me?' He blew out a breath. 'Kind of ironic that a week ago it was me who didn't believe you, wouldn't you say?'

Aspen's chest felt tight. 'No. I wouldn't.' Nothing seemed ironic to her right now. More like tragic.

Cruz pushed a hand through his hair and Aspen wished he was a thousand miles away. So much easier to deny her feelings when he wasn't actually right beside her.

'I know you're angry, Aspen, and I don't blame you. I thought I knew about human nature. I thought I had it all covered. But you showed me I was wrong. After your grandfather kicked me out I vowed never to need anyone again. I saw money as the way to ensure that I was never expendable. I was wrong. I understand why you didn't want me to give you The Farm now, and if you want we'll consider it a loan. You can pay me back.'

Aspen felt a spurt of hope at his words. But that didn't change their fundamental natures. She couldn't afford to be in love with him. She'd become needy for his affection and he'd do it again. At some point he wouldn't listen to her and they'd be right back where they started. Better to save herself that pain now.

'I can't.'

'I know you were hurt, Aspen. By your grandfather's expectations, by the lucky-to-still-be-breathing Anderson. Me. But I promise if you give me a chance I won't hurt you again.'

Aspen shook her head sadly. 'You will.' Her cheeks were damp and Cruz brushed his thumbs over the tears she hadn't even known she was shedding. 'You won't mean to, because I know deep down you're kind-hearted, but—' She stopped. Recalled what she had said to Delta. He *would* take care of her. But could she trust his love? Could she trust him to listen to her in the future? Could she trust that she wouldn't get lost in trying to please him? 'I'm not great in relationships.'

'Then we really are perfect for each other because I'm hopeless. Or at least I was. You make me want to change all that. You make me feel human, Aspen. You make me want to *embrace* life again.'

Aspen's nose started tingling as she held back more useless tears.

'I know you're scared, *chiquita*. I was too.'

'Was?' She glanced at him.

Cruz leaned towards her and kissed her softly. 'Was.' He gave a half smile and reached inside his jacket pocket. He pulled out a small red velour pouch. 'You asked me last week what I would get you for your birthday and I had no idea. It took me a while, but finally I realised that I was imposing my way of fixing things over yours.'

Aspen gazed at the small pouch he'd placed in her hand.

'One of my flaws is that I see something wrong and I want to fix it. My instinct is to take care of those around me. The only way I knew how to do that without getting hurt was to remain emotionally detached from everything.

But no matter how hard I tried I couldn't do that with you. You fill me up, Aspen and you make me feel so damned much. You make me want so much. No one else has ever come close.'

Aspen's mouth went dry as she felt the hard piece of jewellery inside the pouch. She'd guessed what it was already and she honestly didn't know what her response should be. She wanted to be with Cruz more than anything else in the world but the ring felt big. Huge, in fact. Oh, no doubt it would be beautiful, but it wouldn't be *her*. It wouldn't be something she would ever feel comfortable wearing—especially with her job—and it was just one more sign that they could never make a proper relationship work.

'Open it. It's not what you think it is.'

Untying the drawstrings with shaky fingers, Aspen carefully tipped the contents of the pouch into her hand.

'Oh!' Her breath whooshed out of her lungs and she stared at a tiny, delicate wood carving of a horse attached to a thin strip of leather. 'Oh, Cruz, its exquisite.' Her shocked eyes flew to his. 'It's just like the ones I saw lined up on your mother's mantelpiece. You *did* do them for her, didn't you?'

'I did,' he confirmed gruffly.

Studying him, she was completely taken aback by the raw emotion on his face and her lips trembled as her own deep feelings broke to the surface. 'You *do* love me.'

Cruz cupped her face in his hands and lifted her mouth to his for a searing kiss. 'I do. More than life itself.'

'Oh.' Aspen clutched Cruz's shoulders and welcomed the fold of his strong embrace as the hot tears she had been holding at bay spilled recklessly down her cheeks. 'You've made me cry.'

'And me.'

Aspen looked up and found that his eyes were wet. She

touched a tear clinging to the bottom of his lashes. 'When did you make this?'

'During the week. I couldn't concentrate on anything and my executive team were just about ready to call in the professionals with white coats. I have to say it took a few attempts before my fingers started working again.'

Aspen clutched the tiny horse. 'I'll treasure it.'

'And I'll treasure you. Turn around,' he commanded huskily.

Aspen let out a shaky breath, happiness threatening to burst right out of her. She clasped the tiny horse to her chest as he gently moved her hair aside and tied the leather strap around her neck. Then she turned back to face him.

He looked down to where the horse lay nestled between her breasts. 'You do know that in some countries this binds you to me for ever?'

Aspen smiled. 'For ever?'

'Completely. And in case you're at all unsure what I mean by that I have something else.'

He produced a small box and Aspen knew this time it would be a ring. She also knew that no matter how ostentatious it was she would accept it from him, because she knew it had come from a place of absolute love.

Smiling, she opened it and got the third shock of the day. Inside, nestled on a bed of green silk, was the most exquisitely formed diamond ring she had ever seen. And by Cruz's standards it must have seemed—

'It's tiny! Oh, I'm sorry.' She clapped her hand over her mouth. 'That came out wrong.'

Cruz grimaced and slid the beautiful ring onto her finger. 'It wasn't my first choice, believe me, but I knew if I got you anything larger you'd think it was impractical.'

Aspen laughed and flung herself into his arms, utter joy flooding her system at how well he *did* know her. 'I love it!'

Cruz grunted and then lifted her off the ground and

kissed her. 'I'm getting you matching diamond earrings next, and they're so heavy you won't be able to stand up.'

'Then I'll only wear them in bed.' Smiling like a loon, she rained kisses down all over his face. 'Oh, Cruz, it's perfect. *You're* perfect.'

'So does that mean you're going to put me out of my misery and tell me you love me? Because I know you do.'

'How do you know that?'

'You called my lawyer a supermodel.'

Aspen pulled back. 'You think I was jealous of her?'

'I hope so. Now, please, *mi chiquita*, say yes and become indebted to me for the rest of your life?'

'You'll really lend your wife money and let her pay you back?'

'If she ever gets around to telling me that she loves me I'll let her do whatever she wants, as long as she promises to only do it with me.'

'Yes, Cruz.' Aspen nuzzled his neck and basked in the sensation of safety and love that enveloped her. 'I love you and I will be indebted to you for the rest of my life.'

Cruz touched the tiny horse that lay between her breasts. 'And I you, *mi gatita*. And I you.'

* * * * *

MARRYING
DR. MAVERICK

KAREN ROSE SMITH

To my family and friends who love animals as much as I do—my husband Steve, my son Ken, Suzanne, Sydney, Liz, Jane, Ryan, Heather, Abby, Sophie, Chris. Special thanks to my pet sitter, Barb, whose expertise allows me to leave home with a free heart.

Chapter One

Brooks Smith rapped firmly on the ranch-house door, scanning the all-too-familiar property in the dusk.

His dad didn't answer right away, and Brooks thought about going around back to the veterinary clinic, but then he heard footsteps and waited, bracing himself for this conversation.

After his father opened the door, he looked Brooks over, from the beard stubble that seemed to be ever present since the flood to his mud-covered boots. Tending to large animals required trekking through fields sometimes.

"You don't usually come calling on a Tuesday night. Run into a problem you need me for?"

Barrett Smith was a barrel-chested man with gray hair and ruddy cheeks. At six-two, Brooks topped him by a couple of inches. The elder Smith had put on another ten pounds over the past year, and Brooks realized he should have been concerned about that before today.

There was challenge in his dad's tone as there had been since they'd parted ways. But as a doctor with four years of practice under his belt, Brooks didn't ask for his dad's advice on animal care or frankly anything else these days.

"Can I come in?"

"Sure."

Brooks entered the living room where he'd played as a child. The Navajo rugs were worn now, the floor scuffed.

"I only have a few minutes," his father warned him. "I haven't fed the horses yet."

"I'll get straight to the point, then." Brooks swiped off his Stetson and ran his hand through his hair, knowing this conversation was going to get sticky. "I ran into Charlie Hartzell at the General Store."

His father avoided his gaze. "So?"

"He told me that when he stopped by over the weekend, you weren't doing too well."

"I don't know what he's talking about," his dad muttered, not meeting Brooks's eyes.

"He said you carried a pail of oats to the barn and you were looking winded and pale. You dropped the bucket and almost passed out."

"Anybody can have an accident. After I drank a little water, I was fine."

Not so true according to Charlie, Brooks thought. His dad's longtime friend had stayed another hour to make sure Barrett wasn't going to keel over.

"You're working too hard," Brooks insisted. "If you'd

let me take over the practice, you could retire, take care of the horses in the barn and help out as you want."

"Nothing has changed," Barrett said angrily. "You still show no sign of settling down."

This was an old argument, one that had started after Lynnette had broken their engagement right before Brooks had earned his degree in veterinary medicine from Colorado State. That long-ago night, his father had wanted to discuss it with him, but with Brooks's pride stinging, he'd asked his dad to drop it. Barrett hadn't. Frustrated, his father had blown his top, which wasn't unusual. What *was* unusual was his warning and threat—he'd never retire and turn his practice over to Brooks until his son found a woman who would stick by him and build a house on the land his grandmother had left him.

Sure enough…

"Your grandmama's land is still sitting there with no signs of a foundation," his dad went on. "She wanted you to have roots, too. That's why she left it to you. Until you get married and at least *think* about having kids, I can handle my own practice just fine. And you should butt out."

He could rise to the bait. He could argue with his father as he'd done before. But he didn't want his dad's blood pressure to go any higher so he stuck to being reasonable. "You can issue an ultimatum if you want, but this isn't about me. It's about you. You can't keep working the hours you've been working since the flood. You're probably not eating properly, grabbing donuts at Daisy's and potato chips at the General Store."

"Are you keeping track of what I buy where?"

"Of course not. I'm worried about you."

"Well, don't be. Worry about yourself. Worry about the life you don't have."

"I have a life, Dad. I'm living it *my* way."

"Yeah, well, twenty years from now you just tell me how that went. I'm going out back. You can see yourself out."

As his father turned to leave, Brooks knew this conversation had been useless. He knew he probably shouldn't even have come. He had to find a way to make his father wake up to the reality of his deteriorating health. He would…one way or another.

Jasmine Cates—"Jazzy" to her friends and family— stood outside the Ace in the Hole, Rust Creek Falls' lone bar, staring up at the wood-burned sign. She glanced around at the almost deserted street, hoping she'd catch sight of her friend Cecilia, who was tied up at a community meeting. They were supposed to meet here.

On the north side of town, the Ace in the Hole hadn't been touched by the devastating July flood, but Jazzy didn't know if she felt comfortable walking into the place alone. It was a rough and rowdy cowboy hangout, a place single guys gathered to relax. But when they relaxed, all hell could break loose. She'd heard about occasional rumbles and bar fights here.

Feeling as if she'd scrubbed herself raw from her shower at Strickland's Boarding House, attempting to wash off the mud from a disastrous date, she passed the old-fashioned hitching post out front and stared up at the oversize playing card—an ace of hearts—that blinked in red neon over the door. After she climbed two rough-hewn wooden steps, Jazzy opened the old screen door with its rusty hinges and let it slap behind her. A country tune poured from a jukebox. Booths lined the outer walls while wooden tables with ladder-back chairs were scattered across the plank flooring around a small dance floor. Jazzy glimpsed pool tables in the far back. Old West photos as well as those from local ranches hung on the walls. A wooden bar was situated on the right side of the establishment crowded with about a dozen bar stools, and a mirrored wall reflected the rows of glass bottles.

Cowboys and ranch hands filled the tables, and a few gave her glances that said they might be interested in talking…or more. Jazzy quickly glanced toward the bar. There was one bar stool open and it was next to—

Wasn't that Dr. Brooks Smith? She hadn't officially met him, but in her volunteer work, helping ranch owners clean up, paint and repair, she'd caught sight of him now and then as he tended to their animals. She'd liked the way he'd handled a horse that'd been injured. He'd been respectful of the animal and downright kind.

Decision made, she crossed to the bar and settled on the stool beside him. Brooks had that sexy, scruffy look tonight. He was tall and lean and broad-shouldered. Usually he wore a smile for anyone he came in contact with, but now his expression was granitelike, and his hands were balled into fists. It didn't even look like he'd touched his beer.

As if sensing her regard, and maybe her curiosity, he turned toward her. Their gazes met and there was intensity in his brown eyes that told her he'd been thinking about something very serious. His gaze swept over her blond hair, snap-button blouse and jeans, and that intensity shifted into male appreciation.

"You might need a bodyguard tonight," he drawled. "You're the only woman in the place."

He could be *her* bodyguard anytime. She quickly banished that thought. Hadn't she heard somewhere that he didn't date much? Love gone wrong in his romantic history?

"I'm meeting a friend." She stuck out her hand. "You're Brooks Smith. I'm Jazzy Cates. I've seen you around the ranches."

He studied her again. "You're one of the volunteers from Thunder Canyon."

"I am," she said with a smile, glad he'd recognized her.

When he took her hand to shake it, she felt tingles up her arm. That couldn't be, could it? She'd almost been engaged to a man and hadn't felt tingles like *that*. Brooks's grip was strong and firm, his hand warm, and when he took it away, she felt...odd.

"Everyone in town appreciates the help," he said.

"Rust Creek Falls is a tight-knit community. I heard stories about what happened after the flood. Everyone shared what was in their freezers so no one would go hungry."

Brooks nodded. "The community spirit was stoked by Collin Traub and the way he pulled everyone together."

"I heard about his proposal to Willa Christensen on Main Street but I didn't see it myself."

Brooks's eyes darkened at her mention of a proposal, and she wondered why.

"He and Willa seem happy" was all Brooks said.

So the man didn't gossip. She liked that. She liked a

lot about him. Compared to the cowboy she'd been out with earlier tonight—

A high-energy country tune played on the jukebox and snagged their attention for a moment. Jazzy asked, "Do you come here often?"

"Living and mostly working in Kalispell, I don't usually have the time. But I'll meet a friend here now and then."

Kalispell was about twenty miles away, the go-to town for everything anyone in Rust Creek Falls needed and couldn't find in their small town. "So you have a practice in Kalispell?"

"I work with a group practice there. We were called in to help here because my dad couldn't handle it all."

She'd heard Brooks's father had a practice in Rust Creek Falls and had assumed father and son worked together. Her curiosity was aroused. She certainly knew about family complications. "I guess you're not needed here as much now since the town's getting back on its feet."

"Not as much. But there are still animals recovering from injuries during the flood and afterward. How about you? Are you still cleaning out mud from homes that had water damage?"

"Yep, but I'm working at the elementary school, too."

"That's right, I remember now. You came with Dean Pritchett's group."

"Dean's been a friend of our family for years. He was one of the first to volunteer to help."

"How long can you be away from Thunder Canyon?"

"I'm not sure." Because Brooks *was* a stranger, she found herself saying what she couldn't to those closest to her. "My job was…static. I need a business de-

gree to get a promotion and I've been saving for that. I
came here to help, but I also came to escape my family.
And...I needed a change."

"I can understand that," Brooks said with a nod.
"But surely they miss you back home, and a woman
like you—"

"A woman like me?"

"I'd think you'd have someone special back there."

She thought about Griff Wellington and the proposal
he'd wanted to make and the proposal she'd avoided by
breaking off their relationship. Her family had tried to
convince her she should marry him, but something inside her had told her she'd known better. Griff had been
hurt and she hated that. But she couldn't tie them both
to a relationship she'd known wasn't right.

Maybe it was Brooks's easy way; maybe it was the
interest in his eyes; maybe it was the way he listened,
but she admitted, "No one special. In fact, I had a date
tonight before I ended up here."

"Something about that doesn't sound right. If you
had a date, why isn't he here with you?"

"He's a calf roper."

Brooks leaned a little closer to hear her above the
music. His shoulder brushed hers and she felt heat other
places besides there. "What does that have to do with
your date?"

"That *was* the date."

Brooks pushed his Stetson higher on his head with
his forefinger. *"What?"*

"Calf-roping. He thought it would be fun if he
showed me how he did it. That would have been fine,
but then he wanted *me* to do it. Yes, I ride. Yes, I love
horses. But I'd never calf-roped before and so I tried it.

There was mud all over the place and I slipped and fell and I was covered with mud from head to toe."

Brooks was laughing by then, a deep, hearty laugh that seemed to echo through her. She liked the fact she could make him laugh. Genially, she bumped his arm. "It wasn't so funny when it was happening."

He gave her a crooked smile that said he was a little bit sorry he laughed, but not much. "Whatever gave him the impression you'd like to try that out?"

"I have no clue, except I did tell him I like horses. I did try to be interested in what he did, and I asked him questions about it."

"This was a first date?" Brooks guessed.

"It was the *last* date," Jazzy responded.

"Not the last date *ever*."

She sighed. "Probably not."

Was he thinking of asking her out? Or were they just flirting? With that twinkle in his eyes, she imagined he could flirt with the best of them if he really wanted to.

"So you came here to meet a friend and hash out everything that's happened," he concluded.

"My gosh, a guy who understands women!"

He laughed again. "No, not so well."

She wondered what *that* meant. "When I'm at home, sometimes I talk it all out with my sisters."

"How many do you have?"

"I have four sisters, a brother and parents who think they know what's best for me."

"You're lucky," Brooks said.

"Lucky?"

"Yep. I'm the only one. And I lost my mom a long time ago."

"I'm sorry."

He shrugged. "Water under the bridge."

But something in his tone said that it wasn't, so she asked, "Are you close to your dad?"

"He's the reason I stopped in here tonight."

"To meet him?"

"Nope." He hesitated, then added, "We had another argument."

"Another?"

Brooks paused again before saying, "My dad's not taking care of himself, and I can't give him what he wants most."

In her family, Jazzy usually said what she thought, and most of the time, no one heard her. But now she asked, "And what's that?"

"He wants me to marry, and I'll never do that."

Whoa! She wanted to ask that all-important question—why?—but they'd just officially met and she knew better than to probe too much. She hated when her family did that.

Her questions must have led Brooks to think he could ask some of his own because he leaned toward her again. This time his face was very close to hers as he inquired, "So what was the job you left?"

After a heavy sigh, she admitted, "I was a glorified secretary."

"A secretary," he murmured, studying her. "How long are you staying in Rust Creek Falls?"

"I've already been in town for a while, so I guess I'll have to go back soon. I work for Thunder Canyon Resort. I'm in the pool of assistants who handle everything to do about skiing. I had a lot of vacation time built up but that's gone now. I don't want to use all my savings because I want to earn my degree. Someday

I'm going to own a ranch and run a non-profit organization to rescue horses."

Brooks leaned away again and really assessed her as if he was trying to read every thought in her head, as if he was trying to decide if what she'd told him was really true. Of course it was true. A rescue ranch had been a burning goal for a while.

"How did you get involved in rescuing horses?"

"I help out a friend who does it."

Finally, Brooks took a few long swigs of his beer and then set down his glass. He looked at it and then grimaced. "I didn't even offer to buy you a drink. What would you like?"

"A beer would be fine."

Brooks waved down the bartender and soon Jazzy was rolling her finger around the foam on the rim of her glass. This felt like a date, though it wasn't. This felt…nice.

The music on the jukebox had stopped for the moment, and she listened to the chatter of voices, the clink of glasses and bang of a dish as a waitress set a burger in front of a cowboy.

Finally, as if Brooks had come to some conclusion, he swiveled on his stool and faced her. "If you had a job in Rust Creek Falls, would you stay longer?"

She had no idea where this was going since the town had few jobs to spare, but she told him the truth. "I might."

"How would you like to come work for me as my secretary and assistant?"

"I don't understand. You said you work for the vet practice in Kalispell."

"I made a decision tonight. There's only one way to

keep my father from running himself into the ground, and that's to take some business away from him. If I open an office here in Rust Creek Falls, I can take the load off my father and show him at the same time that he can feel confident handing down his practice to me, whether I marry or not."

She admired what Brooks wanted to do for his father. Would working for him move her life forward? She could learn a lot from him.

"Can I think about it, at least until tomorrow?"

"Sure. In fact, take a couple of days. Why don't you come along with me on my appointments to get a feel for my practice day after tomorrow? I'm going to have loose ends to tie up in Kalispell, but then you and I can spend the day together and you can see what my practice will involve."

When she looked into Brooks's dark eyes, she felt something deep in her being. In that moment, the world seemed to drop away.

They might have gazed into each other's eyes like that all night except—

Cecilia Clifton was suddenly standing beside Jazzy saying, "You should have come to the meeting. The town's making plans for the holidays." When her gaze fell on Brooks, she stopped and said a breathy "Hi."

Yes, Brooks could take a woman's breath away. Jazzy thought again about his offer. "I'd like to shadow you for a day and see what you do."

Brooks smiled and so did she. She had a feeling the day after tomorrow was going to be a day to remember.

Chapter Two

Two days later, Brooks pulled his truck to a stop in front of Strickland's Boarding House, a four-story ramshackle Victorian. Its once-purple paint had faded to a lavender-gray. Cowboys on the rodeo circuit had bunked here over the years, but right now, many of the folks from Thunder Canyon who had come to help were staying here. Melba and Old Gene Strickland cared about their guests in an old-fashioned family way.

He switched off his ignition, thinking he must have been crazy to ask Jazzy Cates to work for him. He really knew nothing about her except what she'd told him. He'd followed his gut instinct as he often did in his work. But that didn't mean he was right. After all, he'd been all wrong about Lynnette. He'd thought she was the type of woman who understood fidelity and loyalty and standing by her man. But he'd been so wrong.

He knew, however, he was right about opening the local practice and taking some of the workload from his father. After all, it was for the older man's best interests. Still…asking Jazzy to become involved in that undertaking—

She was so pretty with that blond hair and those blue eyes. When he'd looked into those eyes, he'd felt a stirring that had practically startled him. It had been a very long time since a woman caused *that* reaction. However, if he hired her on, he'd have to forget about her natural prettiness and any attraction zinging between them. He'd be her employer and he'd have to fix his mind on the fact that she was just a Girl Friday who was going to help him, maybe only temporarily. She might hightail it back to Thunder Canyon sooner than he expected. After all, Lynnette hadn't wanted to live in a small town like Rust Creek Falls. How many women did?

The wooden steps leading to the rambling porch creaked under his boots. He opened the front door with its glass panel and lace curtain and caught the scent of something sweet baking. Forgetting all about Melba's well-deserved reputation as a terrific baker, he'd picked up donuts and coffee at Daisy's Donuts, never thinking Jazzy might have had breakfast already.

Jazzy had told him the number of her room—2D, on the second floor. He climbed the steps to the second floor and strode down the hall to her room. He gave a double knock on her door and waited. Maybe she'd forgotten all about going with him today. Maybe she wasn't an early riser. Maybe she was down at breakfast. Maybe she'd decided going along with him today was tantamount to calf-roping!

She opened the door before he could push aside

the flap of his denim jacket and stuff one hand in his jeans' pocket. She was wearing an outfit similar to what she'd had on the other night, a snap-button, long-sleeve blouse and skinny blue jeans that molded to her legs. He quickly brought his gaze up to her face.

"I was running a little late," she said breathlessly, "but I'm ready."

She'd tied her wavy blond hair in a ponytail. Her bangs straggled over her brow. Forgetting she was pretty might be a little hard to do. "I brought donuts and coffee from Daisy's if you're interested."

"Oh, I'm interested."

They couldn't seem to look away from each other and her words seemed to have an underlying meaning. No. No underlying meaning. He just hadn't dated a woman in a very long time. He was reading too much into cornflower-blue eyes that could make a man lose his focus.

Brooks never lost his focus. Not since his mother had died. Not during his years at Colorado State. Not during his engagement. His focus was the reason his engagement had gone south.

"Let's get going, then. I have an appointment with Sam Findley at his ranch at seven-thirty to check on a couple of horses that almost drowned in the flood. One of them has PTSD and gets spooked real easy now."

"Were they hurt physically?" Jazzy closed and locked the door to her room, slipping the key into her hobo bag that hung from her shoulder.

"Sparky had a few deep cuts that have taken their good time healing. I want to make sure he hasn't opened them up again."

"Is most of your work with horses?"

"Lots of it is with horses and cattle because of all the ranches around here. But I do my stint in the clinic, too. Or at least I did."

At the end of Jazzy's hall, Brooks motioned for her to precede him down the steps. When she passed him, he caught a whiff of something flowery. Could be shampoo. Could be lotion. He didn't think she'd wear perfume for this little jaunt, but what did he know? Women mystified him most of the time.

Jazzy clambered down the steps in a way that told him she was high-energy. She went outside to the porch railing and stared up at the sky that was almost the same color as her eyes. She pointed up to the white clouds scuttling across the vista, hanging so low they looked as if a person could reach them.

"Isn't that beautiful? I never appreciated a day without rain as I do now."

She wasn't just pretty. She was gorgeous. Not in a highfalutin-model kind of way, but in a prettiest-gal-in-town way. He crossed the distance between them and stood at the railing with her.

"I know what you mean. I've never seen so much devastation. Half the town was affected. Thank God for our hills. The General Store, Daisy's and Strickland's were all on the higher side. The other side of Rust Creek is still recovering, and that's where we're headed." Standing beside her like this, his arm brushing hers, talking about the sky and the flood, seemed a little too intimate somehow. Weird. He had to get his head on straight and do it fast.

Jazzy gave him one of her quick smiles. He'd seen a few of those the other night at the Ace in the Hole.

Then she headed for the steps. She was a woman who knew how to move. A woman with purpose.

In his truck, he said, "You didn't wear a jacket. Even though we're having a bout of Indian summer, the morning's a little cool. Want the heat on?"

Glancing over at him, she motioned to the coffee in the holder. "If one of those is mine, that's all I need."

"Donut now or later?"

"One now wouldn't hurt."

He chuckled and reached for the bag in the back. "Cream and sugar are in there, too."

He watched as she poured two of the little cream containers into her coffee and then added the whole pack of sugar. She wasn't a straight caffeine kind of girl, which he supposed was all right.

"Dig around in the bag until you find the one you want."

She came up with a chocolate glazed, took a bite, and gave him a wink. "Perfect."

Brooks found his body getting tight, his blood running faster, and he quickly reached for his black coffee. After a few swallows that scalded his tongue and throat, he swiped a cream-filled donut from the bag and bit into it. Halfway through, he noticed Jazzy watching him.

"Daisy's Donuts are the best," she said a little breathlessly.

He was feeling a little breathless himself. Enough with the donuts and coffee. Time to get to work. Focus was everything.

Ten minutes later, Jazzy wondered if she'd said something wrong because Brooks had turned off the conversation spigot. He was acting as if the road was an enemy he was going to conquer. She supposed that was just as well. Eating donuts with him had gotten a little…sticky. She'd seen something in his eyes that had, well, excited her…excited her in a way that nothing Griff had ever done or said had. Downright silly. If she was going to be working for Brooks—

She hadn't decided yet.

Veering to the left, Brooks drove down a rutted lane that had been filled in with gravel. Yet, like on many of the Rust Creek Falls streets, there were still a lot of potholes. Paving crews had been doing their best, but there was only so much money and only so much manpower. Lodgepole pine grew on much of the property. Larch, aspen and live oak were color-laden in October with gold and rust. A couple of early snows had stripped some of the leaves and there were still a bunch fluttering across the ground as they climbed out of the truck and headed for the large, white barn.

"Does Mr. Findley run cattle?" Jazzy asked to soothe the awkwardness and start conversation between them once more.

Brooks responded without hesitation. "No. No cattle. Sam's livelihood didn't get affected like some. He's a wilderness guide. Hunters and tourists stay at the farmhouse, and he has two cabins out back. He stays out there if he has women guests who would rather be alone in the house."

"Sounds like a gentleman."

Brooks shrugged. "It's good business. A reputation goes a long way out here. But then you should know that. I imagine Thunder Canyon is the same."

"It is."

A tall, good-looking man with black hair and gray eyes came to meet them at the barn door. Brooks introduced Jazzy. "She's one of the volunteers from Thunder Canyon, but she's hanging with me today."

As Sam opened the barn door for Jazzy, he said, "Brooks has some kind of magic touch that I haven't had with Sparky ever since the flood." Sam shook his head. "I was the one who rescued him along with a couple of others, and maybe I hurt him without knowing it."

"Or maybe you just remind him of what happened," Brooks said easily. "Horses remember, just like cats and dogs. It's why a visit to the vet is so traumatic for some of them."

"He lets me feed him, but he won't take a carrot or sugar cube like he used to," Sam added regretfully. "And getting into his stall is a major undertaking. Are you used to being around horses?" Sam asked Jazzy, looking worried.

"Yes, I am. A friend rescues them and I help her out. I promise I won't go near Sparky if he doesn't want me near him."

"Do you want me to stay?" Sam asked Brooks.

"If you have things to do, and I'm sure you do, there's no need. We'll be fine."

Sam nodded, tipped his Stetson to Jazzy and headed back toward the house.

She watched him thoughtfully. "For a small town filled with gossip, I never heard anything about his tours while I've been here."

"Sam keeps a low profile, mostly advertises on the internet, attracts a lot of tourists from back East."

"Is he from here?"

"Nope, and nobody knows where he came from. He doesn't talk about himself much."

"Are you friends?"

Brooks thought about it. "We're something between acquaintances and friends."

"So that means you talk about sports and livestock."

Brooks chuckled. "I guess you could say that. You can add the goings-on in Rust Creek Falls, which is a topic of conversation for everyone. Come on, let's see Sparky. Sam has it rigged up so the stall doors open to the outside corral. He can come and go as he pleases."

"That's smart. Freedom's important to an animal that's been traumatized."

Brooks eyed her again as if trying to figure out who she was. *Good luck,* she thought. *She* was still trying to figure that out herself. Coming to Rust Creek Falls had changed her in some elemental way. Sure, in Thunder Canyon she had her family and her job. But she didn't want to live vicariously through her sisters and brother. She didn't want her family to be her world, and she certainly wanted her job to be more exciting than the one she had, or at least promise a better future. She couldn't get promoted without a degree, so she was going to get that degree.

"Let's take a look at Mirabelle first. Sparky will hear us and get used to us being around."

Jazzy had made a quick judgment about Brooks when she'd met him at the Ace in the Hole. The more she learned about him, the more she realized she'd been right. She'd been able to tell he cared about his dad. Now she could see he felt deeply about the animals he cared for. Just why did this man never intend to marry?

Mirabelle, a bay, was cavorting in the corral beside Sparky's. When she saw Brooks, she neighed.

Jazzy smiled. "She likes you."

"What's not to like?" He almost said it with a flirting tease, but then he sobered. "I've been treating her for a few years. One weekend, Sam had an emergency and couldn't reach my dad, so he rang up our practice. I was on call. Since then, I've been taking care of his horses. Gage Christensen's, too."

"The sheriff," Jazzy said, knowing Gage a little. They'd had a dinner date, but things never went any further.

"Yes."

"While I was at the elementary school working, I heard that he and Lissa Roarke are engaged." When she and Gage had dined at his office, his mind had definitely been elsewhere. Probably on Lissa, who'd flown in from the East to organize volunteers in Rust Creek Falls on behalf of an East Coast relief organization.

"So that's all around town, too?" Brooks asked.

"Lissa has been doing so much to get help for Rust Creek Falls that her name pops up often, especially with the volunteers."

"Gage went through a tough time after the flood, but he sure seems happy now."

"We had dinner," Jazzy said.

"Dinner? With Gage?"

"I stopped in at the sheriff's office to ask for directions. He and I started talking and one thing led to another. But his mind was elsewhere—I think it was on Lissa. That was soon after she arrived."

"You mean he asked you out because he didn't want to think about her?"

"Something like that, though I don't think he realized it at the time."

Brooks looked pensive as Mirabelle trotted toward him. He glanced at Jazzy. "Do you feel comfortable being out here with her?"

"Sure. Is there anything special you want me to do?"

"I'm just going to check her overall fitness, and make sure nothing insidious is going on. After a flood, all kinds of things can develop."

When Mirabelle came up to Brooks, Jazzy let the horse snuffle her fingers. That ritual completed, she petted her neck and threaded her fingers through the bay's mane. She talked to her while Brooks examined her. He checked one hoof after another, then pulled a treat from his back pocket and let her snatch it from his palm.

"She's the easy one," he remarked. "Now let's go check out Sparky."

Jazzy could easily see Sparky eyeing them warily, his tail swishing. "How do you want to do this?" she asked.

"We're going to sit on the fence and let him come to us."

"Do you think I should be sitting there with you, or should I go inside?"

"Let's give it a try. You can't force a horse to communicate with you. If I'm patient with Sparky, he usually comes around."

"He hasn't for Sam?"

"Sam was on a guiding tour when the rain started, but he got back in the nick of time. Sparky's tolerating Sam. But I think that has to do with the flood and the rescue, maybe a sense of abandonment. Animals have it, too."

Had Brooks felt abandoned when his mother died?

Had his father been there for him? Maybe that was at the root of their discord.

Brooks opened the gate at the rear of Mirabelle's corral, and they walked out.

"Sparky was watching us while we were tending to Mirabelle, so he knows we're here." Brooks went along the fence a little ways then climbed the first rung and held his hand out to Jazzy. She thought a man's hands told a lot about his character. Brooks's hand was large, his fingers long. Staring at it, she felt a little quiver in her stomach.

"Jazzy?" he asked, and she lifted her chin, meeting his gaze.

Zing.

Something happened when she looked into those deep, brown eyes. She took his hand and felt an even stronger buzz vibrate through her body. She could feel the calluses on his fingers that had come from hard work. She was curious about him and his life and she was afraid it showed.

They were both sitting on the top rung when Sparky froze midtrot and eyed them warily. He was a paint pony with dark brown swaths on his cream-colored coat.

"Now what?" she asked.

"We wait."

"Wait for what?"

"You'll see."

The horse did nothing for at least five minutes. He just stared at them. When Jazzy glanced at Brooks, she saw he wasn't the least bit impatient. Wasn't *that* a novelty. She shivered suddenly. The morning air *was* cool and she rubbed her arms.

"Are you cold?"

"The sun's warm."

"Not what I asked you." Brooks was wearing a denim jacket that fit his broad shoulders way too well. It was loose at his waist. She concentrated on the brass buttons on his jacket instead of contemplating other things about him.

He started to shrug out of the jacket and she clasped his arm, saying in a low voice, "No, really. I'm fine."

He chuckled. "You don't have to whisper around Sparky. He's not afraid of our voices, just of us getting too close when he doesn't want us to."

She felt herself blush, but she still held his arm because her hand seemed fascinated by the muscles underneath. Ignoring the fact that she said she was fine, he removed his jacket and hung it around her shoulders.

"You can give it back once the day warms up."

So he was protective, and…thought he knew best. What man didn't?

Although she protested, his jacket held his warmth and his scent. It felt good around her. She snuggled into it and watched Sparky eyeing them.

It happened slowly, Sparky's acceptance of them into his world. The horse tossed his head and blew out breaths. He lifted his tail and ran in the other direction, made a circle and then another that was a little closer to them. After about ten circles, he was only about five feet from them.

Brooks took a treat from his back pocket and held it out to the horse, palm up.

"Sam said he wouldn't take treats from him anymore."

"That's Sam. Sparky and I have an understanding. I

don't try to do anything he doesn't want me to do when he takes the treat."

"Rescue horses are often skittish like this," she said. "I mean, horses rescued from abuse, not floods."

"Trauma in whatever form has to be treated with kindness most of all, as well as a gentle hand and a firm determination to overcome whatever happened."

She'd seen that, working with the horses at Darlene's place.

It took Sparky a while but he finally came within a foot of Brooks's hand.

Jazzy didn't move or even take a breath.

Sparky snatched the piece of biscuit and danced away then looked back at Brooks to see if he had more.

With a smile, Brooks took another piece from his back pocket. "These get crushed by the end of the day, so you might as well eat them," he said in a conversational tone to the horse.

Sparky must have understood because he made another circle, but didn't dawdle this time. He snatched the biscuit and didn't dance away.

"How many times have you done this before?" Jazzy asked, completely aware of Brooks's tall, fit body beside her.

"Too many to count," he said, shifting on the fence but not moving away. "He and I go through this routine every time I come over. I'm hoping someday he'll see me and just trot right on up. I thought about buying him from Sam, but I don't think it's advisable to move him to another place right now.

"Can I look at you a little bit?" Brooks asked the horse.

Sparky blew out a few breaths but didn't move.

"I'll take that as a yes." Brooks slowly slid down off the fence, taking care not to jump too heavily onto the ground. The sleeves of his snap-button shirt blew in the wind, the chambray looking soft.

Jazzy was fascinated by man and horse.

Brooks found another crumb of the treat in his pocket and offered it to Sparky. The horse snuffled it up and Brooks patted his neck, running his hand under the horse's mane. He slowly separated the hair there and Jazzy could see a series of scratches and a five-inch long swatch that looked as if it had been stitched.

Although he pawed the ground, Sparky stayed in Brooks's vicinity.

"Come on down," Brooks said to Jazzy. "Slowly."

She eased herself off the fence.

"Stay there," Brooks warned her. "Let him catch more of your scent. Let him get used to you."

Rescued horses mostly needed to be cared for gently, then regularly watered and brushed when they'd let you do it. She'd never become involved with one quite this way before.

Brooks kept talking to Sparky and then gave her the okay to come closer. She did, feeling she was getting closer to Brooks, too.

Brooks gave her the last little bit of treat and she held it in her fingers. When she extended her palm, Sparky took it from her.

By then, Brooks was studying the horse's flanks. "He's looking good. Soon we can put him in the corral with Mirabelle and see how it goes."

"I think he'd like some company. Wouldn't you?" she crooned softly to the horse.

When she glanced at Brooks, he was watching her, listening to her, and her pulse raced.

At the end of the day, would he still believe he should hire her?

As Brooks drove to other ranches, Jazzy could see they were all recovering from the flood. In some fields, alfalfa had survived. Many ranchers had been soil-testing to find out what nutrients the flood had depleted. Some reseeded with fast-growing grasses, while others planted soybeans. All were trying their best to recover. Most were making headway.

She watched Brooks work with calves, with goats, with cattle. She helped however she could and realized she liked assisting him. They grabbed a quick lunch at the diner, talked about Rust Creek Falls and Thunder Canyon. Whenever their fingers brushed or their eyes met, Jazzy felt energized in a way she never had before.

At the end of the day when they were driving back to Strickland's, Brooks said, "I know I'm doing the right thing opening this practice. Dad's going to be angry about it, but in the end I think he'll thank me."

"You're doing something for his best interests, even if he doesn't see it that way. I guess roles reverse as parents age."

"And as children grow wiser."

She thought about that and all the advice her parents had given her. But she particularly remembered one thing her brother Brody had told her. He'd said, "You have to find the life you want to live, rather than settling for the life you've fallen into."

What life *did* she want to live?

Brooks drew up in front of the boarding house,

braked and switched off the ignition. Leaning toward her, he explained, "If you're my assistant, you wouldn't spend all your time in the field with me. Mostly what I need in the beginning is somebody to set up the office, make appointments, get the word out about the practice."

He paused for a moment, then honestly admitted, "At first I thought I'd been impulsive about asking you to work for me, but today I realized it really was good instinct that made me ask. You're great with the animals, Jazzy, and with the clients. You seem to be able to talk to almost anybody. That's a gift, and a great one in a receptionist. So if you take this job, you'll be a little bit of a lot of things—a receptionist, an assistant, a tech. What do you think? Do you want to work with me?"

Brooks was leaning toward her and she was leaning toward him. She felt a pull toward him and thought she saw an answering pull toward her in the darkening of his eyes. But if she accepted, they'd be boss and employee.

"Sure. I'd like that a lot."

Brooks extended his hand to seal the deal. When his hand gripped hers, she found herself leaning even closer to him. Whether he was aware of it or not, his thumb gently stroked the top of her hand, just for a moment.

Then he pulled away. "I'll wait until you get inside," he said gruffly. "Tomorrow I'd like to take you to the practice in Kalispell and let you talk to the office manager. Is that okay with you?"

"That's fine with me."

Looking into Brooks Smith's eyes, Jazzy realized their association was going to be more than fine. The thing was—he was a confirmed bachelor. So she'd better keep her head.

They'd *both* keep their heads because that's what bosses and employees should do.

Chapter Three

Jazzy had no sooner hopped into Brooks's truck Friday morning—he'd waited outside today—when she fastened her seat belt and turned to him. "I have a favor to ask."

Brooks cocked his head and his face said he was ready for almost anything. "I'd guess but I'll probably guess wrong."

"What makes you think you'd guess wrong?" she joked.

"Because I can*not* read a woman's mind. What's the favor?"

"I've been helping Dean at the elementary school when I'm not needed somewhere else, even though my carpentry skills are at a minimum. Still, I don't want to let him down. Can we stop over there on the way to Kalispell? I tried to call last night and kept getting his voice mail."

"He's engaged now, isn't he?" Brooks asked, obviously tuned in to the local chatter.

"He is. He bought a place with some land and he's just moved in with Shelby and her daughter Caitlin."

"Shelby works at the Ace in the Hole, right?"

"Yes, but for not much longer, she hopes. She's going to reapply for a job as an elementary school teacher once the school's up and running again."

"That could be a while."

"It might be, but that's what she wants to do. Anyway, he doesn't always answer his phone in the evenings. So I thought it might be just as well if we could stop at the school. I'll explain I'll be working with you, but I'll still help out around the school on weekends."

"You want his blessing?" Brooks didn't sound judgmental. He actually sounded as if he understood.

"Something like that."

"We can pick up donuts on the way and bribe him."

"Brooks!"

"I'm kidding. I often pick up donuts and drop off a couple of boxes for people who are volunteering. We all do what we can to say thank you."

After a stop at Daisy's, they drove to the elementary school property in a drizzling rain that had begun to fall. The low-hanging gray clouds predicted more of the same. Just what Rust Creek Falls didn't need.

At the school, the building crew had made progress, but it was slow going without money for materials, and work often had to stop while they waited for supplies. Today, however, Dean was there with a crew. They found him easily in the school library, building shelves. He looked up when he saw Jazzy and did a double-take as he spotted Brooks.

After Jazzy explained why they were there, Dean gave her an odd look. "You're not going back to Thunder Canyon?"

"I don't know when. For now working with Brooks will give me experience to open that horse rescue ranch I want to open someday."

"She's good with animals," Brooks assured Dean. To Jazzy he said, "If you're going to be a few minutes, I'll look around."

Perceptively Brooks probably sensed that she needed to convince Dean this was the best move for her. She nodded.

When Brooks left the library, Dean frowned. "What kind of relationship do you have with Brooks? I didn't even know you knew him."

"I didn't before the other night. But we hit it off."

"Hit it off as in—"

She knew she shouldn't get impatient with Dean. He cared as an older brother would. But his attitude was much like her family's when they second-guessed the decisions she made. "I know you think you have to look out for me while I'm here. But I'm thirty years old and old enough to know what I'm doing."

Assessing her with a penetrating glare, he asked bluntly, "Did you hook up with him?"

"No, I didn't hook up with him!" Her voice had risen and she lowered it. "He's going to be my *boss,* so don't get any ideas you shouldn't."

With a glance in the direction Brooks had taken, Dean offered, "Maybe *he'll* get some ideas he shouldn't."

Jazzy vehemently shook her head. "He's not like that."

Dean sighed. "I guess you'd know after a couple of days?"

"My radar's good, Dean. I know if I'm 'safe' around a man."

"Woman's intuition?" he asked with a cynical arched brow.

"Scoff if you want, but I believe in mine."

It was probably woman's intuition that had made her break off the relationship with Griff. Her instincts had told her he simply wasn't *the one*. There hadn't been enough passion, enough of those I-can't-live-without-you feelings. Something important had been missing.

"Okay," Dean conceded. "But be careful. I heard he's a confirmed bachelor with good reason. If you fall for him, you'll only get hurt."

She couldn't let this opportunity to find out information about Brooks pass her by. "Why is he a confirmed bachelor?"

After an assessing look that said he was telling her this for her own good, he kept his voice low. "He has a broken engagement in his history that cut him pretty deep. A wounded man is the worst kind to fall for. Watch your step, Jazzy, or you will get hurt. I don't want to see that happen. Not on my watch."

"I'm *not* your responsibility," she said, frustrated, and stalked out.

Ten minutes later with rain pouring down faster now, she and Brooks sat in his truck again, headed toward Kalispell. Dean's words still rang in her head. *A wounded man is the worst kind to fall for.* She wouldn't fall for Brooks. She couldn't. Besides, she didn't fall easily. Her relationship with Griff was proof of that.

Still, as she surreptitiously eyed his strong profile,

her stomach did a little somersault. To counteract the unsettling sensation, she remarked casually, "Progress is being made on the school, but it's going so slow."

"A ton of funds and a larger crew could fix that. But the way it is now, the elementary school teachers are going to be holding classes in their homes for a long while."

"The town has come a long way since I first arrived, though."

He nodded. "Yes, it has. The mayoral election next month should be interesting."

"Collin Traub against Nate Crawford."

"Yep. They butted heads trying to get the town back on its feet. Their families have a history of butting heads."

"A feud?"

"Some people say so. I don't know how it started. I don't know if anybody remembers. But because of it, the election is even more heated."

She wouldn't ask him who he was voting for. That was really none of her business. But other things were. "How did your clinic in Kalispell take the news you'd be leaving?"

He didn't answer right away, but when he did, he looked troubled. "I don't want to leave them in the lurch, and I won't. The other two vets in the practice understand why I have to do this. Family has to come first."

Her parents had always instilled that belief in their children, too.

Two hours later, Jazzy was still thinking about Brooks's broken engagement as well as everything she'd learned from the clinic's office manager about the computer programs they used, advertising and a multitude of other elements she'd have to coordinate to set up his practice. The rain had continued to pour as Brooks and the office manager had filled Jazzy in on what her job would entail.

Jazzy had worn a windbreaker this morning in deference to the weather and now flipped up the red hood as she and Brooks ran to his truck. He'd gone to her side with her to give her a hand up to climb in, but that meant he'd gotten even damper from the rain.

Inside his truck, he took off his Stetson and brushed the raindrops outside before he closed the door. Then he tossed it into the backseat.

"Where's your jacket today?" she asked.

"The same place yours was yesterday."

His crooked half smile and the curve of his lips had her thinking of other things than setting up his office. An unbidden thought popped into her head. What would it feel like to be kissed by Brooks Smith?

No! She was *not* going there.

Brooks looked away and she was glad because she was afraid he might read her thoughts. As he started up the truck, she said, "You need a name for the practice." It was the first thing that she could think of to say.

"I guess I can't call it Smith's Veterinary Practice, can I? That's what my father uses. Any suggestions?"

"Not off the top of my head. Once you pick a location, we might choose something geared to that."

"I like your ideas," he said simply, and she felt a blush coming on because there was admiration in his voice. When was the last time someone told her they liked her ideas? At work, she just did what was pushed in front of her. Sure, she offered suggestions now and then, but nothing that really mattered. Brooks seemed to make *everything* matter.

The rain poured down in front of them like sheets that they could hardly see through. Brooks didn't seem to be anxious about it, though. He drove as if he drove in this weather all the time, keeping a safe distance from whatever taillights blinked in front of them, making sure he didn't drive through puddles that were growing deep.

They were well out of Kalispell when he asked, "So you think you can handle setting up the office? The printing for flyers and business cards and that type of thing will have to be done in Kalispell, but we can accomplish a lot of it through email. I know this is a big job—"

Was he having second thoughts about her abilities? "I can handle it," she said with more assurance than she felt.

She must have sounded a little vehement because he cut her another glance. "I don't want you to be overwhelmed. There's a lot to think about. We can farm out the website design."

"I can do it. I know I can, Brooks. I've taken night courses that I thought might be useful at the resort, and I've never gotten a chance to use a lot of what I learned, including web design and graphics. I even took a course in setting up a small business in case I ever get the chance to start up my rescue ranch. I've put my life on hold for too long. By helping you, I finally feel as if I'm moving forward."

He was silent for a few moments, then asked, "Did you have other things on hold, other than your job?"

Was he fishing about her personal life? She could tell him about Griff—

And maybe she would have. But the water was moving fast along both shoulders of the road. As she thought about Brooks's broken engagement, how she'd told Griff she couldn't see a future for *them,* the truck suddenly dipped into a hole hidden under a puddle. The jarring jolt would have been bad enough, but a loud pop like a gun going off accompanied it.

Brooks swore and muttered, "I know that sound."

Their blow-out caused the truck to spin on the back tire until they faced the wrong direction. The vehicle hydroplaned on another puddle and they ended up near the guard rail on the opposite side of the road.

It had all happened so fast, Jazzy almost felt stunned, like she'd been on some amusement-park ride that had gone amuck. Her brain was scrambled for a few seconds until she got her bearings and realized they were half on and half off the highway.

Brooks unsnapped his seat belt and moved closer to her. "Are you okay?"

"I think so." Without conscious thought, she rubbed her shoulder. "We blew a tire?"

He nodded. "I'm going to have to change it."

"Oh, Brooks. In this rain? I can call Cecelia or Dean."

"There's no need for that. I've changed tires before. I've gotten wet before. It won't take long, Jazzy, once I get us set up right. Trust me."

Trust him. Could she? She didn't know if she could or not…yet. She'd be foolish if she trusted him on this short acquaintance. Yet she had seen enough to trust in his abilities, to trust that he'd do what he said he was going to do.

His gaze ran over her again. "Let me get us over to the shoulder on the right side of the road so I can take care of the tire."

"I can help."

"Jazzy—"

"We can argue about it or we can change the tire," she said adamantly, not accepting a macho attitude from him any more than she would from Dean, her brother or her dad.

"Are you going to tell me stubbornness is one of your virtues?" he asked warily.

"Possibly. Apparently we both have the same virtue."

He shook his head. "Let's get this done."

Jazzy was more shaken than she was letting on, and her shoulder *did* hurt. But she wouldn't be telling Brooks about it. Testing it, she realized she could move it, and she wasn't in excruciating pain. Those were both good signs. She could help Brooks and worry about her shoulder later.

Brooks managed to steer the truck around and with the thump-thump-thump of the blown tire, they made it to the right side of the highway over to the paved shoulder. Thank goodness the shoulder was wide enough that they wouldn't be in any danger as other vehicles passed.

Brooks touched her arm. "Stay here. I've got this."

But she, of course, wouldn't listen. She hopped out of the truck and met him at the rear of the vehicle.

He shook his head. "You're crazy. You're going to get soaked."

"So we'll be soaked together. I've helped my brother and dad change tires. I'm not inept at this."

He lowered the rear truck panel. "I didn't think you

were. Let me grab the spare and we'll get this done quick."

"Quick" was a relative term, too, when changing a tire in the rain. Jazzy had tied her hood tightly around her face and she felt bad for Brooks when his shirt became plastered to his skin. But he didn't complain and she didn't, either, though she was cold and shivery. That was so much the better for her shoulder because it was aching some. The cuffs of her jeans were protected by her boots, but from thighs to below her knees, she was getting soaked.

Twenty minutes later they were back in the truck with rain still sluicing down the front windshield.

Brooks reached in the back and took a duffel from the seat. "I carry a spare set of duds in case a calf or a horse drags me into a muddy field. It *has* happened. How are you under that jacket?"

Actually, the waterproof fabric had kept her fairly dry. "I'm good. Just my jeans are wet."

He switched on the ignition and the heater. "How's your shoulder?"

"Numb right now from the cold and damp."

He began unbuttoning his shirt.

At first she just stared at the tan skin and brown curly hair he revealed as he unfastened one button and then the next. For some insane reason, she suddenly had the urge to move closer...and touch him.

When his gaze met hers, her breath almost stopped. She quickly looked away.

She could hear the rustle of fabric...hear him reach into the duffel bag.

"Jazzy, take this."

Out of the corner of her eye, she could see he was offering her a hand towel.

"You need it more than I do," she managed to say, her eyes skittering over his bare chest.

"Wipe your face," he suggested. "Then I'll use it."

She took the towel and dabbed at her rain-splattered cheeks, the ends of her hair that had slipped out from under the hood. After she handed it back to him, her gaze went again to his completely bare chest, broad shoulders, muscled arms. Wow!

"Do you work out?" she asked inanely, knowing he'd noticed she'd noticed, and there was nothing she could do about that.

"No need to work out when I wrestle with calves, chop wood for my stove and repair fencing on my dad's property when he lets me."

"Do you have a house in Kalispell?"

"No. Because I fully intended to move back to Rust Creek Falls someday. I'm in one of those double condos on one floor. It's got everything I need."

She handed him the towel and watched as he dried his hair with it. It was sticking up all over. She wanted to run her fingers through it and brush it down, but he quickly did that and swiped the towel over his torso.

"Getting warmer?" he asked, with the heater running full blast.

"Yes. I'm fine. I can't believe *you're* not shivering."

"Hot-blooded," he said with a grin that urged her once again to touch him, test the texture of his skin, and see if there really was heat there.

Before she had the chance to act foolishly, he pulled a T-shirt from the duffel, slipped it over his head, maneuvered his arms inside and pulled it down over his chest. She could see denim protruding from the duffel.

"Is that another pair of jeans?"

"Yes, it is."

"You should change."

"I'm fine. Let's get you back to Strickland's and look at that shoulder."

"You're a veterinarian," she protested.

"I had some EMT training, too. Out here, you never know what you're going to run into. If you'd rather I take you back into Kalispell to the hospital—"

"No! I don't need a hospital or a doctor."

"Great. Then I'm perfect for the job."

After that, every time Jazzy glanced at Brooks, she envisioned his bare chest, his triceps and biceps and deltoids and whatever else she'd seen. He had tan lines from shirtsleeves on his upper arms. He had dark brown hair arrowing down to his belt buckle. He had a flat stomach and a slim waist and—

Okay, heating up her body wasn't helping her shoulder. In fact, it was starting to hurt a little more.

They didn't talk as he concentrated on driving and *she* tried not to concentrate on him. She thought about her sisters and brother and parents, and considered phoning them. She hadn't checked in for a while and they'd want to know what she was doing. However, should she tell them about her job with Brooks? She almost had to, because Dean probably would. Besides that, the news would soon get around to the other volunteers and some of them would be going back to Thunder Canyon. It was difficult to hide anything in a small town.

When Brooks pulled up in front of Strickland's, Jazzy said, "You don't have to see me in."

"I don't have to, but I'm going to. I told you, I want to check your shoulder."

"You're still wet. You'll catch cold."

He laughed. "Everyone knows you don't catch cold from the cold. I promise, this will be almost painless, Jazzy. I just want to make sure you're not really hurt."

Okay, so they were going to have to get this over with because he was persistent and stubborn. In a family as large as hers, she'd learned there was no point in arguing.

Once inside Strickland's, they climbed the stairs. Jazzy took out her key and opened her door. She'd already told Dean that Brooks was "safe," so why was she hesitating in letting him into her room?

Simple. He was half dry, half wet, and all imposing male.

Her room was small and the nice thing about it was it had a bathroom of its own. Standing by the single bed, Jazzy was very aware of it as Brooks came into the room and stood before her.

"I left the door open," he said. "I don't want you to think I have an ulterior motive."

He had left it open about six inches, and she realized how thoughtful it was of him to do that. She simply had to think about him as a doctor right now.

"Take your jacket off," he said gently.

At first her fingers fumbled with the zipper. Her nervousness was stupid. She had nothing to be nervous about. But unzipping her jacket, she felt as if she were letting him into her life in a different way. She shrugged out of it and hung it over the bed post. He took a step closer to her, and she suddenly felt as if she couldn't breathe. Her gaze locked to his for a few seconds, but then he directed his focus to her shoulder and reached out to touch it.

She thought she'd prepared herself. She thought this would be clinical.

The exam *was* clinical on his part as he kneaded around the joint and asked, "Does that hurt?"

"Some," she managed to say.

"Don't soft pedal it if it does."

"It's not that bad. Really."

As he felt along the back of her shoulder, she winced. His fingertips massaged the spot and she found that didn't hurt but felt good.

"You got bumped around and might have black-and-blue marks tomorrow. Put some ice on it for the first twenty-four hours, ten minutes on, half hour off."

"Yes, Doctor," she said with a slight smile.

His fingers stopped moving. His eyes found hers. The room seemed to spin.

No, not really. Couldn't be. But gazing into Brooks's eyes was like getting lost in forever. His hand was on her back now as he leaned a little closer. She felt herself swaying toward him.

But then he straightened. "Take it easy for the rest of the day."

Feeling reality hitting her straight in the face, she asked, "When do I officially start work for you?"

"Let's consider tomorrow the starting date. I've been talking to a real-estate agent and she'll have a list of places for me to look at. Would you like to go along to do that?"

"You bet."

"Unless you don't feel well."

"I'll be fine."

"Famous last words." He went to the door. "Ice the shoulder."

As he opened the door and went into the hall, she called after him, "Get out of those wet jeans."

She thought she heard a chuckle as he strode away from her room. She remembered his shirtless upper body. She remembered the feel of his fingers on her shoulder. She remembered the way his smile made her feel.

Working for Brooks Smith could be the biggest mistake she'd made…lately.

Chapter Four

The sun shone brightly in the brilliant turquoise sky as Brooks let himself into Strickland's Saturday morning, coffee and donuts in his hands. He'd found a property he wanted to show to Jazzy. She'd said yesterday she'd be ready anytime he was, but he hadn't wanted to waste her time, so he'd taken a look at three properties early this morning. He was confident one of them would work, but he wanted to see what she thought.

At the front desk, he greeted Melba who was shuffling papers into a file folder. She eyed the bag from Daisy's Donuts. "Jazzy didn't come down to breakfast," she told him. "Maybe she'll eat some of what you brought her."

He supposed Melba had seen him with Jazzy the past two days. The older woman watched over her guests with an eagle eye.

He climbed the stairs, glad he'd put lids on the coffee cups or he'd have sloshed it all over the box and donuts. He was just eager to show Jazzy the property, that was all.

But deep down, he knew the reason for his eagerness was more than that. When he brought Jazzy back here yesterday and examined her shoulder, he'd had to remind himself over and over again that it was a clinical examination. But he could vividly remember how she'd felt under his fingertips, the look in her eyes. They were attracted to each other and fighting it. Just how difficult was it going to be to work together?

Not too difficult, he hoped. They wouldn't have time for attraction, not if they were going to get a clinic up and running. So the sooner they looked at the property and got started, the better. It was silly, really, but he couldn't imagine doing this with anyone else. Jazzy was so positive and upbeat, so excited about new things. She understood the dedication it took to take care of animals, and she even admired it. Unlike Lynnette. She was so different from Lynnette. Jazzy wouldn't do anything half-measure. Dating Jazzy could be an unrivaled experience. More than dating her could be...

He thought about his dad's ultimatum. Marriage would be a solution. Yet after his experience with Lynnette, he couldn't even think about it.

It was a shame he couldn't erase the shadows of the past from his memory bank.

When he reached Jazzy's door, he shuffled the box into one arm and rapped. She didn't answer. Could she have gone out? Was that why she hadn't appeared at breakfast?

He rapped again. "Jazzy?" he called. "Are you in there?"

To his relief, he heard movement inside. Then Jazzy was opening the door, looking as if she'd just awakened from a deep sleep. Her blond hair was mussed around her face and she'd pushed her bangs to one side. She was wearing a raspberry-colored nightgown and robe over it, but she hadn't belted the robe and the lapels lay provocatively over her breasts.

He quickly raised his gaze to hers. "Are you okay?"

She seemed to come fully awake. Now she belted her robe, cinching it at her very slim waist. That wasn't a whole lot better, but she didn't know that. He'd just have to package his lusty thoughts away in mothballs. He was concerned about her and that concern must have shown.

"Tell me the truth, Jazzy." He didn't want some varnished description of how she was feeling.

"Can I tell you over donuts and coffee?" she asked. "That really smells good."

If she wanted coffee and was hungry, she had to be okay, right?

Without a second thought, he stepped inside the room. She moved over to the nightstand, clearing it of books and lotion. She set them on the small dresser.

After he settled the box on the nightstand, he pulled over the ladder-back chair while she curled up cross-legged on the bed. She was so natural...so unaffected... so pretty.

He opened the box of donuts, pulled out a chocolate-glazed one and handed it to her. "Tell me."

She wrinkled her nose at him. "As the day went on yesterday, I got more sore. Last night I couldn't get to sleep. It must have been about 4 a.m. when I finally did, and I guess I was in a deep sleep until you knocked. You should have called to warn me you were coming."

"You need a warning?"

She shrugged. "A girl doesn't like to be caught with her hair all messed up." She flipped a hank of it over her shoulder.

He laughed. "You look—"

She held her hand up to stop him. "Do *not* say fine. No woman wants to hear she looks fine."

"Then how about you look morning-fresh and pretty."

She'd been about to take a bite of the donut but she stopped and her eyes widened.

"What? You don't believe me?"

"I have sisters who look beautiful in the morning. They don't even get sheet wrinkles on their faces."

"You don't have any sheet wrinkles. Or *any* wrinkles at all."

Her skin was so creamy, he wanted to reach out and touch it. That was the problem. "You do have a few freckles, though. But I like those, too."

She blinked.

He could see he'd definitely surprised her, maybe even embarrassed her a little. He popped the lid off the coffee. "Sugar and cream, just like you like it." As he handed it to her, he asked, "So how sore are you this morning?"

"Just a little, really. I think some of it's from the seat belt."

That made sense.

"Do you feel like looking at a property I found? If you don't, we can do it another time."

"No, I want to go." She was about to lay down her donut, when he said, "Take your time. I told the real-estate agent I'd buzz her when we were on our way."

Jazzy suddenly got a determined look on her face,

and Brooks knew he was probably in for trouble. She pointed her donut at him. "Just because you're tall and strong and seem to know what you want in life, doesn't mean you can look at me as...fragile."

Now where had *that* come from? Honest to goodness, he just didn't understand women. "I don't."

She pointed her donut at him again. "You do. Maybe it's because you take care of animals, but you have some kind of protective streak. It's the same streak that argued with me about help with changing your tire, and being out in the rain and thinking I had to rest today. *You* were in the accident, too. *You're* not resting."

"I didn't bump my shoulder."

She lifted a finger and stroked the air. "Okay, point taken. Still, I'm not some damsel in distress. Got it?"

She was sitting there cross-legged on the bed—with mussed hair and a just-awakened look. Baser urges nudged him to move closer, to climb into bed with her...

As if he needed more proof she wasn't fragile, she said, "And I iced my shoulder yesterday like you told me to. I can take good care of myself."

Whether she could or couldn't remained to be seen, but he wasn't going to tell *her* that. After all, she'd left her home and her family and her job to come to Rust Creek Falls to help.

"You've been fighting having somebody look after you all your life, haven't you?" he asked perceptively.

She finished the rest of the donut and wiped her fingers on a napkin. "With a family as big as mine, it can't be helped. Everyone thinks they know best for everyone else. We do take care of each other, but sometimes it just gets very smothering." She licked one finger then picked up her coffee, took a couple of sips, then asked,

"Do I have time for a quick shower? I can be ready in ten minutes."

A woman who could be ready in ten minutes? This he had to see. "Go for it," he said and stood. "I'll go downstairs and wait. If Old Gene's down there, he'll want an update on how all the ranchers are doing. So if it goes a minute or two over ten, don't worry."

She hopped off the bed. "Ten minutes. Start timing."

He was still shaking his head, amused, as he went down the stairs. Jazzy was a bundle of…something. He wasn't sure what. She had energy and spirit and a smile that wouldn't quit. Maybe, just maybe, their partnership was going to work out.

Fifteen minutes later in Brooks's truck, Jazzy could feel his gaze on her and she knew she was just going to have to get used to that protective streak of his. It didn't feel so bad, really, coming from him—rather than from her brother or Dean or her dad. But she really was feeling better since the shower had loosened her up. Ice had definitely helped last night.

She was a bit surprised when he headed down Buckskin Road toward the creek. The properties in the lower-lying areas in the south part of the town had been the worst-hit by the floodwaters. Some of the properties directly north of the creek hadn't fared so well, either.

He pulled up in front of a refurbished one-story office. Another car was already parked there. When she and Brooks disembarked from his truck, an older woman in jeans, boots and a denim jacket nodded to them. Brooks introduced Jazzy to Rhonda Deatrick, who was a real-estate agent.

Rhonda handed Brooks a key. "Look around as long

as you want. You can drop the key back at the office when you're done. That way I won't interfere in your decision process."

He laughed. "In other words, you're not going to sway me one way or another."

She smiled. "You're just like your daddy. You know exactly what you want. So this will either work or it won't." She nodded to Jazzy. "Nice to meet you." She headed for her car.

"I guess she knows your dad?"

"Actually, she helped out my grandmother on some property issues. But Rhonda has a couple of horses my dad's taking care of, too."

"Everyone knows everybody here. But then Rust Creek Falls is even smaller than Thunder Canyon. Thunder Canyon used to be more like this, before money moved in with the resort and all."

They went up the short walkway that looked as if it had been recently power-washed. The building itself was sided in dark blue. Concrete steps led to the wooden porch with its steel-gray railing.

"Everything looks freshly painted and cleaned."

"From what I understand, there was a foot of mud in this place after the flood, so it was completely gutted and redone," Brooks explained.

"Was this a house?"

"No, it was a dentist's office. That's why it has a lot of good things going for it."

"The dentist didn't want to resume his practice?"

"Nope. He was near retirement age. He'd been renting the property for the past ten years. The owner was the one who decided to put it into tip-top shape again, and see if he could rent it to another doctor."

Brooks opened the door and stepped aside so Jazzy could precede him. She went up the steps, her arm brushing his chest. Even that swift contact affected her. The scent of his cologne affected her. Everything about him affected her.

Inside, everything was white. There was new dry wall in all the rooms, as well as new tile flooring.

"I think I'd leave the exam rooms in white for now," he said. "I can hang framed posters on the walls. But the reception area needs a coat of paint."

Jazzy examined the space. "An L-shaped desk would look good right there." She pointed to the wall across from them. "Or a counter. This would be pretty in a really pale blue, maybe with some stenciling around the ceiling."

"Stenciling?"

"Yes. You use a template and there are special paints. It's not difficult. I helped Mom do it in the kitchen. It could be on one of the walls or two of the walls, just around the doorways and windows. Whatever you decide. I'm sure there are plenty of animal stencils. It would look really cute. We can fill a basket with dog toys, another with cat toys."

"Everything in here has to be easy to clean," he reminded her.

She'd forgotten about that. "What's your dad's office like?"

"Practical."

"Animal owners are practical, but they want their pets to feel at home, too. Coming to the vet is often a traumatic experience. The more pleasant we make it for them, the more they'll be glad to come here."

"I like that philosophy. I'll try to have regular hours

here and make outside visits to ranches during specified times. I know there will be emergencies in both instances. Once I take patients away from Dad and he sees he doesn't have to work so hard, then maybe we can combine our practices. I can take over the majority of the work, and he can help out when he wants. Or else he can handle office visits and I can do the ranch visits, which are harder on him. It would be ideal. I think he just doesn't want to admit he can't do what he used to do."

"Nobody wants to admit that."

"Maybe so, but life is about change, even for, or especially for, older folk."

Before she thought better of it, she clasped his arm. "I think you're doing the right thing."

He covered her hand with his. "I surely hope so. Let me show you the rest. You can see the creek from the backyard."

Leading her into a hallway that led to the back of the office, he opened the door that went outside. The property had a huge backyard and beyond she *could* see Rust Creek.

"This is nice."

"I can imagine kennels out here and runs, which Dad doesn't have. Maybe eventually, if he doesn't give in to a joint practice, I could buy this place. Because of the flood, prices are down in this whole area."

"I imagine it could still be expensive."

After a long look at the creek, and then a glance at her, he said, "I've saved most of what I've made since I graduated. My rent's low, my scholarship paid for schooling. I've invested a lot of it since I've been working."

"How long have you been living in Kalispell?"

"Four years."

She saw something shadowy pass through his eyes and couldn't help asking, "But you really didn't intend to live there?"

"Life hasn't turned out as I expected."

She could keep silent, but that wasn't her way. Softly, she asked, "What did you expect?"

Again, he stared into the distance for so long a time she didn't think he was going to answer. But then his gaze came around to hers. "I expected to be married and practicing with Dad. But my fiancée broke our engagement and everything fell apart."

There was a lot of pain behind his words. From his broken engagement, or from his troubles with his father? If it was the broken engagement—

When she'd broken off her relationship with Griff, had it left this kind of pain with *him?* Brooks had confided in her and she realized that that confidence gave them an even more personal connection. If she reciprocated, their bond would grow. Unless he saw her in the same light as his fiancée. Right now, telling him about Griff just didn't seem to be the right thing to do, any which way.

They stood there in silence for a long time. Finally Brooks said, "I'm going to take it. This property seems perfect and I don't want to let it slip away. I can probably get all the paperwork done today. I'll start painting the reception area tomorrow morning."

"*You'll* start painting? I thought I was working for you now."

"Your shoulder's still sore and…"

The look she gave him must have stopped him. He

held up his hands in surrender. "Right. You don't want me to be protective. Do you want to paint, too?"

"Paint, and anything else that will help you get off the ground. If my shoulder's still sore tomorrow, then I'll decide what I can or can't do. Deal?"

A slow smile spread across his lips. "Deal."

But when they shook on it, Jazzy had the feeling she was agreeing to a lot more than a business arrangement.

The volunteers had carpooled for their initial drive to Rust Creek Falls, so Jazzy had left her car back in Thunder Canyon. She really didn't need it here because everything was within walking distance or she could catch a ride with someone. When Cecilia, who was also staying at Strickland's, dropped Jazzy off at Brooks's new clinic the following morning, she winked. "Have fun."

"We're going to work," Jazzy told her, for not the first time. She'd told Brooks yesterday, after they'd shaken hands on their deal, that she'd find her own way to the clinic.

"You can have fun and work, too," Cecilia reminded her.

But Jazzy was not looking at Brooks in any way other than as an employer. She simply was not. She was going to help him get his office ready. Period.

Glancing toward Brooks's truck, she wondered how long he'd been there. When she stepped inside his new office, she figured he'd probably arrived before dawn. There were tarps covering the floor, a flat of water bottles in one corner and a giant cup of coffee on the ladder.

"Did you have breakfast?" he asked. "I have donuts in the truck."

"I ate this morning. I knew I'd need some energy."

"How do you feel?"

"I feel like I should be here helping you paint. End of discussion, right?"

He gave her a slow smile. "Right. I only have one more wall. It would help me if you would do the trim around the windows."

"So I don't have to lift that heavy roller?"

"No. Because I think you'd be good at the detail work."

She laughed. "Very adept. Just point me to the brushes. What else is happening today?"

"Internet service will be hooked up tomorrow, same with phone. Equipment will also be delivered. I bought a secondhand desk at the used furniture shop and Norm said he'd actually deliver it today, even though it's Sunday."

"That's fast."

Brooks looked so tall and head-over-heels sexy this morning. He'd discarded his Stetson. His shirt might have seen a hundred washings because it was soft and a bit faded. He'd probably worn an old one in deference to the paint splatters he might get on it, she supposed. His jeans appeared worn, too, and fit him *so* well.

"I can't believe how fast this is happening."

"It has to happen fast for Dad's sake," Brooks said matter-of-factly.

"When are you going to tell him?"

"Once we're up and running. I don't want him to think it's something I won't go through with. I intend to present it to him as a done deal."

Brooks's cell phone buzzed. He took it from his belt and checked the caller ID. "I should take this. It's the Kalispell clinic."

Jazzy nodded and went to find the paint brush, but she couldn't help hearing Brooks say, "Clint can't handle it?"

He paused then added, "Yeah, I understand. Okay, it will take me about ten minutes." When he ended the call, he just stared at Jazzy. "I have to drive to a ranch outside of Kalispell, but I don't want to leave you here with this mess."

"No mess, just painting to be done."

"I don't like leaving you here without a vehicle."

"Strickland's is only a few blocks away. I can always call Cecilia or Dean if need be. Go, take care of whatever emergency has come up."

He came closer to her, so close she could see the rise and fall of his chest as he let out a long breath. He looked as if he wanted to…touch her and she wanted him to touch her.

His voice was husky as he said, "You're becoming indispensable."

Seriously she responded, "I don't think I've ever been indispensable."

He cocked his head. "That's hard to believe."

"In a large family, someone's always there, ready to step in. Sometimes when I get home after time away, it feels like no one's missed me. It's hard to explain."

Now he did reach out and touch her face, his thumb rough on her cheek. "I'd miss you if you weren't here."

"I shouldn't have said what I did." She could feel heat in her cheeks.

"You can say whatever you want to me, Jazzy. Sometimes it's easier to talk to strangers about the truth than to anyone else. Maybe that's why we hooked up at the Ace in the Hole."

Hooked up. But they really *hadn't* hooked up, not in that way. Still, she knew exactly what Brooks meant, and she couldn't help but say, "You're not a stranger anymore."

As soon as the words were out of her mouth, she wondered if she should have said them. Maybe he didn't feel the same way. But then his eyes darkened and he seemed as if he wanted to do more than touch her face, as if maybe he wanted to kiss her.

"No, we're not strangers anymore."

She tried to cover the excitement she was feeling, the heat and the speed of her racing pulse. "It's hard to believe we've only known each other less than a week. I feel as if I've known you longer."

"Much longer than a few days," he agreed, seemingly unable to look away. Then he appeared to remember he had something else to do, and someplace else he had to be. Whatever he'd been thinking and feeling got closed off. "I'd better get going. If there's any problem, call me," he reminded her.

There *was* a problem. She was much too attracted to Brooks Smith. *He's a confirmed bachelor,* she chastised herself. That was so hard to remember when he looked at her with his intense brown eyes.

Chapter Five

When Brooks stepped inside his Rust Creek Falls clinic—and he was beginning to think of it that way—he stopped short and just stared at Jazzy. She was sitting at the desk that had obviously been delivered when he was gone…in front of the wall that hadn't been finished the last time he'd looked. She hadn't just painted the trim, the baseboards, the door frames, she'd finished that wall, too. He didn't know whether to shake her or… *Go ahead and think it.* He wanted to take her to bed.

Not going to happen. He was her boss. They could never have a decent working relationship if they were involved, though that didn't keep him from imagining what it would be like—bringing her into his condo, undressing her slowly, leading them both into pleasure. He'd wondered more than once about her romantic past, and maybe it would come up because he had a question for her about it.

She stood when she saw him, all smiles. "I need to know if you're going to rely on word of mouth to get business, or if I should investigate some other advertisement opportunities." She had a pad and pen on the desk, jotting down ideas and the next items on a to-do list.

"Are we going to talk about what you did here this morning?"

"Not right now. There are more important things. I'll need to know your budget for advertising. Maybe you can tell me what's worked with the Kalispell clinic and what hasn't. What I think will serve you well now is to provide some kind of service that your father can't."

He'd been wrestling for the past few hours with recalcitrant cows. He'd washed off at an outside spigot but he still felt grimy, not at all as if he should be anywhere near Jazzy. Still, he approached her.

"You've given this a lot of thought."

"You want to succeed, don't you?"

"Sure, I want the practice to succeed, but more than that, I want Dad to see the success of this practice as a relief for him."

"So what service *doesn't* he provide?" she asked with that perky smile that made his whole body tense.

Keeping his mind on the question, he answered, "Dad doesn't do much work with small animals because he doesn't have time. He sets up office hours but then he gets called away. Ranchers can't bring horses and calves to him, so *he* goes to *them*. Traveling takes time. On top of that, Dad likes to gab. He spends a lot of time with his clients."

"Do you think that helps?"

"Sometimes it might, sometimes it might not. For instance, the first time I went to Sam's to help with his horses, we did spend a lot of time talking. I had to get a good feel for what was going on and what had happened to them. But since then, we talk very little, except if it's about the animals. Dad, on the other hand, would make a point of spending time with Sam with each visit."

"So what you're saying is that your dad's appointments aren't always on time."

"They're *rarely* on time. When he has office hours, his waiting room fills up and patients can be there an hour and a half to two hours before he gets to them."

"So that's a great place to start. His weakness can be our strength. We'll have to figure out a way to make sure you keep your office appointments, and I'll have to be certain I schedule them with the right amount of time."

"That envelope I gave you has a list of Kalispell services and the times that they schedule them. For instance, if you have a cat come in for an ear cleaning and a nail clip, that's a fifteen-minute appointment. A yearly check to discuss problems, get vaccinations, maybe flea treatments, would take a half an hour. Get my drift?"

"But I don't think it can be that cut and dried," she protested.

"You're right. After I get to know my patients, I can analyze their needs pretty accurately. I don't want to overcharge just because they take up my time, either. It's going to be a balance."

"I understand that."

He came around the side of the L-shaped desk unit. Jazzy was using a folding chair because the desk chair he'd bought wouldn't be delivered until tomorrow.

She ran her hand over the walnut finish on the desk.

"I like this. It's quality wood and sturdy. Your computer setup and printer should fit on here just fine."

"We'll see tomorrow. It shouldn't take too long to set up." He studied her. "But right now there's someplace I want to show you."

"Here in the office?"

"No. You've done enough work here today. I just want to show you something I like about Rust Creek Falls, and maybe you'll like it, too."

He was standing behind her as he looked over the desk and suddenly he couldn't keep from placing his hands on her shoulders.

She went perfectly still.

Jazzy felt warm under his hands. There was a comfort in holding her, but he felt a need to claim her somehow, too. Funny he should think of it that way.

He was grateful for her help, for her expertise in painting, for her caring about his practice and his dad. He cleared his throat. "Thank you for finishing this today, Jazzy. Tomorrow we can actually start setting up."

Releasing his grip on her, he stepped away.

She was silent for a moment but then her eyes sparkled in a way that invited him to get to know her better. "As soon as I wash up, I'm ready to go." Her voice was light.

They were going to keep everything between them *very* light.

As Brooks drove to the north of Rust Creek Falls, Jazzy recognized where they were headed—Falls Mountain. Tall evergreens were everywhere.

When the paved part of the road ended, Brooks

glanced at her. "This last stretch has been smoothed out some since the flood, but it could still be a little rough. Have you ever been to the falls?"

"I haven't. There just never seemed to be enough time to ride up here."

Brooks's truck bumped along the narrow road, which became a series of switchbacks under the never-ending groves of pines. One of the switchbacks led out onto a rocky point before doubling back. They could have parked there, she guessed, to get a view of Rust Creek Falls valley below, but they didn't. Brooks kept driving.

Suddenly they rounded a sharp turn and Jazzy could hear a tumbling, echoing roar. Mist wisped in front of them until finally as the sparkling sun reflected off shimmering water, she spotted the falls.

Brooks veered off the road to a safe spot and parked. "Would you like to get out? We can walk closer."

"Is it safe?"

"I promise I won't let you trip and fall over the edge." He grinned at her and she shook her head.

"I've done some hiking, I'll be—"

"Fine," he supplied for her and she had to grin back. There was something about Brooks Smith that made her want to dive into his arms. How could his fiancée have broken up with him?

After Jazzy climbed out of the truck, Brooks took her elbow as they walked toward the falls. They stood there a few moments in silence, listening to the fall of water, watching the mist puff up, admiring the late-day sunlight glinting off the cascade of ripples. They were standing close together. Brooks was still holding her elbow and it didn't feel protective as much as... close...intimate.

Because of that, because she wanted to know more about him, she asked, "Do you date much?" She knew what she'd heard from Dean, but she wanted to hear it from Brooks.

"I don't have time to date."

"If you did, would you?"

Instead of gazing at the falls now, he was gazing at her. "I don't know. Dating is meant to lead somewhere. I don't know if I want to go there for lots of reasons."

She knew she was prying but she asked, "Such as?"

The breeze and the mist wound about them, seeming to push them closer.

"Relationships require time, and I don't have it. Relationships require commitment, loyalty, fidelity and few people know how to give those."

She sorted that one out from all the rest. "You've put a lot of thought into it."

"Because I tried once and it didn't work."

Hmm, just what did that mean? Had Brooks's fiancée expected flowers, poems, rose petals and attention from morning to night? On the other hand, if Brooks really didn't know how to be a partner in a relationship...

She'd find out about the partner part.

"Did your mom and dad have a good marriage?"

"This is beginning to feel like the Inquisition," he grumbled.

"Sorry. I shouldn't have asked." She'd obviously pushed too far and she had a tendency to do that. She just hoped that she hadn't ruined their rapport.

But as if *he* needed answers, too, he asked, "What about *your* parents? Do they have a good marriage?"

She didn't mind talking about her parents. They were the epitome of what a married couple *should* be. "Oh, yes. They still hold hands. They enjoy being around each other. We can tell."

"You talk about it with your brother and sisters?"

She grinned. "Especially when we're trying to point out what we want for our futures. Three of my sisters are happily married. Incredibly lovesick." She sighed. "They sure have had more luck than I've had." Then, because she didn't want Brooks to think she was pathetic not being able to find anybody to love, she said, "But maybe that's because I don't like calf-roping. Maybe if I practiced, a cowboy would lift me out of the mud and he'd become my Prince Charming."

Brooks laughed. "That's a pipe dream if I ever heard one."

"Don't I know it. I limit my pipe dreams to achievable ones." And she could see, even if she'd begun to fall for Brooks Smith, that that road would lead nowhere. Whatever had happened to him had made him sure that a bachelor's life was the one he wanted.

What a shame.

The following morning, Jazzy was at the front desk, setting up the computer program. She glanced over at Brooks as he helped the delivery man move in more equipment and furniture. He was wearing jeans and a T-shirt today in deference to the work he was doing, and he looked good. All brawny, handsome cowboy.

They'd met here today and acted as if they hadn't shared those closer moments at the falls yesterday. But then she knew that was the way men acted sometimes. Her dad, especially, had trouble showing his feelings. And Brody, even though he was supposed to be a modern-day bachelor, didn't often put his into words, either.

In the reception area, Brooks pushed a few chairs into place and then asked Jazzy, "What do you think?"

"I think it's coming together. By tomorrow you should be ready to see patients. Later today, I'll see about putting the word out on local Kalispell sites. Getting the word out isn't always easy, but we'll do it."

Suddenly, a tall, thin woman with fire-red, frizzy hair burst into the office. "Brooks, what's going on here? I heard there was a bunch of commotion down here and came down to see myself."

With an expression of chagrin, Brooks turned to face the newcomer. "Hi, Irene. Have you met Jasmine Cates? Jazzy, this is Irene Murphy. She manages the feed department at Crawford's store."

"It's good to meet you, Mrs. Murphy." She wasn't touching this complication. She was going to let Brooks handle the woman and an explanation that might spread through the town like wildfire. Jazzy was an outsider, but Brooks wasn't, and the news would be better coming from him.

"I'm setting up a clinic here," he explained. "Buckskin Veterinary Clinic."

"You mean, you're like an annex to your dad's practice?" Irene inquired with a puzzled look on her face.

"No, I'm not an annex." Brooks didn't explain more.

Irene gave the place a good looking around, and her nose went a little higher into the air. "It looks like we'll have something to talk about at Crawford's today." Before Brooks could say another word, she'd swept out the door.

"Uh-oh," he muttered. "I'd better get hold of my father. She's the town crier. Nothing escapes her notice."

Brooks took out his phone and speed-dialed his dad's number. He frowned. "Voice mail. He must be out on a call. He leaves his phone in the car rather than carry it with him. That's a mistake for more than one reason. If he had it on him, at least he could dial 9-1-1 if something happened."

"Is there a reason he leaves it in his car?" Jazzy asked.

"He lost his phone once when he was tracking through a field and never found it again. When something happens once, Dad doesn't forget. He doesn't change easily, either."

When Brooks's face darkened, Jazzy suspected he was thinking about his broken engagement and his father's directive to get married or not join him in his practice. She didn't know how she'd feel if her parents gave her an ultimatum, like either get married or move out. But they'd never do that.

Nevertheless, she did often feel their concern that she hadn't met the right guy, that she wasn't settling down like her sisters, that she wouldn't have the grandchildren they were hoping for. That was a constant, steady pressure. She could only imagine the pressure Brooks was feeling with his dad's health being in danger. No wonder he wanted to do something about it.

A half hour later, Jazzy was proud of herself that she'd set up the computer program and it was ready to input patient data.

Brooks circled around the desk and leaned over her shoulder. "Great job, Jazzy."

Turning her head sideways, her face was very close to his.

"Thanks," she said, a little breathless. "Now I just have to round up some four-legged patients for you."

He didn't move away and she wondered if he liked the idea of being close as much as she did. His voice was husky when he said, "Once we get the sign up tomorrow, everyone will know we're here." He'd told her he had a friend who could paint a sign on short notice.

All of a sudden, the front door of the clinic banged opened and a tall, barrel-chested man, who was red-faced and almost looked as if he were breathing fire, came rushing in. "Just what in the hell are you doing?"

When Brooks straightened, he had a pained look on his face.

Jazzy asked, "Should I call the sheriff?"

"The sheriff?" the man bellowed. "*I* should be the one calling the sheriff. My own son is trying to put me out of business."

Now Jazzy saw the light. The irate man was Barrett Smith, Brooks's father. She couldn't believe he'd already gotten wind of what was happening here, but Irene Murphy must have put the word out.

Brooks rounded the desk so he was face-to-face with his dad, or rather boot to boot. "Calm down, Dad."

"Calm down? My own son is trying to humiliate me in front of the whole town!"

"I'm doing no such thing. I'm setting up a clinic to take some of your business away, so you're not working twenty hours a day."

"You've no right to interfere in my business."

"Just as you have no right to interfere in my life?" Brooks asked, a bit of resentment in his tone.

Uh-oh, Jazzy thought. This argument could really damage father-son relations. Yet she didn't feel she had the right to interfere.

"I'm older and wiser. I know best," Barrett blustered.

"You're older, but I don't know how much wiser. You won't see reason so I had to take matters into my own hands. We could see patients here today if we had to. We'll definitely be open soon, then you won't have to take all the night calls. If people in town start trusting me, we'll both have enough business."

"If they start trusting you? You're only four years out of vet school."

"Yes, and I know all the new techniques and new medications. Do you?"

"You think you know too much for your own good. If I put the word out that no one should come here, they won't. Then what are you going to do?"

"You don't have everybody under your thumb, Dad, including me. So just accept the inevitable and think about slowing down."

"The only time I'm going to slow down is when I'm in my grave." He pointed a finger at his son. "And you remember that. This isn't over, but I have someplace I've got to be." And with that, Barrett Smith left as brusquely as he'd come in.

"That went well, don't you think?" Brooks muttered as his father slammed the door behind him. Then he added, "Maybe marrying someone would be easier than all this!"

Jazzy felt bad for Brooks *and* for his dad. "You knew he'd be upset."

Brooks rubbed the back of his neck. "I should know

better than to get into a shouting match with him. It never does either of us any good."

"You weren't shouting," Jazzy reminded him.

"My father thought I was. I wanted to break it to him gently. Irene must have beamed it up to a satellite and disseminated it through the whole town."

Jazzy bit back a smile at Brooks's wry tone. "Did the two of you ever just sit down and *talk?*"

With a sad shake of his head, Brooks admitted, "No. We haven't had a decent conversation in the past four years."

She felt such a need to comfort him. "You know, our families just want the best for us."

"What they think is the best for them is the best for us, and that's not true. You asked if my parents had a good marriage. They seemed to. They didn't fight. I saw them kiss each morning before Dad left for work. He wasn't around that much because he was always working, but my mother never complained. She warmed up his suppers when he got home late. When he missed a school event because of an emergency, she was there for me and enjoyed it. She never wanted him to do anything else. When she was diagnosed with cancer, my grandmother lived with us to help out, but I hardly remember that time. In some ways, it seemed to last forever, and in others it was over in the blink of an eye. Three months after her diagnosis, she died."

Jazzy came from around the back of the desk and stood near Brooks. "I'm so sorry. I can't even imagine losing a mom. My mom…well, she's our glue."

"That's exactly right," Brooks said. "Mom was our glue, and when she was gone, it was as if Dad and I had nothing else to hold us together. I spent time with

Dad with the animals just to be around him because I felt so adrift. But it's not as if we talked about what we were feeling…how much we missed her. It's not as if we talked about much of anything except the cases he took care of. When I wasn't with Dad, I was spending time with the horses. We had three and we boarded a couple of others. I could ride and forget for a little while. I could ride and eventually start to feel happy again. But I felt guilty when I felt happy."

"I don't think that's so unusual. Did you get over the guilt?"

"Eventually, but my dad… After my mom died, he changed. He became more rigid…harder. Sometimes I thought he expected perfection and I just never lived up to that. Now I think, like you said, he just wanted the best for me."

"So when you were a teenager, did you rebel?"

"Nope. I didn't want to give him a hard time. I wanted to keep the waters smooth. I played sports, told myself I didn't care if he was at my games or not. I got scholarships and that seemed to make him happy. So we had a tentative peace until everything went south with Lynnette and I felt as if I had disappointed him all over again."

Jazzy was more curious than ever to find out what had happened with his broken engagement, but he didn't seem to want to talk about it. In fact, he turned the tables on her.

"So did you rebel when you were a teenager?"

"I put a few pink streaks in my hair, got a tattoo, but that was about it."

"A tattoo?"

"It's a butterfly," she said. "But it's not someplace

that usually shows." She wasn't being provocative, but she saw him glancing at her arms. Maybe she hadn't meant to be provocative, but his eyes got that dark look again.

"There's much more to you than meets the eye," he said as if that wasn't a good thing.

"You like simple women?" she asked.

"I like women who are honest."

That gave her food for thought. She was about to follow up and ask him if Lynnette had been *dis*honest, but her cell phone played, announcing a call. She'd laid it on the counter beside the computer. Now she reached for it and saw it was her sister.

"Family," she said. "I'd better take this."

"Go ahead. How about some lunch? I'll go get take-out at Buffalo Bart's Wings To Go."

"That would be great."

Brooks gave her one last look before he grabbed his denim jacket from a chair and left the office.

"Hey, Jordyn," she said as she answered her phone. "What's up?"

"Mom told us you took a real job in Rust Creek Falls with a veterinarian. What's he like?"

Leave it to Jordyn to hone in on that.

"He's a veterinarian," Jazzy said evenly, to stop her sister from wandering further.

"How old?"

"He's twenty-nine."

"Ooh, and you just turned thirty not so long ago. Same age. Now give me the real details. Is he tall, dark and handsome?"

"He's tall," Jazzy teased. "And he's cowboy handsome. He's really great with animals, and he's a...gentleman."

"Are you falling?"

"No, of course not. I'm working for him."

"Those two things *aren't* mutually exclusive," Jordyn concluded.

"He's a confirmed bachelor."

"Uh-huh."

"And his life is complicated right now. He and his dad are arguing and—"

Jordyn cut in, "I hear something in your voice I never heard when you talked about Griff."

Out of all her family, Jordyn had probably been the least enthusiastic about her relationship with Griff. Maybe she'd sensed Jazzy's uncertainty about it.

"I'm working for Brooks," she said again. "Let's leave it at that. How are Mom and Dad?"

"They're fine. So is everybody else. But we're concerned about you. Are you giving notice to Thunder Canyon Resort?"

Wasn't *that* a good question?

"I should know in another week or so. I like working with Brooks and the animals. It's great practice for that horse-rescue ranch I want to start."

"You've given up on the business degree?"

"No, but for now, I don't want to plan. I just want to go with the flow. I'm tired of trying to meet other people's expectations of what my life should be."

"You're mad at the family because they wanted you to marry Griff."

"I'm not mad. I just got exasperated and tired of being watched over. I want my own life. I don't want to make finding a guy a priority because my family wants it for me. Do you know what I mean?"

"I know exactly what you mean. You want Prince Charming to drop out of the sky and land right at your feet."

"Jordyn—" This sister *could* be just as exasperating as the others.

"I get it, Jazzy, believe me, I do. And whatever you want to do, you know you have my support. So take a picture of this veterinarian with your phone and send it to me. I'll decide if he's Prince Charming material or not."

Chapter Six

On Friday, Jazzy printed out Mrs. Boyer's bill as the woman stooped to her beagle, patted a chocolate patch on his head and cooed, "You're going to feel better soon. I'll take good care of you." She looked up at Jazzy as Jazzy told her the amount of the office visit and waited as the woman wrote out her check.

It had only been a few days and Buckskin Veterinary Clinic was already seeing clients. Brooks had put a sign in the window that they were taking walk-in patients, and that had helped business, too.

"You know, your clinic is going to be convenient for me," Mrs. Boyer said. "Barrett is hard to get a hold of in an emergency. And it will be nice to have a practice that focuses on the smaller pets, too."

"I'm glad you decided to give us a try," Jazzy said sincerely.

Brooks came into the reception area from the back, carrying a bag. He handed it to Mrs. Boyer, a brunette in her midforties, who seemed to love her beagle like a child. "If Hilda won't take the whole pill," Brooks explained, "you can open the capsule and sprinkle it on her food. Just mix it in. It's supposed to have a liver and beef taste."

Mrs. Boyer laughed. "Hilda will eat almost anything."

"If anything comes up between now and your follow-up appointment, just give us a call."

"I was just telling Jazzy it's such a relief to know I can get a hold of you on short notice."

Jazzy and Brooks had made a pact that they wouldn't bad-mouth his dad, or say anything derogative about his practice. This was about building up Brooks's practice, and providing service to their clients. If they did that well, they would be successful.

"I saw your father at the General Store," Mrs. Boyer went on, glancing at Brooks. "I didn't know if I should say anything, but he was looking a bit peaked. When he left, one of the men he'd been talking to said Barrett had been complaining because some of his clients were coming here."

"We're just trying to provide an alternative to Dad's practice," Brooks explained. "I think the area has room for both of us."

Hilda began to whine. She obviously wasn't getting the attention she thought she deserved.

"I'd better get Hilda home. I understand we could have bad weather later today, rain into sleet. I think I'd almost rather see snow than more rain."

"A lot of other folks here would say the same thing," Brooks agreed.

After Mrs. Boyer deposited her checkbook in her purse, she led Hilda out the door.

As soon as the woman left, Jazzy turned to Brooks. "Maybe you should have a talk with your father."

"You saw what talking with Dad is like. It just raises his blood pressure."

"But if he's not looking well—"

"Jazzy, he won't listen to me."

"Do you think your practice really is starting to affect his?"

"After just a few days, it's hard to believe. Maybe he's seeing something that isn't there. He's never had much time for small animals. Most people here call our practice in Kalispell for their dogs and cats and bunnies. But if he's heard people are coming in here to us, maybe it's a psychological thing. I don't know. I just know the two of us can't seem to have a conversation about anything that matters, not without his temper— or mine—flaring."

"I haven't said one bad word about his practice," Jazzy assured him.

Brooks put his hand on her shoulder. "I know you haven't. Thank you for that. I want to do this fair and square."

The fact that Brooks was a man of integrity drew Jazzy to him as much as everything else about him. His hand on her shoulder felt warm. In fact, she could feel the heat from it all through her. Every time they were together, they seemed to have a rapport that went beyond words. She understood him a little better now since he'd told her about his childhood and about his broken engagement, though she still wondered why he'd broken up with Lynnette, or why she'd broken up with him. However, looking into his eyes right now, she didn't care at all about his past, just about being with him.

"You did a great job getting the word out about the practice through Dean and the other volunteers at the elementary school," Brooks said with appreciation. "I think that's made a difference. Are you still volunteering there on Sunday?"

She'd told Dean she'd still help out when she could, so she didn't mind giving up her day off to keep her word. "Yes, I am. I don't know how much help I'll be, but Dean says they can use anybody who knows how to swing a hammer."

"You've had practice swinging a hammer?" Brooks's hand still rested on her shoulder.

"Sure. Abby, Laila, Annabel and Jordyn never wanted to get dirty so I'd help Dad with his at-home projects like the shed in the backyard, or even work on the stalls and in the barn. I really am a Girl Friday. I can do a little bit of everything."

"You're proving that," Brooks said, gazing into her eyes.

When Brooks looked at her like that, her tummy did flip-flops, her breath came faster, and sometimes she even felt a little dizzy. It happened at the oddest moments—after he treated a little patient, when they were sharing hot wings over lunch, when he dropped her off at Strickland's. She wondered if that zing in the air whenever they were together was evident to anyone but her. She wondered what he thought about it.

He's a confirmed bachelor, she warned herself again. No sooner had she taken note of the warning, than

Brooks dropped his hand from her shoulder. "I'm thinking about helping out over there on Sunday, too."

"Really?"

"Don't sound so surprised. I told the Kalispell practice I'd be on call for them, but I know how far behind the elementary school is on their progress. It can't be easy for the teachers to be having classes in their homes. I think they're going to have more than the usual volunteers this weekend. I spoke to Dallas Traub from the Triple T as well as Gage Christensen last night. They're going to be at the school, too." He paused then went on, "You said you had dinner with Gage and it didn't go well. Is it awkward when you see him now?"

Was Brooks fishing to see if she might still be interested in Gage? If he was, he could put those thoughts to rest. "No, it's not awkward. We had dinner and that was that. He's a great guy. When anyone sees him with Lissa, it's obvious they're in love. I'm glad he's happy."

Just like her sisters were happy. Just like Willa and Shelby were happy. Sometimes Jazzy wanted what they had so badly that it hurt. Sometimes she could hear her biological clock ticking. Sometimes true love seemed to be a far-away dream that was never going to come true, at least not for her. She thought coming to someplace like Rust Creek Falls, she would stop the constant reminder. Maybe something was lacking in her that she couldn't find the *one,* that Mr. Right might simply not be out there for her.

The phone on the desk rang and she was glad for the interruption. However, before she picked it up, she studied Brooks. "I still think talking to your dad might be a good idea."

But Brooks shook his head. "I've never met a man

more stubborn than my father. He's solid rock once he's made a decision. But I will call his friend Charlie and ask him to keep an eye on Dad for me." He motioned to the phone. "Now see if we just picked up another client."

Brooks was a good man, she thought as he headed for the back of the clinic.

And a man who never intends to marry, she warned herself again as she picked up the phone.

It never should have happened.

Jazzy's dad had taught her to wear gloves when handling wood products. She usually did. But today, with Brooks working with her side by side, she didn't seem to have her head on straight. So when the two-by-four slipped and the splinter cut her, she knew it went deep.

Brooks was beside her in an instant. "What happened? Are you all right?"

"I'm fine," she said, unable to keep from grimacing in pain. "It's a splinter, that's all."

Brooks's steady gaze didn't waver from hers. He took her hand in his and saw the injury immediately. "I'm sure someone has a first-aid kit."

"Don't make a big deal of it."

"Jazzy, it needs to be looked after. Do you always try to fade into the woodwork and pretend everything's okay?"

Brooks's words shocked her somewhat until she realized they were sort of true. At home, she didn't want to cause anyone any trouble. It was simple as that. That's why she'd dated Griff as long as she had, even though she'd known there wasn't enough passion there. Her family had liked him. He'd come to dinner. He talked sports with her dad. Her parents had liked the fact that his sporting-goods store was doing so well and he was financially secure. She hadn't wanted to upset the family applecart. She'd wanted to be on the road they'd dreamed for her, and she'd dreamed for herself. But Griff hadn't been right. Pretending she was happy hadn't been right. Always standing in the background hadn't been right.

"That's what I do, I guess," she admitted.

"Let me see if I can get it out without a tweezers," he suggested. Taking a close look at it, he manipulated it a little, then pulled it out. "I think I got it all, but you really should ask Dean if he has a first-aid kit and put some antiseptic on it."

Brooks was close enough to kiss. He was close enough for her to see the tiny scar above his eyebrow. His caring and his attention were like a balm that she'd needed for a couple of years and hadn't even known it.

She heard the titter of laughter across the room and glanced at two volunteers who were eyeing her and Brooks. Uh-oh. She didn't want any gossip starting about the two of them.

Spotting a couple of other volunteers glancing their way, too, she sighed. Did Brooks notice how they were becoming the center of attention? Before he could, before any of it could get out of hand, she backed away from him and said quickly, "I'll find Dean and get this taken care of."

Her sudden agreement seemed to surprise Brooks.

She hurried to the hall. Dean was there and when he saw her, he scowled! What was that about?

Approaching him, she asked, "Where do you keep the first-aid kit? I have a splinter I'd like to bandage up."

"You can't leave it in."

"Brooks took it out. I just want to put antiseptic on it."

Taking her by the elbow, Dean guided her up the hall to a bathroom. "We've got running water in there now. Wash it with soap. I'll bring the kit in."

"To the girls' bathroom?" she asked with a laugh.

"It's the only one working. We do what we have to do."

With another smile, she went into the bathroom and did as Dean suggested. A few minutes later he was there with a plastic box. He removed a bottle of antiseptic and a tube of cream.

"I hope you know what you're doing," he said.

"I'm making sure my hand doesn't get infected."

"Don't play dumb with me, Jazzy. You don't do it very well."

She supposed that was a backhanded compliment. "What's the problem, Dean? Every time you look at me today, you're frowning."

"That's because there's been little ripples around you and Brooks today."

"Speak English, okay? What kind of ripples?"

"Whispers, under-breath comments like, 'Doesn't she work with him now? Maybe they're more than boss and employee.'"

"And you listen to gossip?"

"Of course not. That's why I'm asking you. Are you just Brooks's assistant or are you more than that?"

"I'm his assistant," she snapped. Then seeing that this was Dean, and remembering all the times she'd spent with Brooks over the past two weeks—the conversations, the lunches, the concern for his little patients, as well as his big patients, she added, "And his friend. You know how it is, Dean. You work with someone all those hours and you talk about family, friends. You become closer than just two colleagues who push papers around."

"You're sure this hasn't gone beyond friends?"

"It has *not*."

"I spoke with Brody. He said they all know you're working with Brooks, though they don't know much about him."

"Jordyn does. She and I had a conversation about it. I don't want my family thinking up stories about the two of us any more than I want anyone here doing it. I wish everyone would just stop worrying about my life and concentrate on their own. You're going to be married and have a beautiful family, a wife who's going to be a teacher here, a little girl to love. Isn't that everything you've always dreamed of?"

"Yes, it is, actually. I want the same thing for you."

"When you want it for me, it feels like angst. It feels like something I have to live up to. I want to fall into it, not live up to it. I want to follow my bliss and let it lead to my happiness."

Dean started to smile.

"Please don't laugh. Over the past couple of years, I've found that the more I tried to control my life, the less control I had. So now, here, I'm taking what comes day by day. I'm going with the flow. I'm adopting an attitude of seeing a glass more full than more empty. And good things are happening. I lucked into this job with Brooks."

"Does it pay as much as Thunder Canyon?"

"Almost. So please stop being concerned for me, and please stop passing your concerns onto my family.

I'll talk to each one of them individually over the next few weeks. I'll make them understand that being here is right for me."

"You do have a new softness about you, a new mellowness. Does Brooks do that for you?"

"I don't know. I haven't thought about it. Does Shelby do that for you?"

"Yeah, she can, when I've had a bad day. Instead of being all grumpy or silent, she gets me talking and I get back on an even keel. You're still staying at Strickland's, right?"

"Right. Melba is giving the volunteers a good deal on rent, so I'm still saving most of what I'm earning. I'm fine, Dean."

Brooks knocked on the bathroom door and called, "Jazzy?"

"We're in here. It'll soon be a crowd."

Brooks laughed as he opened the door and saw Dean. "What do you think? Do we need to rush her to the emergency room in Kalispell?"

"Nah, I think she'll live."

"You two better think up a new routine," Jazzy muttered. "Something that will make me laugh instead of cry."

At that, they all laughed.

"Okay, I'll take my kit and go." Dean headed for the door.

As soon as the swinging door slapped behind him, Brooks moved closer to the sink where Jazzy stood. "All fixed up?"

"Ointment and a bandage. I'm good to go."

"Are you? Or is the gossip a problem for you?"

"I just don't want the wrong thing getting back to my family. I don't want to cause them stress and worry."

"I understand that. But you have to shut off the gossip. In a small town, it could ruin your life." He took her hand. "We have nothing to hide, Jazzy."

No, they didn't. Not yet. The business relationship was front and center. But she wondered about the other part of their relationship—the heat, the quivering excitement, the pull neither of them could deny. Yet Brooks was trying to deny it. Again she wondered if that was for her sake...or for his.

"Are you still going to be able to work okay, or do you want me to take you back to Strickland's?"

"I can work just fine."

Brooks's cell phone buzzed and they both glanced at the holster on his belt. "I have to get this," he said. "It could be the clinic."

"If you need to make a quick exit, I can get a ride home with Dean, no problem."

"Let's find out." Brooks checked caller ID and frowned. "It's Charlie Hartzell." Brooks answered quickly. "What's going on, Charlie?"

Jazzy watched the color drain from Brooks's face, watched his back straighten, his shoulders square. "When did this happen?" There was a pause.

"Thank God you were there," Brooks breathed. "I'll head to the hospital now. I'll meet you there."

After Brooks clicked off his phone, he said to Jazzy, "Dad collapsed. Charlie thinks it was a heart attack. He's on the way to the Kalispell hospital. I've got to get going."

He'd already started moving and Jazzy walked after

him, catching his arm. "Do you want me to go with you?"

His voice was gruff. "You don't have to do that."

"I want to, Brooks. You should have someone there... for *you*."

His eyes got that deeply dark intensity that she was beginning to understand meant he was experiencing deep feelings he didn't share. All he said was, "I'd appreciate that."

Fifteen minutes later—Brooks's foot had been very heavy on the accelerator—they walked into the hospital, not knowing what they'd find inside.

Much later that day, Brooks and Jazzy sat in the waiting room. Charlie had left and Jazzy was glad she'd come along with Brooks so he'd have somebody with him. The lines on his face cut deep, his expression was grim and tension filled his body. She could tell when she sat next to him. She could feel it when his arm brushed hers.

Brooks suddenly muttered, "I never should have had those arguments with him. I should have stayed detached and calm."

"He's your father, Brooks. How can you stay detached?"

"I've pretty much done it the past few years, and I regret that, too. I feel so guilty about all of it. If anything happens to him—" He shook his head. "Before they took him in for the procedure, I didn't even say what I should have."

That he loved his dad? Those words were sometimes hard to get out, especially in an emergency situation when time was limited and medical personnel were buzzing around.

Jazzy had been part of this push to get Brooks's new practice up and running quickly, and she felt partly responsible for everything that had happened. Maybe if they had handled it all differently, Brooks's dad wouldn't be in the hospital. She laid her hand on Brooks's arm, knowing nothing she said would ease what he was feeling.

A nurse came into the room and said to Brooks, "Your father has been taken to his room. Dr. Esposito would like to see you there. Just follow me."

Although Jazzy had stayed in the background until now, she knew it was hard to absorb everything a doctor said in this type of situation. She asked Brooks, "Do you want me to come with you?"

He didn't hesitate. "I'd appreciate that."

When they stepped into Barrett Smith's room, Jazzy thought Brooks's dad looked ten years older than he had when she'd seen him last. He was hooked up to an IV and he was scowling.

Dr. Esposito, with his wavy black hair and flashing brown eyes, glanced at Barrett's chart and then up at the two of them. "You're Barrett's son?" he asked Brooks.

Brooks nodded and shook the man's hand. The doctor glanced at Jazzy. "And she is?"

"She's a friend of mine," Brooks said.

The doctor eyed Barrett. "It's up to you whether I should discuss this in front of her."

Barrett waved his hand. "After a man goes to the hospital, nothing's private. What's it matter?"

"Is that permission to let her stay?" the doctor asked Barrett.

"Hell, yes," the older man said. "Just get on with it. I want to go home."

The doctor's arched brows and patience said he'd seen this reaction before. "Your father experienced a myocardial infarction. Fortunately, not a severe one. We inserted a stent in a blocked artery."

"Is that going to take care of the problem?" Brooks asked.

"It will take care of the problem for right now. We're of course monitoring him and he'll have to get checkups. I'll set up a follow-up appointment when he's released. But as I was telling your father, I believe his attack was brought on by several factors—exhaustion, overexertion and a lifestyle not conducive to heart health."

Silence reigned in the room.

"What does he have to do to stay healthy?" Brooks asked.

"He has to change his habits if he wants to live a long life."

"I'm here," Barrett said. "Don't talk to them as if I'm not. I have a veterinary practice. I eat when I can. I work because the work's there."

"Yes, well, that doesn't mean you can't make adjustments," the doctor said. "I'll also be putting you on medication—one is a blood thinner and the other is to help lower your cholesterol."

"I hate taking medicine," Barrett grumbled.

"Dad, you'll do what the doctor says."

Barrett crossed his arms over his chest and looked very much like a rebellious teenager.

Dr. Esposito remained passive. "I'll be talking to your father again before he's released, probably tomorrow. I want to monitor him overnight. I also want to set him up with a consultation with one of our nutritionists about diet."

"I already know," Barrett said. "It's all over the TV and news. But I'm *not* going to turn into a vegetarian."

"You don't have to turn into a vegetarian," the doctor protested. "But you *do* have to practice moderation. I'll leave you to talk to your son." He said to Brooks, "If you have any questions, I'll be on this floor about another half hour or so."

After the doctor left, Brooks said to his dad, "You have to take care of yourself. You have to let me take over the practice."

Barrett looked up at Brooks, mutiny in his eyes. "No, I don't. This is just a little setback. I'm not giving up my practice until you're settled down."

A nurse bustled into the room to check Barrett's IV and they all went quiet. But as she began to take Barrett's blood pressure, Barrett waved his son away. "Go! Go home. I need to rest. I'm going to be just fine."

Brooks looked as if he wanted to go to his father, sit beside him, convince him to do what was best. But Jazzy knew Barrett was in no mood for that now. She gently touched Brooks's elbow. "Let's let him rest for now. We can come back."

She could see the torn look on Brooks's face. But when he looked at his dad and Barrett stared back defiantly, Brooks gave a resigned sigh. "All right, we'll leave for now. But I'll be back."

"Famous last words," Barrett muttered. "Go take care of your own life and let me take care of mine."

Outside the room, Brooks stopped in the hall. He

suddenly erupted, "He makes me want to put my fist through the wall."

"You don't need a broken hand on top of everything else," Jazzy reminded him.

Brooks studied her, went silent, studied her again. "He's going to die if he keeps up what he's doing."

"Brooks, all you can do is encourage him to do what's healthy. You can't do it for him."

Brooks stared down the hall, at the nurses' desk, at the tile floor and the clinical surroundings. Then he looked Jazzy straight in the eye. "Will you marry me?"

Chapter Seven

Jazzy gazed at Brooks in stunned silence. Her heart was tripping so fast she could hardly breathe. Had he asked her to do what she thought he asked her to do? *Marry* him?

"Can you repeat that?" she asked haltingly.

He ran his hand down over his face, then looked at her as if maybe he should have kept his mouth shut. "I asked you to marry me. I know you think I'm absolutely crazy."

"No..." she started and didn't know quite how to finish or where to go from there. All she knew was, the idea of being married to Brooks Smith made her feel as if she was on top of a Ferris wheel, toppling over the highest point. "I just wanted you to repeat it so I know I wasn't hearing you wrong. You want to marry me?"

He took her hand in his and looked deep into her

eyes. "This isn't a joke, Jazzy. I'm not out of my mind. Really. But I need to solve this problem with my father. The only way he's going to let me in on the practice, the only way he's going to rest and stop wearing himself down, is if I'm really settled. I thought he was bluffing up to this point. I truly did. But he's not. Something is making him want this for me. A rival practice seems to have made the problem worse. So I can only see one solution. I have to give him what he wants."

"I don't understand," she said very quietly, his assessment not making her feel so tipsy anymore.

"He wants me to be married. Settled. So I need a wife. The way we've worked together the past week, I just know you'd be perfect."

"So you really *do* want me to marry you?"

"It wouldn't be a *real* marriage."

When he said those words, she found herself amazingly disappointed. How stupid was that?

He squeezed her hand and went on. "We would stay together for a year. In exchange, I'll deed over the land my grandmother left me. You can have the ranch you've always wanted, rescue horses, maybe even earn that business degree."

Suddenly Jazzy realized *she* was the one who must be crazy. She didn't want a ranch as much as she wanted a life with Brooks. She was falling for him, and she was falling *hard*. Working beside him for a year, living with him for a year, she'd be altogether gone. On the other hand, if they actually fell in love, maybe he'd change his mind about not wanting to stay married. On the other hand, if their relationship didn't work out, she'd have an out.

Living with Brooks, eating breakfast with him,

working in the office with him, spending evenings with him… What was she thinking?

"What would your grandmother think?"

"She would understand. She loved animals, too. And she'd be proud to watch you use it for good. She'd also understand I want Dad around as long as I can have him. Think about it, Jazzy. I'll show you the land. It's a great place for what you want to do. Imagine how long it would take you to save up to buy your own property."

"I don't even know if I could do it in ten years," she murmured.

"Exactly. We'd both be getting just what we need out of this deal."

The longer Jazzy looked into Brooks's eyes, the longer he told her all the reasons this would work, the more she believed him. She thought about his dad in that hospital bed and how this fake marriage could possibly set his mind at ease. Really, they'd be saving his life.

"Maybe you should think about this a little while," she said.

"I don't need to think about it. I'm not usually an impulsive person, but when I see the solution to a problem, then I take it. You're my solution, Jazzy. We can make this work. We like each other. We respect each other. We'd look at this as a partnership."

Yes, they would. It would be a bargain…a good deal. They'd each be getting something they needed. She'd definitely be moving her life forward.

"But didn't your dad say he wanted you to build a house on that land?"

"We'll have to take this piece by piece. I think he'll just be so overjoyed I'm getting married, that the house won't matter."

"But what happens at the end of the year? With your dad, I mean?"

"By then his health will be stabilized. He'll be on the road to healthier living. I'll be taking care of most of the work at the practice, maybe even bringing in a partner. We'll just tell him it didn't work out. We jumped in too soon. But that's not to think about now. Now, we just need to convince him we fell in love and this is exactly what we want."

"Will you keep the new office?"

"Yes, I think I would. Dad would feel as if he still had a say over what was going on at his place. Little by little, I'd handle the whole load."

"You'd be giving up a year of your life for your father. Is that what you really want to do?"

"Didn't we both say family is what matters most? A year of my life is nothing. I don't know how much longer I'll have him. I have to do this, Jazzy. Will you help me? Will you make it work?"

She thought about a wedding, a bridal gown, vows. She thought about the ranch and the horses that needed to be rescued and a life in Rust Creek Falls. She thought about being far enough away from her own family to have a life of her own without their meddling. This really could work.

And her and Brooks? Well, she'd just have to keep her growing feelings under wraps and pretend this was business all the way. But in the meantime, she'd enjoy every minute she was with him. How much of a hardship could that be?

"There *is* another big advantage in this for me," she confessed with a smile.

"What's that?"

"My family will be getting what they want. They want to see me married and settled down, too. Maybe they'll stop worrying about me, at least long enough that I can put my own life in the direction *I* plan without their interference."

He was still holding her hand and now he squeezed it gently. "So you'll do this? You'll marry me?"

Her heart felt fuller than it ever had before. "Yes, I'll marry you. What do we do first?"

Brooks stood beside Jazzy as they looked up at the pine-filled mountains, snow-capped peaks, the quiet serenity of the property his grandmother had left him. Was he absolutely crazy?

After his father's adamant refusal to do what was best for him, Brooks had known he had to do something drastic, really drastic. He'd asked himself what would settle his dad's mind most; what would provide the opportunity for him to change his health in the right direction? Brooks had realized only one thing would do that—his own marriage.

Of course he wouldn't ask just any woman to marry him. That would be truly stupid. But he knew Jazzy's background. He knew what she thought about her family. He knew she worked hard. He knew she had a goal, but wasn't sure how to get there. A marriage on paper for a year would suit both their purposes.

"What do you think?" he asked her.

They stood by his truck pulled helter-skelter over a rutted lane. This property, like his dad's clinic and ranch, was located on the higher end of town. There had been some erosion from the waters, but overall, it had survived quite nicely.

"How big is it?" Jazzy asked in a small voice, and he wondered if she was anxious or nervous about his proposal and her acceptance. Of course she was. They were stepping into untested waters.

"Ten acres."

"The property looks like it's never been touched by a man's hand."

"It hasn't. My grandmother's ranch, next door so to speak, was sold when she died. She'd subdivided this parcel for me, and I never knew that."

"Are you sure about this, Brooks? You really want to let this property go?"

"It's a pretty piece of land, Jazzy, and, yes, it was my grandmother's. But it's not as if I'd be selling it for a housing development. You want to do something worthwhile with it, and you deserve compensation for giving me a year of your life."

She gazed out over the hills and pine forests, rather than at him. "When do you want to get married?"

Was that a little tremble he heard in her voice? Was she as terrifically unsure about this idea as he was? Maybe so, but Brooks only knew how to do one thing— forge ahead.

"As soon as possible. In fact, the sooner, the better. As soon as we put Dad's mind to rest, the quicker he'll take it easy. I'm hoping we can get this planned and accomplished in a week to ten days."

"That's fast."

"Having third and fourth thoughts? You can back out."

Now she did turn toward him. What he saw in her big, blue eyes made his chest tighten and his throat practically close. She was vulnerable, maybe more vulnerable than he was. Maybe planning this wedding put an impediment in her road instead of clearing it. From what he'd heard, little girls had dreams of Prince Charming and happily-ever-after. He certainly wasn't offering her that. The good thing was, however, she'd be free and clear of him in a year. Then she could resume her search for Mr. Right and think about having babies.

The idea of Jazzy and babies didn't help that tight feeling in his chest. "This wouldn't be a real marriage, Jazzy. You'd have nothing to fear from me. We'll be... housemates."

That caused a crease in her brow. "Housemates," she repeated. Then after a huge breath, she asked, "Where would we get married?"

"Dad won't believe this is the real thing unless we get married in a church."

"I'll have to shop for a wedding dress."

"And we'll have to order a cake. I'm hoping we can use the church's social hall for a small reception."

"You've already planned all this out in your mind."

"Yes, I have, but all the details can be up to you. After all, it's your wedding."

"And yours," she said softly. "There is something I'd like to know before we move on with our plans."

"What?"

"Can you tell me why your fiancée broke her engagement to you?"

The wind sifted in the branches of the pine boughs and Brooks felt snow in the air. Not a big one yet. Maybe flurries tonight. He knew he was distracting himself with the idea of the weather because Jazzy's question turned the knife that sometimes still seemed to be stuck in his heart.

"Brooks?" Jazzy asked, looking up at him, expecting the truth and nothing but. Jazzy wasn't anything like Lynnette. Nothing at all. That was a terrifically good thing.

"There were several reasons. You want me to run down the list?"

"Brooks—"

He shook his head. "Even after all this time, it's still hard for me to talk about."

"Do you ever talk about it with anyone?"

His answer was quick and succinct. "No."

Instead of prompting, poking, or encouraging, Jazzy just stood there and waited, looking at him with those big blue eyes, her blond hair blowing in the breeze.

"We were at Colorado State together and engaged for a year. She was three years younger than I was and I didn't see that as a problem at first."

"At first?"

"She still liked to go out with her friends. Since I was buried in studies or practical vet experience most of the time, she went. I really didn't think anything of it. My parents had had a good marriage and I just expected the same thing to happen to me."

Jazzy's expression asked the question, *Why didn't it?* She didn't have to say the words. A nip in the air made his cheeks burn, or maybe it was just thinking about the whole thing all over again.

"She'd come home with me on holidays and vacations. When we were home, I helped Dad and she knew I expected to join his practice after I graduated."

"So you thought everything was on the table?"

"Yes, I did." He realized Jazzy was getting an inkling of what was coming next. "A few months before my

graduation, Lynnette started asking questions like—
Did I really want to practice in Rust Creek Falls? Did I
really want to live there all my life? I told her that was
my plan. I'd never been anything but honest about it. I
think the real turning point was a job offer I had from a
practice in Billings, and one in Denver. When I turned
them both down, she began acting differently. Or maybe
that had started even before that. I don't know."

He saw Jazzy take a little breath as if she guessed
what he was going to say.

"A month before I was scheduled to graduate, she
told me she'd fallen in love with someone else, someone else who wanted the same kind of life she did. She
didn't want to be married to someone who might work
eighteen-hour days, whose phone could beep anytime
with an emergency, whose small-town life was just too
limited for what she had planned."

"Oh, Brooks."

This was why he didn't talk about what happened.
This was expressly why he hadn't told Jazzy. He didn't
want her pity. He turned away from her to look in another direction, to escape the awkwardness, to bandage
up his pride all over again. He was looking up into the
sky for that snow when he felt a small hand on his arm.
It was more than a tap, almost like a gentle clasp. Her
touch was thawing icy walls that surrounded his heart,
had surrounded it for a long time.

"Brooks?" There was compassion in her voice and
he had to face it. That was the right thing to do. He
turned back to her.

"Thank you," she said simply. "For telling me. I understand a little better why—" She shook her head.
"Never mind. It helps me understand you."

"So you think you have to understand me to marry me?" he joked, trying to shake off the ghost of the past, trying to look forward.

"That would help, especially in front of your dad. If we're going to pretend we're madly in love and this was a whirlwind courtship, understanding each other goes a long way, don't you think?"

Madly in love…whirlwind courtship…pretending.

Just what were they getting themselves into?

"You're what?" Barrett asked, looking stupefied an hour later.

"We're getting married," Brooks said, with more determination than enthusiasm, Jazzy thought.

"Of course we'll wait until you're feeling better," Jazzy explained.

Barrett looked from one of them to the other, his eyes narrowing. "And just when did this romance start?"

"Jazzy's been here since July," Brooks answered offhandedly. Then he took her hand, moved his thumb over the top, and smiled at his dad, though Jazzy thought the smile was a little forced. She was aware of his big hand engulfing hers, of how close they were standing, of how her life was going to be connected to his.

Studying them again, their joined hands, the way they were leaning toward each other, she wondered exactly what he saw. After all, she and Brooks had developed a bond. They wanted the best for his father. They had their own goals. They believed this was a good way to achieve them. Besides all that, they genuinely liked each other. If she could just keep that liking under wraps, if she could just pretend Brooks was a good friend, not a man she was extremely attracted to, everything would be fine.

The flabbergasted expression left Barrett's face, but he still seemed wary. "You two have been spending a lot of time together, haven't you?"

"For more than a week, we've been together most hours in the day," Brooks supplied easily.

"Yes, I know. Setting up a *rival* practice."

"Dad, it doesn't have to be a rival practice."

Barrett took another look at their clasped hands. "We'll talk about that after this marriage takes place. Why is it you don't want a long engagement?"

"You and Mom didn't have a long engagement, did you?" Brooks countered.

Barrett looked surprised that Brooks remembered that.

"Mom used to tell me stories about when the two of you met." Brooks added, "Come to think of it, you had a whirlwind courtship yourself, didn't you?"

"So your mother told you about those days?"

"She did. She was visiting friends in Rust Creek Falls and went to a barn dance. You were there. She told me as soon as you do-si-doed with her, she knew you were the one."

A shadow seemed to cross Barrett's face and Jazzy wondered if he was in pain. But the monitors were all steady. He was silent for a few moments and then said, "Those years were the happiest of my life. She was right. We both knew that night. So maybe...so maybe this sudden engagement of yours is in the genes. Maybe waiting is stupid when life is short."

"But you're going to have a long life, as soon as you change some of your ways," Brooks suggested.

"No one knows how long they have," Barrett said thoughtfully. "I'm going home tomorrow if some blasted machine doesn't beep the wrong thing."

"Are you sure you're ready to go home?" Jazzy asked.

"You know hospitals and insurance these days. I'm sure the doc wouldn't let me go home if he didn't think I could."

"You're not going home alone. I'll stay with you," Brooks concluded.

"There's no need for that."

"Dad, I insist. Even if it's just for a few days…to make sure you're back on your feet. Our practice isn't that busy yet and I can help out with yours. You've got to start taking care of yourself, and this is one best way of doing it."

Barrett assessed the two of them for a long time, then finally he addressed Jazzy. "I heard some of the volunteers are staying at Strickland's. Is that where you are?"

"Yes, sir, it is."

"Then let me propose a bargain. I'll let Brooks come and stay with me if you come and stay, too. I want to get to know my daughter-in-law-to-be."

Jazzy fought going into a panic. Staying with Barrett wasn't all that far-fetched. The problem was, she and Brooks would be under his eagle eye. They'd have to watch themselves every minute they were together. They'd have to watch every word they said, and really, truly act like a couple who'd fallen in love. She wouldn't look at Brooks because that could be a dead giveaway that there was a problem.

Instead, she focused on his dad. "That is an option, Mr. Smith. I'd like to get to know you better, too. But

I do think Brooks and I should discuss it before we decide."

Barrett didn't look at all upset with her suggestion. In fact, he waved his hand at the two of them to go outside the door. "So discuss! Then come back in here and tell me what you decided." He studied Brooks. "I think you chose a gal with a practical head on her shoulders. Go on now. Talk this out."

In the hall, Brooks pushed his hair back over his forehead and his eyebrows rose. "I can't expect you to stay at Dad's with me."

She was quiet a moment but then she decided, "Maybe it's for the best. We have a wedding to plan, and your dad needs somebody to keep on eye on him while you're at work. I can do that."

"Are you sure you don't want to back out of this whole venture? Dealing with two Smiths in close quarters might be too much to ask."

She thought about the horse-rescue ranch she wanted to manage. She thought about Brooks's dad and his health. She thought about staying at his dad's ranch with Brooks. Did she really want to do this?

Her answer came easily and freely. "We'll plan a small, quiet wedding, and we'll take care of your dad. It will be a piece of cake."

A piece of cake, Brooks thought wryly the next day as he handed his father his remote and made sure he was settled in his recliner. "Is there anything you need? A glass of water? Something to eat? Jazzy and I went shopping last night in Kalispell and the refrigerator is stocked with good stuff."

"Rabbit food, probably," Barrett grumbled. "You know I don't like rabbit food."

"I have a copy of the diet the doctor recommended."

"Fine. I'll eat what you want when you're here. But as soon as you two leave—"

Brooks stepped in front of his father's chair and stared him down. "I lost Mom. I don't want to lose you. So try to cooperate a little, all right?"

Barrett was about to answer when Jazzy came into the room with a tray. On it, Brooks saw a turkey sandwich, a salad and a dish of fruit. He didn't know what his dad was going to say about that.

Jazzy glanced around the living room. "This is nice. Homey. This is where you raised Brooks?"

If his father had been about to argue with Brooks, he seemed to have changed his mind. "Yeah, it is. He was born here, in the downstairs bedroom, in the four-poster bed." Barrett waved his hand toward the hall in the back of the house.

"Really? A home birth? Was that planned or an accident?"

"It was in the middle of a snowstorm is what it was," Barrett elaborated. "My mom happened to be here so I didn't have to handle it myself. He came out squalling."

Jazzy set the tray on the table next to his father. "I hope you like this. The turkey is supposed to be the deli's oven-baked kind. The salad is something I cooked up. It's my own dressing. And the fruit—I hope you like apples and strawberries."

To Brooks's surprise, his father looked up at Jazzy and smiled. "It looks great and I think my stomach just growled. Good timing."

Brooks felt like shaking his head and rolling his eyes but he knew better.

"I'm going to make soup tonight if you're okay with that. My mom's vegetable soup can make anybody feel better about anything."

"So you know how to cook?" Barrett asked with a wink, taking a big bite of his sandwich.

"I'm not a wonderful cook, but I can make anything basic. And I can always call my mother to find out what I don't know."

"Did you tell your family about the wedding yet?"

Jazzy's face was serious for a moment then lightened. "Not yet. That's on my list of things to do today."

"I have a couple of Dad's outside calls to make, but then I'll be at the clinic for a few appointments this afternoon," Brooks informed them both.

Barrett scowled. "You think you'll be able to handle that on your own with Jazzy here? I'm really fine alone."

"You're not going to be alone, Dad, not for the next few days. So just get used to that idea. Jazzy, if you need me, or he becomes too bullheaded, call me. I put your suitcase in the upstairs bedroom, the one with the yellow rose-print wallpaper." To his father, Brooks said, "I want to talk to Jazzy about some wedding details. Will you be okay for a few minutes?"

"I'll be fine." His father pressed a button on the remote. "Don't worry about me."

Brooks crooked his finger at Jazzy and they went into the kitchen. She wore khakis today with a red blouse and looked like a million bucks. He'd been trying not to notice but that was hard with her blond hair swishing over her shoulder as she moved, her blue eyes flashing up at him, her smile curling like an old, forgotten song around him. There was something about Jazzy that was starting to make him ache. That was the dumbest thought he'd ever had.

"You want to talk about the wedding?" she asked.

"I called the courthouse this morning and all we have to do is go in and get the license and we're good. I also checked with the church and we can have the service next Wednesday. Is that all right with you?"

"If you think your dad will be okay by then."

"Not okay, but I have the feeling we'll have to tie him down long before then. He listens to you much better than he listens to me. So anything we want him to do is better coming from you. Do you think you can handle that?"

"I'm used to dealing with a younger brother. I can handle it."

Brooks chuckled, and then he looked at her and he wanted to kiss her. No way, but yes, that was definitely what was on his mind.

To change gears and to drive in a different direction away from that train of thought, he asked, "So you're going to call your family later?"

"I suppose I'll have to now. Your dad's bound to ask me about it."

"Do you want to wait until I'm around to do it?"

"No. I'll call Mom and she'll spread the word. Everyone else will probably call me. I might have to turn off my phone for the next few days. What bothers me most is that I can't be completely honest with them, at least not yet."

"It's not too late to back out."

She looked as if she wanted to say something about that, but she bit her lip and didn't.

With that gesture that was both innocent and sexy, he couldn't keep himself from reaching out and pushing her silky blond hair behind her ear. "We're in this together and it will work out."

She turned her cheek into his palm and they stood there that way…in silence. Finally she was the one who straightened and leaned away from his hand. "You'd better get to work. Covering two practices yourself isn't going to be easy."

"At least mine's just getting started. I'll manage. I forgot to tell you with bringing Dad home and all, the Kalispell practice found another vet who's relocating from Bozeman. So now I can focus here."

"That's wonderful news." Jazzy threw her arms around his neck and gave him a hug. "I'm so glad. I was worried about you spreading yourself too thin."

All of his senses registered her sweet smell, her soft skin, her genuine hug. On top of that, he realized he couldn't remember when a woman had last worried about him. That aching took up residence in his chest again. He pushed it away as he leaned away from her.

Taking his jacket from the back of the kitchen chair, he shrugged into it. He felt her watching him as he walked to the door.

"I'm just a phone call away," he reminded her, meaning it.

As Jazzy gave him an unsure smile, he wished he was staying right there in that kitchen with her. That thought drove him out of his childhood home. It drove him to concentrate on where he was going and the animals he'd be treating. It drove him to think about *anything* but Jazzy.

Chapter Eight

"Mom, take it easy, I know what I'm doing."

Jazzy glanced in the living room and down the hall to the first-floor bedroom. Brooks was in there with his dad setting up a baby monitor he'd bought so he'd be able to hear his father if he needed anything. She really didn't want either of them to overhear this conversation.

"How can I take it easy when you broke up with someone recently, and now you're getting married?" her mother asked.

"Griff and I were never right. You and Dad, Abby and Laila and Annabel liked him. Jordyn and Brody liked him, too, but they understood better how I felt."

"And how did you feel?"

"Like all of you were rooting for a relationship I didn't want. When Laila told me she knew Griff was going to propose, I had to break it off."

Her mother sighed. "Griff was such a good catch."

"Mom—"

"How can you be getting married when you haven't known this man very long? What's his name again?"

"It's Brooks Smith. I told you. He's a veterinarian."

"That's about *all* you've told me. You didn't even tell us you were dating him. Dean didn't even mention it."

"Dean doesn't know everything," Jazzy said, holding on to her temper.

"So is this going to be a long engagement?"

Jazzy swallowed. This was the hard part. "No, we're getting married in a week to ten days. I don't have the details yet. As soon as I do, I'll let you know. But Mom, I know this is quick, so it's really not necessary for all of you to come. Really. But if you do, I can reserve rooms at a Kalispell motel."

"A week to ten days! Jazzy. Why the rush? You're not—"

"No, I'm not pregnant. This is just…right. Brooks and I know it." Jazzy was realizing more and more that this marriage *would* be right for her. How Brooks might feel at the end of the year was another matter.

"I wish your father was here." Her mom had mentioned that her father had gone to visit a friend.

"Dad won't change my mind."

"Then maybe your sisters can."

Jazzy knew she was going to have to say what she didn't want to say. However, maybe it was time. "Mom, do you know why I left Thunder Canyon?"

"Yes. You went to Rust Creek Falls to help the flood victims."

"That's true. But I also needed to get away from all of you. I needed to find out who I am on my own without four sisters' opinions, and Brody telling me what he thinks is best, too. I needed to make up my own mind about everything from work to getting a degree to dating."

Her mother was silent for a few moments and Jazzy was afraid she'd hurt her. But then she said, "You never told us any of this."

"I don't think I fully understood what was happening until I was here. I mean, I knew I wanted to get away from something, but I wasn't exactly sure what it was. After I was here, I realized there's so much noise in our family, and its growing in leaps and bounds with Laila, Abby and Annabel finding their dream husbands. I felt lost sometimes. I felt invisible sometimes."

"Oh, Jazzy." Her mother's voice was filled with the compassion she felt for her.

"I don't feel that way here," she murmured. "I don't feel that way anymore. I feel like Brooks needs me— with work, and personal things, too. I feel like an equal…a partner."

Again, her mother went quiet. Finally she asked, "Jazzy, is this truly what you want?"

"It *is*. And as soon as I know more about what's happening, I'll let you know. I promise."

"Your sisters are going to call you."

"I know."

"Brody might, too."

"I know."

"And you won't get upset with them because they care."

"I won't. But you might as well tell them my mind is made up. I'm getting married to Brooks Smith."

After the conversation was over and Jazzy had ended

the call, she felt worn out. This afternoon, she'd made soup and generally checked on Barrett, yet she'd also had to dodge *his* questions about her relationship with Brooks. She'd sidetracked him with anecdotes about her brother and sisters and her family. She'd done pretty well, but she didn't know how long she could keep it up.

At least Barrett was turning in now, and she and Brooks wouldn't have to deal with his scrutiny as they had during dinner and a few games of gin rummy.

She went down the hall to Barrett's room and found Brooks plugging the small monitor into a receptacle.

"So you're going to hear me snore all night?" Barrett was asking his son.

"I'm sure you don't snore all night. I'll sleep a lot better hearing you snore than I would worrying about the fact that you could need something."

Barrett gave a harrumph and turned to Jazzy. "So you called your parents?"

"I spoke with Mom. Dad wasn't there."

"And—"

Jazzy felt her cheeks getting a little hot. "They're concerned, of course, because it's short notice. But my mom just wants me to be happy." She went over to Brooks, took his hand and looked up at him adoringly, though it really wasn't much of an act to do that.

This is what they'd been doing all evening, and he played along with her, too. Leaning toward her, he wrapped his arm around her shoulders. "They'll come around. I can't wait to meet them."

Something in his eyes told her that he was being honest about that. Did he want to meet them to learn more about her? Or because he'd be dealing with them, maybe, for the next year? This was all getting a bit confusing. Boundaries were blurring. Were they colleagues or were they friends?

Taking his arm from around her, Brooks said, "You're all set up, Dad. You don't have to do a thing. Just leave it on, and if you need anything, yell."

"If I yell, you'll hear me without the monitor."

Jazzy had to smile at that.

"So you two are turning in, too?" Barrett asked with a quirked brow, as if he wondered if they'd be sleeping in separate rooms.

"I have a few journal articles to catch up on," Brooks said.

"I'll turn in early because I want to get up and make both of you breakfast," Jazzy added.

"We're both early risers," Barrett warned her.

"No problem there. I am, too. We'll see you in the morning."

But before she and Brooks exited the room, Barrett called after her, "That was a fine right soup. I'm glad there's leftovers for tomorrow."

Jazzy laughed as she and Brooks entered the living room and headed for the staircase. They climbed it in silence.

After Brooks walked her to the guest-room door, he frowned. "I didn't think being around him was going to be so tough."

"That's because we're pretending."

They stared at each other, each weighing the other's motives, needs and ultimate goals. After what Brooks had told her, she understood now why he was a confirmed bachelor. He'd been hurt badly. As far as she knew, he'd never trust another woman. Yet there was something in the way he looked at her that told her he wasn't immune to her as a woman, and she knew there was something in the way she looked at him that told him he was a very attractive man.

"We're going to have to do a lot of pretending with my family, too," Jazzy warned him. "They're probably all going to call me. I told Mom I don't expect them to all make it to the wedding. After all, Annabel's husband is a doctor."

"So from what you've said, there's Abby and Cade, Laila and Jackson, Annabel and Thomas. Brody and Jordyn are still single."

"That's right. I told Mom I could reserve rooms at a Kalispell motel if they want to come up and stay overnight."

"That's probably a good idea."

"How many guests do you think we'll have?"

"Maybe about fifty."

With Brooks's eyes on hers, with him close and the memory of his arm around her still fresh, she said, "So we're really going to do this."

"We really are." He changed the subject before either of them thought too much about it. "Dad wants to help with chores tomorrow morning, but I told him that's out of the question."

"I can help."

"You're making breakfast."

"Breakfast takes about five minutes. I help with chores at home, you know."

He grinned at her. "You do, do you?"

"I'm not a city girl. I'm used to small-town Montana." Maybe she'd said it because she wanted to make the distinction between herself and Lynnette.

Brooks's eyes narrowed. "Are you trying to tell me something?"

"I'm trying to tell you, you can trust me to keep my word. You can trust me to be a partner in this. Helping you look after your dad means taking a load off your shoulders. I'll do that with you, Brooks. After all, it's our agreement."

Even without the agreement she would do it for him if he asked.

Brooks was close, but now he moved a little closer. The nerve in his jaw jumped and his eyes darkened. She thought she knew what that darkening meant. It was his desire. He was fighting it for all he was worth, and she had been fighting hers, too. But now, she didn't know what was more prudent. She wished he'd act on that desire.

As he leaned closer to her, she thought he might.

But he didn't even touch her this time. His lips, that had been so sensual moments before, thinned and drew into a tight line. His shoulders squared and his spine became even straighter.

Then he let out a breath and he shook his head. "I confided in you about Lynnette, but that's not something I do very often. And even though I did, trusting is tough for me."

Although he hadn't touched her, she had to touch him. She clasped his arm. "Brooks, I will help you with your dad. That's the point of all this, isn't it?"

"Yes, it is."

She had the feeling that when he said the words, he was reminding them both of the reason for their marriage. He didn't want either of them to forget it.

* * *

In the barn the following morning, Brooks made sure he concentrated on the chores and not on Jazzy. That was hard, though. Her soft voice got under his skin as she talked to the horses. It was tough not to watch her jeans pull across her backside as she carried feed to the stalls. While he replaced water buckets, he remembered the meal she'd cooked last night, the way the house had smelled so good, the fresh-baked biscuits that had fallen apart when he'd broken them. He found himself easily imagining coming home to her every night.

"Are you going to play gin rummy all day today with Dad?" he asked from across the stall.

"Not *all* day. If you need me to work on anything for the office, I can do it here. Just let me know. I want to cook and freeze dinners so your dad can just pull them out when he needs them."

"There *are* frozen dinners."

"There are. But they have preservatives, and maybe not as tight a watch on calories, fat, all that. I found some good recipes online."

"You're going above and beyond the call of duty."

"If I sit with your dad and talk with him, it's hard to deflect some of his questions. He watches the two of us like a hawk. At least if I'm busy, he can't ask me about…us."

Brooks knew staying here was hard for Jazzy, too, and he shouldn't take his frustration out on her. "Tonight, instead of talking and playing gin, we'll make out the guest list. You can bet he'll have opinions on that. We should also decide on food. The women in the church's social club can provide a down-home meal with fried chicken if we'd like that. After all, your family is traveling all the way from Thunder Canyon. A hot meal would be good."

"That would be nice," she agreed. She studied him for a few moments, then commented, "You were awful quiet this morning while we were doing chores. Are you worried about the wedding?"

He wasn't worried about the wedding. He was concerned about what came after and the attraction he was beginning to feel toward Jazzy that he didn't understand and couldn't deflect.

"The wedding should pretty much plan itself. When are you going to get a dress?"

"I found one online. It should be here soon."

"Won't your mom and sisters be disappointed you chose a dress without them?"

"I don't want to spend too much time around them right now, Brooks, for the same reason I don't want to sit and talk with your dad. They'll understand I have to do this on short notice."

But he saw the look in Jazzy's eyes and knew she wasn't convinced of that. Were they making a mess of their lives? He knew this was right to do for him, but Jazzy? She was the kind of girl who still had stars in her eyes, who dreamed of bridal veils and babies. He'd bet on it.

For that reason, he thought about another errand he should run. He really should buy Jazzy a wedding present, just something small to tell her he appreciated what she was doing. He didn't know if Crawford's General Store would have anything, but they might. Nina ordered some unique gifts simply because Rust Creek Falls inhabitants didn't always want to travel to

Kalispell to find what they needed. He'd stop in there sometime today because things were only going to get more hectic before the wedding.

"Is there anything I should know about the horses? Should I come out to check on them during the day?" Jazzy asked as she stroked a gray's nose.

"No, I'll let them out into the pasture before I'm done here. Why don't you go on up and start Dad's breakfast."

"Trying to get rid of me?" she asked teasingly.

Yes, he was. But he couldn't tell her that. When he didn't answer right away, she asked, "Brooks?"

"Once Dad's up, he doesn't like to wait around for breakfast. I don't want him coming out here and thinking he can help. Maybe you can head him off at the pass."

"I'll do that."

When she swished by him, he almost reached out and pulled her into his arms. But he didn't.

At the doorway to the barn, she stopped. "Sunny-side up eggs, or scrambled?"

"Any way you want to make them."

She flashed him a smile and was gone.

Brooks groaned and picked up a pitchfork.

A wedding present for Jazzy.

Brooks strode through Crawford's, not knowing what he was looking for, just hoping that when he saw it, it would be right. He was hoping he could find that one special thing that he knew she'd like. Jewelry was always the best bet, but thinking about it, he hadn't seen Jazzy wearing much jewelry. Of course she wouldn't to work with animals or painting or helping with construction at the new elementary school.

Pearls were a traditional wedding gift. His dad had given his mom pearls. In fact, he knew they were still kept in his dad's safe. But this wasn't going to be a traditional wedding. It wasn't going to be a real marriage, so traditional didn't work.

He glanced at vases and candy and even boots. He spotted sparkly earrings and a necklace that would have hung practically to her navel. But then his gaze fell on the right thing, the perfect thing, something that was necessary yet something that could be a little fashionable, too. The Montana Silversmith's watch. His gaze targeted the rectangular-faced one with the black leather band and the scrollwork in silver and gold that made the band fancy.

When he saw who was behind the counter today, he smiled. It was Nina Crawford. She was looking as pretty and fit as usual, yet when his gaze ran down over the front of her, even in the oversize T-shirt, he could see the small bump.

"Nina, it's good to see you."

She frowned and laid her hand on her tummy. "It's good to see you, too, Brooks. I guess you noticed." She leaned close to him and whispered, "I just started showing, almost overnight."

"That's the way it happens sometimes. At least that's what I've heard." Though he did wonder who the father was.

Nina asked, "How can I help you?"

"Can I see that watch?" It was inside the case.

"That's a woman's watch."

"Yes, I know."

"Are you dating someone?" She sounded surprised and he knew why. Most everyone in town knew he'd said more than once, he'd never get married. But never say never.

"I'm not just dating someone. I'm going to marry someone."

"Why, Brooks Smith! Who's the lucky girl?"

"Jazzy Cates."

"One of those volunteers from Thunder Canyon?"

"That's right. She's been helping out here since after the flood. I thought this would be a nice wedding present."

"It's a *beautiful* wedding present. Any woman would love to have it." She stood back and eyed him again. "I just can't believe you're getting married. Did the flood change the way you look at life? It did for many folks around here."

He couldn't say it did, really, though Jazzy had maintained it had changed her outlook some. "Not so much. I guess I'm just feeling it's time to put down roots and forget about the past."

"That's not so easy to do," Nina said. "Take the mayoral election for instance. Collin Traub versus my brother. In the past, there was a family feud between the Traubs and Crawfords that no one even remembers anymore. But the bad feelings are still there. Who are you voting for?"

"Collin did a good job after the flood, bringing everyone together."

"You're kidding, right?"

"No, I'm not. I saw him in action."

Nina crossed her arms over her chest, "And my brother didn't do a good job?"

Now he'd set his foot in it. "It's going to require some thought, but I think my vote's going to be for Collin."

"I should charge you extra for the watch."

"But you won't."

She gave him a wry smile. "No, I won't. Do you want it gift wrapped?"

"You do that here?"

"Sure do. I have a pretty gold foil that should do the trick, if you have time to wait."

"I have a few minutes. Thanks, Nina. I really appreciate it."

"I don't need you here," Barrett said for about the tenth time.

Jazzy and Brooks exchanged a look across the kitchen table.

Barrett motioned to the papers Jazzy had spread across the table—pictures of wedding cakes and flowers, a list of guests and a to-do list that ran on for two pages. "You have lots to do and not much time to do it in. And you can turn off that damn monitor, too," he told Brooks. "After tonight, I'm on my own. You have better things to do than babysitting."

Brooks wasn't sure he was ready to leave just yet. But he also didn't want his dad's blood pressure going up every time he thought about them being there. "I'll make you a deal."

"Uh-oh. Sounds like I'm going to get the short end of the stick again."

Jazzy laughed and Brooks realized the sound broke the tension. She seemed to be able to do that easily.

"Jazzy and I will leave, but I come out here to help you with the chores first thing in the morning and at the end of the day. And she stops in at lunch to make sure you're eating properly."

Barrett narrowed his eyes. "I don't mind seeing her pretty face at lunch, and I'll take your help with the chores in the morning. But I'm on my own after that."

"Dad—"

"Don't give me that tone of voice, son. You want to help out with the animals, fine. You want to help out at the clinic, fine. But then I need my private time."

"Another condition, then. You get one of those new smartphones so we can talk face-to-face."

"I don't need—"

"Mr. Smith, I think you need to put Brooks's mind at rest. He won't be able to work if he's worried about you. Is a new phone such a bad thing?"

Barrett sighed. "You two aren't going to give up, are you?" After a lengthy pause, he decided, "All right, a new phone, Brooks helping out with the animals and with the practice, and you keeping me company at lunch. But don't think that's going to go on forever, either."

"We'd never think that," they said in unison, and then they both laughed.

Barrett shook his head. "You're even beginning to sound like a married couple. So did you set the date?"

"I talked with the reverend tonight," Brooks said. "Next Wednesday evening. Jazzy and I are going to the social hall tomorrow to check things out."

"I'm paying for the reception," Barrett said.

Brooks looked at him, surprised. "You don't have to do that."

"That's not a matter of *have to*. I want to. It's the least I could do for all you're doing for me. Why don't you two go take a last check of the barn, so I can watch my TV in peace."

This time, Brooks didn't argue with his father. He hadn't seen Jazzy all day, and he'd missed her. It was an odd feeling, one he couldn't remember having even with Lynnette.

"I'll grab my jacket," Jazzy said and did just that. She pushed all the papers into a pile and slipped them into a folder.

Once they were outside and walking toward the barn, she said, "I think your dad wants some peace and quiet."

"He's used to living alone. I can see why having us around is tough."

"So which cake did you like?" she asked him. "The one with the little pedestal, the layer cake with the flowers in pink and yellow around the border, or the all-white cake with a dove sitting at the edge of each layer? Melba said she can do any of them. She's a terrific baker and offered to do it when I told her we were getting married."

"It really doesn't matter to me, Jazzy. Just choose one. Any one will be all right, as long as the cake's good." He could see that wasn't what she wanted to hear. She wanted him to be enthusiastic. But he was having trouble with enthusiasm for this wedding when it was going to be fake. Certainly he didn't want more than that, did he?

She stopped him with her hand on his arm. "You really don't care?"

The night had turned cool and very damp. Suddenly snow flurries began floating around them. "It's not that I don't care, Jazzy. I want you to have what you want. Doves or pedestals don't make a difference to me. But if they do to you, pick the one that makes you happy."

She gazed up at him, and in the glow of the barn's floodlight, he could see she looked confused.

"So it's not that you don't care, you're just not particular."

"That's the gist of it. Though I do prefer chocolate cake to something...exotic."

"Like white?" she teased.

He took her by the shoulders and gave her a gentle little shake. Her hair fell over his hand, turning him on. When Jazzy was around these days, he got way too revved up. Maybe he should keep his distance from her until the wedding. That wasn't going to be so hard unless...

He had something to ask her...to invite her to do. "We're getting married next week." If he said it often enough, he might believe it.

"I know," she said softly.

At that very moment, kissing her was the top thing on his to-do list. But he had to cross it off. "When we leave Dad's, you'll be going back to Strickland's till the wedding. But when we move in together...I just want you to know you can trust me. I have two bedrooms and you'll have your privacy in yours."

"I wasn't worried about—" She stopped and looked him straight in the eyes. "I trust you."

She trusted him. That was a vote of confidence he had to live up to.

"Are we eventually going to move to Rust Creek Falls?" she asked.

He'd been giving that some thought. "That makes sense, too. Since the Kalispell practice found someone to replace me, there's no need for me to stay there.

After we're married, we'll look around and see what's available."

"It sounds like a plan."

The snow was coming down a little heavier now, and Jazzy raised her face to it. A few flakes landed on her eyelashes—pretty, long, blond eyelashes. She opened her mouth and caught a few flakes on her tongue, giving him a grin.

His stomach clenched, his body tightened and he knew his plan to keep his distance would go along just fine as long as he didn't kiss her.

Chapter Nine

Jazzy stood in the social hall of the church the following evening, still not quite believing she was planning her wedding.

Her wedding.

She'd never thought it would be like this. Her chest tightened and her eyes grew misty.

Standing beside her, Brooks must have realized her emotions were getting the best of her because he asked, "Is something wrong?"

"Not really," she said, her voice betraying her.

He lifted her chin, and his touch excited her as it always did. "What is it?" he asked gently.

She summed it all up the only way she could. "It's our wedding day. I never thought it would be like this—just something to plan and get through."

He studied her for a very long time.

Then he asked, "Do you have that CD you burned at the office today of your favorite songs?"

"Yes," she said warily, glancing toward her purse that was sitting on one of the tables.

"Hold on a minute. I'll be right back."

When he started to stride away, she clasped his arm. "Where are you going? We really should get back to your dad." They would be moving out this weekend. She'd be going back to Strickland's until they married and Brooks would be staying at his condo once more.

"If we're leaving him on his own this weekend, we have to trust him to behave. But I asked Charlie to make an unexpected visit after we left tonight. They're probably deep into a discussion about what teams are going to make it to the Super Bowl this year."

When he turned away from her again, she asked, "But where are you going?"

"Patience, Jazzy. I'll be right back."

Men said they didn't understand women. That was definitely a two-way street.

For a few minutes, Jazzy believed Brooks had deserted her. Maybe that's what she expected. In the end, wasn't this kind of marriage all about that? Leaving each other with no strings? Unfortunately for her, she was going to have strings.

She wandered about the hall, thinking about flowers for the tables. Maybe white mums…

Brooks reappeared. He ordered, "Give me the CD."

She did and he went to a little door mounted on the wall and inserted a small key. He opened it, manipulated whatever was inside, and came back to her without the CD. Moments later, her music began playing and he opened his arms to her. "Okay, let's take a spin and see how it feels."

Was he serious? She felt a little ridiculous.

"Come on, Jazzy. Let's do more than plan. Let's practice our first dance."

When she still hesitated, he offered, "Look, I can understand you don't want me to treat our wedding as if it's just an appointment on the calendar. I'm not. Let's dance."

She felt a bit foolish now. After all, their wedding *was* an appointment on the calendar. It wasn't a *real* wedding. That fact made her so deeply sad.

Gratefully, Brooks didn't see her underlying confusion because he went on, "I think we've been trying to avoid the pretense of the whole thing. You hate deceiving Dad as much as I do. We just have to keep remembering the greater good."

So that's what he thought they were both doing, pretending for the greater good. *She* wasn't pretending. As world-shaking as it was, she'd fallen in love with Brooks Smith! Who knew that could happen in these strange circumstances? All she knew was that she never felt this way with Griff or anyone else, for that matter. She was an experienced dater. Truth be told, she hadn't even gone on anything resembling a date with Brooks. But each time they were together, it felt like a date. Each time they were together, she was sinking deeper into a whirl of emotion—and she wasn't sure how she'd ever pull herself out.

Gosh, she should write a country song.

Stepping closer to Brooks, she let him take her into his arms. His clasp was loose at first as the music swirled around them. As she gazed up into his eyes, however, his hold tightened a bit and then a bit more. She liked the feel of his strong arms around her. She liked the feel of the softness of his T-shirt against her cheek. He was so…so…male and she felt as if she were drowning in that…drowning in him.

She had to distract herself before she started weaving dreams that would never come true. "Do you really believe your dad will be okay if we leave?"

"He's not giving us any choice. I found someone to help him with chores morning *and* evening. He's the son of one of Dad's neighbors. And I'm going to insist Dad keep his cell phone on him at all times. I'll be at his practice during the day if I'm not out on call, so I can check on him between patients. With Charlie checking, too, all the bases will be covered."

All the bases except home base…her heart.

"I really want to rent a place in Rust Creek Falls so we're closer to Dad," Brooks continued. "But I checked with the real-estate agent. Since the flood, a nice place is hard to find. My condo in Kalispell will have to do until something becomes available. In fact, why don't we take a drive there when we're finished here?"

Touring the condo where Brooks lived would tell her even more about him. "Sure."

Suddenly Brooks released her, but he didn't go far. He reached into the pocket of his jeans. "Before I forget." He withdrew a chain with two keys. "There's a key to my place, and a key to Dad's."

She held them in her palm and the reality of living with Brooks shook her a little. She pocketed the keys. "Thank you."

"You're welcome." Taking her in his arms again, he brought her closer.

She'd watched couples dancing on TV. She'd danced with a few of her dates, too. But the pleasure of dancing with Brooks surpassed anything she'd watched or anything she'd ever felt. Now that they were pressed even closer together, she let his thighs guide hers. She let her cheek actually rest against his shirt. She could feel him breathing.

Although she fought against it, a happily-ever-after dream began to take shape and there was nothing she could do about it.

On Friday, Jazzy slipped Brooks's key into his door lock and opened the door. Then she waved to Cecilia who gave her a thumbs-up sign and drove away.

Everything seemed under control in Barrett's clinic, and Brooks was going to be out on calls all day. There hadn't been any appointments at the Buckskin Clinic. For now, any emergencies that came in there were being forwarded to his dad's place, anyway. So Jazzy had told Brooks, barring any unforeseen circumstances, Cecilia would drive her to his place and she could make them dinner. His father seemed to crave more privacy and independence now that he was feeling better, and Brooks had liked the idea.

She picked up the bags she'd rested on the porch while she was opening the door and went inside. It was one floor with two bedrooms, a spacious living room, a small dining area, and a basic kitchen. It was obvious he didn't spend much time here. There wasn't a loose sneaker or a stray newspaper or magazine anywhere. The kitchen looked pristine, as if he never cooked in it. Most of all, she admired the floor-to-ceiling fireplace. She could imagine being curled up on the tan corduroy sofa that sat opposite, sharing a cozy evening with Brooks. Maybe more than a cozy evening.

Thoughts like those were invading her waking as well as sleeping hours now, and she wasn't pushing them away quite as forcefully. After all, love made you think about all aspects of being together. She now knew exactly what had caused those looks on Laila, Abby and Annabel's faces when they'd been falling in love.

Whenever Brooks entered her mind, she had to smile. Whenever she thought about him caring for an animal, her heart warmed. Whenever he got close, her stomach fluttered. All signs she'd never had before. Now she knew what they all added up to—love. This marriage wasn't going to be one of convenience for her. She was going to mean those vows when she said them. And Brooks...well, maybe a year would make a difference. Maybe, in their time together, he'd tumble head over heels in love with her, too.

She planned supper for around six-thirty. The time had seemed reasonable. After all, a pot roast could cook a little longer if Brooks was late. She'd wrapped baking potatoes in foil before popping them in the oven. Blueberry cobbler would stay warm for a while or could be reheated in the microwave. But at seven-thirty, she was still telling herself all that as she worried in earnest. At eight o'clock she got the call.

"Are you all right?" She tried to keep the note of panic from her voice.

"I'm fine. There was a break in fencing at one of the ranches and some calves got wound up in barbed wire. I ended up working by flashlight and I didn't have a cell signal to call sooner. Sorry about that."

"It's okay. I'll have dinner ready for you when you get home."

"It's probably ruined."

"Nope. The meat might be a little stringy, but it's salvageable. What's your ETA?"

"About fifteen minutes."

"Sounds good. See you then."

Jazzy hung up the phone, relieved that Brooks was okay. More than relieved, really.

Fifteen minutes to the dot later, she heard the garage door go up. She heard the door open into the mudroom. When Brooks appeared in the kitchen, she couldn't help but gasp. He was practically covered in mud!

"I haven't been calf-roping, but close to it," he joked.

He unbuttoned his jacket and shrugged out of it. It was wet as well as muddy, and he didn't know where to lay it.

She took it from him and plopped it in the mudroom sink. "I can get clothes from your room if you don't mind me opening your closet or drawers."

"I don't mind. I don't want to track mud in there. Second long drawer in the dresser. Just grab sweatpants and a sweatshirt."

Hurrying off to his room, she switched on the light and looked around. There was a four-poster, king-size bed, a dresser with a detached mirror, a chest of drawers by the closet and a caned-back chair next to the bed. His bedspread was imprinted with mountains and moose, and the blinds were navy like the background of the spread. This was a thoroughly masculine room, and when she thought about that bed and him in it—

Quickly she went to the dresser and pulled out pants and a shirt, then hurried back to the mudroom. He'd shut the door. She could hear the spigot from the sink running, so she knocked.

"I'm washing off," he said. "Just drop them on the other side of the door and I'll grab them."

After they were married, would she be able to open that door and just walk in? Would he want her to?

Crossing to the kitchen, she pulled the food from the oven and arranged their plates. The vegetables had practically disintegrated, but the meat was surely tender. She fixed two plates, but instead of arranging them on the table, she took them into the living room and set them on the coffee table.

When Brooks came into the living room, he looked like a different person from the mud-splattered one who'd come home.

"Soap and water make a difference," she teased.

"Soap and water might not make a difference for those clothes."

"That's why man invented washing machines. You'd be amazed."

He glanced at the meal on the coffee table. "I already am."

She patted the sofa next to her. "Come on. I bet you're cold. It's supposed to go down to freezing out there tonight. A hot meal will help you warm up again."

He smiled and sat on the sofa beside her. That butterfly feeling in her stomach wasn't because of hunger.

They ate side by side. Jazzy was aware of every bite Brooks took, each sideways glance, the lift of his smile that said he approved of her cooking. She finished before he did, and she went to the kitchen for the whipped cream and cobbler.

After Brooks laid his head back against the sofa

cushion for a moment, he eyed her soberly. "Do you know, I've never had a meal like this cooked for me before?"

"So no woman has tried to make inroads to your heart through your stomach?" she asked in mock horror.

To her surprise, instead of taking a lighter road, he admitted, "Lynnette didn't cook. We had takeout or meals at a local diner, much like Dad does." He paused and added, "And I haven't dated much since then."

And she knew exactly why. Handing him the cobbler, she said, "I'll cook when I can, for your dad, too."

"I think you're going to deserve more than a piece of land when our year is up."

Did that mean he could possibly give her his heart? But then he added, "I might have to raise your salary."

She felt her hopes wither but she wouldn't let him notice. "Try the cobbler," she encouraged brightly.

He did and she did. When she glanced over at him, she saw he was watching her with that deep intensity that darkened his eyes. A ripple of excitement skipped up her spine.

"What?" she asked.

He leaned toward her and stroked his finger above the skin over her lip. "Whipped cream."

She could imagine him using that voice in bed with her. She could imagine him using that voice in between kisses, in between—

He lifted his finger to his lips and licked off the whipped cream he'd taken off hers. Then he leaned closer to her.

Jazzy's insides were all a-twitter. Maybe he was going to kiss her. Maybe she'd actually feel his lips on hers, like she'd dreamt about for so many nights now.

But as soon as she had the thought, he must have realized what he was doing. His expression closed down, that dark, male intensity left his eyes, and he was once again essentially her business partner. Nothing more.

That was it, she thought. She'd have to deal with a year of wanting him to kiss her...a year of wanting more than that.

But she had *her* pride, too. She certainly wouldn't throw herself at him. She wasn't going to set herself up for a huge fall. She'd have to be as calm and practical about this as he was.

Calm and practical, she told herself once again. "We really should get back to your dad's."

Brooks's expression didn't change, though she could feel his body tense beside her. "Just let me get my boots."

As he hiked himself up off the couch and strode toward his bedroom, she whispered to herself once more, "Just be calm and practical, and you'll be fine."

But she didn't believe it.

The next few days sped by as Jazzy manned the phones at Brooks's clinic and tried to forget that he'd almost kissed her, tried to stop asking herself the question—why *hadn't* he kissed her? The day before the wedding, she was getting ready for work in the morning when Cecilia came to her room.

After Jazzy let her friend in, Cecelia said, "I'm kidnapping you this morning."

Jazzy ran her brush through her hair. "What do you mean *kidnapping* me?"

"I told Brooks you had something important to do for the wedding this morning. He said that was fine. There aren't any appointments on Buckskin Clinic's schedule and you could take the morning off."

"Then I really should go check on his dad—"

"Nope. You're going with me to Bea's Beauty Salon. *You* are getting a makeover."

Jazzy spun around. "A *makeover?*"

"A hair trim, some highlighting, and I brought a bunch of makeup along. We're going to get you ready for the wedding."

At first she was going to protest, but then she thought about her relationship with Brooks thus far. She thought he found her attractive, yet something was holding him back. Maybe his past romantic history. Maybe his broken engagement. Maybe he just didn't want to delve under the surface of the murky waters of their business arrangement. Maybe all of the above. But Jazzy knew she wanted more than a marriage on paper. If she was going to be married to Brooks, then she wanted to be *married* to him. She was afraid if she told him that, he'd call off the whole agreement. Possibly this whole deal had made her a little crazy. They certainly hadn't known each other very long. But she felt more sure of this marriage than she'd felt about anything in her life.

"My family's arriving today," she murmured. "Abby and Cade are driving my car up and parking it at Brooks's condo."

"All of your family is coming?"

"Everyone."

"But you don't look as happy about it as you should. What's going on, Jazzy?"

Oh, no. She couldn't confide this marriage of convenience to anyone. Not anyone. Not for her sake, not for Brooks's sake, and not for his dad's sake.

"Just jittery, I guess. Maybe a day at the salon is just what I need," she joked.

She'd never been that fashion-conscious or put much store in spending hours in front of a mirror. But Cecilia didn't wear gobs of makeup and she certainly looked pretty. Maybe she couldn't find a guy because she didn't care about all that as much as she should.

Not that she wanted just any guy anymore. She wanted Brooks Smith.

"I have something I want to show you." Jazzy went to the small closet, reached up for a hanger, and brought out her wedding dress for Cecilia to see. It was a Western-cut, three-quarter length dress with just the right amount of fringe. "I bought it online, what do you think?"

"I think it's *perfect* for you. Oh, Jazzy, you're going to look so pretty."

Jazzy reached up to the shelf above where her clothes were hanging and pulled down a Western hat with a bit of tulle around the brim and down the back. "And this goes with it."

"I'm so glad you showed that to me. We'll keep that in mind when we're getting your hair done. I have you set up for a manicure and a pedicure at the same time. A facial first."

"Cecilia, that's too much."

"Nonsense. It's part of my wedding gift to you…and Brooks," she said with a wink. "Believe me, he'll appreciate it when you're done over."

Done over.

"So what are you wearing tonight for the rehearsal dinner?" Cecilia asked.

"There isn't a rehearsal, per se. We're going to dinner

with our families and then the minister is going over the basics at the church. I'm not having bridesmaids. Jordyn will be my witness. Brooks's dad is going to be his."

"So where are you all going to dinner tonight?"

"The diner. They've reserved a big table. I just hope my family behaves. You know how they can get. Mom tried to talk me out of getting married. Dad asked a lot of questions. Laila, Abby and Annabel would have taken over the ceremony and everything about the reception if I hadn't put my foot down...hard. Brooks and I had everything planned and we knew exactly what we wanted. I wasn't going to let my family mess with that. We don't want a big shindig for Brooks's dad to have to deal with. I've explained that to everyone more than once so I hope they'll be on their best behavior."

"You don't want a fuss or argument that could cause a heart attack."

"Exactly. I'm worried about Barrett as it is, how he's going to be, how he's going to feel, what he's going to think."

"Think about you and Brooks?"

"And about my family's attitude. Barrett actually believes in love at first sight. He and his wife had it. So he's going to be right in there rooting for us. He could be at odds with my parents."

Cecilia suddenly took Jazzy's hand. "Jazzy, what do you want?"

"I want a happy, committed, long-lasting marriage with lots of babies."

"Have you and Brooks talked about babies?"

"No. But we have time." They had a year...at least. She had to be hopeful.

Cecilia ran her hand down the delicate fabric of the

wedding dress and the silky fringe at the sleeves. "This really is magnificent. That means everything that goes with it should be, too. Do you have shoes?"

"High-heeled boots. I ordered those online, too. But they're a little big. I'll stuff tissue in the toes and in the back." Pulling them out from the bottom of the closet, Jazzy showed Cecilia the calf-high boots.

"I was hoping you'd have open-toed shoes, so everyone could see your pedicure."

"It's mid-October in Montana. I don't want my feet to freeze."

Cecilia shrugged. "The boots will make you look sexy. Brooks will still be taller than you, even with those heels."

Actually, Jazzy liked the effect of Brooks towering over her. She liked the fact that when he hugged her, he surrounded her.

"What color for the toenails and fingernails? What will you be wearing *after* the wedding?"

Jazzy certainly hadn't thought about *that,* either. They'd be going back to Brooks's condo. It wasn't as if they were going anywhere special. "I guess I'll wear something I brought along."

"You are not talking flannel pajamas, are you?"

"No, I brought along a nightgown and robe."

"Yeah, I bet it's the kind you feel comfortable in. That's not what you need. Something else we're fitting in this morning. We'll be stopping at the General Store. Nina has a rack of nightgowns and robes. Maybe if there's time when we're done, I'll drive you into Kalispell to a cute little dress shop I know there. You need something special for tonight, too, Jazzy. Something that shows your family you know exactly what you're doing…something that shows this town that this wedding isn't of the shotgun variety."

"Is that what everyone's saying? That I had to get married because I was pregnant?"

"I've heard it at the beauty salon, around the General Store, around the volunteers at the elementary school."

"I hope you squelched it."

"You know each one of those gossip conversations is like a little bonfire. It takes a lot of water to douse them out. The best thing would be seeing you looking slim and confident and ready to go into this marriage as if it's just any other marriage. And it *is* like any other marriage, right?"

Oh, how Jazzy wished that were true. "It's a marriage that Brooks and I will work at to make last."

That's what she had to believe.

That evening when Jazzy took off her coat at the diner, all eyes in the place seemed to be focused on her. Especially Brooks's.

Cecilia had insisted she buy a red dress. The one she'd chosen was simple and sleek enough—even understated with its high neckline and just-above-the-knee hem. But there was a slit in the side and when she turned around, there was a keyhole in the back.

But Brooks wasn't looking at her back; he was looking at her front, and boy, was he looking at her front. Not only the dress, but her hair and her face, too. She'd used mascara, lipstick and some kind of powder that almost shimmered on her skin. With her newly highlighted blond hair tapered around her face in a fresh style, she'd never felt more confident as a woman.

Brooks was looking at her as a very stunned man.

"There she is," Barrett said with a wide smile. "I knew she wouldn't run out on you."

But Brooks didn't seem to hear his father. He couldn't seem to take his eyes off her. And she couldn't take her eyes off him. He'd worn a dressier Western shirt tonight with bolo tie and black jeans with boots. Tall and handsome and ultimately sexy, she found herself trembling just standing there.

"Don't you look beautiful," her mother said, motioning to the chair next to her. "Not that you don't always look pretty, but tonight something's...different."

"She's dressed to bowl over any guy she meets," Brody said, not looking as if he approved.

But she squelched that statement right away. "Only one guy," she assured them all. Was she acting or had she really said that? She meant it.

Brooks stepped closer to her like a fiancé would, took her hand and squeezed it.

Leaning close to her ear, he murmured, "You look gorgeous."

Was he acting, too?

He led her to the chair her mother had gestured to and pulled it out for her. She sank down onto it before her legs gave way. This was some way to start the evening with her head feeling as if it were filled with cotton and her mouth totally dry.

Brooks took his seat next to her and they faced her family. He covered her hand with his again and she knew to everyone gathered there, they looked like a loving couple.

Yet her father was frowning as he stared at them. "So tell me again why you're rushing into this marriage so fast, without giving us all breathing space, and time to get used to the idea."

Her whole family had come—Abby and Jackson, Laila and Cade, Annabel and Thomas, Jordyn Leigh, Brody and her parents. Jazzy knew Jordyn was on her side. After she'd seen the phone picture of Brooks Jazzy had sent her, she'd insisted he was too good to let go. But the rest of her family... She had to make this good.

However, before she could open her mouth, Brooks, protective as ever, stepped in. "I'm not sure you can explain the bond that forms when two people just click, sir, the way Jazzy and I did from the beginning."

That definitely didn't allay her father's concerns. "So you're just going to move up here, away from us, without discussing it with the family?"

Jazzy exchanged looks with Abby, Annabel and Laila who'd gone through the process of falling in love. Her look said *Help me out here, sisters!* Abby did. "You know how true love works, Dad. You've seen me and Laila and Annabel go through it. When it's right, it's right."

"We won't see you very much," her mother said, a little sadly.

Brooks assuaged her mom's concerns. "We'll visit you often. Jazzy's going to want to make sure you're part of our lives, and I will, too." The look he sent Jazzy said he meant that.

"You folks can stay with me the next time you're in town," Barrett told them. "Brooks still considers me an invalid and won't let me overdo anything. I'd be glad to have the company." He stared at Jazzy's dad. "I hear you're good with horses. I've got a few."

The tension around the table eased. The two men

began talking ranch life. Jordyn gave her a thumbs-up sign. Brody, however, eyed her suspiciously as if he still didn't believe what was going on. Her sisters and their husbands fell into conversation, too.

Brooks interlaced his fingers with hers on the table, leaned close and said only loud enough for her to hear, "It's going to be all right."

But as she felt the heat between them, as his breath fanned her cheek, as his gaze unsettled her the way no other could, she thought about her vows tomorrow and wondered if everything *could* be all right.

Chapter Ten

Brooks knew he must be crazy. Today he was going to marry a woman he was seriously attracted to, yet he didn't intend to sleep with her! If that wasn't crazy, he didn't know what was.

He adjusted his tux, straightened his bolo tie, wishing all to heck that Jazzy hadn't almost knocked his boots off last night when he'd seen her in that red dress. And when he pushed her chair in and saw her skin peeking through that cutout in the back, he'd practically swallowed his tongue.

There was a rap on the door. He was in the anteroom that led to the nursery area in the back of the church. He knew Jazzy was in a room across the vestibule that was used exactly for situations like this—brides and their bridesmaids preparing for a wedding.

Preparing for a wedding.

After the dinner last night, and the suspicious and wary glances of her family, he'd retreated inward. He knew that. He also knew it had bothered Jazzy. But how could he explain to her that she turned him on more than he'd ever wanted to be turned on? How could he explain to her that this marriage of convenience might not be so convenient, not when it came to them living together?

Still he was determined to go through with this. Their course was set. He wasn't going to turn back now.

After a deep breath, he opened the door. Jazzy's sister Jordyn stood there with an unsure smile. She'd been the one person to treat him like the brother-in-law he was going to be.

"Everything's all set," she said. "Once you're in place at the altar, the organist will start the processional."

Stepping into the vestibule, he saw his dad beckoning to him from the doorway that would lead up to the altar. He also saw Jazzy's dad looking more like a soldier than a father, standing by the door to the room where she'd emerge.

Mr. Cates frowned at Brooks.

Brody stood at the entrance to the church, his mother on his arm. He was ready to walk her up the aisle. But when he glanced over his shoulder and saw Brooks, his mouth tightened and Brooks saw the disapproval in his eyes.

If he were a betting man, he'd bet that someone in Jazzy's family would stand up and protest at that point in the wedding when the minister asks, "Is there anyone who sees a reason that these two shouldn't be joined in matrimony?"

"Abby, Annabel and Laila will give you a chance," Jordyn assured him as if she could read his thoughts.

"And because *they* will, their husbands will, too. Mom and Dad and Brody will come around as long as they see you make Jazzy happy. And you will, won't you?"

After the way he'd left Jazzy last night, with him all silent and brooding, he'd wanted to do something nice to reassure her. So he'd bought a bottle of champagne to celebrate when they got back to his place tonight. That's when he'd give her the watch. He wanted her to be happy, and he'd do his best to see that happen. But no one could *make* someone else happy. Everyone had choices, and those choices either led to success or failure.

So he was truthful with Jordyn. "I want Jazzy to be happy."

Jordyn gave him an odd look, as if she suspected everything might not be what it seemed. Then she confirmed it when she said, "I trust Jazzy to make the right decisions for herself. I'll be around if she needs me. Don't you hesitate to call me if she *does* need me."

"I won't," he promised, and he meant it.

Brooks crossed the vestibule and approached his father. When they were standing next to each other, Barrett pounded Brooks on the back. "I'm glad you asked me to be your best man. You could have had Gage Christensen or even Dallas Traub, for that matter."

He and Dallas had been friends for years, but since his divorce and gaining custody of his three kids, Dallas had had even less time for friendship than Brooks had.

"I wanted *you,* Dad."

"This day makes me happier and prouder than you'll ever know. Jazzy will be good for you. She'll ground you like your mother grounded me. You and me—we're going to have to have a talk one of these days, about marriage and everything that goes with it."

"I think I learned the facts of life a long time ago, Dad," Brooks said with a smile, trying to lighten the atmosphere a bit.

His father's face grew a little red. "That's not what I mean. There are things…there are just some things we need to talk about."

The minister emerged from behind the altar and Brooks nudged his father's arm. "We can talk. But right now, I think it's time for me to get married."

His father chuckled and side by side, they walked up the aisle to the front of the church.

Jazzy felt like a princess. It was silly, really. This dress wasn't all tulle and lace. It was more like a dressy, Western dress. But it was white and her boots were white with three-inch spiked heels, and Cecilia had made sure her hat was tilted just right on her head with the tulle flowing down the back of her dress. Mostly she felt like a princess because she could see Brooks waiting for her at the altar, all handsome and starched and pressed, with shiny black boots, and a look in his eyes that was lightning hot.

Last night she'd been worried because he'd turned so quiet, so expressionless, so unlike the Brooks she knew. What would he be like today after they were married?

That thrill of anticipation ran down her spine. He was going to be her husband.

Her dad stood beside her and held out the crook of his arm for her to put her hand through. She knew he wasn't on board with this wedding, but she couldn't keep living her life to please her parents. At thirty, it was well past time she flew the coop. She could see her mom sitting in the front pew, her sisters and their husbands in the pew behind that.

Jordyn Leigh, however, was going to lead the way on the road to this future. She'd worn a pretty, royal blue dress that, in Jazzy's estimation, was just right for this ceremony. She and Brooks hadn't wanted pomp and circumstance and long gowns. They'd wanted simple and quiet and just plain friendly.

The organ music began and with a spray of yellow mums clenched in her hands, Jordyn glanced over her shoulder at Jazzy and then started forward.

Jazzy held on to her bouquet of lilies and white mums even more tightly, afraid she'd drop it. She was that nervous. As the scent of the flowers wafted up to her, she used the look in Brooks's eyes as her guiding light. He couldn't look at her like that and not feel something, could he?

Whether he felt something or not, she was going to marry him and see where the future led them. Exciting couldn't even describe the ripple of emotion inside of her. Everything about today was going to be memorable.

Just as she reinforced the thought, Laila turned toward her and snapped a picture with her camera. Abby and Annabel had cameras, too, and knowing her sisters, everything about today would be recorded.

Tears pricked in her eyes. She blinked fast and smiled.

The church aisle really wasn't that long, but her walk down toward the altar seemed to take forever. But she didn't falter as the look in Brooks's eyes drew her forward.

Once Jazzy was at the front of the church, her father solemnly kissed her and she took her place beside Brooks.

"You look beautiful," he said in an almost awed voice.

"You look pretty spiffy yourself."

At her words, the awkwardness they both seemed to be feeling drifted away. He smiled, one of those Brooks smiles that affected her in a way she didn't understand, that made her feel hot and giddy and altogether a woman.

Beside Brooks, his father beamed at Jazzy and in that moment she felt a few doubts about what she was doing. What would happen to Barrett's feelings about her in a year if she and Brooks separated? But she couldn't think about that now. Today they were joining their lives. Somehow this would work out.

The minister welcomed their family and guests.

Jazzy handed her bouquet to Jordyn as she and Brooks joined hands. His was warm and dry and firm, decisive in its hold on hers. She felt fragile and beautiful and supportive beside him. The words of the ceremony became a blur as the minister talked, as she and Brooks responded.

They each said "I do" calmly as if they knew what they were doing.

Then Brooks's voice was low but strong as he said, "I, Brooks Smith, take you Jazzy Cates to be my lawfully wedded wife…to have and to hold from this day forward…for better or for worse…for richer, for poorer…in sickness and health…to love and to cherish until death do us part."

She repeated those same words, looking straight into his eyes so he'd know she meant them. Now his reaction was more stoic, yet the nerve in his jaw worked. The ceremony was affecting him, too. He just didn't want anyone to see that.

As Brooks slipped the gold band onto her finger, she could hardly breathe. When she slipped the gold band onto his finger, a hush over their guests seemed to emphasize the importance of the moment. They held hands and gave their attention to the minister as he said a few words about love and marriage, bonds, promises and a union that made the world go round.

They bowed their heads as the minister bestowed a blessing, and then he said the words the whole church was waiting to hear.

"I now pronounce you husband and wife." In a low voice, he said to Brooks, "You can kiss her now."

Well, of course, they *had* to kiss. They had to show everyone they meant what they'd said...the promises they'd made.

Brooks's arms went around her and there was only a moment of hesitation before he bent his head to her. His lips found hers unerringly as if this had been a long time in coming. She certainly felt as if it had, but then maybe he was just determined to get it over with. Yet as his lips settled on hers, it certainly didn't seem as if he wanted this kiss over with quickly. This meeting of lips took on more than a perfunctory air. It went on longer than she thought it would. In fact, she didn't know how long it went on because she lost track of time and place and the fact that there were guests watching them.

Apparently, Brooks forgot, too, because his arms held her a little tighter and he didn't raise his head and break their kiss until the minister cleared his throat.

She should feel embarrassed, she really should. But

she was so awed by the desire behind what had just happened that she couldn't even think of anything else. She probably couldn't have found her way out of the church. But Jordyn handed back her bouquet. Brooks took her arm and, in the next moment, they were walking down the aisle to the smiles and applause of their family and friends.

She was married. Brooks was her husband. The full reality of that hadn't set in yet.

They walked down the aisle to the back of the church, through the vestibule to the reception hall. Once inside, Brooks took her elbow and spun her around. "I had to do that, Jazzy. I had to make it look good." There was something in his voice that was a little unsettled as if making the kiss look good had unsettled him. And here she'd thought the kiss had really *meant* something.

"You certainly made it look good. I'm not sure what my parents thought of it, but afterward your dad was grinning from ear to ear."

"They'll all be in here in a minute. We just have to be clear about how we're handling it. No honeymoon now because of taking care of Dad's practice, as well as setting up mine. We'll be moving back to Rust Creek Falls as soon as we find a good place. Not a house, though. Not yet."

"Your father's going to think we're planning to build on your grandmother's property."

"I'm not going to tell him we will. If that's what he thinks, fine."

Her hand on his arm, looking up into his eyes, she said, "Brooks, I don't like deceiving anyone, especially not him."

But Brooks didn't have a chance to respond because

their guests started pouring in and they began receiving them like a newly married couple would.

Brooks's dad pounded him on the back, congratulating him. Jazzy's sisters gathered around and gave her a group hug. She and Brooks got separated more than once as guests migrated to their tables and conversations abounded. They had almost greeted the last of their guests and Brooks had stepped aside to speak to the minister, when Dean took Jazzy's arm.

"I can't believe you went through with this so quickly."

"You're going to be doing the same soon."

"That's different and you know it. I'm still getting the feeling that something's off here. That all of this happened too fast."

"Dean, Brooks and I just got married. Why can't you simply wish us well?"

"Maybe you married Brooks to escape Thunder Canyon and your family, but is that a valid reason? Shelby and I are getting married because we can't live without each other."

"Are you judging what I feel?" Dean was an old enough and good enough friend that she could ask the honest question.

He shook his head. "I'm just hoping you're head over heels in love and this isn't something other than that."

Looking him straight in the eye, she assured him, "I'm head over heels in love." That thought still shook her up, made her feel queasy, instilled in her the knowledge that she could easily be terribly hurt.

But it was absolutely true. She loved Brooks Smith.

Dean's eyes widened a bit as he could see the truth.

He gave Jazzy a big hug. "Then congratulations. I hope the two of you have a lot of happy years together."

She was hoping for one year that would stretch into a lifetime.

Jazzy sat beside Brooks during their wedding dinner, wondering what he was thinking. He smiled, but the smile didn't light up his eyes. He spoke to their guests, but there was a surface quality about it that troubled her. Every once in a while, he'd reach over and squeeze her hand or drop his arm around her shoulders. But the gestures felt forced. She just wanted to give him a hug... nestle in his arms. That's what a wife would do when she was feeling unsure.

Jordyn, who had taken over as facilitator for the day—and Jazzy was so grateful because this sister wanted to help, not interfere—tapped Jazzy on the arm and addressed Brooks, too. "It's time to cut the cake. Are you ready?"

She and Brooks hadn't really talked about this...or prepared a script. This would be a go-with-the-flow moment.

Brooks stood without a word and held Jazzy's chair for her. Once she'd gotten to her feet, he took her arm and escorted her to the table where the multilayered cake stood.

"You can have the top layer to take along," Jordyn told them. "For a midnight snack," she teased with a wink as if she imagined what they'd be doing then.

What would they be doing at midnight? Jazzy wondered. Sleeping? Pacing their separate bedrooms, thinking about whether or not they'd done the right thing? How many doubts was her new husband having?

"I bought you a special cake-slicing knife so you'll remember this moment," Jordyn said with a smile and handed them a cake knife with their names and the date engraved on the handle.

"Oh, Jordyn," Jazzy said with tears filling her eyes. "Thank you."

As she hugged her sister, flashes from cameras went off and she realized her family was recording the moment. She heard Brooks sincerely thank Jordyn, too.

Then it was time. With friends and family looking on, Brooks's hand covered hers over the handle of their first wedding gift. There was a stack of presents on the table beside the cake. Even though this was a sudden wedding, their guests were taking the opportunity to give them something to start them on their way.

Brooks's hand was large, warm and encompassing. When he gazed down at her and gave her a half smile, Jazzy's breath hitched.

Brooks himself took care of the slice of cake, sliding it onto a paper plate. Then he offered it to her. They each broke off a piece, knowing what they were supposed to do.

Brooks lifted the bite of cake and icing to her lips, never taking his eyes from hers.

Flashes from cameras again burst around them.

She opened her mouth, and when she took the bite from his fingers, her tongue touched his thumb and icing slid along her upper lip.

The sound of a spoon tapping a glass rung in her ears. As if the sound had to be translated, a woman called, "Kiss that icing away!" More tinkling on glasses. After all, this was a wedding reception.

Brooks leaned in and kissed her. The icing became

the sweetest confection she'd ever tasted as Brooks's tongue slipped along her lips and she kissed him back.

When he broke away, she blinked, tried to find her equilibrium and realized it was *her* turn now. If he kissed her like that again... She was careful picking up his piece of cake. He was careful as he ate it from her fingers. Everyone clapped. She tried to smile along with Brooks as they both seemed to be relieved that tradition was over.

As Jordyn oversaw the slicing of the cake for guests, some of them chatted with Jazzy and Brooks. Dallas Traub, who Brooks had introduced in their receiving line, approached them. "I just want to tell both of you not to be strangers. We've all been so focused on recovering from the flood, we haven't had time for anything else. After spending so much time with my rug rats, I could use adult conversation."

Earlier, Jazzy had learned that Dallas lived on his family's ranch—the Triple T—but had his own house on the property that had seen some damage from the flood, but not the devastation others had experienced.

"I'd like to see your ranch sometime. And meet your children." After all, it was only polite to make Brooks's friend feel comfortable.

"We'll set up a time soon," Dallas assured them. Then he clapped Brooks on the back and walked away.

"He's been through a rough time," Brooks said almost to himself. "That's when family counts most."

Jazzy imagined he was thinking again about the reason for this wedding—not true love, not a lifelong commitment, but rather his dad's health.

Had they done the right thing?

* * *

A short time later, as Brooks and Jazzy were mingling with their guests, Brooks watched Jordyn go to the podium and pick up the microphone. She tapped it and smiled. "It's time for the first dance between Jazzy and Brooks as a married couple," she announced. Turning to the CD player on the wall, she started the music.

It was one dance, Brooks thought, as he offered his hand to Jazzy. Surely he could get through one dance.

He thought of the first time he and Jazzy had danced when they'd looked over the social hall. And their kiss after the ceremony, not to mention the sensual tasting of the wedding cake—

He had to look at this logically. This day was simply an exception to the agreement they had made. Today, they were pretending in front of a larger audience than his dad. Today would be over before they knew it.

His wedding day. When he'd imagined it with Lynnette, he'd had dreams. Now he just wanted his dad's good health. He just wanted the year to pass quickly so he and Jazzy could get on with their lives.

As Brooks forced a smile and took Jazzy in his arms, he was glad they'd had that one practice dance. That way this wasn't so awkward.

Just like last night when Jazzy had appeared in the diner in her red dress, he'd been bowled over by the way she'd looked in her wedding dress as she'd walked down the aisle on her father's arm. It was so feminine with its lace and high neck. Yet it had a touch of Western sass, too, with its fringes and peek-a-boo sections that gave him a glimpse of skin. And those boots with their heels...

Taking her in his arms and bending his head to her,

he said, "I don't know how you can dance in those things."

"These boots were made for dancing," she joked, but her smile wobbled just enough that he knew this day wasn't easy for her, either. He was glad he'd bought the roses, champagne and watch for tonight.

When he leaned toward her, he got caught in the fragrance of her perfume. It was musky-sweet and fit Jazzy perfectly. "Are you okay?" he asked seriously, in spite of everyone watching.

"As okay as you," she returned with her usual spunk. But then she added, "Though I'm glad we're not in a fishbowl all the time. It's downright unnerving."

"Now you know how celebrities feel," he bantered, hoping to make her smile again.

She didn't just smile. She laughed. And he realized how much he enjoyed the sound of it.

"Maybe I should simply think of my family as groupies!"

Flashes popped as both Laila and Abby took photos of them.

"They're going to make an album for us." Jazzy was watching him for his reaction.

"Your family is just doing what families do."

"Maybe we should have gotten married by the justice of the peace. It would have been simpler the whole way around," she murmured.

Tearing his gaze from Jazzy's, he caught sight of his father watching them. His broad smile said it all.

"Just look at my dad, Jazzy." He maneuvered them so she could see Barrett.

After the moment it took for her to absorb his message, she sighed.

Brooks didn't know what that sigh meant because everyone began clinking their spoons on their glasses so he and Jazzy would kiss.

"Here we go again," he said, tightening his arms around her, drawing her close so her body was pressed against his. She didn't resist or try to lean away.

When his lips met hers, he intended to make the kiss quick. He intended for it to simply be a brushing of lips on lips.

But with Jazzy, nothing was ever exactly as he intended it to be.

Her perfume was like a magic spell, drawing him into its aura. Jazzy was so femininely alluring, his hand came up to caress her cheek. Careful not to disturb her hat, he angled his mouth over hers and almost forgot about "pretend." His lips felt so right on hers.

In the nick of time, before he took their public kiss into the private realm, he pulled away. Jazzy almost tripped over his boot and he caught her up against him so they didn't have a mishap.

Charlie called out, "Careful those kisses don't knock you off your feet!"

Everyone laughed. Everyone except him and Jazzy. They couldn't seem to unlock their gazes.

And they didn't until Jordyn announced, "Now my dad will dance with Jazzy and Brooks will dance with my mom. Everyone else, join in and enjoy the music."

Brooks had to let Jazzy go. Tearing his gaze from hers, he realized he didn't like that idea at all.

That night on the porch at Brooks's condo, Jazzy held the top layer of foil-wrapped wedding cake, still not quite believing what had taken place. She and Brooks

had said their vows, he'd kissed her so passionately
her hat had almost popped off. When he'd licked that
icing—

He set her suitcase down on the porch and unlocked
the door, glancing at her. "You packed light when you
came to Rust Creek Falls. One suitcase? Most women
would have three."

"I'm not most women." She wanted to say, "I'm your
wife now," but she didn't.

He gave her a very long look that made her shift
the layer of cake from one hand to the other, then he
opened the door.

Jazzy caught the scent of roses as soon as she walked
inside. Immediately she spotted the vase on the side
table and went straight to it. The blooms were huge and
red, giving off a beautiful scent.

"They're wonderful!"

"I thought you might like them."

She wanted to cross to him and kiss him all over
again in a way that wasn't simply for show, but she
didn't have that freedom.

While he carried her suitcase to the guest bedroom,
she looked around the place and noticed a fire was laid
on the grate. Maybe they'd cozy up together in front
of it.

Brooks returned to the living room. "I'll light a fire.
I have champagne, too. We can celebrate. I've never
seen my dad happier."

His dad. That was the reason they'd done this, and
she couldn't forget it. "Champagne would be nice," she
agreed.

When Brooks started for the kitchen, she followed
with the cake. "I'll find a plate."

"Top left cupboard. You'll have to learn your way around," he said with a smile.

That smile. She sighed, found two plates and unwrapped the cake.

Five minutes later they were sitting on the sofa with a fire dancing on the grate, sharing bites of cake. Brooks had taken off his jacket and rolled up his sleeves.

"It was a nice wedding," she said as a preamble.

"Yes, it was," he agreed. "But I'm not sure your parents approve of me, or your brother, either."

Her dad had questioned Brooks about his practice and so had her brother. They hadn't smiled much and Jazzy wished, as she had in the past, that they'd just trust her judgment.

Brooks took the bottle of champagne he'd pulled from the refrigerator, unwrapped the foil around the top, and then popped the cork. It bounced across the room and they both laughed. He poured the champagne into two tumblers, only filling them about a third of the way. As he picked up her glass, as well as his, and handed it to her, the bubbles danced and popped.

"Before today, I hadn't had champagne since my sister's wedding."

"Then it's about time." He clinked his glass against hers. "We pulled it off."

Yes, they had. "My parents will be harder to convince if and when we visit them."

"It will be fine, Jazzy, really it will. Jordyn's on our side. She still lives at home, right?"

Jazzy nodded and took a couple of swallows of her champagne. "She'll be a good buffer. I wish I could confide in her, but it's difficult for sisters to keep secrets from one another. I'm afraid if I tell her, she'll tell Abby, Abby will tell Laila, Laila will tell Annabel..."

"You can talk to *me*."

Yes, she could talk to Brooks about everything but what she felt for him. She took another swallow of champagne and realized she'd drained her glass. He drank his, too, picked up the bottle, and poured more for both of them. They were sitting close together, the sleeve of her dress rubbing the sleeve of his shirt, their knees brushing every now and then.

"I spoke to Charlie tonight," she said.

"He keeps Dad on track as much as he can."

"Did he tell you your dad wants to do the chores himself?" Jazzy asked him. "He doesn't want Travis helping him."

"Travis has his orders from *me*. He's supposed to listen to me, not to Dad."

"Charlie insists your dad's stubborn."

"He doesn't know how to sit still unless his favorite program's on the TV," Brooks grumbled. "He's eating the meals you're making him, though. That's a good sign. And he walks up and down the drive, going farther each day. When bad weather sets in, I don't know what he'll do. Maybe I can get him a treadmill for Christmas."

"Do you think he'd use it?"

"I can set it up in the basement and make him a gym area. If I have to, I'll go there and work out with him."

She drank more champagne, then laid her hand on Brooks's arm. His forearm was as muscled as the rest of him, the dark brown hair there was rough under her fingertips. "You're a good son."

"We haven't been close enough in my adult years. Maybe now that will change."

"I think it will…if you both want it to."

Brooks reached to the shelf under the coffee table and brought out a wrapped package. She hadn't noticed it under there, though now the gold foil gleamed in the lamplight.

"Brooks, what's this?"

"Just a little something for you to remember today. Open it."

Jazzy's fingers fumbled as she tore the paper off the box with a Western scene. "Montana Silversmiths." Taking the lid from the box, she saw the watch inside. Lifting it out, she examined the scrollwork on the band, the pretty face.

"Oh, Brooks, it's beautiful! Thank you."

"Put it on and see if it fits."

It fit her wrist as if it had been made for her.

Brooks poured more champagne into the two glasses. Then he looked at her as he'd looked at her when she'd walked up the aisle toward him, when she'd taken his hand and faced the minister. "You've been a good sport about all of this."

"I have a dream, too," she said, knowing Brooks would think she was talking about the rescue ranch, not about their marriage.

The longer they gazed at each other, the more the fire crackled and popped, the more the electric tension in the air seemed to draw them together. She didn't want this moment of closeness to end. Maybe those champagne bubbles had gone to her head, but she thought she saw desire in his eyes.

He took a strand of her hair in his hand and then

played with it between his fingers. "So silky and soft. In that hat and your dress, you looked as if you'd just stepped off the pages of a fashion magazine."

"I'm just Jazzy," she said with a small laugh, feeling all trembly inside. "The same girl who got to know Sparky because of you. The same girl who got scratched by Mrs. Oliver's cat. The same girl who will never be a calf roper."

He laughed at that and leaned a little closer. "I have no doubt you could be a calf roper if you set your mind to it."

"I'd rather set my mind on other things."

It seemed as if he would, too, because instead of just touching her hair, his hand delved under it and slid up the back of her neck. She tilted her head up to gaze into his eyes and he leaned even closer.

Something in the air changed. Instead of conversation and banter, Brooks seemed to want something else, and so did she. The kiss after their ceremony flashed in her mind, right before his lips settled on hers. Their kiss with the taste of icing between them was still a sweet memory. But this time as he kissed her, he didn't stop with the pressing of lips on lips or a slight lick of his tongue. Now Brooks's tongue slid along her lips, and she didn't hesitate a second. She opened her mouth to him. He tasted her and she tasted him. He was champagne and icing, and she was tempted by both.

Apparently, he was, too, because his tongue explored her mouth, searching, asking, maybe even demanding. She gave in to his desire…and hers. She responded with everything she had. Her arm went around him and she became intoxicated by the scent of his cologne and the scent of him and the idea that they were husband and wife. She could feel every bit of Brooks's desire. When his fingers went to the zipper on the back of her dress, she anticipated what might happen next. But the sound of the rasp of the metal changed everything. Brooks's fingers froze as he did, too.

He broke their kiss, raised his head and looked as if he'd done something terribly wrong.

Before she could tell him that she liked what they were doing, that after all, they were married, that maybe something new could come of their partnership, he gruffly said, "I'm sorry, Jazzy. I know we have an arrangement and I never intended for this to happen. I just wanted to celebrate a little and show you how much I appreciate what you're doing. This is essentially a business deal, and neither of us should forget that."

A business deal. She'd really never thought of this as strictly business, but clearly, *he* had. The flowers and the champagne and watch were just to show his appreciation.

And the kiss? Well...

She was a woman and he was a man, and he had needs that he apparently wasn't going to satisfy.

"I guess the champagne went to our heads," she murmured.

"I guess," he said gruffly.

"Thank you for the watch. I really like it."

"Good."

So Brooks had once again turned into the monosyllabic remote man he'd been the night before their wedding. Because he felt he'd done something wrong?

So she said the one thing that she knew would make this easier for both of them. "I'd better turn in. I have to unpack and…set up my alarm. Do you want me to go to your dad's with you in the morning?"

"That's up to you."

"I'll go with you. We wouldn't want him to think something's wrong." She stood, feeling a little shaky from everything that had happened today, just wanting to make a fast exit.

He stood, too. "I'll have to make sure the fire's out, so I might be up for a little bit. Good night, Jazzy."

She murmured, "Good night," and headed for her room. As she did, she felt the air on the back of her neck where her zipper had been lowered a bit, and she wondered just what would have happened if both of them had had one more glass of champagne.

Chapter Eleven

The next morning, breakfast was awkward and quick. Jazzy cooked scrambled eggs while Brooks fried bacon. She put the toast in and waited for it to pop while he took everything to the table.

Halfway through eating, Brooks said, "You don't have to go along to check on Dad. I can drop you at the clinic."

That certainly would be easier with this tension between them but not necessarily the best thing to do. "I don't mind. Besides, wouldn't your dad think it was odd that we weren't together the day after our wedding?"

As she'd watched yesterday, Brooks had done some fast talking to both their parents about why they weren't taking a honeymoon yet—what with setting up both clinics and so much to do, they thought they'd wait. With a sigh, Jazzy realized she didn't even know where

Brooks would like to *go* on a honeymoon. She wouldn't care. Anyplace holed up alone with him overnight would be terrific.

If last night had really been their honeymoon—

Once outside in Brooks's truck, their gazes met and she could easily see Brooks was thinking about last night's kiss, too. Yet he obviously didn't want to talk about it or their marriage. He started the truck and aimed it in the right direction.

This tension between them was more than she'd bargained for. This tension between them felt as if it could explode at any moment. She just hoped when it did, they were both ready for the consequences.

When they arrived at the Bar S, Brooks pulled around back to the clinic. But when he rounded the curve in the driveway, he spotted his dad's truck and his father climbing into it.

"What the hell?" he mumbled, as if this was one more stress he didn't need.

Jazzy clasped his arm. "He might be just driving into town to get something at the General Store. His doctor said it was safe for him to drive."

"Jazzy, I know what the doctor said," Brooks snapped. "But I also know Dad always pushes the boundaries, so it's never as simple as it seems. He wouldn't have driven the truck around back unless he wanted to load up a few supplies. I know him. You don't."

That stung because she felt as if she'd come to know Barrett pretty well over the past couple of weeks. True, she didn't know all of his habits, but she did know he wanted to feel better. The two of them had talked about what he needed to do for that to happen. She was hurt Brooks would dismiss her so cavalierly.

"I might not know your dad as well as you do, but during the time we spent together, we talked, probably more than you've talked to him in the past few years."

Brooks looked startled at that observation, but he obviously didn't want to have a conversation about it now. He climbed out of the truck and jogged over to his dad.

Jazzy got out and followed him. All right, so she was going to let *him* handle it. Let's see how well he did that.

"Where are you going this early, Dad?"

With the door to his truck hanging open, Barrett looked from Brooks to Jazzy. "The better question is, what are you two doing here so early? It seems to me you'd be late on the day after your wedding." There was a twinkle of slyness in his eyes that made Jazzy feel uncomfortable.

"Off-topic, Dad. Where are you headed to?"

"It's not like I'm going to drive across the state. Stewart Young called. He has a horse that went lame and he wants me to look at him."

"I can do that," Brooks said in an even voice that told Jazzy he was keeping what he really thought under control.

"Stewart doesn't want *you,* he wants *me. I'm* the one who's handled his horses for thirty years. *I'm* the one he trusts. Besides, I've got to start getting out again. I'm not going to sit in that house like an invalid. That's no better for me than doing too much."

In a way, Jazzy knew he was right. Yet she could also see Brooks was afraid his dad would do something he shouldn't, get involved in something he shouldn't, overexert himself in a way he shouldn't.

Mediating, she suggested, "Why don't both of you go?"

They both swung their gazes toward her in a challenging way. All right, she'd take on two Smith men at once if she had to.

Focusing on Brooks's dad, she suggested, "You can consult with Stewart while Brooks does the actual physical exam. That way you can get out, but Brooks won't worry about you. I can hold down the fort here until you get back. If something comes up at Brooks's clinic, I'll call you. That's what cell phones are made for."

Barrett didn't look happy but he wasn't protesting, either. Still, he eyed them suspiciously. "So tell me again why you're here so early."

Brooks pushed up the rim of his Stetson. "We're here early so maybe we can finish early."

Barrett harrumphed. "I guess the whole evening together would suit the two of you." He noticed the watch on Jazzy's wrist. "That's pretty."

"It was a wedding gift from Brooks." She knew that would please Barrett.

"It's good to know my son *does* have a romantic bone in his body. I guess there's hope."

When Jazzy looked down at the watch, but then back at Brooks's expression, she wasn't so sure.

With troubling insight, Brooks realized whenever he was with Jazzy, he felt like a different person. Sometimes stronger. Sometimes way too unsettled. Their kiss last night weighed on his mind. His brusque attitude this morning did, too. Somehow they had to figure out this marriage.

After his visit to Stewart Young, he'd dropped her

at the Buckskin Clinic. She'd taken care of calls that had come in and referred patients to his dad's clinic where Brooks could see them. It was all a bit confusing for now, but they'd get into a routine, and slowly as his dad came back to work, he'd spend more time at his own clinic.

Eventually his father would say to him, "Let's join our practices," and then they'd get a partner that would take some of the load off them both. It was easy to see the way this should go. He just wished his dad wasn't being so stubborn about it.

After he finished at his dad's, he picked up Jazzy. On the drive home, they decided to order pizza instead of worrying about cooking. They'd been silent in the truck again, though, and Brooks wished they could get back the easy camaraderie they'd had at the beginning of their relationship. What had happened to their friendship?

It had gotten sidetracked by circumstances that had taken on a life of their own.

At his place, he decided against a fire tonight. No more cozy atmosphere. No more thinking about pleasing Jazzy with flowers or champagne. That had given off the wrong signals. He wasn't interested in romance, he told himself, just in an easy companionship between them. Jazzy got herself a glass of water, and he called the pizza establishment he favored most.

He put his hand over the phone. "What do you want on your pizza?"

"It doesn't matter," she said without her usual enthusiasm.

"Tell me *something,* Jazzy, or I'm going to load it up with what I want."

"Pepperoni," she shot at him. "And plenty of onions."

Okay, so she wasn't interested in romance, either.

After he placed the order, she said, "I'm going to give Jordyn a call in my room. Let me know when the pizza arrives."

Before he could blink, she was gone from the kitchen into her bedroom and had closed the door.

For some reason, that closed door annoyed him. Not that he wanted to listen in on her conversation, but it set up another barrier between them.

Restless, he grabbed two plates and set them on the table. Then he rummaged in the drawer for silverware and pulled napkins from the counter. Next on his list was to find an apartment in Rust Creek Falls. It would definitely be more convenient. He could call Rhonda Deatrick now and leave a message. Going to the phone again, he was about to do that, when his doorbell rang.

Couldn't be the pizza already.

When he opened the door to Gage Christensen, he smiled. He'd invited Gage to the wedding but he hadn't been there.

"I know, I didn't show up for the big shindig. I had an emergency call and had to go out. And Lissa's in New York. So I thought I'd stop by now and congratulate you both." He had a package in his hands. "Something I thought you could use other than a toaster."

"Come on in." But as soon as Brooks said it, he realized he shouldn't have. Not because he didn't want Gage there, but because Jazzy was in her own room, not his master suite. Gage had been here before. He knew the setup.

At that moment, Jazzy emerged from the guest bedroom. When she saw Gage, she stopped. Gage handed her the wedding present, but exchanged a look with Brooks.

"You two haven't known each other very long. You weren't dating when Jazzy and I had dinner."

They both kept silent.

"You fell hard overnight?"

"Didn't *you?*" Brooks shot back.

Gage's face turned ruddy. "Maybe. I suppose it does happen." After another long look at both of them, he said, "If the two of you need to talk about anything, I'm around."

Suddenly, his cell phone beeped. He gave a shrug and said, "Excuse me," and checked it. "I've got to get back to the office. Now."

Halfway to the door, he stopped. "Are you coming to the meeting tomorrow night at the town hall? Nate Crawford is supposed to have an important announcement."

They hadn't talked about it, but the meeting would give them something to think about other than this marriage of convenience. "Sure, we'll be there," Brooks responded.

After Gage was gone, Jazzy looked at Brooks. "Do you think he guessed that…this isn't a real marriage? Are we doing the best thing for everyone?" she asked.

"It's too late to have second thoughts now." Though he *was* having second thoughts. Being married to Jazzy for a year and keeping his hands off her was going to be torture.

"Why don't you open Gage's present? We really should open the rest of the stack tonight."

Jazzy sat on the sofa, the box in front of her on the

coffee table. She tore off the wrappings and on the outside of the box they could read PRESSURE COOKER.

"Oh, it's one of those advanced foodie pressure cookers that're supposed to be easy. You can brown everything right in it then let it steam. A meal is supposed to be ready in about half the time," she explained.

"Sounds practical."

"Gage put some thought into this. It's a great newlywed gift."

Yes, it was. When Gage had decided on it for them, he hadn't realized how appropriate it would be. A pressure cooker. Brooks felt as if he were inside a pressure cooker right now, just waiting for it to blow.

The community meeting was just getting underway when Brooks and Jazzy slipped inside the town hall. Jazzy kept stealing glances at Brooks to try to guess what he was thinking. Gage's visit stretched like a wire between them. Was what they were doing wrong, or simply advantageous to them both, as well as Brooks's dad? She wasn't sure anymore. But if it was right, why didn't it feel right?

The folding chairs were packed tight together to fit the most people in. Jazzy's shoulder rubbed against Brooks's but he didn't look her way, though she did look his. He'd dropped her at his clinic this morning while he went to his dad's. All of the appointments Jazzy had made for Brooks at Buckskin Clinic were set up for tomorrow. That seemed to be the easiest way to handle this for now. So they'd be working together tomorrow. Maybe some of this tension would dissipate then.

Irene Murphy saw them and waved. "Congratulations," she called, a few feet from where she was sitting.

A gentleman seated in back of them clapped Brooks on the shoulder and wished them all the best, too. Gage was across the room and just raised his brows. Jazzy didn't know what he was thinking.

Nate Crawford was running the meeting. He banged his gavel on the podium for some order. After thanking everyone for coming, he read a list of the community's accomplishments since the flood. Utilities had been restored, roads repaired, bridges rebuilt.

He went on, talking about the progress on the elementary school and how volunteers had come from all over to help.

The side door to the town hall opened and shut. To distract her attention from Brooks, Jazzy turned to look to see who the newcomers were. A couple walked in followed by—

Jazzy felt her whole body go a little cold. Oh, my. What was Griff Wellington doing here?

As if his eyes were drawn by a magnet, they came to rest on her. It didn't take a genius to figure out he was here to see her. He must have heard about her marriage.

Nate was still speaking and everyone was listening to him. Jazzy raised her hand to Griff, an acknowledgement that she'd seen him, but she wasn't going to disrupt the meeting to go to him. That would look odd.

Brooks nudged her shoulder. "Who's that?"

Maybe he was as aware of her as she was of him. She stayed silent, trying to figure out how to explain.

Before she could, Brooks noted, "You've gone pale."

"Don't be silly. It's just a little cold in here."

"Not with all these people, it isn't. Who is that guy?"

Some of the other meeting-goers had turned to look

at them. Jazzy whispered, "Not now. I'll explain later, okay?"

Brooks gave her a look that said he would indeed expect an explanation later. She wished now she had told him about Griff and her almost-engagement. She wished now she'd told Brooks *she'd* broken it off. But it just hadn't seemed important. Or had the real reason for not telling him been she didn't want him comparing her to the fiancée who had broken her engagement with *him*. Whatever the reason, the die was cast and she'd have to figure this out as she went.

She felt Brooks's gaze on her from the side and she felt Griff's gaze on her from the back. He must have found a seat behind them. The hairs on her neck prickled and she had the feeling she was in for a stormy night. Not at all what she'd planned. She'd hoped she and Brooks could talk and maybe get back on an easy footing. But now this.

Jazzy tried to concentrate on Nate's words once more.

"The reason we called this meeting tonight, the main one, anyway, is that I have some good news for this town. Lissa Roarke's blog and personal diary about life in Rust Creek Falls since the flood has gotten some attention back in New York City. She's going to be on a national morning talk show. I spoke with her myself this afternoon, and she believes that once she's on that show, donations and even more help are going to come rolling in, which will be an even greater help with the reconstruction efforts. So maybe we can really be the town we were before the flood, even better."

Everyone applauded. Gage looked proud enough of

Lissa to burst. But all Jazzy could think of was Griff standing in the back of the hall, waiting for her.

Jazzy grew more antsy the longer the meeting went on. Brooks glanced at her more than once, and she tried to stay calm. She realized, although she'd dated Griff, she didn't really know him very well because she didn't know why he was here and she had no idea what his reaction was going to be to seeing her, to talking with her, to hearing the news of her marriage, if he hadn't heard it yet. But she did know Brooks and the fact that she hadn't told him about Griff weighed heavily on her.

After the road construction foreman spoke, after a couple of ranchers had their say about what they still needed to get their places back to running in top shape, after Nate thanked everyone for coming, the meeting finally ended.

Jazzy tapped Brooks's arm. "I have to speak to someone. It will only be a few minutes."

After Brooks gave her a piercing look, she added, "I'll be right back." Then she slipped away before he could ask her any questions.

When Griff saw Jazzy, his expression was somber. "Can we step outside?"

This was a small town full of people who knew each other. At gatherings like this, they liked to chat. They started forming groups now, doing just that.

Jazzy nodded. Though she started to follow Griff, she glanced back over her shoulder and saw that Brooks's gaze was tracking her.

Once outside, Jazzy glanced up at the beautiful full moon that was lighting up the front of the town hall. It was a momentary distraction before she had to face Griff. However, squaring her shoulders, she did.

"How are you?" she asked.

"I'm good. How are *you?*"

"I'm great," she said brightly, but then dropped the pretense. "Why are you here, Griff?"

"I ran into Abby, or rather she ran into me at the store. She made some excuse about needing new running shoes, but I don't think she runs, does she?"

"She might have taken it up lately." Jazzy always defended her sisters and brother, no matter what.

He nodded his head in concession. "Fair enough. Anyway, she told me you got married. I couldn't believe it. I wanted to ask you myself. Is it true?"

"She wouldn't have lied to you."

Griff looked up into the thousand stars, and then back at her. "No, I suppose not. Is it that guy you were sitting next to?"

"Yes, Brooks Smith. He has a veterinary practice."

"Ah," Griff responded, as if that made sense somehow. "A love of animals. Is that what bonded you together? This is awful quick."

"A love of animals is one of the things that brought us together."

"You never looked at me the way you look at him."

"Griff, don't."

He sighed. "I should have seen our breakup coming. But I guess I was just hoping that I was as right for you as you seemed to be for me."

"Was I really *right* for you? Think about it. We became friends, but—"

"We never had grand passion? I suppose not. Maybe I just wanted to settle down and start a family so badly that I ignored what I *should* have in favor of what we *did* have."

Jazzy had shared embraces and kisses with Griff, details of their lives, the hopes for a future, so it didn't seem odd for her to take his hand now. "I never wanted to hurt you. That's why I broke off our involvement when I did. Don't you see?"

"And you didn't know this Brooks Smith before you left Thunder Canyon?"

"Oh, no! I never would have dated another man behind your back."

"I didn't think so, but I had to have that question answered, too. So you love him?"

"More each day."

Griff gazed into her eyes for a moment, squeezed her hand, then leaned in and kissed her on the cheek. "I wish you well, Jasmine Cates Smith, I really do. Once I get over some hurt pride, maybe when you come back to Thunder Canyon, we can stay friends, and I can meet your guy."

Leaning away, she responded, "I'd like that."

Griff gave her a little salute and then he walked away. She watched after him, knowing he was a good man, knowing he'd make someone a wonderful husband.

She jumped when Brooks's voice startled her. "So… who is he?"

Jazzy glanced around at the people who had started to trickle out of the town hall. Nina Crawford stopped and said to the two of them, "Congratulations on your wedding." She whispered to Brooks, "Even if you don't think you're going to vote for Nate." She'd moved away when another burly gentleman waved to Brooks.

"Can we talk about this when we get home?" Jazzy asked. "A little privacy would be good."

"We can talk in the truck. I don't think I want to wait until we get home."

He was right about that. Or maybe he just didn't want to have to look at her while they were having the talk. He'd have to keep his eyes on the road.

They had parked some ways down the street and they walked that way on what Jazzy knew could be a romantic evening, with that big, full moon and all the stars.

Brooks waited until they were in his truck, buckled up, and then out on the road toward Kalispell. "So spill it," he said in a brook-no-argument voice.

She figured the best way to tell it was just to tell it. "Griff and I dated back in Thunder Canyon."

"Dated, or were dating when you left?"

"Past tense. Laila saw him looking at engagement rings and she told me. He and I had been going out for a few months and I just didn't feel— I just knew he wasn't the one. So I broke off our relationship." She could see Brooks's mouth tighten, his hands wrap more securely around the steering wheel.

"So he thought you were serious enough to get married, and then you broke up with him."

She knew what he was comparing this to. "It's nothing like your relationship with Lynnette."

"Isn't it? And even if it isn't, you didn't tell me about it. I thought you were an honest woman, Jazzy."

That hurt. It hurt terribly. "I *am* honest. I *was* honest. Did you want me to tell you about everyone I dated in the last five years?"

"I told you about Lynnette."

Yes, he had confided in her about his fiancée, and why hadn't she told him about Griff?

"Brooks, I didn't intentionally keep it from you. It

just never came up. It didn't seem important." Not after she'd met him. Not after she'd realized the difference in being around Brooks. It had been nothing like being around Griff.

But she could see he wasn't buying it. She could see he still thought she'd been dishonest with him. There was really no way to change his mind.

When they arrived back at Brooks's place—Jazzy couldn't quite think of it as home yet—he took off his jacket and went to the kitchen. There he pulled a bottle of beer from the refrigerator.

Jazzy followed. "We can talk about this more if you want."

"There's nothing to say, Jazzy. You lied by omission. I don't know if I can forget that."

"Maybe I did it because I didn't want you comparing our friendship or relationship or whatever it is, to yours and Lynnette's."

He gave her a hard stare and unscrewed the cap of the bottle. "That's an excuse but I don't know if it's a good one."

If he understood she'd been falling in love with him, it might be, but she certainly couldn't tell him that now.

"I didn't tell you about Griff because it was over, because I had started a new life here in Rust Creek Falls. You're acting so self-righteous, telling me I'm not an honest woman. Yet you're lying to your father. *We're* lying to your father. How do you account for that? Are *you* a dishonest man?"

He looked totally taken aback as if he'd never put those things in the same category. "That's not the same at all, Jazzy, and you know it. My dad's health was at stake."

"And your relationship with him, and my relationship with my family and friends, too. Maybe my relationship with you is at stake here. Think about it, Brooks, then tell me if we're so different."

His attitude rankled. He was as stubborn as his father. But she loved him, anyway. That, most of all, was what made her turn away. That, most of all, was what made her hightail it out of the kitchen and head for the guest room.

Chapter Twelve

Jazzy stood in the exam room beside Brooks, their bodies not touching if they could help it. She was there because she was more aid to Maggie Bradshaw and her son Timmy who'd brought a rescued kitten in than she was to the vet who had only monosyllabic replies to anything she said. Well, two could play that game. There wouldn't be any conversation. There wouldn't be any closeness. There might not even be a marriage of convenience for much longer.

The little boy, who was about five, was crying. "Momma says if she's sick, we can't keep her!"

Brooks knelt down beside Timmy, making eye contact. "When you first brought her in, I took a blood sample to do testing. I'll find out in a few minutes whether she's sick or not. So how about if you wipe those tears until we find out if we have something to worry about?

I'm giving her a flea treatment, but I have a little comb here, and I'd like to show you how to use it. Do you think you could do that?"

Timmy looked at Brooks as if he'd given him the biggest job in the world. "I can do that."

Brooks nodded to Jazzy. "Can you help him with that?"

It was the first, since last night, that his voice had held a little bit of tenderness…that gentleness she knew so well.

"Sure, I can. I have a stepstool over here, Timmy. You can climb up on that and you'll be right in line with the table."

Timmy glanced over his shoulder at his mom. "I want to keep her."

His mom looked pained as if she wanted to say yes, but yet didn't know if she could take care of a sick cat. The fuzzy, yellow tabby hadn't shown any symptoms yet, but she was only about a month old, and had somehow survived the outdoors. Maybe she was sturdier than she appeared.

"We think she's been sleeping under our porch," Mrs. Bradshaw said. "Timmy came in and got me as soon as he saw her so we could feed her, and she was hungry. If we keep her, is there anything we should know about food?"

"Food in small portions with water in between. Always make sure she has plenty of water, and make sure it's kitten food," Jazzy instructed, then she checked with Brooks. "Right?"

"Right on," he admitted. "I'll go check on the test."

Jazzy showed Timmy how to lift the comb through the fine fur, looking deep at its roots for dirt and any fleas they might find. In about twelve hours, the treatment would take care of the pests, but it would be good to get the dirt out.

Jazzy explained, "In three days, you should give her a bath in no-tears baby shampoo with tepid water, a warm room, and a nice fluffy towel for drying afterward. Some cats don't mind a bath as much as you think. You might want to have a pitcher of water there to pour over her to rinse her. It would be better to start in the morning so she could dry off in a patch of sunlight."

A short while later Brooks was back and he was smiling. "She tested negative for feline leukemia and FIV."

"I told her about the bath," Jazzy said.

He glanced at her. "Right. I understand you don't have any other animals?" he asked Mrs. Bradshaw.

"No, we don't. With food costs the way they are, it just seemed better not to. But this little one found us."

"Do you have a room you can keep her in for the next couple of days? One that you'll be able to clean up fairly well, just in case a flea or two escape."

"We have a sunroom. Would that be all right?"

"In October, that should be perfect. Keeping her there will serve two purposes. It will make sure the fleas are gone. You can also give her a small space to explore a little at a time. In a few days, she'll learn every aspect of that room, then she'll be ready to go exploring elsewhere. She's scared, dehydrated and malnourished, so she's going to need a few days to perk up and feel like her real kitten self again. You're sure there weren't any other kittens close by?"

"Not that we could find. And we did look."

Brooks plucked the kitten from the table and knelt down again in front of the boy. The kitten had curled in Brooks's arm looking up at him with little golden eyes that were trusting and innocent. "Want to hold her?" Brooks asked.

It was obvious Timmy did, but hadn't known if he should. Now, however, Brooks helped him and showed him the best way to hold the kitten so she wouldn't slip away.

"This is good when she's sleepy," he said. "If she gets squirmy, just forget holding her and let her down. She won't want anyone to hold her then and she'll be able to get away, no matter what you do. But when she's sleepy, she'll probably want to cuddle with you."

Timmy looked at his mom. "Can she sleep on my bed, Mommy? Please…please?"

"Maybe it will be a good idea if she does," Mrs. Bradshaw answered. "You won't be so lonely. Ever since his dad left, he's had bad dreams."

"I'm sorry to hear about your husband leaving Rust Creek Falls," Brooks empathized. "You're certain he's not coming back?"

"This place was just too small for him to begin with. He never stayed in one place long before I met him. We came from New Mexico."

"That's a long way," Jazzy said.

"Oh, we stayed in a few states in between, but when we got here, I settled in. I joined a quilting club and a knitting club. Jay wasn't enamored with the place *before* the flood. After the flood, he said there was simply no reason to stay. But I disagreed. Now more than ever, this is a real community. We have to stick together. But he didn't see that. He just wanted to go his own way and said it was time."

"I'm sorry," Jazzy said.

"Being a single mom isn't so bad," she said to Jazzy. "I don't have to consult anyone else about my decisions. But Timmy misses him, and maybe this kitty is the answer to a prayer."

"What are you going to name her?" Jazzy asked.

"Porch," Timmy answered quickly, as if he'd already thought about it. "That's where we found her. Wouldn't that be a good name?"

Brooks laughed. "I think that's a great name. You'll never forget how she came into your life. You've got to promise me you'll help take good care of her, that you'll help to feed her and give her water. A kitten like this has to eat even more often than you do. Do you think you can be that responsible?"

"I can feed her."

"I'm sure your mom will help and show you at first. But then we'll see how much of a big boy you can be."

It was obvious to Jazzy that Brooks would make a wonderful father. When he looked up, their gazes met, and she wondered if he guessed what she was thinking. They'd never talked about children because they never expected their marriage to be a real one. She wanted children, but she wanted to do it right.

Brooks was helping the kitty back into her box. "I'll take her out to the desk for you. Jazzy will give you an itemized bill."

"My husband would have had a fit if he had seen what this was going to cost. But I figure, I'll just use the money he would have spent on beer this month."

Jazzy typed a few things into the computer and printed out the bill. Maggie wrote a check and handed it over.

Just as Timmy and his mom were leaving, Paige Dalton came into the office, surprising Jazzy. Paige was a fifth-grade teacher who was holding classes in her home. But she couldn't be holding classes if she was out and about. Jazzy had seen her over at the school several times and had liked her, though she really didn't know too much about her.

"Paige, it's good to see you. What brings you here? Do you have a small animal in your purse?"

Paige laughed and pushed her dark brown hair away from her cheek. "No, I don't. Not this time, anyway. I have a question for Brooks."

Brooks was watching mother and son leave, and Jazzy wished she could read his mind. Was he wondering what it would be like to be a father someday? Did he want to be a dad?

At the sound of his name, he turned toward Paige. "Hi, Paige. How can I help you?"

"The children have off today to work on special projects at their own homes. We're doing holiday customs around the world. Some of them are making baked goods. Some of the guys are building structures like the Eiffel Tower. Some of them are writing reports or recipes. Anyway, I gave them the day to work on them at home. And tomorrow is their presentation to the rest of the class. It should be fun. I'm taking our curriculum as is and trying to make it suit to what's happened around here. Teaching from my home is different from being in a classroom. Actually, they seem to be learning well in a relaxed atmosphere, but they do miss the socialization with their friends."

"I imagine they would," Jazzy said.

"So what do you need?" Brooks asked.

"Would you come talk to the class about being a veterinarian? I'm sure they'd love to hear. We're trying to do a different career each week, and I want to broaden their outlooks." She took a step closer to him. "I understand how busy you are, helping out with your dad's practice as well as this one. I'd only need about an hour of your time, and I think it would mean a lot to the children."

"I can't say no to the children now, can I?" Brooks asked with a smile. "Sure, I can spare an hour. What day next week would be good for you?"

"How about next Friday? Late morning...around eleven?"

"Jazzy will pencil it in." He motioned to the exam room. "I'm going to clean up in there."

Paige and Jazzy were left alone in the reception area. As Brooks disappeared, Paige put her hand over her mouth. "Oh, my gosh, I didn't even congratulate the two of you on your wedding. Best wishes!"

Jazzy didn't know what to say, so she just said, "Thank you."

"You got married really fast. It must have been a whirlwind romance."

Jazzy wasn't a mind reader, but she could see Paige seemed a little wistful. Was it because she wanted a whirlwind romance of her own? Or because her own heart had been broken?

Jazzy just hoped this marriage of convenience wouldn't break *her* heart.

* * *

The following evening, Jazzy made supper—soup again, so she could take some to Barrett—wondering how she could break the tension between her and Brooks. Clamping the lid on the soup, she turned it down to simmer, hoping Brooks wouldn't be too late.

As soon as she thought it, the garage door opened. She realized she was nervous and anxious as he came from the garage into the kitchen and strode into the mudroom.

She called a "hello" but he must not have heard her over the water running because he didn't call back. When he appeared in the kitchen, he'd discarded his jacket. There wasn't a welcoming expression on his face. He looked so serious, she was afraid of what might come out of his mouth next.

However, all he said was, "Do I have time to take a shower before dinner?"

"Sure. The soup can keep. The longer it cooks, the better it tastes."

Usually he bantered back. But after their argument last night, he obviously wasn't bantering. Had that been their first fight? Was he going to forgive her for not telling him about Griff, or for the things she'd said about what they were doing concerning his dad?

Chopping vegetables for a salad, she heard the shower running. She imagined him standing naked under that shower. She imagined tan lines from his working outdoors, let alone the muscles that would ripple when he moved. She imagined his wet hair, brown and slick, his smile as he beckoned her into the shower with him...

Abruptly, she cut off the fantasies. From what was

going on between them right now, that kind of envisioning belonged on another planet.

She'd finished making the salad and was slicing a loaf of crusty bread that she'd picked up at the bakery when she realized the shower had gone off a long while before. Was Brooks staying in his room to avoid her? Maybe he was making phone calls.

Leaving the kitchen, she walked down the hall to his bedroom. His door was partially open, and when she peeked inside, she saw him standing at the window, sweatpants riding low on his hips as he stared out into the black night. Something was off. Something was wrong.

She simply couldn't stay away. She had to know what was going on in his head. He didn't seem to hear the door when it creaked open because he didn't turn toward her.

"Brooks?" she called softly.

He still didn't turn toward her.

Crossing to the window, she touched his arm. "Is something wrong?"

His face still had the strained expression she'd seen when he walked in. His eyes bore a look of turmoil as he finally turned to look at her. "I'm a veterinarian and I'm supposed to stay detached from the animals I treat."

She had a bad feeling and dreaded what was coming. "It's hard to stay detached."

"I'm usually good at compartmentalizing—keeping the business of being a veterinarian on one side, patient care on the other side, personal life underneath it all. But today— I lost a foal. It was stillborn. Nothing I could do."

Looking away from her again, she knew he didn't want her to see the emotion he was feeling.

"I'm sorry, Brooks." She really could think of nothing else to say. No words helped in a situation like this.

He must have heard the heartfelt understanding in her words. He must have seen the longing in her eyes…her desire for everything between them to be right again. His voice was deeply husky as he said, "Jazzy."

Impulse led her to wrap her arms around him in a hug, to lift her face to his. Impulse must have gotten to him, too…because he bent his head and kissed her.

This wasn't a light, feathery kiss. This time, Brooks's mouth on hers was decidedly masterful, absolutely possessive, totally consuming. His tongue breached her lips in a way that said he needed—wanted—this kiss as much as she did.

She didn't need to breathe. All she wanted to do was feel—feel Brooks's desire in the way his arms tightened around her, feel it in the way his tongue swept her mouth, feel it in the way his body hardened against hers. His skin was hot as her hands explored his bare back. His muscles were taut under her fingertips. He was strength and desire and gentleness…and she loved him. Oh, how she loved him.

She thought it over and over again though she didn't say it. Too much was happening at once. Had he forgiven her for not telling him about Griff? Were his feelings going deeper, too? Did he want exactly what she wanted tonight?

He certainly seemed to because as she stroked her hands down his back and around to his hips, as her thumbs fingered the drawstring on his sweatpants, he groaned and broke off the kiss. For a moment she thought he might want to part like he had the other night, but tonight he looked at her differently.

Tonight he shook his head as if he couldn't fight desire anymore. Tonight he said, "I want you, Jazzy. Do you want me, too?"

No words of love there. Yet she heard deep emotion in his voice and saw it on his face. She was going to give in to it...give in to passion and hope for love.

"I want you." She put as much feeling into those three words as she could manage.

With a deep groan, he lifted her into his arms and she wrapped her legs around him. His fervent kisses distracted her so she didn't even realize he had carried her to the bed. As she sat on the edge of the bed, she clung to him, rubbing her nose into his neck, letting everything about him encompass her. His large hands slid under the hem of her sweater.

"You're going to have to let go of me if I'm going to get this off you."

She didn't want to let go of him, not ever.

He swiveled their bodies until he was sitting beside her on the bed, too. Lifting her sweater over her head, he made quick work of her bra and stared at her as if she were a beautiful piece of artwork...or a fascinating sculpture...or a woman he cared about. Maybe even...loved.

"You can touch me," she said softly, so wanting to hear what he felt about her.

He gave her a wry smile. "So can you."

They reached for each other at the same moment.

She untied the drawstring at his waist. He unsnapped her jeans.

In no time at all, they were naked on his big bed, facing each other, touching. Every stroke and every kiss meant so much because it had been taboo for so long. Ever since that first night when they'd flirted at the Ace in the Hole, they'd experienced the sexual electricity that had brought them to this moment.

When she laced her fingers in his hair, he caressed her thigh, his hand doing enticing things she could feel down deep inside. Her fingers played in his chest hair. After a speaking glance that said he was going to get serious now, he lowered his head to her breast. The tug of his lips on her nipple inspired sensations she'd never felt before. His tongue laving it made her call his name. His smile, filled with deep male satisfaction, led her to reach for him, enfold him in her hand, and feel the pulsing of his blood. He let out a long breath that told her she affected him just as he affected her.

But apparently he'd had enough of the foreplay. Sliding his palm to the apex of her thighs, he knew she had, too.

"Don't move," he rasped, as he reached for the nightstand and pulled out the drawer.

She kept her eyes closed, her breaths coming in short, shallow pants because each kiss and touch had readied her for what came next. She heard the rustle of foil, the packet tearing. A moment later, he was back with her, kissing her lips until she clung to him like a vine.

He rolled her onto her back and rose above her, but he didn't move to enter her. Gazing at her, he said, "I was jealous of that man you dated, and I took it out on you. I shouldn't have. You're the most honest woman I know."

It was an apology, and she knew saying he was jealous was hard for Brooks. There was no reason to dwell on it, or their argument. She reached for him and when he entered her, she felt wonderfully whole. She arched up to Brooks, wrapped her legs around him, and took him deeper. His groan of satisfaction made her feel proud, made her feel driven to give him everything she was and everything she could be. Each of his thrusts took her to a new plane of sensation. The melding of their bodies created a swirl of emotion she couldn't begin to grasp.

When they'd stood at the falls a couple of weeks ago, she'd felt awe near to this. But not anything this wide and deep and high. Not something as cataclysmically earth-shattering. This was *love*. It was so totally consuming that she didn't know if she'd ever be herself again.

As she held on to Brooks, light shattered, feelings washed over her, her body trembled and then shook with a climax so overwhelming, tears came to her eyes. Brooks's release came immediately after, and as they gasped for breath together and held on to each other, she knew their lives would never be the same.

The first sign that something was wrong was the way Brooks rolled away from her, with his eyes closed, and without a smile. The second was his terse "I'll be right back," as if they had something important to settle.

Jazzy's head was still spinning from making love

with him, and she hoped she was wrong about the feeling of doom that was stirring in her heart. Moments before, it had been filled with hope.

When Brooks returned from the bathroom, he didn't slide into bed with her, but rather sat on the edge. "That was a huge mistake."

She didn't know what she had expected to hear, but that wasn't it.

She was about to tell him she didn't regret anything about making love, when he said, "I think we should split up. We'll tell my dad it didn't work out. I'll still give you my grandmother's land, though."

Stunned, she couldn't begin to make sense of his words, let alone respond to them.

He went on, laying out his case. "Even if we tried to make a real marriage of this, I can't give you the marriage you deserve. With my own practice, watching over Dad's, I won't have time to sleep, let alone nurture a relationship. My mom had to cover for my dad more times than I can count. Whenever I had a school function, or sports event, she didn't complain, but he wasn't around. He was always working. When she got sick, my grandmother was there more than he was."

"Are you saying that I'm so different from your mom?"

"Oh, you're different all right, Jazzy. You say what you think. Even if she resented the time Dad worked, she never said. You couldn't be like that."

"How do you know I'd resent it?"

"I just know."

To her dismay, she realized he was thinking of

Lynnette again. He might not be comparing her to his mother, but he was comparing her to another woman who'd let him down. And that just made her angry.

"This isn't about your mom *or* your dad working too much. It's about *your* broken engagement. It's about a woman being unfaithful to you and walking out."

His silence told her she'd hit the mark. Still, he concluded, "No matter what it's about, we'd end up hating each other. I don't want that. Do you?"

Reaching for the sheet, she pulled it up, feeling the need to cover her body where she hadn't such a short time ago. But now everything was different. Brooks had succumbed to desire in a moment of weakness. He didn't love her. He couldn't, not if he wanted to end their marriage.

To top it all off, he began dressing quickly. And then he pulled his duffel bag from the closet.

"What are you doing?"

"I'm going to give Dallas a call and go bunk with him and his kids. I'm sure he won't mind, and he won't ask any questions."

"That's all you're concerned about, questions?" Brooks was building a new wall around himself, and Jazzy knew there wasn't anything she could say to knock it down. She'd found the man of her dreams and he didn't want her. He didn't need her.

All she could think of to say was, "Your father's going to be so upset."

Brooks gave her a long, hard look. "Not any more upset than he would be at the end of the year. This was a crazy idea. We were both foolish for thinking it could work."

With his boots on now, jeans and sweatshirts in his duffel, he was ready to go.

"I'm not going to stay here, Brooks. It's *your* place, not mine."

"Stay as long as you need to. This is *my* fault, not yours, Jazzy. I'll see a lawyer and get that land transferred over. I'll keep my word."

Then as if he couldn't stand to look at her another moment longer, he left.

Chapter Thirteen

Jazzy absolutely didn't know what to do. She'd cried most of the night. This morning she was trying to look at her options. But her feelings kept getting in the way. Should she go back to Thunder Canyon? Should she leave Brooks forever? She really couldn't think about that in spite of what he'd said.

Yet she knew she couldn't stay here in his condo. She couldn't walk into his bedroom and remember what they'd done…how she'd felt…how he'd claimed her. It would be impossible to stay here without envisioning the future she'd hoped they'd be able to share.

Tears threatened again. She swiped them away, knowing this was her own fault for risking her heart. Maybe she should have married Griff who was safe. But, no. She hadn't wanted safe and she still didn't. She wanted Brooks. But if he didn't want her, what could she do?

Picking up her cell phone, she dialed the number for Strickland's Boarding House. Fortunately, Melba answered. She certainly hadn't wanted to leave a message. "Melba, it's Jazzy Cates."

"Hi, honey. How are you? Getting used to married life?"

So what could she say to that? She could hang up and think of something else. She could drive herself back to Thunder Canyon.

Not yet.

"Melba, I need to know if you still have the room I was renting."

Silence met her question.

"You want your room back?"

"Is it still available?"

"Yes, it is. Did you and your young man have a fight?"

If it had been a fight, they could make up. If it had been a fight, maybe she would have gotten out all of her feelings. If it had been a fight, there could still be hope.

"You could say that. I just need to be by myself for a while."

"Well, come on back, honey. You know that coffee is always brewing and there's hot water for tea. I baked apple bread, too. Comfort food."

"Thanks, Melba. I'll be over soon."

After Jazzy packed her suitcase, after she got into her car and switched on the ignition, she backed out of Brooks's driveway. Instead of heading for town and Strickland's, she headed for the Bar S. She didn't expect Brooks to be at his dad's clinic this early. In fact, she didn't want to see him. She couldn't see him. Not until she felt as if she had her emotions all under control. But she *did* want to see his father. She had something to say to him and she just hoped he was in a receptive mood.

Barrett had a mug in his hand when he opened the door. "It's tea," he said with a broad smile. "Herbal. I've still cut caffeine out of my diet."

"Good for you," she said with as much enthusiasm as she could muster. She knew Barrett missed his coffee as much as he missed donuts. She'd brought him soup because she and Brooks hadn't eaten any last night, and she knew his dad liked it. Besides, it was a good excuse for stopping by.

She had two containers in the bag, and she said to him, "I brought you soup, enough to eat and freeze. Do you have a few minutes?"

"Sure. That teenager Brooks hornswoggled into helping me with chores won't get here for about an hour. He's catching on, but I still have to supervise."

Jazzy went inside the house to the kitchen. She stowed a container of soup in the refrigerator and the other one in the freezer. Barrett's freezer was still fairly stacked with other dinners she had made for him. Maybe they'd be the last. Maybe she wouldn't be seeing Barrett again. That thought deeply saddened her.

"Okay, missy. Sit down and tell me what's going on. You don't have the usual spring in your step. What did my son do now?"

For some reason, Barrett's comment made Jazzy angry. "You've got to stop blaming Brooks for trying to do the right thing."

Barrett looked a little surprised at her explosion. "You *do* need to sit down. You need some of this herbal tea more than I do." He pulled out a chair for her and pointed to it.

As she sat she said, "Brooks didn't do anything wrong. He tried to do something right."

Barrett sat across from her and hiked up one brow. "And—"

"He's the most honest, value-oriented man I know. The only thing he did was try to…try to protect *you*."

After a long pause, Barrett's voice was wary as he encouraged, "Go on."

She was going to get it all out. Every bit of it. There was simply no reason why she shouldn't. Simply no reason why Barrett shouldn't know all of the truth. "If you had just trusted Brooks enough to hand down the practice to him…if you had been reasonable about your own health, then I never would have gotten caught up in a pretend marriage that turned out to be not so pretend!"

Barrett leaned back in his chair and eyed her. "Let's slow down a bit so I can make sure I understand what you're saying. You think I should have handed the practice down to Brooks?"

"Of course you should have. Or at least formed a joint venture after he graduated. It wasn't his fault Lynnette took up with another guy. She didn't have what it takes to be a veterinarian's wife. She didn't have what it takes to live in a small town. You blamed him for that."

"Is that what he said?"

"Of course that's *not* what he said. He blamed himself, too. And that was reinforced by *you* blaming him."

"I never knew why they broke up," Barrett muttered. "He didn't tell me. He just said something about long hours and her not wanting to live in a small town."

"That was only part of it. And she blamed the breakup on that. But she hurt him badly, Mr. Smith, and that's why he hasn't wanted to get involved with anyone since."

"Until you came along."

She sighed, took a deep breath and plunged in. "The night I officially met Brooks, he'd argued with you about your health. He was so frustrated and so worried. That's why he decided to set up a private practice. I happened to be on the bar stool next to him. We'd run into each other before that, but not officially introduced. That night, we talked. He asked me to come work for him."

"Must have liked you right away to do that."

"Maybe so. I don't know. But the icing on our wedding cake was because you wouldn't listen to reason when you were in the hospital. That day, Brooks asked me to marry him. We made a deal. He offered me his grandmother's land if I married him for a year. He figured in a year, he could help get your health turned around and then everything would go back to normal."

She shook her head. "There is no normal. Last night, he realized…he realized it's not going to work. He wants to split up. He doesn't want to be married."

Barrett cocked his head, studied her carefully and she suspected he could see way too much. He cleared his throat. "I can see the Smith pride has gotten us both into a peck of trouble. I *do* trust Brooks. But the truth is—I could see him going down the same road I took. I'd been a true workaholic all my life. I saw my family suffer because of it. I knew only one thing could save Brooks—if he found a woman he cared about as much as he cared about himself…as much as he cared about his furry patients. I wanted him to find that woman and build a life with her. I wanted him to marry and settle down so he'd have a reason to come home."

Jazzy's dejection must have shown on her face.

"He said the marriage isn't going to work out, huh? Do you believe that?"

When Jazzy didn't respond, Barrett leaned across the table and patted her hand with his. "Do you love him?"

She couldn't keep the tears from her voice. "I do."

"You know what? I think he loves you, too, whether he admits it or not. I've seen the way he looks at you. And you can't tell me he would have gotten himself tied up to a woman if he didn't care for her. I don't know what happened between the two of you, but give him a little time and maybe he'll come to his senses."

"What if he doesn't?"

Barrett's heavy brow hiked up. "Then he's a danged fool."

Brooks finished with his last patient of the morning at Buckskin Clinic, checked out Mr. Gibbs with his Doberman pinscher, handled the man's check and watched him leave. Then he glanced around the empty reception area, heard no sounds of Jazzy moving around in the exam rooms and realized how much he missed her. He not only missed her by his side here in the office… he missed her, period. Had she driven back to Thunder Canyon? Or was she still at his place?

His place. He had begun thinking of it as *their* place. Everything—every memory, every touch and kiss—that they'd experienced last night came back to haunt him. Thinking about it all was like a punch in the gut. He thought about staying with Dallas and his kids again tonight. The boys had been a distraction, that was for sure. But even Dallas's kids couldn't distract him from the memory of the look in Jazzy's eyes when he'd said he wanted out…when he'd said their deal was no longer a deal…when he'd said his father might as well know sooner rather than later.

His dad.

Brooks had to settle everything with him now. He didn't want his father finding out about the breakup of his marriage from somebody else.

Fifteen minutes later, Brooks was in his father's kitchen, watching his dad ladle soup from a plastic container into a bowl. "You look as if you need some lunch," Barrett said. "What's up?"

Brooks didn't know where to begin. "Jazzy and I… we—"

Barrett pushed the soup into the microwave, shut the door and set the timer. "You and Jazzy what?"

"We don't…we didn't have a real marriage. She's probably on her way back to Thunder Canyon."

With those words the rest of Brooks's sorry tale poured out—how they'd connected at the Ace in the Hole, how she'd agreed to work for him, how he'd come up with the brilliant idea of a marriage of convenience. "I made an appointment to see a lawyer this week and transfer Grandma's land to her." He expected a blowup from his father at that, but he didn't get it.

"Are you sure you want to do that?" was all his father asked.

"Jazzy deserves it for putting up with this whole situation. For—"

"*Why* does Jazzy deserve it? She went into this thing with open eyes just like you did. Fools, both of you. But consenting fools."

"Look, Dad, we just never realized what was going to happen. We thought we could keep it a business agreement and we couldn't."

"So feelings got involved?" his father asked.

"Hell, yes, feelings got involved," Brooks erupted, standing up, walking around the table. "And there's not a thing I can do about them. I'm not marriage material. Working the two practices is going to keep me swamped up to my eyeballs. Besides, there's a reason Lynnette broke our engagement. There's a reason she fell for someone else. She said it was the hours, but it was something deeper than that. I was missing something—something as a man—that would keep her there."

Had this been the real reason he hadn't dated for the past four years? Was this the real reason he kept himself guarded where women were concerned? He was clearly lacking some special ingredient he needed to be a good husband and maybe a father someday.

"Brooks," his father said sharply.

He stopped pacing and stared at his dad.

"You're missing *nothing*. Did it ever occur to you that your relationship with Lynnette was missing something? Maybe *she* was missing a loyalty factor that led to her infidelity."

Brooks's mouth dropped open.

"Jazzy was here earlier. She explained what the two of you did. She gave me a dressing-down because I didn't trust you enough to hand over my practice. She told me about Lynnette and added that my lack of faith in you didn't help the situation. I've got to tell you, son. I *do* have faith in you. I *am* proud of you. But I wanted you to find a woman like your mom who could ground you. I wanted you with a woman who could make a home for you. I wanted you to have a wife to be the center of your world…who could keep you from working too long and too much. I should have made your mom the center of my world and I didn't. If I had, maybe she wouldn't have died so soon. If I had, maybe I would have seen the symptoms. *I* would have, should have been taking care of her at the end, not your grandmother. I did everything all wrong, and I didn't want you doing it wrong, too."

Brooks had never known any of this. But that's because he and his dad had never really talked. Not about the kind of things that mattered. Stunned, he asked, "So you blame yourself for Mom's death?"

"I blame myself for not loving her the right way. I blame myself for being pigheaded, in denial and too focused on work that served like a shield so I didn't have to give too much of myself. Don't you make the same damn mistake."

The microwave beeped. Barrett removed the soup bowl and put it on the table. "So what happened between you and Jazzy that made this whole thing blow up?"

Oh, no. Brooks wasn't going there.

Barrett narrowed his eyes. "Fine. My guess is your marriage of convenience got a little inconvenient. You're both confused because things happened so fast."

"I'm not confused," Brooks said, realizing now he had been miserable since he'd left Jazzy in his condo.

"Do you want out of the marriage?" his father demanded to know.

Last night when he'd made love to Jazzy, he'd realized in a blinding flash of earth-shattering proportions that he *had* been making love to her. It wasn't just sex. It had been so much more that the experience had rattled and disconcerted and even panicked him. He'd given her his word their marriage would be a business deal. He'd gone back on his word, which was something he *never* did.

"Not confused, huh?" his father asked with a sly smile. "Seems to me you're *plenty* confused. So think about a few things. How would you feel if Jazzy left for Thunder Canyon and never came back? How would you feel if you didn't see her every day? Just how would you feel if Jazzy Cates Smith got involved with someone else?"

Brooks didn't know where to turn. Facing those questions made him want to ram his fist through a wall. And why was that?

The fact was that the sexual electricity between him and Jazzy had wired him since he'd met her. But even more than that, her sweetness and caring, her perky outlook, lifted him up above a place where he'd been. She'd become the sunlight in his days, the moonlight in his nights. She'd become someone he treasured, a woman he respected…and *loved*. Jazzy had become the epitome of everything he'd been running from and everything he'd hoped for.

She was everything he wanted.

"So," Barrett drawled. "If you're not confused, just what do you feel for her?"

Brooks sighed. "I love her."

"Then why are you sitting here eating lunch with me? Go get her."

"I don't know where she is. She might have driven back to Thunder Canyon."

"She didn't. Not yet. She's at Strickland's."

Brooks started for the door.

Barrett called after him, "For what it's worth, she's in love with you, too. She has to be to put up with me."

Brooks prayed his dad was right as he climbed into his truck and picked up his cell phone. He skimmed through his contacts and dialed Strickland's, hoping to get Melba. He did.

"Melba, its Brooks Smith. Is Jazzy there?"

"I just took her a cup of tea a little while ago. Do you want me to get her?"

"No. I just wanted to make sure she was there."

"She's pretty upset," Melba told him. "Are you going to upset her more?"

"I certainly hope not. Can you keep her there if she tries to go out? I should be there in about twenty minutes."

"She's not going anywhere. She doesn't want anyone to see her crying."

Brooks felt as low as he could possibly feel. The last thing he'd ever wanted to do was hurt Jazzy. So he told Melba, "I'll see what I can do about that."

Twenty minutes later to the minute, he stood in front of Jazzy's door, a bouquet of roses in his hand. Thank goodness Nina had had some fresh flowers. Maybe they'd at least get him in to talk to Jazzy. He knocked.

Jazzy called through the door, "I'm okay, Melba. Really. I don't need any more tea."

"It's not Melba," he called back.

When Jazzy opened her door, slowly, as if she was afraid to let him in, he could easily see she was miserable, too. He held out the roses to her, taking in everything about the woman he loved, trying to absorb the fact that she held his future happiness in her hands.

"I know these will never be enough to make up for all the mistakes I made. But I want you to come home with me."

Jazzy's expression changed from cautious to defiant. "I did that before and you left."

"That's because I was a fool."

She didn't take the roses, and she crossed her arms over her chest. "You're not a fool anymore? What's changed?"

He deserved that. He deserved her not making this easy. He stepped inside her room, closed the door and laid the roses on the bed. Then he faced her, knowing this couldn't be done in half measure. "I didn't ask you to marry me on a whim."

Jazzy's arms uncrossed as she dropped them to her sides…and she waited.

Taking a risk, he took her hands in his and pulled her closer. "I might not have realized it the exact moment I sat on that stool at the Ace in the Hole, but you're everything I should have been looking for, everything I missed, everything I want. I love you, Jazzy. I don't know when it happened and I don't know why. Maybe it was when you first smiled at me. Maybe it was when you painted my office. Maybe it was when we went to the Falls. I know now it was before I said 'I do.' Making love with you was absolutely incredible. But I felt overwhelmed with desires I didn't even understand. But now I do."

Since she wasn't pulling away, since she seemed to be listening, since her eyes were glistening with unshed tears, he pulled her arms up around his neck and held her in a loving embrace. "I want a real marriage with you, Jazzy. I want to build a life, a future, a home with you. Can you forgive how stupid I've been and be my wife through thick and thin, better and worse, today and forever?"

"Oh, Brooks…"

When she said his name like that all he wanted to do was love her forever—

His heated kiss exposed his longing, his desire, the love he felt and the love he hoped to feel in the future.

She broke off the kiss, cupped his face in her hands, and said, "I love you, too, Brooks. I want to stand beside you, work beside you, fall asleep in your arms every night and have your babies."

"Babies?" he asked with a quirked brow.

"Babies," she assured him.

Sweeping her into his arms, he laughed and carried her to the single bed. When he kissed her again, he didn't stop and neither did she. They'd found their future in each other's arms.

Epilogue

Jazzy and Brooks walked through the field, holding gloved hands. The weather had turned colder, but they didn't care about the chill. This was something they wanted to do. They glanced at each other often, then studied their surroundings.

When they stopped in the midst of field grass about two hundred yards from the road, Jazzy said, "I can tell Mom and Dad are accepting our marriage now. They want to know how they can help with plans for the house."

"Our visit with them over the weekend brought us closer. When your dad and I went riding, he was almost friendly!"

"They could see we're in love."

Brooks grinned at her. "Because we didn't leave our bedroom till late Saturday morning?"

"Maybe," Jazzy said with a laugh. "Or maybe it's because when we look at each other, anyone within fifty feet can tell. We give off signals like Laila and Jackson, Abby and Cade, Annabel and Thomas do."

"Give me a signal," Brooks said, teasing her and bringing her close for a kiss. Their passion caught fire until Brooks broke away and raggedly stated, "If we don't want to make love in the middle of a field in freezing weather, we'd better concentrate on why we came." He waved to the east. "I can see the house sitting on that rise. Do you want one story or two?"

"I like those plans you found for a two-story log home. And I was thinking…"

"Uh-oh. Always dangerous."

She swatted his arm.

He hugged her, amusement dancing in his eyes. "Just teasing. What were you thinking?"

"I could start taking business courses online so I know how to run the operational side of a horse-rescue ranch. What do you think?"

"I think that's a terrific idea. Self-serving on my part because I want as much time with you as we can manage. To that end, I'm interviewing two possible partners this week. One is driving all the way from Bozeman. I'm video conferencing with the other. Dad's going to sit in."

Suddenly they heard a truck rumbling down the access road. "Speak of the devil," Brooks said in an amused tone.

Barrett climbed from his truck and leisurely walked toward them. "I thought I'd give you two a little time out here then come put in my two cents before you go back to Kalispell. Which, by the way, seems like a commute you don't need."

"Nothing in Rust Creek Falls is available, Dad. I spoke with the real-estate agent again this morning."

"Actually, something *is* available," his father assured him.

"Just what do you know that we don't?" Brooks kept his arm around Jazzy's waist.

"I was thinking," his father said.

"It's going around," Jazzy joked with a glance at Brooks.

Barrett ignored her comment and went on, looking a little...nervous? "It will take at least six months for you to get a place built. Especially if we have a rough winter. In fact, you might have to wait until spring to start construction."

"That's possible," Brooks conceded.

"So why don't you come stay with me?" Barrett hurriedly continued. "You can have the whole upstairs and as much privacy as you want. You can even make a spare bedroom into your own sitting room with a TV. After work, you can go your way and I can go mine. What do you think?"

Jazzy was totally surprised by the offer and Brooks seemed to be, too.

Brooks said, "I can't give you a decision right now. Jazzy and I will have to talk about it."

"Talking is a good thing when you're married. I'll let you to it. But don't stay out here too long or you'll freeze your tails off."

As quickly as Barrett had appeared, he gunned the engine of his truck and drove away in a spit of gravel.

Brooks squeezed Jazzy nearer to combine their warmth. "We could go sit in the truck."

"You think this is going to be a long discussion?" she asked, studying his face.

"I don't know. Is it? Tell me what you honestly think. Shouldn't newlyweds have total privacy?"

"That depends. It seems to me if we want privacy, we can find it—in the barn, in the clinic at the end of the day, in an upstairs hideaway. I really think your dad means what he says. We could have our own place up there. And...we wouldn't have to worry about him."

"It would be temporary...just until we get the house built."

"Exactly. Who knows? Till then maybe we can convince him to date."

"You are *such* an optimist."

"Isn't that why you married me?"

He shook his head. "I married you because I was falling hopelessly in love with you."

"And I with you."

As snowflakes began a fluttering shower around them, they kissed again with a fire that could warm any cold winter day...a fire that could last a lifetime.

* * * * *

JOIN US ON SOCIAL MEDIA!

Stay up to date with our latest releases, author news and gossip, special offers and discounts, and all the behind-the-scenes action from Mills & Boon...

 millsandboon

 millsandboonuk

 millsandboon

It might just be true love...

MILLS & BOON

True Love

Romance from the Heart

Celebrate true love with tender stories of
heartfelt romance, from the rush of falling
in love to the joy a new baby can bring,
and a focus on the emotional
heart of a relationship.

MILLS & BOON
MEDICAL
Pulse-Racing Passion

Set your pulse racing with dedicated, delectable doctors in the high-pressure world of medicine, where emotions run high and passion, comfort and love are the best medicine.